A TEAR FOR JUDAS

By LeGETTE BLYTHE

A
TEAR *for* JUDAS

by
LeGETTE BLYTHE

THIS BOOK PROPERTY OF
JESS F. BAGLEY

THE BOBBS-MERRILL COMPANY, INC.
INDIANAPOLIS   *Publishers*   NEW YORK

First Edition

TABLE OF CONTENTS

✠

A TEAR FOR JUDAS

PROLOGUE

"BEZEK! O God of Israel, my brother!"

"Simon. It's . . . it's you, Simon? I . . . I cannot see . . . so well. But your voice; I'd know——" The man stretched naked on the cross was struggling to lift his head, focus his glazing eyes on the man ten paces in front of him. "Come nearer, Simon; I cannot . . . Yes . . . " He twisted his head sideways and by apparent great effort held his bulging, bloodshot eyes steady. "Yes, it's you . . . and the boy. I thought that you would be coming, Simon. I . . . I . . . " His head dropped again to his chest, his gaunt frame, white beneath the blackness of the hair that covered much of it, sagged on the block that protruded between his thighs.

"We got the word only late in the morning watch, Bezek. It was almost sunrise when Azariah knocked on the door."

"Then Azariah got away from the Roman dogs? Are you sure, Simon? I don't see how that can be." Bezek was straining to lift his head again, and a twisted half-smile lighted the pallid, set face.

"He bolted into the rocks and quickly outdistanced the soldiers, he told us. They had unbound him to nail him to the cross. He told us that no hart could have overtaken him."

"May the God of Israel be praised! That is good. I rejoice that Azariah escaped the Romans and old Herod, may hell take their souls forever!" Bezek clamped his thighs together against the supporting beam and labored to lift high his heavy head, but the movement sent a new searing pain along his legs from the darkly swollen feet held fast to the upright by a huge spike that transfixed them. With a muffled scream he settled again on the crude support.

"God in Israel, Bezek! Endure but for a while longer and it will be dark, and we will get you down and slip you away. Then you will have a mightier story to tell even than Azariah."

"No, Simon, that cannot be," said the man on the cross weakly.

11

"I have already endured many terrible hours. It was yesterday when the sun had not yet reached his highest climb that the foul pagans did this to me. Now it must be nearing dusk, or else my eyes are fast failing me. Some of those hours I was mercifully in a faint, but during too many of them I was fully conscious. No . . . no, Simon . . . " He faltered, for the effort of his long speaking had wearied him. "I am soon finished, and I pray our God—if there be one—that He spare me much more of this torment."

"Doubt not God, Bezek, and endure," said Simon, coming nearer the cross, while the boy, his eyes on the ground, kept to his place. "The soldiers are down the slope at the other crosses. For the time being it may be that they have forgotten you. It will soon be dark. Then we can bring you down and steal you away."

"No, those villains have not forgotten me," Bezek said. "Only God has forgotten me. He has forgotten us all—all who took up the sword to drive those pagans from our land. He has forgotten Judas of Galilee and those who fought beside him, has He not, O Simon? Is not Judas even now groaning on one of these crosses sown on the troubled soil of Galilee? Is it not so, Simon? Have you not heard it?"

"I know not, Bezek. I have heard that Judas of Galilee has been taken. Others say that he escaped like Azariah and fled back across the lake into Gaulanitis. But speak not thus of God, my brother. He will never forsake His children."

"In later years, perhaps, in the fullness of time, as has been promised, He will send one to save Israel, to drive out from the land these swine that pollute it. But us who have followed Judas of Galilee He has certainly forgotten. It must be so."

Spent once more by the effort of talking, Bezek sagged on the block, his head hanging, his beard sunk into the black wool of his chest.

"Try to rest, Bezek. The sun is fast sinking. Soon it will be dark. The soldiers are occupied. They have forgotten you. We will get you down and be long gone before they discover it. Try to hold your strength."

"No, Simon, there is no such chance. I am already spent. I cannot much longer endure this——"

He stopped short. From below a sudden spate of oaths, loud imprecations, silenced the muffled groans and weakening cries of other pinioned men. Then a thud, as if someone with a heavy maul had driven a wedge deep into a log, and a sharp scream split the darkening coolness and fell away into echoes along the rocks.

The boy sidled toward his father. "What—who is it, Father?"

The man on the cross twisted his head to peer at the child and smiled wanly. "The sound is not so terrible, lad, as it seems. I think it was Elam who screamed. I saw little Dysmas pass this way this morning, searching among the crosses for his father. But weep not for Elam. His agony is past now. He is already unconscious, and soon he will be dead."

"But, Uncle Bezek——"

"It is a hard lesson for one of your few years, my boy," Bezek interrupted, "but these are hard days in Israel. The Romans, dogs that they are, have just done a merciful act, though their hearts did not will it. Tomorrow is the Sabbath, and shortly now it will be here, and it would be a sacrilege to permit men to hang on crosses on the holy Sabbath. So the soldiers are breaking the legs of the crucified that they may die before the sun sets and be taken down before the Sabbath is come." He raised his head, which had sagged again. "Soon it will be here, and they will come ahead of it. God decree that they come quickly!"

"No, no, Bezek," Simon protested. "That must not be. We shall get you down before they come. Below in the glade there are others who will help us. It will not be too difficult to get you down, and——"

Another scream cut short Simon's speech.

"See," said the man on the cross, "they move fast, those devils. There is not much time left for me, thank God!" He fought to fasten his eyes on his brother's sorrowful countenance. "Listen, Simon. I will soon be gone, and so will all of us who followed Judas of Galilee. We fought to rid the land of the hated conquerors. We have failed. Galilee is shattered. But there is still in Galilee the spirit of rebellion. There is still——"

His head slumped forward, but he shook it slowly, struggled to look again at Simon. "There is still revolt in the heart of Galilee. But that is not good—now. It will mean only death, more—more crosses. The time will come, but it is not yet. So listen to me, Simon. Move down from Galilee, my brother. Go south from Jerusalem, beyond Hebron, into the desert country, perhaps even to Kiriot. There is peace. There you can rest in safety. Gain riches, if you can, for possessions bring strength. And then someday—some better day—you or your sons can come back into Galilee and organize the new rebellion, and—please the God of Israel, Who has turned His face from us of this day!—Galilee will be freed of the damnable Romans."

His head fell forward, his whole body slumped outward from the cross, and it seemed that he might even slip from the support between his thighs. Thus he hung inert for a full minute. Then he pushed his tortured frame back against the upright and slowly raised his head until his eyes were centered on the boy. "Come nearer, lad. It is hard for me to look on you standing back there."

The boy edged nearer the cross, looked up into his uncle's haggard face.

"You must go southward into Judaea with Simon your father and the others," Bezek said to him. "And then, my boy, when you have become a man and this ill-fated venture of Judas of Galilee is forgotten and the Romans have fattened on the land and grown soft and have lost an edge of their cunning, then you . . . you . . . "

He faltered, but only for a moment. A fierce light flashed into his swollen eyes and his spirit shone out through their glazing heaviness; his voice, too, was renewed. "Then, my boy, promise me this: promise me that you will return to Galilee and raise another revolt, if need be, that will drive these beasts from our ancient land. Promise me this, my boy—" he hesitated again and his head bobbed downward, but he raised it quickly and summoned new fire to his dying eyes—"promise me this, and I die . . . happy."

Below him the boy raised his right hand toward the darkening heavens. "I promise, Uncle Bezek. Hear, O God of Israel, my promise!"

The man on the cross smiled and for an instant held his head high, until it pushed back against the crosspiece. "Did you hear the lad, Simon?" he asked, and there was in his voice a tone of triumph.

"I heard," said Simon.

"And now, get you gone," Bezek warned, the surge of his emotion abating, "before the Roman soldiers come."

"But, Bezek, we are not willing to leave you here——"

Simon stopped suddenly, for along the path that curved downward to disappear behind a great upthrust boulder they heard the sound of voices and the slog of heavy boots climbing the slope.

"Quick!" Bezek's voice was urgent. "They are coming! Begone, Simon; away with you and the lad! And peace be with you, my brother, and with your household."

They turned away without further protest. At the edge of the slope they raised their hands to salute Bezek, whose head was now braced grimly against the upright of the cross. Four Roman soldiers were striding toward him, their short swords clanking at their sides. One carried a large wooden mallet. Simon and his son darted into the shelter of the rocks and the fast-falling shadows.

"Father, are the Roman soldiers going to——?"

"Yes. But when they have left we shall get help and carry him home. They must still be awaiting us below. If he can but manage to live until we——"

"Sons of perdition! Evil spawn of Rome!" It was Bezek's voice, fierce, strong and malignant. "You kill us now, but there will come another sunrise. And then, you vultures of odious Caesar, our sons will drive you and your lewd and idolatrous brood into the sea!"

A babel of Roman voices, strident, furious, drowned Bezek's imprecations. Then, before Simon and his son were prepared for it, came the muffled thump as the heavy mallet struck. Bezek's agonized scream gashed the gathering night. But only for an instant. His cry ceased as though someone had abruptly shut a door upon it.

"Bezek did not want us to suffer. O God—" Simon's voice was a moan—"have mercy on Thy suffering people Israel!"

"And damn to bottomless hell those dogs of Rome!" The boy, turning about, shook his fist toward the soldiers beyond the rocks. "I hate them! God in Israel, how I hate them! Nor shall I forget my promise, Uncle Bezek. I shall never leave off hating them!"

The man, his face drawn and suffering, clutched the sleeve of the boy's tunic. "Come, let us join those in the glade below. Nor is it good that one so young as you should hold such a hate even for the Romans, Judas."

Part I

THE ZEALOT

✠

Chapter 1 ✠

"Hold, Cush!" At the top of the rise, where the path twisted between two sharply upthrust boulders, Judas stopped suddenly, held out a warning palm. The man two paces behind stopped too, and then moved cautiously abreast of the leader. "Roman soldiers?"

"Yes. Likely the ones we seek, too. We must be careful not to be seen by them." Judas turned about to face the other five men bunched on the path just below him. "Stay behind the rocks. The sun's on us. Keep your swords under your robes. One flash could betray us."

Silently they pushed forward, keeping low among the rocks, until they could look out across the great plain of ancient Philistia, its level cut through by the brook Besor far toward the left. Straight before them the sun hung an hour high above the Great Sea, and beneath them, a little way out from the foot of the precipitous slope, its rays glinted on the helmets, the cuirasses and the stacked shields of Roman soldiers busily making camp for the night.

"But, Judas, why do you think that those soldiers—" Lamech pointed down the slope—"are commanded by the Centurion Longinus?"

"Haven't I told you, Lamech, that Elimilech fetched news from Jerusalem that Longinus would command a detachment bearing the tax money to Gaza to be put aboard the next galley for Rome? Isn't this about the time we'd expect him to have come this far south in his journeying from Jerusalem?"

"I thought he'd hardly have got so far by now, not so far even as Hebron."

"Longinus is a good commander. He works with dispatch.

19

That's why I hate him so." Judas scowled. "Among all the Romans in our land, in my opinion, there's no centurion abler than this Longinus."

"And there's none I hate more."

"You have reason enough, Seba," said Lamech. "Didn't soldiers of his century slay Isaachar your brother above Beersheba not two years ago? You should remember that day well, Judas; you still bear a scar from the battle, don't you?"

"Yes," Judas answered, "and I bear just as clearly the memory of that fight. And so do Tola and Nadab, and you too, Pethuel."

"I should," said Pethuel. "I carry a scar from it, too, and I wasn't two paces from you when the Roman gave you the sword cut. But Longinus wasn't stationed then at the Tower of Antonia, was he? Didn't he command a detachment from Gaza?"

"Yes, he was transferred to the Tower just before the last Feast of the Passover." Judas smiled wryly. "He's one Roman I try to keep my eyes on—and his off me."

Tola, crouched behind a rock a few paces to the left of Judas, had been keeping his attention on the soldiers. Suddenly he pointed. "They are raising a larger tent. It's probably the centurion's. He'll likely sleep in it tonight."

"With the bags of coins beside him, no doubt," Judas added, "and sentries posted every fifty paces."

"If we had but a score more Zealots and weapons to match the Romans', we could go down and take that money," Cush ventured.

"No, a score more would hardly be enough," Judas countered. "The Romans must number almost two score, and they have shields and heavy cuirasses and they know how to use them."

"But are we going to let the pagans take away the coins snatched from the pouches of Israelites throughout Judaea?" Nadab protested. "Must we stay hidden while they steal away Israel's blood?"

"No, Nadab." Judas' tone was sharp. "Can anyone justly say that Judas of Kiriot is disposed to avoid a fight with Romans? But we must use discretion, man. Would you have us rush into their camp, screaming and waving our swords? That would be nothing

less than madness. It would be but the wasting of more Zealots'
lives when already there are too few of us to harry Rome."

"You're right, Judas," Nadab agreed. "But I so hate the usurpers
that when I see a company of them, like those down there on the
flat—" he pointed—"I can't judge things coolly. We'd be no
match for them even for a few minutes. Yet it's hard to let those
robbers send our sorely earned coins off to Rome without even
challenging them."

"They may not send them, Nadab," Judas said. "I have a plan."
He beckoned to the others to draw nearer. "When darkness has
fallen and the soldiers are sleeping, I'll slip down the slope, get
past the sentries—if I have to slit a throat or two, that will be all
the better—and crawl stealthily into the centurion's tent. Then I
can slip out with the bags of coins and maybe at the same time leave
Longinus with his throat cut."

"But what is there for us to do?" Cush protested. "You'll be
taking all the risk."

"You men will help get the money away, and that will be a dangerous task, for the Romans won't be long in discovering its loss. I'll
bring it to the foot of the slope, and you'll make off with it into the
rocks. See that it is hidden well so that later we may recover it and
dispose of it properly."

"But, Judas—" Pethuel's countenance betrayed a sudden concern—"would we not be breaking the law of Moses against stealing
if we carried off coins by stealth, even from Romans? As Zealots
mustn't we see to it that we pay heed to the laws of the fathers?"

Nadab's forehead creased in a heavy scowl. "God in Israel,
Pethuel, do you count it stealing when one recovers from a thief
one's own stolen property? Our father Moses would not call it
stealing, I'd venture, if we took from any Roman whatever we could
lay our hands on. Haven't those thieves stolen all our ancient land?"

"You're right, Pethuel, to caution us as Zealots to be scrupulous
in upholding the laws of the fathers," Judas said. "But recovering
from the Romans the money they've snatched from the hands of
suffering Israelites isn't stealing. I'm inclined to hold with Nadab,

too, that we'd be justified in taking from the Romans anything we could get, for they've robbed us, and the whole world, to enrich themselves. They've fattened on robbing the poor and grown strong by plundering the weak."

He was silent a moment as he watched the Romans in the camp below. When he spoke it was more to himself than to the others. "Nor is it murder to twist the heel of your sandal on the head of a snake."

"Suppose you get into the tent of Longinus and manage to steal out with the bags of coins and then in the darkness we fail to find them? Or you may be discovered before you can get away with them and have to fly. What must we do then?" Cush asked.

"Lie quiet among the rocks until the tumult in the camp has ceased. Then you can start northward. But be careful, for the Roman may send out patrols. Travel singly or by twos." Judas paused, his forehead knit. "On the morrow, about the third hour, meet me at the khan of Meshach this side of Hebron. But don't all come together. Leave your weapons off, too. Hide them in the rocks over beyond the khan. Be cautious."

Nadab smiled grimly. "You, Judas, are the one to be listening to your words."

Chapter 2 ✠

CROUCHED behind a stunted acacia bush hardly thirty paces from the tent, which was now faintly outlined in the darkness by the flickering light of a small lamp inside, Judas listened to the measured pacing of the sentry.

The Roman is beyond the tent, Judas reasoned, for his moving shape is not silhouetted on the tent's wall even though the sound of his steps shows that he is walking past it to the right and again to the left. If he is on the other side of it, then the opening of the tent must also be on that side.

That is good, he told himself, his eyes focused on the tent, his ears straining to measure the sentry's course. I can slip up to the tent, keeping it between him and me, and when he's walking away toward the smaller tents where the soldiers are sleeping I can steal around and enter.

He eased forward noiselessly, keeping low to the ground, for now he was away from the protection of the acacia. When he had reached the tent he lay flat a long time and listened.

Longinus is asleep, he deduced, and he must be the only person in the tent, for there is no other snoring. Nor does he snore heavily; it may be that the centurion sleeps lightly.

The sentry now was moving away from the tent, westward toward the Great Sea that an hour ago had swallowed the thin sliver of the new moon to leave the Judaean plain in midnight darkness. Judas could measure the soldier's slow pacing only by timing the footsteps, for beyond the tent he could see nothing. He crawled around to the other side, found the opening, raised the flap cautiously, eased inside.

The lamp, he was glad to discover, was attached to one of the tent posts near the entrance. It would be between him and the guard; there would be no revealing moving shadows. But he must be cautious. He glided to one side of the opening, now sealed again by the lowered flap, and stood still, looking and listening.

He could not discern the occupant. A heavy drapery, thrown over a rope suspended between two posts, divided the tent's interior into two compartments. The sleeping area was on the other side. Beyond the drapery, perhaps with the bags of coins beside his couch, the centurion must be sleeping. But was he asleep? Suddenly Judas realized that he no longer heard the slow snoring. Had he awakened Longinus? Was the centurion, his sword ready, poised to spring on him the moment he lifted the drapery to slip in? Now he heard a light stirring, as though Longinus had turned on his side, and the snoring began again. He is asleep, Judas thought with relief. Then a new doubt assailed him: Is the centurion feigning sleep? Has he stirred on his couch to reach for his sword?

Judas stood motionless. Maybe Longinus has caught a glimpse of my shadow on the drapery. Maybe he is now watching that shadow, though the lamp on the post gives but a dim light.

But the snoring continued. Longinus was either sleeping or being a good actor. . . . He must be sleeping. Judas relaxed and looked about the small room, though he kept to the corner. He saw against the opposite wall a chest with heavy rope handles at the ends, and beside the chest a campstool. To the left of the chest was another stool and, at the corner across from him, a low table. On the table were bottles, jars, a hand mirror, a hairbrush ornate and intricately carved—he could tell this even in the weak, flickering light—a comb, other toiletries.

Then he realized that the air was heavily perfumed. He had been so intent on getting in undiscovered that he had hardly been conscious of a sweet, pungent odor that seemed strangely out of place in an overnight camp of Roman soldiers.

Judas moved silently toward the table and looked down on scissors and tweezers, files, a razor, the looking glass—whose rim was studded with brightly colored stones, some of them apparently gems of value—a strigil carved from bone, and an array of bottles of colored glass, phials and jars, several of them opened and revealing creams, oils and ointments in pale colors and highly scented.

Surely these cosmetic vanities are not the centurion's, Judas reasoned. Surely Longinus would not be rubbing himself with creams, spraying his uniform with perfume, even though stories from Rome tell how certain effete men of that evil city have been willing thus to emasculate themselves. But surely not Longinus!

Would Longinus have a boy? Would he be fetching such a creature with him on a military mission? Men in Rome had boy favorites, Judas had been assured, even men of high repute. But hardly Longinus.

Nor would he be fetching along a mistress. Judas knew that even profligate Rome would never permit that sort of conduct in a soldier engaged in an important and potentially dangerous mission. And Longinus had no wife. He had been too busy enforcing Rome's rule in the region of Jerusalem and lower Judaea to dally with love-making.

But here, nevertheless, Judas told himself, is a table filled with the instruments and the ointments of vanity and beyond the dividing drapery someone lies sleeping or feigning sleep. A pleasure youth it must be, for the snoring is not the sonorous breathing of a mature man like the centurion. But where then is Longinus? Is he also be-yond the thin partition, perhaps awake and waiting, gripping his sword?

Judas stood a long moment, listening. Then he crouched, lifted the drapery's corner stealthily and peered into the small chamber. Only one person was sleeping there, he could tell, for the couch was wide enough for one only. He was too low to the ground to see the person, and a large pillow lying askew further obscured his vision. Quietly he pushed the heavy cloth aside, glided into the sleeping room and stood up.

A woman lay on the couch. The thin light, coming through the narrow slit between the drapery and the tent wall, fell across her.

She lay almost full on her back, her right leg drawn up slightly so that the sheer black nightdress, twisted and crumpled in her tossing, had been pulled to her knee, leaving the soft whiteness of her leg and one small foot exposed. Her other foot was hidden beneath covers awry at the foot of the couch.

Judas stood above the sleeping young woman—the centurion, the moneybags, the sentry outside momentarily forgotten. A sudden strange tenseness held him; his breath was coming in short, quick gasps, as though he had been running a great way, and he breathed through the flattened circle of his open mouth. He stood hardly an arm's length from the couch, and his eager eyes searched out the symmetry of the woman's figure, which was little concealed by the diaphanous silk of the twisted gown.

A double thickness of the black silk, fashioned perhaps in dia-mond shape though hard to define now in the disarray of sleeping, formed a girdle at the waist that went up in a point to her bosom, outlined clearly beneath the gossamer sheerness.

She was young, Judas saw when his eyes went to her face, smeared now with night cream. She was fair, and her hair, the color of ripened grain, was long and curling.

A gentile, he thought. A pagan, perhaps a Roman even though she is blonde; maybe a captive from distant Gallia or Germania. I should not be here. This is not the tent of Longinus. No bags of coins here. Only this pagan woman, and I should not be looking on her. It is evil for me to feast my eyes on the perfection of her body. This is sin against the Lord of Israel, and sin against Shelomith, my beloved. This is sinning grievously. And yet, by the beard of the High Priest, this woman is a beautiful creature, and tempting, and who am I but a young man warm and eager and filled with the red wine of life? Who am I not to look on a pagan woman, maybe from foul Rome? Is that indeed sinful? She's not of the chosen race. Is it wrong even to——

Suddenly her rhythmical light snoring ceased. She stirred and thrust out her right arm, which had been crooked across her stomach. Bracelets on her wrist and halfway to the elbow tinkled against one another.

I must get out before she awakens, Judas told himself. I must slip quickly from the tent.

But now she moved again, and he stood motionless, his eyes still on her. As she drew up her knee, the lace hem of the sheer nightdress slipped upward along the whiteness of her leg. Judas suddenly fancied that the girl was awake but feigning sleep. His eyes moved again to her cream-smeared face, glistening even in the thin light.

Yes, she must be asleep, he thought. She was only stirring in slumber. Her breath comes evenly. Her face—I've hardly noticed her face—must be beautiful when cleansed of the creams and pastes. Her hair spreads like a golden fan beneath her head, her lips show red even beneath the cream.

What a gorgeous, what a perfect woman! Judas moved a step nearer, stood above her. His eyes traveled the length of her, came again to study her hair, her face, her sharply chiseled lips.

Suddenly the girl opened her eyes. "Longinus, I—I——"

She sat up quickly, reached for the cover crumpled at her feet, drew it over her legs to her neck. "I was hoping you'd meet me. I——" She stopped speaking, squinted. "A redhead! By all the gods, you're not Longinus! Who—who are you?" Her voice was shrill. There was anger in it, but little fright, Judas noted even in his own astonishment.

He stepped back into the shadows of the corner. "I mean you no harm. I got into this tent by error."

"But who are you? Where is Longinus? Are you of his century?" She was peering intently into the gloom into which he had retreated. "You wear no Roman uniform. Speak up, man!" she demanded, her voice rising.

"No, I'm no cur of a Roman. Nor am I interested one penny's worth in what the Centurion Longinus would have come here seeking."

"By Jupiter, you're a Jew!" The girl let the cover drop past her thinly veiled bosom to her waist, held her head back and laughed. "By all the gods, what insolence, what beautiful insolence!" Suddenly she stopped laughing. "I'd heard you Jews are a spirited race. I'd heard——"

The sound of a man running, his sandals slapping fast against the graveled earth as he came toward the tent, stopped her. Judas had already jerked his sword from the girdle that held it to his side and had darted through the narrow slit between the tent wall and the dividing drapery. Behind him, as he pushed aside the flap at the entrance, he heard the girl scream.

The sentry aimed a lunging blow at his skull as Judas plunged through the opening, but he was off balance from running and Judas parried the thrust. Then, peering at his assailant in the light from the tent, Judas side-stepped, thrust with his sword and felt its point

scrape along the bone of the sentry's sword arm. He turned and
fled into the darkness. Past the acacia bush he ran, across the flat,
until he had reached the foot of the declivity. Nor did he pause to
catch his breath until he had climbed high among the rocks.

Chapter 3 ✠

THE innkeeper poured Judas more wine. "And you didn't come on
any of the others?"

"Not one. But I didn't go back into the rocks at the place where
I had come out. And I didn't dare call out a name. The Romans
followed me up the slope a way, but they soon lost me. They don't
know these rocks."

"No, but you and Cush and Seba and the others know them like
mountain goats."

"We should, Meshach. We've done much fighting among them,
and we've had our share of harrying Romans journeying this way.
I told the others to meet me here."

"They aren't fetching their swords, I hope." Meshach showed
alarm. "Do you have yours inside your robe?"

"No, Meshach. Don't be alarmed. I told them to hide their
swords in the rocks; and I hid mine between the manger and the
wall in the stable behind the khan."

"That's good, Judas. I'd want no fighting should Romans happen
by here. If a fight started, my place would be well-nigh ruined in
no time."

"Wouldn't you be willing to have your wineskins burst and your
tables and stools splintered if at the same time Roman skulls were
bashed in and Roman blood flowed, Meshach?"

"I'm a good Jew and you know it well, Judas of Kiriot. But this
too you should know—that there's no virtue in a weak man's openly

offending a strong man. I wonder if sometimes you and Cush and these others don't show more courage than good judgment. Don't you know that Israel can't defeat Rome?"

"It may be that at times my hate outweighs my caution, Meshach. And I know, of course, that we can't defeat Rome. But maybe we can so harass and sting them that they'll think it prudent to call home their legions and leave us to govern ourselves. At any rate, I have such a great hate of them that I can't leave off fighting them. You know I've reason to hate them."

"I know it, Judas. I know that you have a greater reason than most of us to wish damnation on them. I know how you've fought them, how you crave to see Israel freed of them, and how——" Meshach stopped. From where he sat he could look through the doorway along the road to Hebron until it disappeared behind an outcropping of dark, rounded boulders. He pointed. "Dust. Much dust, too much for a solitary traveler, or even half a score. They may be Roman soldiers coming from the Tower of Antonia. Hadn't you better get gone before they come?"

"No." Judas was calm. "If they come from that direction they're not of the century of Longinus. I'll sit here quietly, and if they stop they'll think me but a simple man of the earth. They'll pay me no attention. I'll keep my eyes and ears open, and I may get information of value."

"Then sit there in the corner and be discreet, Judas. Don't let your hot anger against them betray you."

Judas walked to the doorway and watched until the soldiers had come out from behind the boulders. Then he went back to the corner and sat down. "There must be two score," he said. "I wonder what mission they're on."

Soon they heard the leader's command halting his men in the courtyard before the khan, and in another instant they were swarming inside, calling for watered wine.

"Quick, innkeeper!" one fellow commanded jocularly. "Can't you turn faster? Wine, Jew, from your best stock, and hurry with the pouring. A cup for Centurion Longinus and one for me!"

Judas, from the corner, kept a close eye on the soldiers as he
sipped his wine. None of them appeared to have noticed him.
Longinus had not recognized him, he was glad to discover. I only
hope he continues not to observe me, he said to himself. It may be
that he actually doesn't know me even by sight. Perhaps he forgets
faces seen in the heat of battle, and bearded Jewish faces at that. But
how was it that Longinus came from the direction of Jerusalem?
He'd been camped on the plain below Hebron and should have been
already well on the road toward Gaza with the tax money. The girl
had evidently been expecting him to come to her after the camp
grew quiet. He must have doubled back. Why?

Sipping his wine, Judas tried to solve the puzzle. Could it be that
he's still searching for me? Did he head a detachment that left
camp early and went toward Hebron only to circle around? But
surely there are as many Romans here as there were in the camp.
Certainly he would not have brought them all back. He would have
sent out a small patrol.

Longinus was speaking. "Are you certain, Aemilius, that the tax
money is carefully guarded?"

"It is safe, Centurion," answered the soldier who had ordered
the wine; "safe as it will be when it's aboard the galley at Gaza."

"I'm holding you responsible," said Longinus. "It's in your care.
See to it." He tasted the cup Meshach handed him. "The wine's
good. I'm indebted to you, Aemilius." He lifted the cup, smiling.
"I drink to you, and to the success of our mission to Gaza."

As they set down their cups there was a sudden commotion at the
door and other Roman soldiers came striding in, their light cuirasses
rattling. In the lead was a square-set fellow with closely cropped
hair blanched and streaked by the sun. He pushed toward the middle of the room. "Are you men soldiers of the century of Longinus?"
At once Longinus turned and showed his face. "Ho, my friend!"

"Sergius, by Apollo! What favorable omen brings you here from
Gaza? I'd no thought of this good fortune. Why should you be
over here nigh to Hebron?"

"Well you might wonder, Longinus. And you'd never guess, never!"

"You're being transferred to Jerusalem to take my place there? And I'm to remain at Gaza?"

"You're going to Gaza?"

"Yes." Longinus laughed. "I'm taking a large consignment of gold and silver coins—tax money—to Gaza to be put aboard the next galley for Rome. But you, Sergius—say, did I guess it?"

"In part, yes. I'm being transferred to Jerusalem. But I'm not taking your place, Centurion. Nor was that the part of the mission I was speaking about."

"Well, then, Centurion, come, speak up! What—what is it?"

Centurion Sergius smiled broadly. "I'm fetching a beautiful young woman from Rome to visit you."

"A woman to visit me?"

"Yes, a woman to visit you. She arrived last week on the vessel from Rome in time to come with us to Jerusalem. And beautiful she is, too."

Longinus was incredulous. "Sergius, I don't understand. A woman coming out from Rome to visit me in Palestine?"

"That's right, Longinus. She's—she's your sister."

"My sister! You don't mean Cynara?" Longinus stared, his mouth open. "By all the gods——"

"Yes, Cynara. Aren't you surprised?"

"I'm amazed, Sergius. Did she come alone? Wasn't her husband—?" He hesitated.

Sergius nodded. "She was alone, yes. She said nothing about a husband. I didn't know she had one."

"She had one the last I heard from home. But that doesn't mean that she still has one—or the same one." Longinus grinned. "Where is she, Sergius?"

"She's somewhere about the khan. I left her a moment ago in the care of the innkeeper's wife. But I'm forgetting to tell you, Centurion. She had a harrowing experience last night while we were

camped below here in the plain before you reach the hills beyond
Hebron. But no harm came of it."

"What—what happened?"

"A man slipped into her tent, perhaps intent on stealing——"

"A man! By Mercury, Sergius, did you catch him?"

"No, the knave got away. We ran him into the hills, but in the
darkness he got away from us."

"Had he offered to molest Cynara?"

"No, she said not, Longinus. I think he meant only to steal her
jewels. But the sentry discovered him before he had time to get
away with anything."

"All the same, it's unfortunate that he escaped. These thieving
Jews who flout the laws must be punished. But say, Sergius—"
Longinus' expression suddenly changed—"let's see if we can find
Cynara."

They had been gone but a moment when Judas saw coming
through the doorway a soldier with a bandage on his sword arm.
Could he be last night's sentry? Judas dropped his eyes, pretending
to be interested only in his wine. The newcomer strolled about the
room among the shoving, chattering soldiers. Suddenly he spied the
innkeeper. "Has a big redheaded thieving pig of a Jew come here
today?" he asked Meshach. "Just let me get my hands on him——"

"I don't know such a man," Meshach answered. "I try not to
have thieves stop here. Do you know his name?"

"No. I'd never seen the knave until last night. But I saw him
then, and I'd know him if I saw him again. By Jupiter, if I do see
him I'll slit his throat!"

"If first he doesn't slit your other arm, eh, Flavius?" A red-
necked Roman clapped his hand on his comrade's shoulder and
guffawed. The soldiers about him joined in the laughter.

"I wasn't expecting the fellow to have a sword——"

"Or to use it so quickly," another added.

"He won't use it the next time I see him," the bandaged soldier
promised. "I'll have him stuck like the pig he is."

"How'll you stick him, Flavius, with both arms sliced up?" The others roared at the raillery.

"But Flavius will still beat the Jew," another declared. "He can still butt him in the belly like a bull, or one of these mountain goats about here. The Jew'll never be able to dent Flavius' skull with a sword; it's too thick!"

They were still laughing when one of the Romans, lifting his wine to his lips, saw Judas. He set down the cup and pointed. "What about that fellow over there, Flavius?" The soldiers turned to look. "He's redheaded. Does he look like the fellow who sliced you last night?"

Flavius came over to Judas and stood in front of him, hands on hips, studying him. "By all the gods, he's the rogue. Here's the pig that was in the girl's tent!" With a sweep of his hand he knocked the cup of wine from Judas' upraised hand. The red liquid splashed on the table. "Stand to your feet, Jew! How dare you sit when Romans are standing?"

Striving to control his wrath, Judas stood up, faced his accuser.

Meshach came waddling on his short fat legs over to the group that was closing about the man of Kiriot. "Soldier, this fellow could not have been the man of whom you speak," he said. "He's a poor sheepherder who wouldn't venture even into a neighbor's hencoop. Never could he summon enough courage to enter the camp of Roman soldiers and draw his sword when——"

"Silence, fat Jew! You needn't try to defend the knave. Do you think I didn't see him? He's the man." Flavius looked around the circle of soldiers. "His headcloth had dropped and I saw him clearly. Do you suppose I wouldn't recognize that red hair?" He whirled on Judas. "Why did you slip into the tent, Jew? Were you seeking money or hoping to bed with the young woman? Speak up!"

Judas made no movement to say anything. He stood calmly before the Roman, his lips set in a thin line.

Suddenly the soldier smote Judas in the mouth with his left hand. "Didn't I tell you to speak, Jew? Talk quickly or I'll slit your throat.

By Hercules, I'll not be trifled with!'' Flavius reached for his short sword and thrust its point almost against Judas' throat.

"Hold, Flavius! Put down your sword. You may have the wrong man.'' The bull-necked fellow nodded toward another soldier, signaled with his thumb. "Go fetch the centurion. And now, Flavius, calm yourself. Waving that sword around you might cut somebody.''

"By the gods, Varro, you'll not tell me what to do! This is the redheaded pig who was in the girl's tent last night——''

"And who sliced you as he came out.'' The soldiers guffawed again. "That's why you're so interested in seeing justice done, eh, Flavius?''

"This is the knave,'' Flavius insisted. "But if it weren't the right Jew and I cut his throat, what harm would be done, I ask you?''

"Calm yourself, Flavius,'' another soldier commanded, "and put up your sword. You might cut one of us—or your other arm. There's no great hurry to be slitting the Jew's throat. He can't get loose.''

"Make way!'' Someone near the door that led to the women's quarters yelled to make himself heard above the ribald laughter. "Here come the centurions.''

The soldiers opened a way through the pushing throng for Sergius and Longinus.

"Is he the fellow?'' Sergius asked as they approached the group about Judas and Flavius.

"Centurion,'' Flavius answered, "this is the knave.''

"You're certain, Flavius?''

"I'm as certain that this redhead is the one who was in the tent as I am that you're the Centurion Sergius.''

"But how do you know? It was a dark night. The moon had set.''

"But the light from the lamp fell full on him, Centurion. His headcloth fell down. And are redheads like this common in Judaea?''

Sergius confronted Judas. "What do you say, Jew?''

The man of Kiriot looked him full in the face. "I am no thief. I am a herder of sheep. I work for the coins I get.''

The innkeeper, whose round black eyes had been fastened on the centurion's face, could remain quiet no longer. "It is as he says, Centurion. I know this man. He's a herder of sheep, as he tells you. He's no thief. He wouldn't have the courage to steal away a new-born she-lamb from his neighbor's fold were the neighbor and his wife sleeping and the watchdog dead."

"The innkeeper is trying to protect the wretch," Flavius protested. "I tell you, Centurion, he's the man I saw last night as he came rushing from the young woman's tent. I'd know him among ten thousand. I'd pick him out from all the Jews in Jerusalem's Ophel. I tell you, this is the man."

Sergius faced Longinus. "What do you think, Centurion?"

"This fellow has denied that he's a thief. But he hasn't denied that he slipped into Cynara's tent with the evil design of forcing himself on her."

Judas' face flushed. "I do not know what the centurion is talking about," he said warmly. "But I strongly deny having entered any tent anywhere to attempt to molest any woman. I am a Jew, son of an ancient heritage. I uphold strictly the laws of our father Moses, and the centurion must know that they condemn lust with great harshness."

"The laws of the Jews do condemn all lustful conduct, Sergius," Longinus declared, "but that doesn't mean, of course, that he's not the guilty man. Your soldier says he's positive this Jew was in the tent. You say that my sister screamed. I'm reluctant to have her brought into this matter, but justice should be done. That is what Rome wishes and demands, and nothing more. Rome does not crave one drop of innocent Jewish blood. Why not call Cynara? It may be that she can identify him, or else say that your sentry is mistaken."

"An excellent suggestion, Centurion. I had thought of it, but I did not wish to embarrass your sister. Go, Varro, and say to her that her brother and I desire her to join us. And tell her why."

Varro nodded and withdrew.

"It may be, Centurion," Flavius suggested, "that the young woman didn't see the intruder clearly. The light maybe did not reach into the sleeping compartment. But I saw him, and unmistakably. Centurion, the light fell directly on him as he came out. I swear by the nine gods that this is the knave who——"

"You've said all that before, Flavius. Hold your peace now and soon the sister of Centurion Longinus may be able to confirm your story. She may——" Sergius stopped and looked around. The inn-keeper, having seen new guests entering from the Hebron road, had begun to chatter in a torrent of Aramaic as he rubbed his fat hands together and bowed low. Longinus too had noticed the fat little man's ecstatic antics; he twisted about on his stool to glance toward the door.

Three men had entered, two of whom, by their dress and manner, were evidently servants. The third, a man of middle age with a fan-shaped gray-flecked beard carefully curled and oiled, was elegantly dressed in the priestly garments of Israelites of great affluence. As he came toward the center of the room followed by the servants, Longinus arose, and the newcomer, seeing him, smiled and walked forward to meet him. "Centurion Longinus, I am happy to see you. But what fetches you so far southward from the Tower of Antonia?"

"Rabbi Nicodemus! I too am happy in this meeting." Longinus bowed, smiling. "As for the business that brings me into lower Judaea, I'm on a mission to Gaza," he added evasively. "These are my men, along with members of a detachment commanded by my friend the Centurion Sergius of the Gaza constabulary. I'd like to present him to you. He's being transferred to duty at Jerusalem." He turned half around and nodded toward his comrade. "Rabbi Nicodemus, this is the Centurion Sergius. The rabbi is a member of the Sanhedrin, Sergius."

Sergius curtly acknowledged the introduction. The Rabbi Nico-demus, bowing, was more courteous. "I am happy to know you, Centurion Sergius. I trust that my acquaintance with you will be as rewarding as has been my association with Centurion Longinus." As he raised his hand to his flaring beard he caught sight of Judas within the circle of Roman soldiers. Longinus saw the rabbi's ex-pression change, but only for an instant; then he was bland and smiling again. "Judas! I had not seen you. I hadn't expected you to arrive here so quickly. You must have traveled swiftly. Have you awaited me long? I'm sorry if I've kept you unduly."

"That is of no importance, Rabbi Nicodemus," Judas replied. "I have been here but a short time. I was resting and having refreshment when these men came in, and now I'm——"

"Is this man your friend, Rabbi Nicodemus?" Longinus interrupted.

"Indeed, Centurion. I've known him since his birth. His father, Simon of Kiriot, is one of my dearest friends. Judas is an upright young man of fine habits and has ahead of him a life of great promise."

"He's now in great difficulty," Longinus said. "He's under arrest, and gravely charged."

Rabbi Nicodemus stood openmouthed. "Under arrest? I cannot understand. On what charge, Centurion?"

"He's charged with having entered the tent of a young woman— my sister, in fact, Rabbi—who was being escorted to Jerusalem by Sergius. It was last night while they were encamped on the plain below here. He's charged with having attempted to steal from her, or, worse, to—to bed with her."

"But surely, Centurion, a mistake has been made. Surely Judas of Kiriot is not guilty of such offense. Certainly it cannot be proved against him."

"The sentry who stood guard is positive that this is the man who invaded my sister's tent."

Flavius had been listening intently. He stepped a pace nearer the rabbi. "He's the man. By the gods, I saw him! That redhead there——"

"Silence, Flavius!" Sergius commanded. He was scowling.

"We have sent for my sister, Rabbi Nicodemus," Longinus said. "We expect her to say if it was he. She was awakened by his intrusion and no doubt can tell." He arose. "Here she comes now. My sister Cynara," he said, as the girl came over to the group; "the Rabbi Nicodemus of Jerusalem."

The girl smilingly acknowledged the introduction, and the rabbi bowed low. "She is on her way to Jerusalem," Longinus explained. "I'll join her there when I return from Gaza. Perhaps you two may see each other again."

"When your sister is in Jerusalem, we would be most happy to have her visit us on Mount Zion," Nicodemus said. "I shall send my daughter Rebekah to fetch her to our house if she will be so gracious as to come."

"I'll be delighted," she assured him.

Longinus was suddenly serious. "We must proceed. I'm sorry that your friend is under suspicion, Rabbi Nicodemus. But the law of Rome knows no favorites. It must be upheld. My friend Sergius has his duty. Centurion, my sister awaits your command."

"I wish to ask her a few questions," said Sergius. He turned to Cynara, and at once the tenseness of the situation could be sensed. "Did you see a man in your tent last night?"

"Yes, after I had been asleep and was awakened."

"Did you hear him enter?"

"No, he was standing beside my couch when I awoke."

"Was there any light inside the tent?"

"Yes. The lamp near the entrance was burning."

"Did you get a good view of the man? Did you see him well enough to identify him should you see him again?"

"Yes, I'm certain I'd know him."

"Look about this room. Stand up, if you will, and see if you can find the man who was in your tent."

Cynara stood up and turned about slowly, studying the faces of the men who stared at her silently. Then once more she circled the chamber with her eyes. "I don't see him."

"That Jew over there. The redhead——"

"Silence, Flavius!" Sergius, his frown fierce, his voice angry, glared at the soldier with the bandaged arm. "One more word from you and I'll have you punished severely!" Flavius slunk back into the ring of watchers.

The centurion turned again to Cynara. "You say you do not see the man?"

"I do not."

Sergius pointed to Judas of Kiriot. "Stand up, you!" Then he faced the girl again. "Look at him. Is he the man who was in your tent last night?"

Cynara half turned. "I had not noticed this man," she said. "I must have overlooked him." She stared at Judas, and the tall tanned man of the desert country faced her without blenching. If he was fearful, he did not betray it. He stood squarely on his feet looking into her face, which was even more beautiful now that the cream had been wiped away and the insolent, tempting lips had been newly reddened. He looked with apparent indifference and waited to hear her words.

"This fellow—" Sergius was gently pressing her—"is he the one?"

She stood another moment silent, a cold smile on her lips, her eyes sharp, intent, drilling. She raised her arm, so that the stones in the rings on her fingers flashed and sparkled, and, rising on the balls of her small sandaled feet, she pointed toward Judas of Kiriot.

"That man," she declared, "is not the one I saw."

Chapter 4 ✠

"Now that the Romans have gone, Judas—" the Rabbi Nicodemus punched his thumb vaguely in the direction of the road to Hebron—"and my servants are outside—" he smiled—"why did you slip into the Roman woman's tent last night?"

"But, Rabbi Nicodemus, didn't you hear her say that I wasn't the man?"

"Yes, I heard her. And I watched her carefully. She was too dramatic, Judas; she overacted the part. I think Longinus saw that, too."

"But why would she, a Roman, wish to protect me, a Jew?"

"That's what I wondered. I've long known that trying to fathom the mind of a woman, Jew or gentile, married or single, is futile, Judas. Maybe, though she's a pagan, she has a kind heart and didn't wish to see you punished. Perhaps—" his eyes lighted, and merry wrinkles ran out from the corners—"she had a sudden liking for you and hoped that your visit to her would not be the last. I don't know why she lied to protect you, but she . . . she did."

Judas laughed. "Yes, Rabbi, she did, of a truth."

"But, Judas, why did you, a Zealot, reared in the strict rules and practices of your good father Simon, go into that woman's tent? It couldn't have been that you were tempted."

"No, Rabbi Nicodemus. I didn't even know she was there. I thought I was slipping into the tent of Centurion Longinus." He peered about cautiously, lowered his voice. "I'd got word that Longinus was coming with the tax money to put it aboard a vessel at Gaza, and when I saw the Romans making camp in the flat below the rocks from which we were watching, I thought they were the detachment of Longinus. So after darkness had fallen I slipped down from the rocks and got into the tent, expecting to carry away the money."

"And you found yourself in the sleeping apartment of the woman, and she awakened and discovered you?"

"Yes, Rabbi. It was the other company coming from Gaza, and not Longinus' soldiers."

"The woman saw you plainly?"

"Most likely. A lamp on the post was burning."

"And did you see her plainly?"

Judas felt himself coloring. He wondered if the rabbi noticed. "Yes, Rabbi, quite clearly."

"She screamed when she saw you?"

"Not at once. She first asked me who I was. In a moment we

heard the sentry running toward the tent, and then she screamed."

Nicodemus smiled. Then he was serious again. "But why did you wish to steal the money from the Romans?"

"I didn't count it stealing. Hadn't it been stolen from us? I meant only to get it back into the hands of the Israelites from whom it had been taken. The conquerors had forced it from our pouches, hadn't they?"

"They wouldn't so term it, Judas. They'd say the money had been levied to bear the expenses of administering the government."

"But, Rabbi, it's their government, not ours. It was forced on us by the Romans. We didn't choose it. I hate the Romans, Rabbi. I've sworn to do them all possible evil. Aren't they our enemies, the enemies of God's chosen people?"

"They are our political enemies," answered Nicodemus, pursing his lips and speaking slowly, "but would it be His will that His children do evil to any soul made in His image?"

Judas leaned forward, his expression intense. "Rabbi, the Romans have done us nothing but evil. They are our foes. Are they not also foes of God? My hate of them grows by the hour. I would delight to see them drowned in the Great Sea. I crave the day when the Messiah comes to drive them forth and deliver us from our bondage. Until that day I'll do the pagans all the ill I can."

"You speak, Judas, of the coming of the Messiah. Do you expect him to be a great warrior and lead us through fire and blood to deliverance? Or do you look for another, a Messiah who in humility and gentle ways will save our people?"

Judas leaned his elbows on the board, gazing in deep earnestness at the member of the Great Sanhedrin. "How can the Messiah be other than a splendid warrior, Rabbi, if he is to deliver our nation from the oppressors, for are they not powerful and relentless? How could a humble man of gentle ways destroy the Romans? The Scriptures promise that our enemies will be overcome and the children of Israel once more be gathered together and become again a mighty nation."

"That, plainly, Judas, is the interpretation placed on the sayings of the ancient prophets by many of our most learned leaders, who look for the coming of a mighty king to restore to us our lost glory."

"You are learned in the Scriptures, Rabbi Nicodemus, and I am certainly not so learned as I'd like to be—though all my life, as you well know, I've been taught to honor and give heed to the prophets' sayings. You know that there are many prophecies concerning the coming of the Messiah and what we of Israel may expect. To me they indicate that the Messiah will be a great and all-powerful king of his people, a conqueror of the pagans and a restorer of Israel."

"Yes, there are many such prophecies, Judas, though others seem to describe a Messiah of quite another sort. It is a matter of interpretation. Some hold one way and some another."

"Rabbi, I may not recall the exact words of the prophet, but our father Jeremiah spoke to the effect that the days will come, 'saith the Lord, that I will raise up unto David a righteous Branch, and a King shall reign and he shall prosper, and he shall execute judgment and justice in the earth.' "

"Those are indeed the words of Jeremiah, and a great prophet he was."

"Well, then, Rabbi, the words of Jeremiah indicate that a descendant of the great King David will become king in Israel, and the land will be prosperous and happy and he will rule in wisdom and with justice. If this be true, how could such a king be a man humble and of gentle and yielding manner?"

Rabbi Nicodemus showed he was impressed. "You know the Scriptures well, Judas, and you interpret them with a logical mind. But another of the great prophets of ancient times wrote of one whom many believe he counted the Messiah, and his prophecy seems counter to the picture drawn by Jeremiah. The Messiah of Isaiah is a man of suffering and humility. Listen to Isaiah's description."

Nicodemus set down the wine cup and leaned forward on his arms, his hands clasped one in the other. "Let me try to repeat them in the exact phrasing, Judas. You may not like his words, but to me they are surpassingly beautiful and they paint a thrilling picture. Listen:

" 'Who hath believed our report, and to whom is the arm of
the Lord revealed?
For he shall grow up before him as a tender plant,
And as a root out of a dry ground:
He hath no form nor comeliness;
And when we shall see him, there is no beauty that we
should desire him.

" 'He is despised and rejected of men, a man of sorrows, and
acquainted with grief:
And we hid as it were our faces from him;
He was despised, and we esteemed him not.

" 'Surely he hath borne our griefs and carried our sorrows:
Yet we did esteem him stricken, smitten of God, and
afflicted.
But he was wounded for our transgressions, he was
bruised for our iniquities:
The chastisement of our peace was upon him;
And with his stripes we are healed.

" 'All we like sheep have gone astray; we have turned every
one to his own way;
And the Lord hath laid on him the iniquity of us all.
He was oppressed and he was afflicted, yet he opened not
his mouth;
He is brought as a lamb to the slaughter, and as a sheep
before its shearers is dumb,
So he openeth not his mouth.' "

The modulated, resonant voice of the rabbi was silent, as if he were trying to recall further the words of Isaiah. He closed his eyes and then, opening them, he began again:

" 'He was taken from prison and from judgment, and who
shall declare his generation?

For he was cut off out of the land of the living;
For the transgression of my people was he stricken.
And he made his grave with the wicked, and with the rich
  in his death;
Because he had done no violence——'

"Hear those words, Judas: 'Because he had done no violence.' "
Then Nicodemus continued:

" 'Neither was any deceit in his mouth.

" 'Yet it pleased the Lord to bruise him; he hath put him to
    grief;
When thou shalt make his soul an offering for sin, he shall
    prolong his days——'

"Listen to these great words, my son:

" 'When thou shalt make his soul an offering for sin, he shall
    prolong his days,
And the pleasure of the Lord shall prosper in his hand.

" 'He shall see of the travail of his soul, and he shall be
    satisfied;
By his knowledge shall my righteous servant justify many;
For he shall bear their iniquities.'

"Now hear the conclusion of the Prophet Isaiah, Judas:

" 'Therefore will I divide him a portion with the great,
And he shall divide the spoil with the strong:
Because he hath poured out his soul unto death:
And he was numbered with the transgressors; and he bare
    the sin of many,
And made intercession for the transgressors.' "

Nicodemus unclasped his hands, leaned back from the board. "My
young friend," he said after a while, "you don't like the words of

the Prophet Isaiah, I take it. They do not draw the picture of the Messiah you have in your mind. But to me they are marvelous words and the Messiah of the Prophet Isaiah is a supremely great conqueror though he would seem but a sufferer. What say you to that, Judas?"

"They are beautiful words, though they seem heavily burdened with pessimism and grief. I cannot comprehend how such a Messiah could restore God's own people to their rightful inheritance. No, Rabbi, I hold rather to the visions of the other ancients, Jeremiah and Ezekiel and Daniel. Recall the words of Daniel: 'And in the days of these kings shall the God of Heaven set up a kingdom, which shall never be destroyed: and the kingdom shall not be left to other people, but it shall break in pieces and consume all these kingdoms—' would not that be the Romans and their spreading empire?—'and it shall stand forever.' And you recall the words, too, of Amos foretelling the destruction of Edom—and is not Edom Rome?—and the still plainer words of Zechariah: 'And it shall come to pass in that day, that I will seek to destroy all the nations that come against Jerusalem.' Surely they foretell the destruction of Rome, Rabbi."

"You know Scriptures well, Judas. You must have studied them diligently."

"My father required it," Judas replied. "You know with what zeal he has sought to learn the law and to require his household to learn it."

"I do, indeed. None has been more faithful than Simon your father. I'm happy you follow his teaching and his example, Judas. I trust you'll not depart from them. But do not water the seeds of hate. Remember that the great God is love, and there is nothing stronger than love, for hate must yield in the end to love, as all the enemies of the Lord must one day yield to Him."

"I love Israel, Rabbi, but I hate the enemies of our land." Judas shook his head slowly. "I'll continue to hate them and seek to do them evil until our land is free of them."

One of the servants of Nicodemus had entered. He approached the rabbi and bowed. "Our preparations for departing for Jerusalem are completed, sir."

"I'm ready," Nicodemus told him. He arose. "Won't you change your mind, Judas, and accompany us? You'd be most welcome to lodge with me. And there are those in Jerusalem who'd be happy to see you."

Judas laughed. "Shelomith?"

"Yes, Shelomith. And—" Nicodemus' eyes were merry—"what of the girl they called Cynara, the sister of Longinus?"

"I'd not thought of seeing her again. But I hope to go to Jerusalem as soon as I can finish my task at Kiriot. Then I'll see Shelomith. You knew we're betrothed?"

"Yes, Judas, and I'm glad. I was only enjoying a little levity when I spoke of the Roman girl. It was wrong of me. Be wary of her, Judas. She is clever, and beautiful, and doubtless as loose as other Roman women. She—she might be tempting."

"I don't expect to see her again, Rabbi. But should I come upon her—" he smiled— "I'll be careful."

"You'll be coming to Jerusalem soon then?"

"Yes. First I must find my Zealot comrades from whom I was separated last night, and then I'll go home for a short while to help my father. After that I'll go to Jerusalem, and on into Galilee. I've business there. On the way I wish to see the Prophet John. I've heard so much talk about his preaching."

"The prophet is a man of mighty words. He draws great numbers to the fords of the Jordan, and there are some, I've heard, who even think him the promised Messiah."

"I also have heard that report. But to me it's plain that the Prophet John is not the leader long promised. I understand that he has never been a soldier, knows nothing about leading men to war——"

"Have you dismissed Isaiah? Must the Messiah lead men to war? Why not to peace?"

But Judas was not confused by the words of the smiling Nicodemus. "First to war and the destruction of Israel's enemies," he answered; "and then to peace."

Chapter 5 ✠

AFTER the Rabbi Nicodemus and his servants had left, Judas went out to the stable at the rear of the khan and recovered his sword. At a pass between the rocks two miles southward in the direction of Beersheba he came on Cush and Seba. "Where are the others?" he asked.

"They are over toward the west—" Cush pointed— "with their eyes on the departing Romans. Longinus seems now to be heading toward Gaza. But we can't understand why he went back to Meshach's inn after having passed it going south from Jerusalem. We've been watching from afar, but we couldn't make out——"

"It was not Longinus' men we saw encamped last night. They were the soldiers of Centurion Sergius coming up from Gaza. They're on their way to Jerusalem now. Sergius and Longinus met at Meshach's, and Longinus is moving on toward Gaza."

"Then Longinus hadn't reached this far south last night? Lamech said he doubted Longinus would have got so far so quickly."

"Lamech was right," Judas said. Then he related to them what had happened in the girl's tent, his flight and the morning encounter with the Romans at the inn of Meshach.

"Had the girl recognized you this morning——" Seba grimaced, shrugged.

"—I wouldn't be here now." Judas grinned.

"Perhaps she did recognize you," Cush suggested. "Maybe you disappointed her last night and she has further plans for you."

"No." Judas laughed. "She'll never see me again."

"I don't know how the woman looked. But if she had the beauty
I judge she had—from your description, Judas—" Cush thrust
forth his hands, palms up— "I'd not censure you if you went to
Jerusalem and sought her. In fact, I don't doubt she's expecting to
see you again."

"I don't like her being in our land," Seba said, interrupting. His
countenance was stern. "Her corn-colored hair and red lips will
be a menace to the youth of Israel. She's an evil woman, no doubt,
and certainly she's a pagan. It would be better if her throat were
cut; there'd be one fewer slut to bear whelps for Rome."

"You're probably right," Cush agreed. "Perhaps she is an evil
woman, but for all that she must be beautiful, and perfectly
formed." He was looking at Judas, his eyes merry. "You saw
just how perfectly, didn't you, Judas? And wouldn't it be a pity,
Seba, to cut her throat before he'd finished last night's interrupted
visit?"

"You counsel a brother Zealot into sinning with a woman,
though she's heathen!" Seba glared at him. "Don't you know, Cush,
that——"

"I'm not counseling Judas," Cush declared, grinning. "I'm just
indicating the course I'd be inclined to take if I'd stood over her
couch last night. I suspect that already I'd have taken the road to
Jerusalem."

Judas laughed. "I am taking that road. But not until I've returned to Kiriot for a while. And it's time that we were on the way
southward. Let's find the others and get started."

At the rocks from which the afternoon before they had looked
down on the Roman camp they came on the other four Judaean
Zealots.

"There go the Romans—" Pethuel pointed to the thin haze of
dust rising far to the west— "but we can't understand why Longinus
turned toward Jerusalem and then came back."

Judas explained this mistake to the four, as he had to Seba and

Cush. Half an hour later they came out on the road from Jerusalem to Beersheba and Kiriot.

As they trudged southward they talked of the sad state of their ancient land prostrate under the rigid rule of Rome and her new representative in Israel, Pontius Pilate. "He has no regard for our customs and traditions," Seba said. "He does not honor our religion. He is the enemy of Israel and Israel's God."

Judas agreed. "Yes, you're right, Seba. But we'll drive him out. We'll submit no longer to his tyranny."

"But how, Judas?" Pethuel asked, his countenance sober, thoughtful. "How can Israel, even though every man should spring to his weapon, stand against the might of Rome?"

"We can't stand against Rome's might, that's true," Judas answered. "No nation has been able to stand against Rome. That will not be our method of fighting the conqueror. We could never defeat the Romans on a battlefield. But there's another way of ridding ourselves of them."

"But how? We have few weapons, Judas. The Romans rob us of our money. The number of our young men capable of bearing arms is small. How can we hope to fight with success?"

"We must organize the resistance better," Judas replied. "In every section we must band together. We in lower Judaea must work with those around Jerusalem and up in Galilee. Now even the leaders barely know one another. We must seek a more effective system and setup. We can't fight the Roman openly, that's true. But we can harry him and molest him day and night. We can sally out against him from the rocks and then escape back into them. We can ambush his supply trains. In Ophel we can send a sudden arrow winging to the heart of a legionary or a spear expertly thrown from a high window or a rooftop. From Galilee's hills we can dart——"

Pethuel was not convinced. "Yes, but how could that be effective against the powerful army of Rome, Judas? How can harrying and molesting defeat the enemy?"

"I don't tell you that they could, Pethuel," Judas admitted. "But
they are Israel's only weapon. Maybe our everlasting harassment,
our unwearied pricking of the enemy's hide, may so worry and ex-
asperate him that he'll withdraw his soldiers from Israel and let us
govern our land ourselves, even though he may continue to exact
tribute. I can't say. But this I know: we must fight with whatever
weapons we can muster."

Nadab slowly nodded his head. "Judas is right. It may be that
we can swarm out on the enemy from time to time and so sting him
that he'll be glad to leave our land. They say we're well organized
in Galilee. If we could arrange things as well south of Jerusalem
and then all our groups everywhere work better together, we might
have hope of success. The resistance in Galilee, I've heard, is fierce."

"I've so heard, too," Judas added. "When I've finished the
spring planting I'm going up there to seek out the leaders. Perhaps
there's where the rebellion will begin."

"And end, too—as it did a score of years ago under Judas of
Galilee. You should remember that, Judas. You were a child when
Sepphoris——"

"Speak not of those terrible days, Tola." The tall chieftain's
countenance darkened. "I don't like to recall them. When I remember my Uncle Bezek and Elam the father of Dysmas and those
countless others who died on crosses, I almost go mad with rage at
the Roman beasts!"

He said nothing more for a long moment as they walked southward through the lengthening shadows from the hills between them
and the Great Sea toward which the sun was slowly dropping. After
a while he smote a fist in the palm of the other hand. "We must
better design the rebellion down here in Judaea! Organize! Organize!
Organize! Our efforts heretofore have been too much without plan.
You—Tola, Nadab and Cush—and you others, must go about
through the country and enlist young men. They must be ready
against that day! You must help them find weapons. You must drill
them in secret warfare. You must inflame them against the usurper.
We'll sting the Romans! We'll never let them rest. They'll know

anxious days and sleepless nights. And it may be—God will that it comes to pass!—that we shall so pester them they'll withdraw from Israel. Dysmas, I hear, is one of the leaders in Galilee. I'll learn from him the methods they use. None, I know, is hotter than he in hatred of the Romans."

Judas was silent again. They trudged along the rough and ancient way. Suddenly he stopped. "Have you men heard of the strange prophet who preaches at the fords of the Jordan above Jericho—the Prophet John?"

"Yes," answered Nadab. "And there are some who hold that he may be that one long promised us. But I think not, Judas. What do you think of such report?"

"I don't know. I've heard it, too. If this John should be the Messiah—" Judas hesitated a moment— "if indeed he is that one, then Israel soon will be restored and once again our land will be free. And if John is not he for whom we look—" he faced the sun settling lower toward the distant sea and his eyes were lighted by an inner fire— "then it can be that even in our day, at an hour not far distant, in the person of some other, our hope—Israel's great Saviour—may yet appear. May the God of Israel will it!"

Chapter 6 ✠

THREE days after Centurion Sergius lodged Cynara at the apartment of Longinus in the Tower of Antonia, the Rabbi Nicodemus' daughter Rebekah came to visit the Roman girl.

With Inacha, Sergius' wife, they sat in the afternoon sunshine at the southwest corner of a gallery that flanked the fortress wall. In the foreground sprawled the stone Palace of Herod, stern and forbidding, and beyond it, street on cobblestoned street, rose the gently rounded mass of Mount Zion, set thickly with the substantial houses of Jerusalem's aristocracy.

Around the corner of the gallery, as they looked toward Mount Zion, and almost below them, was the great white marble Temple, ornate and resplendent, the very center and soul of Israel's life. Past the Temple edifice itself was the partially uncovered assembly place known as the Court of the Gentiles.

"This is an excellent spot from which to view Jerusalem," Cynara observed, as she leaned forward to look. "I'll confess I was surprised to find it such a large city."

Inacha laughed. "If you think Jerusalem is large now, stay with us till the Feast of the Passover and you'll think it rivals Rome. The Jews, a devoutly religious people, swarm into the city from every part of Palestine and even far distant provinces to attend the celebration. That whole district beyond the walls and behind us along the slope of the Mount of Olives—" she indicated with a sweep of her arm— "and, in fact, all the circumference of the walls is filled with the tents of pilgrims. Down among the hovels of the poor in Ophel, and up there on Mount Zion where the rich have their houses, every home overflows with guests."

"The Feast of the Passover? Is that a sort of Saturnalia among the Jews?"

Inacha laughed. "No, indeed, Cynara. It's nothing like the Saturnalia." Then she was serious. "It's a religious observance, a—a period of worship. I hardly know how to explain. It's . . . it's . . . you tell her what it is, Rebekah. It's your religion. I'm still a Roman, though I've been out here in Palestine for years and even a long time in Jerusalem before Sergius' last assignment at Gaza. You tell her."

"It commemorates the ancient deliverance of the people of Israel from Egyptian bondage and the sparing by the angel of death of the first-born of each Jewish family on whose doorpost the blood of the lamb had been sprinkled——" Rebekah flushed.

The Roman girl was laughing. "Angel of death . . . blood sprinkled on a post. Really!" She was laughing as though Rebekah's simply stated explanation had been high jest. "I'd heard you Jews were delightfully naïve, but I wasn't prepared for anything so amusing. Blood on a post to keep away an angel of death! And Jews from everywhere flocking into Jerusalem to celebrate such a weird superstition!" All at once she stopped laughing. "Tell me honestly, do you believe such things? Is that the sort of religion you practice? I'd thought the stories that went around in Rome must be greatly exaggerated—the tales about Jewish religious customs. But they couldn't have been."

Rebekah said nothing. She continued to look solemnly across the roofs of Zion Hill.

"Forgive me," Cynara said. "I didn't mean to offend you. But your story of a death angel failing to kill a child because blood had been——"

"To our people it's not a cause of merriment," Rebekah replied. "We're a devout people. The Passover was the beginning of our nation as a free people. On that occasion we were delivered from bondage to the Egyptians. Now we're enslaved once more. Now another conqueror has his foot on our necks. Now once again we are——"

"You speak of us Romans," Cynara said, gently interrupting. "You call us enemies. Perhaps the Emperor, perhaps old Sejanus—maybe they are enemies of your country. But this does not mean that I am. I know little of politics, Rebekah, and I care less. Politics are for the leaders. But we can still be friends. I certainly have no ill will toward the Jews, toward any Jew. I meant no offense. Perhaps I blundered because of the strange difference in our religions—" she smiled— "if we in Rome have any religion."

"The Jews, as I told you, Cynara, are deeply religious," Inacha repeated. "They take their religion seriously. Now and then even a Roman living in these provinces becomes interested in it. The centurion at Capernaum, for instance, has——"

"A Roman centurion!" Cynara's expression was incredulous. "A soldier interested in such beliefs!" She held her head back and laughed. "Excuse me, Rebekah, but imagine Sergius afraid of an

angel! Or Longinus, by the gods! Imagine their sprinkling blood
on a post to keep an angel away! Does this centurion at Capernaum
do that?"

"Listen, Cynara," said Inacha, who had not joined in the laughter,
"the Jews don't do that now. The Passover is only a commemoration
service. The original incident, which the festival celebrates, happened hundreds of years ago—more than a thousand, wasn't it,
Rebekah?" The daughter of Nicodemus nodded. "As for the centurion at Capernaum, I've heard that he helped the Jews build a
large new synagogue there. That's what the Jews call a temple
where they worship."

"Indeed. To what god was it raised?"

Inacha smiled. "You have much to learn about the Jews, my dear.
Don't you know that they have but one god? Isn't that right,
Rebekah?"

"Yes. We worship the only living God. We believe that the
worship of more than one is pagan worship."

"That's probably better than our system," Cynara said. "We
have so many gods we can't possibly remember them all. And in
worshiping many we may overlook some and thereby gain their
enmity. It would be certainly more convenient and less hazardous,
too, to worship only one. If you could have only one, and stick to
him——"

"Just as it might be less hazardous, perhaps, if a woman should
have but one husband and stick to him," Inacha said, laughing.
Then Rebekah, watching, saw her color slightly. "I beg your pardon,
Cynara. I wasn't thinking of you and Cassius. I——"

"Nor of me and Flaccus." Cynara winked. "Or had you heard
of Flaccus?"

"No, I hadn't heard of your divorcing another——"

"Of his divorcing me, you mean. Well, Flaccus came and went in
the same way Cassius did. I don't think you ever knew Flaccus."
She shrugged. "Flaccus was all right. It wasn't his fault. He ought
to have divorced me, no doubt. At any rate he did."

"Why, Cynara?"

The Roman girl gestured with an open hand, shrugged. "He maintained that I kept other beds warmer than his."

Inacha's expression was amused. "Did he charge you—falsely?"

"Not altogether. He was perhaps too flattering." She looked out over the rooftops, turned again to Inacha, smiled. "He gave me credit for more beds than I really occupied."

"Don't you suppose he's suffering now for the lack of your warm back?" Laughing, Inacha faced Rebekah. "You're amazed to hear women talk like this, aren't you?"

"Well, I——" Rebekah stopped.

"Don't be alarmed," said Cynara. "In Rome I'd hardly be called a—an abandoned woman. As a matter of fact, in some of the better circles I might be considered slow, somewhat old-fashioned. Rome must be considerably more—more relaxed over morals in general and sex in particular than Jerusalem."

"Then I'm afraid——" Rebekah's black eyes snapped—"that you'll find Jerusalem somewhat—uninteresting."

"No, strangely enough, I'm expecting to find it highly interesting," Cynara countered. "I want to learn your customs here, and also in Galilee, of which I've heard much. The people there, I understand, are somewhat different. I'm looking forward to my stay in Palestine. It certainly began excitingly."

"Rebekah, has your father said anything about a man who slipped into Cynara's tent as they were camping overnight on their way here?"

"No-o. No, of course not. My father would never speak to me of such a thing."

Inacha tugged at the sleeve of Cynara's stola. "Go ahead, tell her."

"Absolutely nothing happened." Cynara grinned. "Sad to say!" She related the story of the night's adventure and the discovery of the man the next day at the khan.

"And you're sure it was the same man, Cynara?" Inacha asked.

"Positive."

"But why did you say that he was not the man?" Rebekah wanted to know.

"He had done nothing to me." Suddenly Cynara's merry laugh ran along the gallery. "May Venus plague him!"

"And he had stolen nothing?"

"No. In fact, I don't know why he slipped into the tent. But had I identified him, Sergius and Longinus would no doubt have had him scourged severely—maybe killed."

"You didn't want him killed because—?" Inacha raised her eyebrows.

"Because I thought I might see him again, yes, and——"

"Next time he wouldn't be so—so timid and scared?"

"He didn't seem timid or frightened, Inacha. Had he acted so, I'd have identified him the next day. But he wasn't fearful in the tent or at the inn. He appeared uninterested, disdainful—maybe challenging is the word."

"And you mean to find him—and try your wiles on him, eh?"

"If I should come upon him again, Inacha, it would be interesting to see what . . . what might be done."

They laughed. Inacha, reaching over, slapped Cynara lightly on the back of the hand. The sun's rays sparkled in the gems of Cynara's ring. "The poor man wouldn't have a chance against you," Inacha said. "By the way, did you ever learn his name?"

"Yes. It was Judas. Judas of—" she hesitated— "I can't remember the place. He was a tall and sinewy fellow. And he had red hair."

Rebekah sat up straight in her chair. "It couldn't have been Judas of Kiriot?"

"That was the name—Judas of Kiriot. Your father called him that and seemed to know him well."

"Indeed he does. His father and my father are dear friends. Judas is a leader in lower Judaea, where his father is a wealthy man with great flocks. Judas is a strong Zealot."

"The Zealots," Inacha interrupted to explain, "are members of a

Jewish party strictly orthodox in religion and violently opposed to Rome's rule."

"So he's a religious person. Perhaps that's why he seemed so— so uninterested. Well, by Cypris——"

"Judas is betrothed," Rebekah said.

Cynara eyed her sharply. "What!"

"Yes, to one of my best friends—Shelomith, the niece of the High Priest Joseph Caiaphas."

"Well, by all the little gods," said Cynara, and her smile was thin, "that makes the redhead doubly interesting!"

Chapter 7 ✠

WHEN Judas finished his task at Kiriot he came north again and lodged at an inn on Mount Zion near the bridge that spanned the valley of the Tyropoeon. This great structure joined the Mount Zion region with the Mount Moriah area on whose crown rose the still unfinished Temple built by Herod.

Having rested a short while from the tiring journey, he bathed and dressed in fresh clothing and went to the house of Benjamin the merchant, Shelomith's father. He and his betrothed sat on the terrace in the late afternoon's waning sunshine. The terrace looked off southward above the rooftops toward the city's wall.

"The tree—see, Shelomith, over there to the left." Judas leaned forward on the stone bench and pointed with lean brown forefinger. "See it? Look, straight above the place where the wall dips to cross the foot of the Tyropoeon."

"I think I see the tree you mean." Shelomith shielded her eyes with her hand. "On the far slope of the Vale of Hinnom, just to the right of that thin column of smoke rising out of the valley?"

"That's the one. There's the place I've been talking about. Often I've noticed it as I came along the Hebron road. I'd like to set the house some two dozen paces southwest of the tree, between it and the road, so that from the bedroom window I could see that tree the first thing of a morning."

"Silly man!" Shelomith's merry laugh rang along the terrace. "Can't you see that it would be on the very edge of the ravine, Judas, and dangerous for the children playing about the yard and——"

"Ah-hah!" Judas leaned his head back against the coolness of the high bench and combed with long fingers through his thick red-brown hair. "Always trust a woman to get along faster than a man. I'd only staked off the house's foundations, but you've already built it and filled the yard with children. Now some of them are getting pushed off into the gulch!" He looked at her with mock seriousness. "Just how many children had you planned, my sweet?"

She tossed her head to look away from him, so quickly that her long black curls whirled out from the white stem of her neck.

"Good girl!" Judas could maintain no longer his feigned solemnity. "You know, I like spirit. I like that saucy way of yours. In fact, Shelomith, I like everything about you, my dear. And your name—I love it. Shelomith—it's pretty to say, and it fits you. 'My happiness, my reward, my recompense'—certainly you are all those to me."

"But you just said you'd rather see a twisted old tree than your wife the first thing of a morning as the sun rose above Kidron Valley."

"I've heard it said—and by married men—that a tree's looks suffer less during the night than a woman's."

This time Shelomith laughed. "There's nothing that looks more bedraggled than a woman rising from a night's sleep, I'll agree. But tell me, why would you want to set the house so?"

"That tree affects me strangely, Shelomith. I always look at it when I pass along the road. I've been over to it several times. Every time I see it, it reminds me that a heavy task remains to be done in Israel, one I've sworn to help do."

"Why must you always be thinking of that task, Judas?" Shelomith's expression betrayed her concern. "Why must you always be talking of freeing Israel of the Romans? That must mean war, and bitter fighting, and the legions of Rome dashing through the streets with bloody lances, and homes burning, and women screaming, and children being trampled by horses."

"Yes, it would mean those things—and more. But we must drive the heathen into the sea!" His sunburned face grew grim. He thrust forth his arm, pointed across the valley. "Shelomith, do you know why I want to build my house near that tree? So I can see it often. And why would I want to see it often? This is why, my dear: I want to be like it."

"But, Judas——"

"I want to be tough and hard, gnarled, twisted and unyielding. Look at the tree, Shelomith. It has stood many a year there on the slope, at the edge of the gulch. It has been buffeted by the winds— the burning sirocco from the east, the blasts from the Great Sea, the hot desert winds from below Kiriot, the wet winds that rush down from the north. It has been buffeted, Shelomith, and it has bent beneath the fury of the tempest, but it has never yielded. Still it stands. It will stand for many a day."

He was quiet a moment, reflective, nor did she speak. He resumed: "Yes, it has always lived in danger. Danger presses upon its roots. It stands on the rim of the precipice. It has never been away from the very brink of destruction. Yet it has stood." He knotted his right hand into a bronzed, hairy fist and smote the heel of it against the stone bench. "May the God of Israel grant me such a life! May I be hard and tough and unyielding, and may I tread the borders of destruction and yet not fall into the abyss! Then I shall accomplish what I swore to do."

"I do not like those words nor those thoughts, Judas, or your scowling face. I don't want to be married to a man hard and twisted and walking forever close to destruction. You aren't that sort of man—unless you choose deliberately to make yourself one."

Judas turned to face her. "Yes, I am that sort of man, and that is

how I want to be. You know that I swore to my uncle stretched
on the cross——"

"But you were only a child, Judas. You can't be held accountable
for an oath sworn as a boy. No one expects you to hazard your
life for it."

"That oath, even though I made it as a child, is still binding,
Shelomith. I have repeated it a thousand times. I have battled the
pagans up and down Judaea. I bear the scars of their swords. And
I'll continue to fight them, my beloved, as long as I have breath to
keep me going. That's why I want to be tough, twisted, hard and—
and enduring. That's why I'm going back into Galilee, and there
I'll——"

He stopped, for a woman servant had come out with a tray of
fruit. She set it on the small table near them and, bowing, turned
toward the house.

"Thank you, Hagar," Shelomith said.

"She's new?"

"Yes, from Cyrene. That accounts for her being so dark."

"It would be best if no one knew my plans, Shelomith——" Judas
smiled wryly—"especially your dear uncle the High Priest."

"I'll tell no one. You know what I think of the High Priest.
But this frightens me, Judas—your going into Galilee to get involved in fighting. You know what a terror Pontius Pilate is—
how the dust of the streets has hardly dried the blood of our people
slain when he marched into Jerusalem flaunting his ensigns." She
hesitated, then put her hand lightly on his knee. "I fear something
else too, Judas."

"What, my sweet? What do you mean?"

"That girl, Judas, that Roman girl."

"The girl in the tent? Longinus' sister? I'm not afraid of her,
my dear. I'll likely never see her again."

"But I'm afraid you may, Judas. I—I don't want you to see
her again."

"But if I should, Shelomith, why need I fear her? I told you she
said I wasn't the man in her tent."

"Yes, but she knew you were."

"She probably suspected it, but why do you say she knew me?"

"Rebekah visited her at the Tower of Antonia. She told me the Roman woman said she recognized you the minute she saw you at the inn. She told Rebekah much more than you told me." Her tone was vaguely reproving.

Judas laughed. "What else?"

"She told Rebekah that she awoke but pretended she was still asleep, and that you stood over her and looked at her a long time, and——"

"I told you that I stood over her couch before she screamed."

"But you didn't tell me——" she tossed her black head again and thrust her chin forward—"that you took a long time about it." She glared. "I suppose you saw her—completely?"

"The light from the lamp wasn't strong."

"And she screamed too soon."

"Listen, Shelomith, wasn't she a Roman, and——?"

"Yes, and wasn't she a seductive woman? Wasn't her hair the color of ripened corn, lightened with dyes from Germania? Wasn't she reeking with perfumes and rubbed with creams and fragrant oils? Oh, I know about women like her—and I know something about men!"

"The creams on her face certainly didn't add to her beauty, my dear." Judas' eyes twinkled, but only for a moment. "Look, Shelomith. Am I become a friend of Rome, or of any Roman woman? Do you think you have to set *me* against those dogs? Why, I hate them with a violent hatred. In fact, I count this woman's brother Longinus my particular enemy, because he's one of the cleverest of all the Romans in Palestine. Do you suppose his sister could attract me?"

"You know I wouldn't try to inflame you against the Romans, for already I fear you hate them too much for your own good. As for me, I shouldn't hate this woman, though I'm—I'm certain that I do. I—I wish she'd leave and——"

"That's one enemy you'd like to see driven into the Great Sea."

She laughed, her annoyance vanished. "I'd like to see her driven back *across* the sea. Her brother may be your enemy, but politics and war are quickly forgotten by a man when he sees a piquant face and golden hair."

"Very neatly put, Shelomith. But most likely I'll never see them again. It was only by chance I got into that girl's tent. Hereafter I'll be careful about slipping into tents."

"But she'll be seeking you out. I know it, Judas."

"I'm going into Galilee, Shelomith. Don't worry about the Roman woman. I'm not going there to head a revolt; I'm not wanting to be captain of Israel's army. I'm going to look things over. And on the way I'm going to stop and hear a man who's preaching these days along the fords of the Jordan. He's reported to have great power with the multitudes."

"The Prophet John? I've heard of him. Many have gone out from Jerusalem to hear him preach, among them the Rabbi Nicodemus and my father. But John's certainly no warrior, Judas. He'd never lead an army, or even draw a sword. He's preaching repentance, submission to God, forswearing of sin. He's a plain rabbi of the Wilderness. He knows nothing of war, nor would he be willing to provoke it."

"Don't be too sure of that. Listen, Shelomith: haven't we been promised a Messiah to deliver us? This John appears to possess great powers. Maybe he's the long-promised——"

Shelomith shook her head. "No, not the Prophet John. Not he."

"How can we tell yet, Shelomith? Maybe the deliverance of Israel through him may be near. Who knows?" He shrugged. "At any rate I'm going to seek him out, hear his words, study him."

"John isn't the Messiah for whom we look."

He ignored her positive words. There was a faraway look in his dark eyes. "If I should join this John and he is indeed the Messiah of the ancient promise and Rome should be overthrown and Israel restored, then I'd be a great man in the new kingdom."

Judas sat musing a long moment, hardly noticing the girl beside him. Of a sudden he sprang lightly to his feet and with a quick backward twist of his head flipped the unruly hair from his face. "Then, Shelomith, my beloved—" he raised his hand and pointed beyond the walls of Jerusalem, past the gorge of Hinnom from which the smoke of burning rubbish forever floated upward— "then we can build our house over there in the center of many acres, with a wall raised high to keep the children from falling into the ravine, and with windows that look out on the tree."

Chapter 8 ✠

WHERE it went through the narrow pass between the rocks the road from Jerusalem to Jericho fell away steeply. But though Judas was going downhill he was tired, for he had walked a long way and the sun was still warm on his back.

He was passing a huddle of large boulders on his left when he saw the shade race out ahead to engulf his own trudging shadow. In that same instant heavy weight came suddenly down against his shoulders and back. He sank to his knees and fell on his face in the gravel.

"Grab his sword, Doeg! While I hold him down see to the money pouches, Chittim!"

Half stunned by the furious attack, Judas, if he had not heard the voice, would have imagined a boulder had toppled on him. Pinioned to the ground by huge arms and the weight on his middle, he lay unprotesting.

"Get up, Shishak," he heard another voice command. "You've likely caved in his ribs already. Get up! We've got his sword and the pouch."

Judas felt the great burden lift itself from him. As he turned on his side one of the men bent down to grasp his hand. "Rise, stranger, and count yourself lucky Shishak didn't burst you asunder."

Judas clambered to his feet, felt himself over. Then he glared at the man who had jumped on his back from behind the boulders. He was immense—a great obese, hairy fellow whose soiled brown robe bulged out over the sagging rope girdle. "What does this mean, you brazen sow's belly?"

The big man seemed not to take offense. His thick lips rounded in a quick smile. "Our visitor shows my belly little respect. Indeed, it's ample, and it's natural that it would be noticed. Certainly it's no sow's belly, and if it were of the swine family, stranger, I insist that it would be a boar's belly and not a sow's."

"Come now, Shishak," one of the others said. "We've no time to discuss the nature of anything so obvious. We must get this fellow back into the rocks before other travelers come along."

"Where are you taking me, ruffian?"

"The fellow has spirit to be a renegade Jew," the man declared. "We're taking you to the leader." He motioned with his head. "He's over there, out of the range of hearing from the road."

"Renegade? What do you mean?" Judas asked, as he straightened his disheveled robe. "Why would roadside robbers call me a renegade?"

The man glared back at Judas. "All Jews who stand with Rome against their own nation are renegades. And it would be better for you to command your tongue to be discreet."

With the two escorting him between them and Shishak walking behind, they started off toward the slowly dropping sun. Then the fat one spoke. "Hold! Chittim, shouldn't you stay and watch the road for the coming of the others? We can take him. You stay and watch."

The man on Judas' left loosed the grip on his arm. "You're right, Shishak," he said. "I'll stay. And when I give the signal, come quickly. There may be several in the company." He walked back toward the road.

Three hundred paces westward, in a small level place among

straggling shrubs, they came upon a company of rough-looking men, perhaps a dozen altogether, sprawled on the ground or seated with legs crossed, leaning back against the rocks. A large barrel-chested fellow got to his feet and ambled toward them. Judas saw sharp black eyes study him out of a shrubbery of black beard. He returned the scrutiny. A coarsely woven and crumpled robe, heavy with dust and sweat, opened in front to reveal knotty legs. Crude sandals were buckled on feet large and roughly knuckled. A round, bearded head sat on the thick, squat column of a neck thrust upward from the black mat of the chest.

This giant paused two paces in front of Judas. "Well, men," he said, "you got him. You're certain he's the right one?"

"Sure of it," Shishak said. "We watched him from the rocks a long way as he came down the Jericho road." He reached up and snatched off Judas' headcloth that had been held in place by black goat's-hair rings. "See?"

"Yes, it's red—that's plainly to be seen. What of the money, Doeg? Is the pouch well filled with gold coins?"

The slender man, a solemn-miened Jew, held up the leather bag he had taken from Chittim to fetch to the leader. "I've only glanced inside. There are few gold pieces, though the money is considerable. But this can't be all the receipts from the sale of merchandise to Benjamin."

Judas caught the name. "Benjamin? The merchant in Jerusalem? What do you mean? He's well known to me. In fact, he's the——"

"He should be well known to you, you filthy traitor," the barrel-chested leader declared. "Haven't you done much business with him as agent for your pagan employer in Tyre?"

Judas, still angry at having been waylaid, was even more puzzled. "I can't understand you," he said. "I'm agent of nobody at Tyre— or anywhere else. I'm a loyal Jew on my way to Galilee. Of a sudden I'm set upon by three ruffians. They rob me and, not content with taking my sword and money, berate me for an unpatriotic Jew. And you speak of Benjamin, the merchant, who's the father of my betrothed, and——"

The giant's black eyes stared. "Who are you, then?"

"I'm Judas of Kiriot, raiser of cattle. Who're you, and why am I so dealt with?"

"God in Israel be praised!" The fellow clapped a weighty hand on Judas' shoulder. "I've heard of you. You're a leader of the Zealots in lower Judaea!" Then his beaming smile vanished and he was cautious. "But how do I know you're Judas of Kiriot? That you aren't the agent of the manufacturer at Tyre? I've never seen Judas, though I've heard much of him."

"As for that, how can I know you aren't an enemy? Do you have the sign?"

Judas saw the big man reach into his unkempt robe. He stopped with his hand still in the fold. "Well, how do I know that you know it?" he retorted.

Judas pointed to his pouch in Doeg's hand. "It's there in the bag."

"Hand him his pouch, Doeg. Stranger, let me see if you can match my sign. Bring it out if you can."

Judas took the leather bag, opened the mouth after he had untied the drawstring, searched through the coins, picked out a denarius, handed it to the leader. "See what is scratched across the face of old Tiberius?"

The big man examined it, handed it back to Judas, then pulled from the fold of his robe a coin which he dropped into Judas' palm. "Look you at the sign on that one."

Judas held it so that the light of the lowering sun fell full on it. "The sign of the cross." He turned to look searchingly into the bearded face. "Who are you, friend?"

"Have you ever heard of Bar Abbas?"

"Indeed! Are you Bar Abbas?"

"None other," the massive chieftain said, displaying a wide grin through the black beard which covered almost his entire face. "What have you heard of me? Report ill or good?"

"According to the man who brought it. Among the Zealots in our region of Israel, Bar Abbas is hailed as a great patriot. Among the Romans, I hear, the mention of his name provokes both wrath and fear."

"That's as I would have it." Bar Abbas turned his gaze on the two men who had brought Judas before him. "Now, you two unworthy sons of the wise King Solomon, what defense have you to offer for waylaying our Judaean leader?"

"But we would have sworn he was the man from Tyre," Doeg hastened to declare. "Doesn't he look like him? The red hair, the wide shoulders, the——"

"All the same, he's not the man from Tyre, he's not a disloyal son of Israel. And you two—and Chittim—might have bashed in his skull and thrown his dead body among the rocks. Doubtless by now the man of Tyre and his whole company have passed and the money is lost to our cause."

"What do you mean, Bar Abbas?" Judas asked.

"A week ago, my friend of Kiriot, the agent of a wealthy manu-facturer of Tyre, a Roman who makes gorgeous textiles and fine glassware, came southward. He brought a train of asses loaded with merchandise for sale at Jerusalem, principally to the merchant Benjamin, who has a shop on Mount Zion——"

"My prospective father-in-law, as I've said."

"Indeed. Well, we watched the man, a redheaded Jew, and his servants as they came through the rocks. I had it in mind to ambush him and take the merchandise, but then I thought of a better plan. I knew I'd have poor chance to dispose of his fine cloth and thin glass goblets among those with whom I associate. So I decided to let him take his merchandise to Jerusalem, sell it and get the cash; then I'd rob him as he came back toward Tyre. In that way I could dis-tribute the money among those who need it, return some of it to Benjamin and those others who bought the Roman's wares—" he grinned— "and perhaps allow some of the coins to stick to the lin-ings of my own pouches, eh?"

Judas laughed. "A novel scheme, Bar Abbas."

"Had it worked, yes." He glared at the two members of his band. "But this pair of light brains——" His glance fell on Shishak.

"God in Israel! Judas, if my men don't use their wits better than they've been doing, the Romans will have all of us nailed on crosses one of these days!" He scowled.

But only for a moment. Then his expression relaxed. "It's getting on toward late afternoon. Soon darkness will fall. It's dangerous to be on this road at night, Judas." He gave his characteristic grin. "You might be waylaid. Stay the night with us, and begin your journey again by tomorrow's first sun. There's much I'd like to ask you about our affairs in lower Judaea."

"I was going up into Galilee to find out what's going on there," Judas said. "And I wished to stop and hear the words of the Prophet John and study his demeanor."

"John is preaching on the Jordan well above Jericho—nearer Bethabara. Not a week ago I mingled in the throngs that were following his strong words." Bar Abbas paused. "I was one of the many blind beggars crying for pennies. I try—" his smile warmed his rough features— "to keep informed on what happens in this region. I see much, too."

Judas ate the evening meal with them. They built their low fire behind great rocks well back from the Jericho road. After they had finished their supper Judas sat down with his back against a stone that had been warmed by the fire. Bar Abbas lay full-length close by, cradling his head in the heel of his left hand, his right arm lying free beside the short sword thrust into his girdle.

"You said you had observed the Prophet John and heard his words," Judas said. "Tell me, what do you think of him?"

"He holds sway over the multitudes. If he inveighed against the Romans as he does against sinning, he'd doubtless aid our cause greatly."

"But he shows no interest in politics?"

"I think not. He limits his words to calls for repentance."

"Answer me this." Judas leaned forward. His eyes searched the black eyes of Bar Abbas. He saw the flames of the low-burning fire dance in them. "Do you think that this John may be the promised Messiah?"

Bar Abbas sat up. "John the Messiah? No! No, indeed, Judas. Why do you ask such a question?"

"Only because the idea had come to me. I've never seen him."

"The Messiah will be a great one, a leader, Judas, who will drive out the enemy and establish once more the might of Israel. Don't you believe that?"

"Yes, that's my belief, though there are some—among them the Rabbi Nicodemus—who suggest that the Messiah may be a spiritual leader, even a suffering one, as the words of the Prophet Isaiah may be interpreted to mean."

"I think not. I hold, as my father and his fathers before him held—I come of a line of priests, though you'd hardly believe it, Judas—that the Messiah will restore the ancient glory of Israel."

"Yes, I agree—and I so hope." He hesitated. "Bar Abbas, how came you to be a leader of the Zealots?"

"It's a reasonable question, Judas." He twisted around to get his back against a shrub. "It goes back to the days of Judas of Galilee and the destruction of Sepphoris. My mother's brother was killed in the fighting."

"He was more fortunate than my father's brother, who went to the cross."

"Then that explains why you became a revolutionary?"

"It was one reason—a good one, don't you think?"

"Yes. We shall never forget, eh, Judas? I shall never be blind enough not to see the vision of my father's house burning, or deaf enough not to hear my mother's screams in the night. No, I shall never forget. I hate them, Judas. I hate them, the damnable beasts!"

"I too hate them. Nor shall I ever relent in my hating!"

They sat a moment in silence. Then Judas, his whole countenance questioning, turned again to the Zealot chief. "If you were reared at Sepphoris, then perhaps you knew one Dysmas, whose father, too, perished on the cross?"

"Dysmas! I know him like a brother, Judas. Do you?"

"I knew him years ago as a child, but I haven't seen him since

those days. I was told to find him in Galilee, that he could tell me
how our cause is faring."

"Right. Dysmas is one of the Galilee leaders. Yes, he's my
friend, though I'm somewhat older than you and he. He has always
been more than kind to my son."

"I didn't know you had a family, Bar Abbas."

"I have only the son, Judas, and he's a cripple—helpless."

"I'm sorry. I didn't know, my friend."

"Few know, Judas. The boy's mother died when he was born.
My sister Eunice at Nain took the baby to rear. Most of her neighbors think the boy hers, she's had him so long. One day—he was a
handsome child, Judas—one day when he was eight—he's seventeen now—he and his comrades were playing in front of my sister's
house when the Roman soldiers came charging down the street on
their horses."

Bar Abbas' eyes gazed into the dying flames. "One boy was
killed. Others were grievously hurt. My boy hasn't walked since,
Judas. Eunice, who's been a widow many years now, has cared for
him."

He stood up, walked around the low fire. Suddenly he knotted
his hairy fist and raised it high. "Damn them, O God of Israel!
Damn the dogs to eternal hell!" He lowered his fist, shook it before
his face. "I hate them! Oh, Judas, how I hate the pagans!"

Chapter 9 ✠

JUDAS first saw the people. They were crowded into a small clearing
some fifty paces below the ford where the road crossed the river.

Then, as he passed beyond a clump of willows that had shut off
sight of the Jordan, he saw the prophet. John stood on the side of

a gentle slope that rose from the cleared place. He was preaching to the throng in words resonant and thunderous.

The Baptist was a tall, gaunt fellow. As Judas moved unobtrusively into the fringe of the crowd he saw that long months of sun and wind had burned John to a leathery darkness. His skin was the color of the coarse, heavy girdle about his loins. The girdle served to hold against his hips the heavy brown camel's-hair robe which was thrown across one shoulder to leave bare his hairy chest and long, muscled arms. So absorbed were his listeners by the flaming words that few noticed Judas' arrival.

John dropped his long arms to his sides, surveyed with bright piercing eyes the crowd fanned out before him. Then with a sudden motion, like a leopard springing, he darted a pace forward, thrust forth his arm to stab with lean, bronzed forefinger toward the throng.

"Repent!" he shouted, and a frown wrinkled his dark forehead. "Repent, O you brood of vipers!" He turned slightly to glare at a small group huddled together apart from the others. Judas judged them to be Pharisees and Sadducees, perhaps sent from Jerusalem to gather reports concerning the Wilderness prophet. "Repent, I say unto you! For has not the great prophet written, 'Woe unto them that are wise in their own eyes, and prudent in their own sight'? Has he not declared that woe shall come upon them that call evil good, and good evil; that put darkness for light, and light for darkness; that put bitter for sweet, and sweet for bitter?"

Again John stopped, to give emphasis to his words. Then he smote his big, gnarled hands together and wheeled to face the hearers on his right hand. "You have cast away the law of the Lord of hosts and despised the word of the Holy One in Israel, as the prophet wrote of old," he shouted. "Therefore, as the great prophet warned, 'is the anger of the Lord kindled against His people, and He hath stretched forth His hand against them, and hath smitten them: and the hills did tremble, and their carcasses were torn in the midst of the streets.'

"I call you to witness that the words of the prophet have come to

pass. Has not the hand of the enemy been heavy upon us? Do not
the children cry in the streets for the fathers slain by the intruder?
Yes, and whence cometh help? 'What will ye do in the day of
visitation, and in the desolation that shall come from afar?' Did not
the prophet thus question his generation and did they not go unheeding and unrepentant? 'To whom will ye flee for help? And
where will ye leave your glory?' Did he not ask them thus in his
day?"

Now the frown deepened on his dark and furrowed brow, and
he raised his gaunt arms toward the heavens and thundered: "Repent, men of Israel! Fall on your faces and cry to the Lord of hosts,
lest He fling you into the bottomless pit of His great displeasure!
Pray, and cleanse your hearts, prepare yourselves for the coming—
and that right soon—of the mighty one of God!"

He lowered his voice, and the frown was wiped clear, leaving
only the deep burn of the sun and the wind. He lifted his arms as
if in blessing.

"Cleanse your hearts, O men of Israel, for the great prophet
declared that 'unto us a child is born, unto us a son is given: and
the government shall be upon his shoulder: and his name shall be
called Wonderful, Counsellor, the mighty God, the everlasting
Father, the Prince of Peace.' And I declare unto you that soon he
will come to bless Israel, that he may even now be at hand! Be you
therefore ready!"

He lifted a corner of his robe to wipe the sweat from his face.

"Tell us, Rabbi——" The man's voice was as suave and oiled
as his luxuriant beard and as soft as the robe that swathed his stout
frame. He stepped forth a pace from the knot of Pharisees and
Sadducees, and Judas had the feeling that he wished to be seen by
the throng. "Tell us, are you that mighty one? Are you the one for
whom we look?" He stood, arms folded across his bulging stomach,
a faint smile of derision curling slightly the corners of his thick lips.

The prophet's scowl deepened. He raised his arm, so that the
robe fell away. Judas fancied the arm a broadsword, nicked and
dulled and rusted along its length, smeared with the darkened

blood of battle. He thought the sword would flash and fall now
once again and smite the scornful Sadducee with fury.

But John did not lash out. Instead he lowered his arm, and the
scowl vanished. When he spoke his words were calm and carefully weighed. "No," he said. "I am not the Christ. I am not that
mighty one of God."

"Well, Rabbi——" Now another man, a tall beak-nosed fellow
almost as angular and sparse of frame as John, spoke from the
huddled group. "If you are not the Messiah, what then? Are you
Elijah returned to restore Israel?"

"I am not," said John.

But the man was persistent. "Are you a prophet of old? You
have been speaking the words of the great Isaiah. Can it be that
you're Isaiah come again to our day?"

"No, I am not he."

"Then, Rabbi, who are you? What report of you can we give
those in Jerusalem who have sent us to hear your words and observe
your bearing? What do you have to say about yourself?"

"Say to them that I am the voice of one crying in the Wilderness. I am he to whom the Prophet Isaiah spoke when he exhorted,
'Prepare ye the way of the Lord, make straight in the desert a high-
way for our God.' And more he said: 'Every valley shall be exalted,
and every hill shall be made low; and the crooked shall be made
straight, and the rough places plain. And the glory of the Lord
shall be revealed, and all flesh shall see it together.' I am he who
proclaims to you, O men of Israel, that glory which is shortly to
come.

"But the prophet declared another thing: 'The voice said, "Cry,"
and he said, "What shall I cry?" and the voice said, "That all flesh
is grass, and all the goodliness thereof is as the flower of the field:
the grass withereth, the flower fadeth; because the spirit of the
Lord bloweth upon it: surely the people is grass. The grass withereth, the flower fadeth, but the word of our God shall stand
forever." '

"Thus said Isaiah the prophet to those Israelites of old. Thus he

speaks to us of this adulterous and idolatrous generation. And thus
I speak to you: Repent, for the kingdom of God is at hand. He for
whom so long you have looked is even now here and near. I baptize
you with water. But this other one will verily baptize you with the
spirit of God. He is the mighty one of God!"

The prophet was standing on the small mound, tense, his eyes
looking out beyond the rapt listeners to the uplifted hills of Galilee.
Now his voice was rising again, and the ring of his words echoed
on the slopes and died away in the gorge of the small, twining river.
"This one it is who, coming after me, yet is preferred before me,
and rightly so, I tell you, for I am unworthy even to bend down and
unloose the latchets of his sandals! Repent, O men of Israel, repent
that your eyes may be whole to see him when he comes, that your
hearts may be clean and pure to know him!"

He turned abruptly to speak to a slender young man a few paces to
his right, and then he stepped down from the mound. The other
man raised his hand, signaled for the throng's attention. "The
Prophet John is very tired," said he. "All day he has been preaching and baptizing. Now it is nearing night and he is greatly spent.
He bids you go in peace. Tomorrow he will be here again to preach
and to baptize."

The spell of the gaunt prophet broken, the crowd began to break
up into small groups. Some moved slowly, talking in quiet words,
toward the river crossing that led over into Peraea; others sifted off
along small paths that pushed through the heavy growth of willows
and tall grass screening the bends and twists of the stream. But the
greater number trudged up the gentle incline toward the road which
roughly paralleled the Jordan till it joined the Dead Sea at its south
end and the Sea of Galilee at the north. Some would find shelter in
homes along the road, others would go into Bethabara seeking food
and lodging for the night. Many would return on the morrow, for
this strange Essene, this stormy sun-baked wind-beaten preacher
whose fierce words summoned them to a new life of right living,
this man of the desert come northward, had gained a strong hold on
them.

Judas, watching them go, realized that he was about to be left with the prophet and his group of personal followers. Turning his head, he saw that they had slumped down on the fallen trunk of a large willow. At the same time they noticed him.

The young man who had dismissed the multitude arose and came toward Judas. "Peace be with you!" he said, smiling.

"With you be peace!" Judas answered.

"I'm called John son of Zebedee," the man said. "I'm a fisherman from Bethsaida."

"I'm Judas son of Simon, from Kiriot down in the desert country of lower Judaea."

"Kiriot, did you say?" The Prophet John had arisen and was walking toward them. "Peace be with you! I too come from Judaea. I'm the son of Zacharias the priest, and I was brought up at Juttah near Hebron. You've heard of my father?"

"Of course!" Judas beamed. "With you be peace! My father Simon has long been a friend of Zacharias the priest of God. We were neighbors and did not know it, though doubtless you are——" He paused.

The prophet laughed. "Older. I'll finish your saying. But not so much older. My father and mother were old when I was born. I've lived hard. The hot sun, and the wind—always the wind—" he held up his right arm, pulled the robe away— "it tans the hide like leather. See? Yes, I've lived hard."

His smile melted the hardness of his years. "Nor have I eaten of the fat of the land," John went on, "especially since I left my father's home to live in rough places. There's little food to choose from in the forsaken land between Jericho and the Dead Sea. A little fruit now and then, a dried fig or two, knotty and hard and bitten by the wind and sand, and sometimes a comb of wild bees' honey, and locusts. Locusts, my friend. Ah—" he smiled again—"I could live a long life right gladly without pulling the wings from another locust! But say, friend Judas, where are your companions? Or did you come alone?"

"Yes," said Judas, "I journeyed alone all the way from Kiriot."

"And you came to hear me?"

"I was going into Galilee, but I wished to hear you first. Your fame has spread even to the desert south of Kiriot. We had glowing reports of the power of your words and the size of the throngs that flocked to you. Now I find the reports true."

"They follow me with their eyes and their ears. As to their hearts I cannot truly testify. But if no friends accompany you, Judas, surely you must have no plans for the night, and darkness will shortly be upon us. Can't you abide with us? We have a shelter down the river a short distance, and ample food for you. I trust, Andrew—" he smiled wryly as he glanced toward another young man near them—"no locusts."

"If I wouldn't be intruding——" Judas started to say.

"You're most welcome. Come, let's be going. I'm not a little tired, and hungry. So are my friends here. And so must you be, too."

"I thank you," Judas told him. "I am wearied with much traveling. I could eat even locusts. But most of all, I'd value the opportunity of talking with you."

"We'll walk together."

John settled his camel's-hair robe about his shoulders, with a quick tug adjusted the leather girdle, picked up his staff that lay against the log and started stalking down the trail, Judas beside him and the others behind.

"Why did you break your journey to see me and hear my message?" John asked, after they had gone a few paces.

"All my life—even from childhood—I've longed to see Israel happy and free, cleared of the Roman rule. As a youth and man I've often raised a secret sword against them. I'd heard in these recent days that you are a man of power who draws people to you and holds them captive under the spell of your eloquence. I'd thought you might be the one to lead us in overthrowing the intruder, in restoring Israel to her ancient glory."

"Even as Judas of Galilee years ago sought to do?"

"And more. You would not fail. The cross would not be for

you, as it was for Judas and those who fought with him—like my father's brother."

"I am sorry, my friend. Perhaps that explains your great interest, your longing. You seek . . . vengeance?"

"I seek the restoration of Israel, the freeing of her people. I look for the promised deliverer. But you told the throng that you were not he."

"No, Judas, I am not that great one. No, no, indeed." John was silent awhile as they walked through the willows. Then he said very gravely, "Judas, I perceive that in your heart there is the longing for revenge." He thumped the ground with his staff to give emphasis to his words. "That is not proper, my friend. 'Vengeance is mine,' saith the Lord of Israel. That is not the way, Judas. You must not hold dark things in your heart. You have reason, indeed. You have suffered. But you must not be vengeful. You must repent, Judas. You walk in error."

In silence they walked the tortuous path, their eyes on the brown earth beneath their sandals. When John resumed, it was as though there had been no break in his speech. "And if that were the way— the way of vengeance and force—I would not be the one to lead Israel. I am but the voice of the forerunner. But shortly there will come another, Judas, and he will lead Israel into the great way, on the road that runs along the heights, the road that binds the mountain peaks together. His is the straight way, and the right way, my brother. You will see it, and I pray you walk in that way."

"He is the one of whom you spoke?"

"Yes, he is that one."

They trudged on.

"But, Rabbi," Judas inquired, suddenly looking up, "how are we to know him? Do you know him as yet?"

For a long moment John was silent. "He is near, in the region hereabouts. I—I am convinced, Judas—" he seemed to be talking more to himself than to Judas—"yes, I feel within myself that he is the Messiah of God."

"You've seen him then?" Judas could not conceal his excitement.

"Yes, I have seen him. It was more than a month ago—five or six weeks—that I saw him. He came to me among the crowds that swarmed along the Jordan, and he sought of me baptism in Jordan's waters. He was a fair young man to look upon, with a smiling countenance and a straight young body, not burned and gnarled like mine, but powerful nevertheless, and graceful. As he came forth from the baptism I looked into his face, and I was strangely moved. It seemed to me that the love of God and His power were settling down on this young man, even as a dove settles to her nest. I tell you, Judas——" John suddenly stood still and stopped Judas with his hand. The men walking behind almost fell against them. John looked Judas full in the face. "Yes, I am convinced that this young man is he whom we seek. I felt that day that he should be baptizing me instead. A glory shone on him, a glory not of this earth." John resumed his walk along the path. "His face shone like the face of God. I saw it."

Judas said, "Where is he now?"

"I don't know, except that I seem to sense he is near. I have not seen him since well-nigh forty days ago. He walked away, seeming in a sort of daze, a profound communion. He went straight toward the Wilderness."

Judas would have questioned him more, but he was reluctant to break the spell into which the prophet seemed to have fallen. John was striding along, his head down, his staff fending the bushes and tall grass from his pathway. "We must have our supper and get an early rest," he said after a while. "The throng may be large tomorrow. And it may be that Jesus will return."

"Jesus—that is his name?"

"Yes, Jesus of Galilee. A kinsman of mine, in fact, though I didn't recognize him as my cousin at the baptism. We may have met as children, but I don't know. We were reared apart, though our mothers were first cousins. Both families are poor. His father Joseph was the carpenter of Nazareth, and mine, as you know, a humble priest. . . . I've learned this about Jesus since he has been gone."

"Then the Messiah will come out of Galilee!" Judas' voice and eyes betrayed his mounting excitement. "How fitting that the saviour of Israel should come from Galilee! Nor is it strange, for in all Israel who have been more eager for freedom than the Galileans?"

"I'm convinced he won't be the sort of leader you want," said John. "I think he'll be a man of love."

"But you said he would be a man of great strength."

"Yes, I saw strength in his face as he came forth from the water—great strength and power—the strength of legions of angels."

"But must he not have legions of men, stout Israelitish men of arms, if he is to vanquish the evil of Rome?"

"No, I think not. He will prevail, if I judge him aright, through the exercise of a power greater than that of a Caesar and all a Caesar's armies. He will conquer the earth through love. And what, my friend, is stronger than love? Is not God himself love? Who can stand against God?" John laid his gaunt, knotted hand on Judas' shoulder. "Be not perverse, my friend. Seek not your own way. Repent. Seek the way of God. Listen until you hear his voice. He is near you, Judas, very near. Hold not out against him."

Chapter 10 ✠

"Repent! Repent!"

John the son of Zacharias stood on the small rise above the ford of the Jordan where the road crossed into Peraea. He shook a leathery fist. Sweat ran down the creases in his weathered face and slipped into the mat of his beard. It reflected in tiny balls of fire the sun which was now fast dropping behind the hills.

"Repent, you men of Israel!" he cried. "Repent, you men of the

vineyards and the fields, of the shops and the countinghouses, of the
fine dwellings on Mount Zion and the squalid dens of Ophel! Tear
your garments and anoint yourselves with ashes, O you vipers even
from the Mount of the House itself!" He thrust high his right arm,
and the naked desert burn of its long leanness was revealed as his
robe fell back. "Have I not told you, O you hypocritical pietists
who know not and care not for the spirit of the law but limit yourselves to a blind worship of cant and tradition—have I not warned
you that a new day approaches, indeed is here, is even already
upon us?"

The prophet is fearless, Judas told himself, watching the dark,
flashing eyes and hearing the inflamed words. He is a man of
strength. He has a commanding presence. If he is not himself the
man to lead Israel, can this other of whom he spoke yesterday so stir
the people?

"Yea, I have told you—" now John's voice was calmer, less
threatening—"that I am the voice of one crying in the Wilderness.
I have told you that I am not that promised one; I am the voice that
hath been ordained to proclaim the glory of the one who comes, and
shortly. I am he that brings tidings of——"

The prophet's voice suddenly was stilled, as though his throat had
been shot through with a swift arrow. Judas, looking quickly toward him, saw him raise his arm and point off toward the left,
above the little dale in which they stood, to the road that led upward from Jericho toward the Sea of Galilee.

Along that road a man was approaching.

"Behold!" Now the prophet's tongue was loosed. "Behold!" he
shouted. Excitement gave way to awe. His voice grew deep and
soft. "Behold the Lamb of God that taketh away the sin of the
world!"

The man walked with an easy stride, Judas noticed, as though
walking great distances was not unusual for him. He was tall, erect.
A soft brown robe thrown about his shoulders and gathered at the
waist with a rope girdle could hardly conceal the depth of his chest
and the smooth strength of the muscles in his arms and legs.

The throng had turned to watch the stranger approach. Not a man uttered a word. Silence had fastened their tongues.

The tall young man in the dusty robe looked quickly toward them when the prophet's shout pointed him out. But he said nothing, offered no salute in return, and when he reached the place where the path turned down into the glade he continued steadfastly forward along the road. In an instant he was lost behind the tall, thick shrubs that fringed the road.

"That fellow! Hah! I know him," said a man over at the left of the crowd, punching his thumb toward the road. "The prophet must be so tired he's seeing things. He's lost his balance. The 'Lamb of God' indeed! That was a young carpenter who lives over at Nazareth. I've known him many a year, and his father before him."

"Nazareth! May the Lord be praised!" said a squat man standing beside him. "Nazareth—" he nudged his neighbor in the ribs—"the lamb of God—whatever that means—coming from such a hovel of huts on a hillside as Nazareth in Galilee! That's something to make one laugh, yes?"

In an instant the throng was talking and gesticulating. Nor were all those who had seen the young man walking the highroad scornful of the prophet's words. Some were nodding gravely; others were solemnly silent.

"The prophet has seen aright."

Judas turned. It was the son of Zebedee who spoke. His countenance, the man of Kiriot saw, was aflame. Perhaps it was the light from the dying sun. Perhaps it was an inner joy. But his face glowed.

"Yes, may the God of Israel will that it be true!" John bar Zebedee saw Judas regarding him with a puzzled expression. "The man you saw was indeed Jesus of Nazareth. I've known him from my earliest youth. He's my cousin, the son of my mother's sister Mary. He has always been the noblest of young men. I'm devoted to him."

The Prophet John was raising his arm to still the mounting chatter of the throng before him. "It is enough. You have seen this

day him of whom I told you aforetimes. The day is at hand. It has
come. Repent you before it is too late. And now—" he held his
hand aloft in benediction—"go you in peace."

They walked back along the river's bank to their shelter, prepared the evening meal, ate it with few words. John's mood invari-
ably set the tone of his followers' talk. Tonight he was saying little.
He sat apart, rapt in thought.

Can it be that he doubts his own words today? Judas wondered.
Can he be puzzled at the failure of the young man to come down the
path into the glade and before an assembly of Israelites acknowl-
edge himself the awaited Messiah? Can John fear that he was in
error when he pointed out this Nazarene as the holy one of Israel,
the Lamb of God long sought by God's people?

Having finished munching on a broiled fish and a fragment of
hard bread, Judas put the imagined doubts into words: "If this
young man, this Jesus of Nazareth, is the Messiah as you proclaimed,
why was he afraid to appear before the multitude and be acclaimed?"

"I do not know why he went his way," John answered. "But this
I do know—that he is truly the one of whom the Prophet Isaiah
spoke in his day. He is the one of whom I am sent to bear witness,
and I am not worthy to unloose his sandals, as I have said. He has
his reasons for what he does. I don't know them. It may be that
tomorrow he will declare his mission."

"Tomorrow by the coming of the dawn I'll be on my way into
Galilee," said Judas. "I too have a mission, and I must be about it.
I can't stay too long away from Kiriot. My father is old and his
flocks are large. There is much to be attended to there. And—"
he smiled—"I trust there will soon be much to do in Galilee." He
turned to the son of Zebedee. "Do you happen to be acquainted
with one Dysmas of the region of Cana?"

"I know him well. He's been a friend of mine since childhood.
He's a friend of Jesus, too. As children we three played together
in Nazareth and the region roundabout. Lately Dysmas has become
one of the most enthusiastic of the Zealots. He's fairly ablaze

against the Romans, as well as against anything that smacks of un-
orthodoxy in our religion. Do you know him?"

"No, but I was told to find him."

"Then you seek a meeting with the Zealot adherents? There's
another in that region whose hate of the Romans and hate of anything contrary to the ancient traditions is as pronounced as
Dysmas'—perhaps more so. He's called Simon—Simon the Zealot.
He damns the Romans with every breath."

"Then I'll be wanting to see this Simon the Zealot, too. I'm
anxious now to find those two—Dysmas and Simon—and discuss
plans with them before I start south again."

Chapter 11 ✝

JUDAS trudged mile after mile along the greening valley of the
Jordan. After a while he came to an opening in the jutting, rocky
wall on the western side. He climbed through this wide pass in the
granite wall and walked along the border of a small stream through
the narrow defile between Mount Tabor on his right and Little
Hermon to his left.

Striking now westward and a little toward the north, the man of
Kiriot headed through fields of waving grain, already promising a
burdensome harvest for the reapers and a bounty to the gleaners
following behind. Past vineyards on the gentle slopes he walked,
and along the banks of meandering streams lined with oleanders,
where a little later would burst into brilliance myriads of poppies
red as the sacrificial altars of Herod's Temple, and innumerable
other wild flowers and the blossoms of fruit-bearing trees.

It's a beautiful land, Galilee, he said to himself as he mounted a
small, rounded rise and saw the great range of Carmel towering

straight ahead of him until it ended precipitately at the Great Sea; his brow was furrowed, and he clenched his brown fists as he kicked a stone from his path. But still it shelters only slaves of Rome! Even here on this smooth tableland between the great mountains where our fathers fought a thousand years ago, where Saul and Jonathan battled, where Deborah uttered her dire prophecies, and where the legions of Varus murdered our fathers—here abide now only vassals of the conquering hordes of Caesar. How long, O God of Israel? How long?

After a while he came to the foot of the slope up which he could see little Nazareth. Then he began to climb, mounting through vineyards that clung to the steep incline. When he was far up and almost within the borders of the village he turned and looked eastward toward the Sea of Galilee. It lay low and long, a blue sheen, on the rim of the horizon, framed by the somber granite headlands of the region of Bashan. He fancied he could see the flash of the dying sun on the roof of the white marble palace in the new city of Tiberias. Herod had built it at the edge of the sea near the center of its western shore, a resplendent residence on polluted soil— polluted because it had been the burial land of countless persons long dead; polluted even more because it housed the adulterous apostate lover of Rome.

Then Judas looked up the slope to Nazareth, but in his mind's vision he saw beyond the mount to the blackened ruins of Sepphoris on the other side. It was about Sepphoris that the revolt of Judas of Galilee had swirled. Here had gathered ten thousand Jewish youths, proud in their visioned strength, to overthrow the armies of the conqueror. Judas, thinking back a score of years, remembered them as they had come swinging along the mountain paths, their crude weapons on their shoulders, their ringing songs on their full red lips. He remembered, too—a scowl scarred his forehead and pulled down the corners of his mouth—the legions of Varus closing in behind them from the garrison of the Procurator at Caesarea and from Capernaum and from Decapolis beyond the Sea of Galilee. He remembered the great blazing fires of the homes and shops of

Sepphoris—among them the house of Bar Abbas' father, he knew now. He could hear again the shrieks, the shouts, the screams in the night. He could see the Jews being marched forth in chains, and suffering the lashes of the Romans. He beheld again the men—two thousand of them—struggling beneath the crosses—one of them Bar Abbas' uncle—and the crosses sowed through the land and among the desolate places. Once more in his ears ran the groanings and the curses, always the curses on the swine from the fetid city by the Tiber. And . . . and he remembered his Uncle Bezek:

I have not forgotten! I shall never forget! Never! Never! Though I live a thousand years, Uncle Bezek, I'll never forget the promise. Until the Roman dogs rot in hell I shall never forget!

He started up the trail again. The night was coming on fast now. He would stop at the tavern in Nazareth, and tomorrow he would go on toward Cana to seek out Dysmas and Simon the Zealot.

Chapter 12   ✠

Two days later Judas, still searching in the hills between Cana and Capernaum for the Zealot leaders, was rounding a steep vine-covered hillside when suddenly he heard a babel of voices, excited and angry. He stepped behind a bush and listened.

They were Jewish voices, he was relieved to discover. Likely a sudden altercation between neighbors. Maybe several brothers quickly fallen to quarreling. Judas stepped back into the trail, moved forward cautiously. At the bend he saw a small stable and beyond it another building, old and in sore need of repair, perhaps a farmer's storehouse. But he could see no one, though now he could hear their words plainly.

Judas stole toward the stable, keeping bent over within the protection of the bushes that bordered the narrow road. He darted through the low doorway which opened on the road, and slipped over to a narrow window.

"Hold, Abishai! He deserves to have his throat cut, but let us have no bloodletting just now."

"But my fingers itch to slit it."

Judas, peeping through the window, saw several men in the level between the storehouse and a modest cottage. One fellow was waving a short sword under the nose of another man, while two heavily bearded Jews whose headcloths had fallen to the ground pinioned him. "And I don't see why a little bloodletting, Dysmas, wouldn't be sufficient warning——"

"No, put away your sword. And loose him. Let him go."

The two released their grips.

A stout Jew ran up to the man who had just commanded the others to free the prisoner. "But he'll run away, Dysmas, and then when you and your comrades leave he'll return with more soldiers and take all I have and doubtless slay me and my wife and children!"

"Oh, no, Zur, he won't be back." Dysmas crossed his arms on his chest. "Will you, Jonadab?"

The prisoner—thoroughly frightened, Judas could clearly see—ventured a thin smile. "No—no, no. This man will never see me again, if—if—if only you let us return to Capernaum un—un—unmolested."

The band's leader—there seemed less than a dozen in the farmyard; several stood with swords drawn on three legionaries—threw his head back and laughed. Then he stepped forward a pace toward the scared fellow, and his countenance was menacing now. "If you ever come back, Jonadab, we'll hear of it, and some dark night, if we haven't the numbers to do it in the daylight——" He drew his forefinger quickly across his throat. "Do you understand?"

"Yes," Jonadab answered, swallowing.

So that is Dysmas, thought Judas as he studied the leader. I didn't know him well when we were children, for our homes were not close, and after these many years I wouldn't have recognized him.

Now Dysmas let loose at the three legionaries. "And you spawn of hell, you whelps of Israelitish bitches, if ever you come into these hills again escorting an agent of that traitorous Levi the publican to rob our people, I warn you to bring a full century. And, listen: when you return to Capernaum you would do well to hold your peace. If the centurion should send others to punish Zur or to entrap us—" he took a menacing step toward them— "then one dark night three dogs will be found with their throats cut. Remember that we well know who you are."

The comrade he had called Abishai was gesticulating with both hands. "But, Dysmas, why not cut their throats now? Then there'll be four less traitors to Israel to deal with."

"No, that would bring the legionaries fanning out into the hills, and much suffering to our people. It will be the prudent thing to let them return. But—" Dysmas turned again upon the four, his frown dark—"remember, you rats, if but one hair of Zur's head is harmed we'll know with whom to deal!"

"But, Dysmas, my hard-earned coins, my lambs and the young goat——" It was Zur again. He was pointing to the frightened animals. "If they take them I'll be ruined. My children will lack for milk, and without those coins how can we live? I do not owe any coins or any animals for the taxes. They've already been here once for what I rightfully owed and they took even more."

Dysmas waggled a finger at the still trembling agent of Levi the publican. "Open the bag and count out to Zur every penny of what you've taken from him! See to it, Zur, that he returns your money to the last mite." He looked again at the fearful Jonadab. "Unloose the lambs and the goat, and be quick about it!"

Already Jonadab had begun to count out the coins, and when he had handed them to Zur he started cutting the cords that bound the bleating animals.

"Now get you gone," Dysmas commanded, when Jonadab had finished, "and tarry not in your going, you carrion despoilers of your own land, you traitorous sons of wild boars, lest we repent of our charity and run you through with our swords!"

"I don't see why, Dysmas, we shouldn't do it any———"

"No, Abishai! It's better for Israel that we show them undeserved mercy." But he glowered at the unhappy four. "If any one of you ever breathes a word———" He swished his forefinger across his throat. "Now get out!" He pointed along the way that ran from the farmyard past the stable.

The servant of Levi and the three Jewish legionaries came swiftly toward the stable. As they were passing his corner Judas leaned forward at the narrow window the better to see them. One of the men with Dysmas, watching the retreating hirelings of Rome, saw him.

"Look! There in the stable! That fellow!"

"Maybe he's another agent of Levi!"

Dysmas jerked his thumb toward the stable. "Fetch him here."

Judas walked out quickly through the stable doorway and went around the corner to meet the approaching men. "I'm a friend," he said. "Take me to your leader."

The men grinned. "That's exactly what we were going to do," one of them said.

"Peace be with you," Judas greeted, when they came up to Dysmas and the others.

Dysmas eyed him sharply. "With you be peace if your mission is friendly. You were in the stable watching. Why, and how long?"

Judas calmly returned his questioner's inspection. "You're called Dysmas, aren't you—Dysmas of the region of Cana?"

"Why do you ask?"

"I was told to find Dysmas, and by the description given me and what I have just seen and heard from the stable, I judge you're the man I want." Judas pulled out his leather pouch, opened it deliberately, and drew forth a coin, which he handed to Dysmas. "Do you know a man named Gesmas? He suggested I find you. Do you see on the coin a familiar sign?"

"Indeed." Dysmas' frown had vanished. He held up the coin so that the others might see it. "The sign of the cross scratched across the face of Tiberius, the dog. The sign of remembrance." He handed back the coin. "So you come from Gesmas, eh? Where did you strike up with that friend? He's one of the fiercest Zealots in all Galilee."

Judas laughed. "I saw him in Jerusalem not two weeks ago. I was on my way to Galilee and paused there. I'm from lower Judaea—Kiriot."

"A Judaean?" Dysmas' smile vanished. "You're not of Galilee? What might be your purpose in journeying in these hills?"

"I was born in Galilee and lived here as a child. It was then that I knew you, Dysmas."

"You knew me? I don't recall you. Who are you, friend? What's your name?"

"I'm called Judas—Judas of Kiriot, son of Simon. Your father was Elam. The last time we met, Dysmas, was the day your father and my Uncle Bezek died——"

"On the crosses, yes." Dysmas' eyes were on the ground. "I remember you, Judas. We were children. We weren't often together. But I remember you now. We met down the hill below the crosses . . . after they'd broken their legs. I'll never forget that day—never. May God give us vengeance on the devils!" He was silent. But when after a moment he glanced up the dark look was gone. "And I've been hearing of you in recent times, too, Judas, and of the fighting down in Judaea. Why have you come here?"

"My purpose in life is the same as yours, Dysmas. I want to rid the land of the invaders, as you do and the others. We're not so numerous in Judaea as you Zealots in Galilee, but even so there have been many to give their blood for the cause. We've harried the Romans and done them all the ill we could. I thought that by coming into Galilee I might learn ways of better organizing our rebellion, and Gesmas suggested that I have a talk with you."

"I knew he'd gone south, through Samaria, looking for support for us. I didn't know, though, that he'd ventured to Jerusalem. He's taking chances. I fear for him. There's much danger there— the Romans and the priests, too, as you know. I wouldn't give a fig for the difference between Caiaphas and old Annas—" he spat— "and Pontius Pilate." He spat again. "They're all against us."

"That's right. They're against us, the Temple leaders as surely as the Romans at the Tower of Antonia. I know well Caiaphas and Annas his father-in-law. Of the two, I'd say old Annas is the more dangerous because he has more brains."

"I think so. But how is it that you know the High Priests so well?" Dysmas' eyes clouded.

"My betrothed is the niece of Caiaphas."

Dysmas frowned. "Then it would be dangerous——" He hesitated. "What you might learn could get back to the Temple leaders. You know, a woman's tongue——"

"She's discreet. And so is my tongue. And she has no high regard for her uncle."

"Does Gesmas know this?"

"Yes. And it pleases him. Isn't it a good thing to be able to go in and out of the enemy's camp?"

"It is. But isn't it also dangerous? One must be cautious. Well I know it. And so should you. Didn't my father and your uncle—? We should both know well what failure means."

"Well I know, indeed. But we shouldn't hold back because of that. I swore an oath as a child that day as my uncle hung on the cross. And I've never relented in my determination to do Rome all the hurt I can."

"We have all sworn oaths," Dysmas said. "My friends here and others throughout Galilee, and beyond Jabel Jermuk in the north, and southward past Shechem and Mount Gerizim even among the Samaritans. Many are ready to make the new attempt to free our land." He stopped, a sudden puzzlement revealed on his face. "How much did Gesmas tell you of our plans? Did he say he'd be the leader?"

"He told me little, except that I should find you and you'd tell me how things go in Galilee. I wish to help. I supposed you were the leader."

"No, I head only this band. Did Gesmas say nothing of Bar Abbas?"

"I think not. But I'd heard of him, of course. His forays against

the Romans have carried his name to Kiriot. You and he must oper-
ate somewhat alike, judging by the way the publican's man and I
have been received by the two of you." He grinned. "I was with
Bar Abbas just a few days ago. In fact, I was waylaid by his men as
I came north. They took me for the agent of a Phoenician manufacturer. But unlike your followers here, Bar Abbas' men grabbed
the wrong fellow. It was between Jerusalem and Jericho, where the
road runs sharply through the rocks." He related his experience
with the giant chieftain.

When he had finished his story, Dysmas declared, "Bar Abbas, I
think, is the man to lead the Zealots of all Israel. He's a powerful
man, as you must have observed, a natural leader, and he has for the
Romans an inveterate and unrelenting hatred."

"So have I." Judas thought this over. "It might be that Bar
Abbas is the man. I'd been thinking of others."

"Bar Abbas is a great one to sting the enemy. The Romans never
know where to expect him next. You saw him only a few days ago
beyond Jericho, but that's no reason to think he's in that region now.
Somewhere in these hills at this very moment he may be swooping
down on some unsuspecting caravan of Roman traders, servants of
Herod or ordinary rich Jews who hold with the Temple despoilers.
He takes their money and with it helps feed poor widows and children in Galilee and Judaea. And he might let a crumb fall to
Samaria. So they tell of him." Dysmas laughed. "I wouldn't be
surprised if he also let a denarius or two stick to the lining of his
own pouch."

"Well, why not?" Judas, grinning, looked along the circle of
Dysmas' men. "Is not the laborer worthy of his hire? Anyone who
robs a Roman, I say, deserves to keep a sizable portion of the loot."

Dysmas cast a glance at the sun, still high above the rounded rim
of the hills. "We must be going, if we are to reach Nazareth in time
for the wedding feast. Judas, you must go with us. You have no
other plans for lodging tonight, have you?"

"My plans came to an end when I came on you," Judas said,
laughing.

"Then you must go with us."

"But I wonder if——"

"If you'd be welcome? Of course. The bridegroom is my brother. The feast will be at his new home at Cana. He's marrying his childhood sweetheart, a girl from Nazareth—Esther the daughter of Cleopas."

"Nazareth? Have you heard of one Jesus from Nazareth?"

"Jesus? Yes, I've known him all my life. We're the same age. We played together as children. He's the son of Joseph the carpenter, who died some ten years ago. Why do you ask about him?"

"For the last few days I've been thinking that possibly he'd be our leader, that he might even be the promised Messiah of God to——"

"Jesus!" Dysmas stood, mouth open, gawking. "Jesus the leader against the Romans—the Messiah of Israel? Man, what do you mean? You must have had too much sun down in the desert. Jesus heading our revolt!" He shook his head. "I could never see Jesus leading any such movement. How did you come on such a notion?"

"I've just come from the ford of the Jordan below Bethabara where the Prophet John has been preaching repentance and baptizing great numbers and——"

"I've heard much of him," Dysmas said.

"John told the people with great emphasis that the Messiah would shortly appear. The next day when Jesus came walking along the highroad above the ford John pointed to him and shouted that he was the Messiah."

Dysmas smiled. "What did Jesus do?"

"Nothing. He kept on walking." Judas smiled. "I'm not holding with John. I've just been mildly wondering. I take it you certainly don't hold with him either."

"I know nothing of the prophet except what I've heard, but it's ridiculous to speak of Jesus as the Messiah." Dysmas' expression changed. "Don't misunderstand me. I think well of Jesus. He's my friend. I've played many a long day with him and the other youngsters at Nazareth. He's a most worthy young man, from his earliest youth upright in every way. But that Jesus should be the Messiah—the son of old Joseph the carpenter, a poor boy and from Nazareth——" He broke off, smiling. "Doesn't that sound beyond believing?"

Judas agreed. "I thought that, too. Maybe it was the Prophet John who had too much sun. But though I saw this Jesus only from a distance, I'll confess there seemed something strong, something—something majestic, about him."

"He is strong. He could outrun, outswim and outwrestle any of the other boys at Nazareth. He's got strength of will, too. But he could never lead a military expedition. That's foreign to everything about him. He'd never engage in shedding blood. I tell you—" Dysmas' tone grew enthusiastic—"I believe we'll find that Bar Abbas is our man. He's a fellow truly eaten up with hatred of the Romans. He's the opposite of Jesus. Jesus doesn't hate anybody, even Romans."

"Doesn't he love Israel?"

"He loves Israel, yes. But he loves everybody else, too. He has no hate in his heart for anybody. He's—he's the most softhearted man you ever saw."

"Then Bar Abbas and not this Jesus is our man?" Judas asked.

"I think Bar Abbas is. I know Jesus isn't the man to lead us." Dysmas pointed toward the sun. "But we'd best be getting started. There's much walking between here and Cana." He turned around. His eye lighted on the fat, short farmer. "I don't think they'll be back, Zur. Should they come and take your possessions or otherwise molest you, get word to me."

"I'll do it, Dysmas. And may the God of Israel bless you and your band for what you've done for me this day!" He bowed low and Dysmas smilingly bowed back.

Then Dysmas turned to his Zealot comrades. "Hatach, you and Shinar were going with me to the wedding, weren't you?" They nodded. "You others had better be getting home. Be careful. I'll summon you when it's needful." Dysmas hitched up his brown homespun robe, tightened the girdle about his middle. "Let's be going. We wouldn't want to be late for the festivities. Come along, Judas. There'll be wine and much merrymaking, and you never know what other excitement might develop at a wedding feast." He turned about abruptly. "Listen, Abishai," he said: "be careful with your sword. We don't want to bring the legionaries of the Capernaum centurion down on our heads until—" he grinned at Judas— "our plans are better made, eh, Zealot?"

Chapter 13 ✠

ALREADY the lamps had been lighted when they turned into the courtyard at the home of Dysmas' brother.

"Let's go around the house to the gallery at the back," Dysmas suggested. "It's well to know who's in a house before one enters. Judging by the merriment, many are already here."

At the hitching rack several animals were pawing the earth and switching their tails to dislodge annoying flies. Dysmas pointed to four horses tied near the more patient asses. "Romans at the feast," he said. "But not many."

A woman came out on the gallery. For a moment she was plainly revealed in the light of the lamps inside the chamber. She was slender, slightly stooped, as with the weight of years and much toil, and her hair that a few years ago must have been black as a raven's wing was now streaked with gray.

The light now was also on the four men approaching the gallery, Dysmas in the lead. As soon as the woman looked toward them she recognized him. Instantly her face lighted, and she came forward to greet them. "Dysmas! It's good you've come!"

"And it's good to see you again, Mary. How are the marriage festivities going?"

"Most enjoyably, Dysmas, I think. We were afraid you wouldn't get here. Several times your brother has inquired for you, and so has Esther."

"How is the little bride?"

"She looks lovely, and she seems so happy! It is a happy match, isn't it? We're all glad for them, Dysmas. It is our good fortune that you've come for the feast, though others have come ahead of you. Go wash your feet and hands after your journey, and take your friends with you, for they're most welcome." She smiled warmly.

"Forgive me, Mary. The excitement of the wedding has robbed me of my manners. These with me—" he singled them out—"are Hatach and Shinar, and this is Judas, who comes from Kiriot down in Judaea." Then he bowed as he presented her: "Mary of Nazareth, my beloved neighbor."

"Peace be with you!" she said, inclining her head graciously.

"With you be peace!" Shinar answered, and Hatach and Judas in turn acknowledged the introduction.

She flicked back several strands from her perspiring forehead. "Now all of you begone, for you are missing the feast. Dysmas, the waterpots are along the gallery, and there are servants there, and towels. Hasten, before they consume the food and the wine." She started into the chamber and then turned to them again. "Dysmas, I'd forgotten the best news of all. Jesus is here!"

"He is?"

"Yes." Her face was beaming. "He came with the bride's procession. He and his friends got to Nazareth this afternoon and they came on with the wedding party! Wasn't that a wonderful surprise for me? I was so happy to see my son again."

"I'll be glad to see him, too. How is he?"

"He seems in excellent spirits, Dysmas, though I've had little chance to talk with him because I've been so busy preparing for the feast. He does look very thin. He's been far south in the Wilderness, he told me, and I think he's had little to eat since he left home. He's been away almost two months."

"I heard that he visited the Prophet John at the Jordan."

"Yes, he told me so. I'm very proud of John. But what I hear keeps me in continual anxiety for him. He has no guard on his tongue, they say, and he doesn't know what the word fear means. I'm afraid he'll get into trouble with the authorities. He's the son of my cousin Elizabeth, the wife of Zacharias the priest. Or did you know that?"

"Yes, I'd heard it, Mary." Dysmas, who had begun to go along the gallery, paused. "These friends of Jesus you spoke of—who are they?"

She wiped her forehead with the back of her hand. "They came with him. One is my nephew John, son of my sister Salome and Zebedee. You know him, don't you, Dysmas?"

"I know John well. The others?"

"All young men, like John, from Bethsaida—except Nathanael. Don't you know him, too?"

"He's that learned young rabbi—or he's studying to be one—isn't he?"

"Yes, that's the one. And another is called Philip, and the two others are brothers, Andrew and Simon. Simon's a big heavy-bearded fellow who talks all the time. If you listen——" She paused. "Yes, I can hear him above all the laughing and talking in there—every now and then." Mary motioned suddenly with her hands as though she were trying to drive chickens back from the courtyard. "But you four must be getting yourselves ready for the feast. If you don't hurry, I'm afraid everything will be gone before you get inside the chamber."

"But, Mary, those horses out there at the rack——" Judas motioned with his thumb. "Aren't there Romans here?"

"The centurion of Capernaum. But he isn't wearing his uniform."

"There are four horses."

"The others bore the son and daughter of Chuza—you know, old Herod's steward—and a young woman some said had come from Jerusalem to visit the centurion." She smiled. "He hasn't a wife; it may be that she's hoping to snare him. But I've hardly seen them, for I've been busy with the serving. But make haste, Dysmas; wash, and go in to the feast."

They went along the gallery to the stone waterpots that stood against the wall. A servant dipped water for them from one of the vessels. He had to lean far down into the pot to fill his pitcher.

"There must be many guests," Dysmas said to the servant.

"Indeed there are, sir. They were all dust-covered from long traveling. It has taken much water." He pointed to the vessels. "You can see for yourself, sir. There are six waterpots, five borrowed from the neighbors. They must hold two or three baths each, and several are well-nigh empty."

"Yes, and Sepphoris baths, at that," Dysmas agreed. "The guests must have required much cleansing."

They washed their hands. Then they sat on the bench for the servant to wash their tired, soiled feet. He dried them with a towel that had been tucked into his girdle. One by one he took their robes to the terrace beyond the gallery and shook them.

As they were going toward the chamber where the wedding feast seemed now to have reached its height, a woman came out and walked past them. Dysmas recognized her as a woman of Nazareth. She went straight to Mary.

"Mary," she said, "the wine is about to give out. What must we do? There were so many more guests than we had expected—Jesus and the five with him, and more from Cana than we had prepared for, and the centurion and his friends." She glanced toward the four in the gallery. "There are still others coming. It would be disgraceful to have the wine give out."

Mary mopped her face and forehead with a corner of her apron. "He had no way to fetch wine with him," she said. "And likely he had no money, nor those with him." She reflected a moment. "Go back into the feast chamber and speak privately with my son. Tell him that his mother bids him come to her."

Without a word the woman turned back to the feast.

"Let's wait here and stand back in the shadows," Dysmas said.

They moved out of the circle of light that fell on the floor through the doorway from the kitchen. If Jesus saw them when he came from the chamber he did not indicate it. "Mother," he said, "you sent for me?"

"Son, there's no more wine—" her distress was in her voice— "and still the guests come. What will they say when they see we have no more? What will the governor of the feast say? And what of the bridegroom, and little Esther?"

Judas, leaning forward, looked at the Galilean standing lean and tall before his mother. Jesus seemed even taller than he had last week on the highroad above the Jordan ford. The expression on his bronzed thin face was solemn and remote; it appeared as if he were trying to bring some distant scene into clear focus.

Then Jesus looked straight into his mother's eyes. "But my dear woman," he said quietly, "how does this concern me? Do you not know that my time of authority has not yet come?"

She lifted her tired, perspiring, perplexed face to her son.

Saying not a word, Jesus walked the three paces to the window and stood a moment gazing out across the night toward the far unseen heights of Kurn Hattin. His back was to Mary.

"Whatever he tells you to do," she whispered to the servants, "do it."

Jesus turned to her again. Judas, watching from the shadows of the gallery, saw the sternness of the tall Galilean relax, and a warming smile drive it away. Judas fancied he could see a film of tears brightening his eyes.

Now Jesus walked over to pat his mother's shoulders caressingly, and then he spoke to the servants who had ceased their bustling to listen. "Take your vessels out to the well and draw water. Clean the waterpots out there and then fill them to the brim."

Immediately they began to obey him. He caught his mother's elbow. "Mother, sit down and rest a moment. You are tired and distraught from much serving." With the sleeve of his white robe he wiped the perspiration from her face. He sat down beside her, put his arm lightly about her shoulders.

After a while the servants began bringing the water and pouring it into the waterpots.

"What's he going to do?" Judas whispered to Dysmas.

"I was wondering. But soon we'll see."

The door to the feast chamber opened, throwing a square shaft of light across the floor of the gallery. The four men saw coming through the doorway the woman who had first warned Mary that the wine was nearly exhausted. She went past them into the kitchen.

"The wine," she said to the mother of Jesus, "is now all gone, and some are already calling for more."

Jesus at once came out onto the gallery. "Have you filled the waterpots?" he asked.

"We have, sir, to the very brim," a servant replied, "so that each is running over."

"Now get your pitchers," Jesus said, his voice louder so that all the servants might hear, "and draw from the waterpots, and bear them to the governor of the feast. See that all are properly served."

As Jesus turned to go along the gallery he spied Dysmas. Instantly his deeply tanned face lighted, and with outstretched hand he walked across. "Dysmas!" He clapped his hand on his friend's shoulder. "I am glad to see you! It has been many months since our paths crossed. How are you?"

"I've fared well, Jesus," Dysmas answered, smiling. "I too am happy in this meeting. I saw Mary and talked with her a moment ago. She told me you'd come to the feast."

"And these friends of yours——"

"You know Hatach here, and Shinar, I think," Dysmas said. "They are of this region and you may have come upon them in various parts of Galilee."

"Yes, I do remember them. I am happy to see you again." He turned to Judas. "And this brother——"

"—is Judas of Kiriot. Judas, I've spoken to you of Jesus, my childhood friend of Nazareth."

Judas felt the penetrating gaze of the Nazarene, almost as if it

were looking through him into the dark courtyard. He felt his
cheeks flush; he wondered if his confusion were noticed by Jesus.
Then with a strange suddenness a warmth flooded through him,
the confusion was gone, and he looked deep into Jesus' eyes.

"My brother," the Galilean was saying, "I am happy to know you
and to bid you welcome to Galilee. Have you traveled before in
this section?"

"Sir, I was born here," Judas answered, "and lived here until
after the—the days of Sepphoris. Then my father moved us southward and settled at Kiriot."

A cloud crossed the face of the tall man. "Sepphoris—yes, I well
remember. I too well remember. . . . And so does Dysmas," he
added with a grave compassion. Then instantly the cloud was gone.
"But let us go into the feast chamber," he said brightly. "Your
brother the bridegroom will want you to share in the festivities,
Dysmas, and he will welcome you, Hatach and Shinar, and you too,
Judas."

"At the hitching rack, Jesus, we saw Romans' horses———"

"They belong to the centurion of Capernaum and his party. They
came as friends, Dysmas. They are sharing in the merriment."

They walked along the gallery. At the doorway to the chamber
they stopped. "You go in to your place, Jesus," Dysmas said. "Then
we'll slip in and find places. After the feast has ended we'll meet
again."

Jesus nodded, opened the door and went inside. After a moment
Dysmas nudged Judas. "Let's go in now. We can move softly
inside without disturbing the merrymaking. I wonder———" He
said nothing more. The four pushed through the doorway.

The room, they saw, was thronged with guests who reclined
about the table, set in the form of a square with one side open. It
was not difficult, because of the music and the revelry, for the four
to ease unnoticed along the wall to a small table with vacant
couches.

The governor of the feast and the bridal couple—with the princi-
pal guests, including Jesus, ranged on either side of them—reclined

at the head of the table on the farther side of the chamber. Dysmas
whispered to Judas, "That's the centurion of Capernaum with the
beardless face and the cropped head . . . not far along the board
from the bridegroom. He's left off his cuirass and is wearing a
plain white tunic. See him?"

"Yes, I see the one you mean, I think. He has taken off his toga.
Is that the one?"

"Yes, that's the centurion. He's a decent person, too, for a
Roman, though I hold no sympathy for any Roman."

"Nor do I. I'd favor——" Judas stopped abruptly. A stout
fellow within arm's length moved slightly, so that he had an entirely unobstructed view of the woman seated beside the centurion.
She was Cynara! The light from the lamps on the walls was reflected
in her bright yellow hair gathered in a filmy net and knotted at the
back of her neck. Her lips looked as red as the meat of a ripened
pomegranate. At her other side sat a young man and beside him
another young woman; Judas knew from what Mary had said that
they must be the son and daughter of Chuza, steward of the household of the Tetrarch Herod.

The servants were moving about the chamber, filling the cups,
placing new helpings of small wheat cakes before the guests, re-
filling the trays that held the fruit—grapes, figs, pomegranates.
Hardly had Dysmas and Judas and the two others settled themselves
when the governor of the feast arose and lifted his cup. The commotion quieted.

"I am about to propose a toast," said he, "but before I do so I
make this observation: We've been enjoying a notable wedding
feast. It has grown better and better as the evening has drawn on.
The food tastes better the more we eat, and the women——" he
smiled with delight at the sound of his own voice—"grow more
beautiful the longer we look at them. And that is——" he paused
again, as if to make a statement of great significance—"as it should
be." He laughed at his wit. "What was I going to say? Oh, I remember! I was going to make an observation. It is this: I have
noticed heretofore at wedding feasts or other convivial gath-

erings that the host sets out the good wine first, and then the wine that is not so good, and finally the wine hardly fit to be drunk. But, my friends, our host the bridegroom has departed from that custom. He set out good wine at first, but now, after we have drunk much, he reserves for the last the finest wine I have ever tasted!"

He raised his cup higher. "Let us drink once more to the health of the bridegroom—" he bowed to the beaming new husband and lower to Esther—"and his beautiful bride."

"The governor of the feast has had so much already that he can't tell water from wine," said Dysmas, grinning. He beckoned to a servant who was entering with a large pitcher held high. "We've just arrived at the feast and wish refreshment. Is that some of the new wine?"

"It is, sir. I've just drawn it from one of the waterpots." He filled the four cups.

Dysmas raised his. "Now, my friends, let's drink this sparkling cold water from the well of my brother the bridegroom." As he moved the cup the light from one of the wall lamps shone on the liquid. "It does have good color," he said. "That's strange." He took a sip, licked his lips. "Men," he said, the cup poised, "this is wine, and good wine!"

Shinar tasted, then took another swallow. "I've never had better."

"You mean—?" Judas sipped, rolled the red liquid on his tongue, swallowed. "This is unbelievable! It can't be wine . . . and . . . yet it is." He swung half around in his seat and beckoned to the servant who had filled their cups. "Are you quite certain that this wine came from one of the stone waterpots just now filled with water?"

"Indeed I am, sir. I drew it out myself."

"My friend Dysmas, how can this be?"

Dysmas shrugged. "I don't know. But it's good wine—I know that."

Judas leaned over on the couch so that nothing would stand between him and the tall Galilean in the white homespun robe. Jesus appeared to be enjoying himself. Though Judas could not hear his words because of babbling tongues loosened by the wine, he could see that Jesus was joining in the talk; once he heard his melodious laughter above the jovial tumult.

How can it be? Judas wondered. Who is this young man? What is he? There seems something—something majestic about him, in his countenance, in the spread of his shoulders, in the way his shapely head sits firm and straight on the column of his neck. Or do I fancy more than I see? . . . This red and sparkling liquid was a few minutes ago cold water from the well of Dysmas' brother. How can that be? One may speculate and philosophize and offer conclusions based on premises, and the conclusions may fall on one side or another. But here in this cup is fact. Here is no argument. This is indeed wine. Yet it has never seen the juice of one grape.

Suddenly in remarkable clarity the words of the Prophet John came back to Judas. Is this Jesus the Messiah of God? Who else could make good wine of plain water? Yet the Scriptures teach that the Messiah will spring from the seed of David the great king. They teach that he will himself be a powerful king and a mighty warrior to deliver his people. Then how can this carpenter son of a carpenter be Israel's deliverer? How can one look to a poor youth from a mean village on a hillside, a young hewer of beams, to fashion a new kingdom?

Yes . . . but the liquid in the cup nevertheless was wine.

What would Bar Abbas say? How would the uncouth, hulking preyer on the privileged look on this gracious Galilean? How would the Rabbi Nicodemus, that learned Sanhedrinist, explain the wine? Or Shelomith?

Thinking of his betrothed, Judas thought also of the Roman girl, and he turned about to see her again as she reclined in her seat of honor across the chamber. Why is she here among Jews at a wedding feast? Why has the centurion come? To spy on us? They say he befriends the Jews at Capernaum. Yet this very morning his hireling soldiers aided the thieving agent of Levi the publican to collect unowed taxes from the fat farmer. Is this girl hoping to marry the centurion?

But the woman is beautiful! By standards of the Jewish women
at the feast—and all are Jews but her—Cynara is lightly clad. But
not so lightly as the other night in the tent! The other night?—no,
weeks ago. Perhaps it's the sight of her that brings that night back
so vividly. That strange, exciting night . . . when nothing happened!

In the safety of laughing and chattering guests between them he
stared at her. Staring, he hardly saw the loose, light-blue waist-
length jacket of shimmering silk cut low at the bosom and held
together at the front by a jeweled clasp. Looking at her with newly
aroused warmth, he fancied her as he had first discovered her. The
silken blue jacket became the sheer black nightdress, and though
she reclined on the other side of the board and actually he could
see nothing of her below her waist, he imagined himself looking
through the intervening guests and the table to see her once again
outstretched in feigned slumber.

She's Roman, yes, he thought, and the sister of Longinus the
enemy of Israel and my enemy. She's pagan, lustful and evil, and it
isn't right for her to be here consorting with sons and daughters of
Israel. But all the same her hair is the color of corn beginning to
ripen in the sun. Her eyes burn into my being, and her lips are red
and tempting. In the arms of a lover she would be warm and yielding yet spirited and challenging. Oh, that I might——

A commotion outside, beyond the gallery, the sound of strident,
demanding voices instantly dispelled the alluring vision. The door
had been left open to provide fresh air in the close chamber. The
guests near it sat up on their couches.

"What caused that outcry?" Shinar asked Dysmas. "Do you
suppose—?"

"Brigands to rob the wedding guests," Dysmas ventured. "Or it
might be——"

Mary was in the doorway. "Dysmas, come quickly! And will
one of you men ask my son to come? Tell him to make no stir, but
to come quietly. I do not wish to disturb the feast if it can be
prevented."

Dysmas, with Judas and Hatach following—Shinar was pushing

through the diners to give Jesus his mother's message—went hurriedly out on the gallery. In the shadows Judas snatched out his sword. He could see skulking figures outlined faintly in the gloom of the courtyard. "We'll have them!" an angry voice shouted. "Stand back! We're coming in to get them."

Judas stepped from the gallery to the courtyard and started to run. From the darkness a leg was thrust out to trip him. He fell heavily on his face. His sword flew from his hand. It landed in the square of light that fell on the ground from the opened kitchen door. Out of the corner of his eye Judas saw Dysmas recover it. And at the same moment a crushing weight landed on his hips.

"Get up, you foul assassin! Get off him before I thrust this sword through your carrion hide!" Dysmas' voice. Judas twisted his head around to look up. Dysmas was waving the sword dangerously near a plump stomach. "God in Israel," Judas murmured, "it can't be for a second time that fat fellow of Bar Abbas' band! Twice within a week!"

"I thank you for the compliment of being referred to as possessed of carrion hide," the man was saying to Dysmas as he clambered panting to his feet. "The last one I landed on called me a sow's belly. To a good son of Israel that's far worse than——" Judas was erect again. Dysmas handed him his sword. The light, as he moved a step, was on his uncovered head. "May God in Israel be praised! It's the same redhead! Bar Abbas'll have me boiled and my bones picked clean!" Shishak waddled nearer. "I'm awfully sorry, friend Judas. Bar Abbas will be glad to see you, though he'll curse me beyond all bounds for falling on you again. But we didn't——"

"Bar Abbas, did you say?" Dysmas strode up. "Where is he? Doesn't he know better than to come here disturbing my brother's wedding feast?"

A huge, dark, bearded fellow came into the square of light. "Dysmas!" he shouted. "Ho, fellow, has this pot of spoiled sheeps' gut molested you, my friend? Say the word and I'll——" He spied Judas. "By the great God of Israel! Judas of Kiriot! Who'd have thought we'd find you here? How're you, Judas?"

Judas was straightening his disheveled robe. "All but flattened, Bar Abbas, by that fat slob of sow's belly." He smiled wryly.

"You don't mean that Shishak sat down on you again!" Bar Abbas roared with laughter.

"He tripped me in the dark and fell on me—with all that weight of undeserved belly. The third time I may not be in as good humor."

Shishak protested, "But, Bar Abbas, he charged out swinging his sword. I feared he might destroy us all."

Dysmas was in no jesting mood as he confronted the other Zealot leader. "How is it, Bar Abbas, that you and your men come storming uninvited to my brother's wedding feast? If you'd come in a mannerly way you know you'd be welcome. But coming like a skulking thief in the night and then creating a great commotion and uproar——"

"We didn't know it was a wedding feast, or your brother's, Dysmas," answered Bar Abbas spiritedly. "We did know that Romans were here——" he pointed toward the rack where the horses were tied—"and we were told that even the centurion of Capernaum was in the group. We came for them. And we aren't leaving until we get them—and their money pouches. That centurion will be worth much in ransom money."

"Bar Abbas, I didn't know you were such a fool. I'm no lover of Rome, and you well know it. But the centurion came to this house as a friend, not wearing his uniform, and he was received as a friend. He'll leave in the same manner. That's the first law of Israel, and any good Israelite knows it." With his forefinger Dysmas punched Bar Abbas in the chest, emphasizing each word with a new thrust. "And you know too that, though we waylay Jewish hireling soldiers of Rome and swoop down on Roman agents and drive them ragged by every means we can, your assaulting a centurion tonight in a Jewish home would be taken by Rome as a sure sign that a general revolt is near. With certain swiftness it would bring destruction to this house and the full fury of the legions on every Zealot they could lay hands on—before we're ready! So, if you won't come in to the feast as a guest——"

"I'll go in, but it will be only to fetch out those pagans whom no good Jew would permit at his wedding feast. And, Dysmas, though you're a Zealot and my friend, you'll not stop me!" Bar Abbas called into the darkness: "Chittim! Doeg! Habbakuk! Nun! All you men! Bidkar! Come here! Meshelemiah! . . . Now stand aside, Dysmas, or you'll be hurt, I fear!"

Dysmas jerked his sword from his girdle. "You'll have to kill me before you go in there with drawn sword, Bar Abbas! You'll not so dishonor my brother and his bride, or the customs of ancient Israel!" He stepped immediately in front of the hairy Zealot chieftain.

"Why, you foolish young goat of the mountains! Would you have your skull cleft defending Israel's enemies? Out of my way, Dysmas! You see these men at my back, don't you? To one side, Dysmas, while your head is still on your shoulders, while you can still——"

Suddenly Bar Abbas was silent. At the edge of the gallery, in the center of the square of light, with the lamps behind him outlining his tall white-clad figure, stood the young carpenter of Nazareth. Jesus said not a word. But his eyes were staring straight into the startled countenance of the brigand chieftain.

"Who's—— Who are you?" Bar Abbas asked, his belligerent manner gone.

From the shadows Judas watched curiously. Does Jesus know this man's reputation as a fierce partisan of Israel, a hater of all Romans? And does Bar Abbas know—but of course he can't—that this Galilean standing so calmly at the gallery edge has just transformed water from the well into wine of finest flavor?

For a moment Jesus gazed deeply into Bar Abbas' eyes. "I am your brother," he said after a while. "Are we not all children of the Father? Peace be with you, Bar Abbas! Won't you and your friends come in to the wedding feast——"

"But there are Romans——"

"—or if not, will you depart peacefully and not longer violate the honor of Israel and this house?"

Bar Abbas started toward the gallery. Will he attempt to thrust Jesus from his way? Judas wondered. And what will the Galilean do? . . . The Zealot leader stopped. The wonderful eyes held him. Jesus raised his arms, held them away from his body and somewhat forward. Judas, looking from the darkness, saw the black shadow of a cross flung outward in the patch of light on the ground in front of the Nazarene. Bar Abbas, his eyes momentarily cast down, must have seen it also. He seemed almost to cringe from that silhouette.

"Bear not in your heart malice against any man, my brother," Jesus said. "Seek rather to love all men." On his countenance Judas saw strength and an infinite tenderness.

Bar Abbas stood an instant. He opened his mouth as if about to protest, but he said nothing. Then he slowly walked away from the gallery toward the little group of his men in the shadows. Judas saw him motion to them to follow him. In another moment they had disappeared through the gateway in the courtyard wall.

Jesus was turning gravely to go back to the chamber. Judas ran forward. "Rabbi, it took great courage to speak that way to Bar Abbas. He too is courageous and it's said he's quick to anger. The Prophet John must have spoken truth when he said——"

Jesus' face brightened. "John is a great man. He is brave. He fears no man." He gestured along the gallery toward the doorway. "Let us return to the festivities." Briefly his eyes fastened on the man of Kiriot. "Judas, when you have gone back to your home and finished the task there and at Jerusalem, then come again into Galilee and join me and these other friends of mine." Smiling, he went into the chamber.

Judas and Dysmas followed, sat down again at their places.

"Jesus doesn't seem difficult to talk with, and yet——"

"Difficult to talk with Jesus!" Dysmas laughed. "Of course not. I know of no one more approachable."

"Yet if he's the Messiah of God——"

"How can you think he could possibly be the Messiah? He's a

plain village youth, son of poor parents, reared with frugality. The Scriptures teach that the Messiah will come of the royal lineage and be a great one in Israel."

"Yes, I so understand. But—" Judas tapped his cup—"how do you explain this?"

"I'll confess I don't understand," Dysmas said. "Perhaps Jesus has learned the art of the magicians. Yet I'd never suspect him of interest in necromancy."

Judas had been sipping the wine. He set down the cup. "Another thing: How did Jesus know—" his eyes were wide with sudden questioning—"that I was going down to Kiriot and then again to Jerusalem to finish a task? How did he know that?"

Dysmas laughed. "Perhaps he just suspected it. Are you?"

"Yes. I must be getting the lambs ready to take to Jerusalem for the sacrifices at the Temple. We're hoping to have a profitable business this year."

"Do you deal with the sons of Annas, or directly with the pilgrims who come to the Passover trusting to buy there the animals for sacrifice?"

Judas toyed with the wine cup. "Generally we sell to old Annas and his sons directly, but lately my father has been threatening to set up his own booths and sell to the pilgrims himself. The priestly family have grown so miserly that it's hard to make a profit dealing with them. They require their overseers to inspect every lamb, beat down the price for blemishes real or imaginary, and haggle over every mite."

"But there are no blemishes when they sell to the pilgrims the animals they've bought from you? And the prices they set then are high even for animals without blemish, aren't they?"

"You're right. It's a shame to Israel how the High Priest and his sons and his son-in-law Caiaphas are fattening on the poor ones who come up for the Passover. They're adding weights to the backs of our people already overburdened by the Romans. That'll be another matter to be considered when——"

"When the new day dawns, eh, Judas?"

"Yes, when the Messiah comes to lead us out of this bondage. I'm not so sure that——"

"That yonder Nazarene friend of mine," Dysmas interrupted, smiling, "isn't the Messiah." He seemed to consider this; then he said, "No, Jesus isn't the Messiah. He may have turned water into wine. It must have been water, and now it's wine, that's certain. Whatever he did was to bring joy to the guests here, and to please his mother." Dysmas lowered his voice. "He didn't thrust his sword to make Roman blood flow. Nor will he. I'll wager he doesn't own a sword, or even a sling and a few rounded pebbles."

Judas shook his head solemnly. "Yes, but he has great power. If we are to succeed we must have, more than anything else, power. The legions of Rome can't by our wishing it be made to walk into the sea or disappear in the darkness of night——" A sudden excitement flushed his face. "Or could they? Listen, Dysmas: if a man by merely wishing it could change six stone waterpots of water into that same amount of wine of potency and flavor, he could also——"

"Judas, you must have drunk too heavily of it." Dysmas laughed softly. "I don't know how Jesus accomplished this trick of wine making, but you can never convince me he's the Messiah."

Soon the guests began to leave the feast. When Judas inquired if they also should depart Dysmas proposed that since he was the bridegroom's brother they remain and join those who would escort the bridal pair to their bed. "When they've pushed us from the chamber and barred the door we'll stay awhile in the gallery outside and tease them."

So they stayed, and when the feasting was ended they went with the laughing, chattering throng. After the last shout of good-natured raillery at the happily embarrassed pair Judas walked along the gallery toward the window at its darkened end. He was peering out when he felt someone brush against him lightly. He turned around.

"Well! The bashful redhead of the tavern—and the tent!"

"I saw you at the inn of Meshach, yes."

The Roman girl, her face almost against his in the gloom of the gallery, laughed merrily. "Yes, you did. And you saw me—much more of me, too—in the tent. But why are you so hesitant, Judas? Why didn't—?"

"Cynara!" The centurion of Capernaum was calling her from the other end of the gallery.

"I'm coming! I'm coming!" she answered, but her eyes never left Judas' face. "I must be going, or he'll come after me. I saw you across the chamber, and you saw me, though you pretended not to. Oh, Judas, come to Capernaum!" She pulled the sleeve of his robe lightly. Her face was very close to his, so close that he could see the redness of her lips even in the deep shadows, so close that the mingled fragrance of her perfumes and her body enveloped him. "Come again to see me, Judas, and then . . . then I won't scream!"

Chapter 14 ✠

As HE went down toward Kiriot Judas paused in Jerusalem to see Shelomith. He found her at the shop of Benjamin her father.

"My father has some most wonderful things brought lately— about the time you were here last—from Tyre," she said, after she had greeted him warmly. "Wouldn't you like to look at them?"

"No," he said, smiling, "I'd much rather look at you. Besides, that merchandise almost caused me to have the life crushed out of me." He told her how he had been waylaid by Bar Abbas' men who had taken him for the agent of the Tyre manufacturer.

"But, Judas," she said when he had related the incident, "you might have been killed!"

"But I wasn't, my dear girl." He grinned. "In fact, Bar Abbas was a gracious host. I spent the night with him, and early on the next morning as I was leaving to visit the Prophet John——"

"Oh, Judas, tell me about him! Did you see him? Did you hear him speak? And do you think now that he may be the Messiah, as you suspected when you were here?"

"Not so fast! One question at a time." He laid his hand on her arm, laughing. "Yes, I saw him and heard him calling on the multitude to repent." As they left the shop and walked along the cobblestones toward her home he reviewed the visit to the Wilderness prophet and tried to make clear his impressions of that strange and impelling preacher.

"But did you leave satisfied that he is the Messiah?"

"No. On the contrary, I'm convinced now that John is not. In fact, he said so himself. He pointed to another as that one for whom we look."

"He did? Did he say his name and where he's to be found?"

"Yes, Shelomith, John said all that. And more." Judas continued the recital of his lively journey into Galilee and of all that had occurred there down to the changing of the water into wine at the Cana wedding. Shelomith was astounded.

"That's what happened," Judas reiterated. "I saw the servants pour the water from the well into the waterpots. I drank what came forth a moment later. It was wine, and good wine."

"This Jesus must be a clever magician. What did he claim?"

Judas reflected a moment. "He didn't claim anything."

"Why then did he do—whatever he did?"

"His mother had just told him the wine was about to give out. He did it because they needed the wine, I suppose."

"Then you think this Jesus is the Messiah?"

Judas didn't answer for a moment. "Dysmas doesn't think so. But how else can you explain the wine?"

"Perhaps it isn't necessary to think it more than a trick of magic."

"That's what Dysmas said. He says Jesus is too—too soft to be our leader. Dysmas leans toward Bar Abbas, even though they quarreled in the courtyard the night of the feast."

"If Bar Abbas becomes the leader of the Zealots throughout Israel he'd better be cautious, for the Romans will be all the more determined to catch him. A man here from Capernaum this week told how Bar Abbas was growing bolder day by day and——"

"This man from Capernaum, Shelomith—what business had he here?"

"Oh, something about the taxes. He came to see the High Priest, who was calling on my mother."

"Who was the fellow?" Judas scowled.

"A publican at Capernaum. I think he was called Levi."

"A notorious Jewish traitor who fattens on money forced from his own people! It was one of his agents that Dysmas had caught robbing a farmer in Galilee the day I came on him."

"I talked with the man but little. I don't know——"

"You talked with a despised publican!" Judas' expression was incredulous.

Shelomith smiled. "But he was in my house. And so was the Centurion Longinus, who brought him."

"And you talked with Longinus too?"

She nodded, smiling still.

Judas shook his head, his eyes on the cobblestones. "Shelomith, I didn't know that you held with the High Priest in his scorn for his own people, his violation of Israel's traditions, his . . . his . . . oh, Shelomith!"

"I don't hold with my uncle, as you know, Judas, and I have no love for the Romans as a race of conquerors. Nor do I respect publicans as a profession. But here and there one may come upon a Roman, even a soldier, and sometimes a publican, whom one finds it hard to hate as an individual."

"Then you hate Romans as a race, but you may think highly of particular persons, even Longinus?"

"I didn't say that, Judas. I hardly know the centurion. But he seemed a friendly man." Suddenly her eyes were different. "You thought well of his sister, didn't you?"

"Now you know, Shelomith———"

"Did you see her in Capernaum? Longinus said she visited there."

He avoided her eyes. "I was not in Capernaum."

This time she smiled. "You hate the Romans as a race, too, eh, but you find it hard to hate a Roman woman with hair the color of grain newly ripened, and lips red as cherries, and oh, such a figure?"

He ignored the challenge. "I don't like your talking with Romans, Shelomith, particularly this Longinus. There's only one good Roman, yes, and one good publican. Both are in Sheol. I hate all Romans."

They were nearing her house. "All Romans, did you hear? Pontius Pilate, old Sejanus the prefect, who rules in Rome in the Emperor's stead, even Tiberius himself, and, here in Israel, Longinus, the centurion at Capernaum—all of them—rich, poor, high, low, the doddering old man gnawing his fish with toothless gums, and the baby brat mewling in his crib. I'd like to see the whole damnable tribe hurled into the sea!"

"You hate violently, Judas. It is not good to hate."

He threw back his red head, bleached to a lighter shade by the sun in his traveling, and laughed until passers-by turned to stare. "Yes, I hate them! My hate grows by the day. I'm glad you see my hate for them increasing."

His voice grew calm again. "Hate and strength, Shelomith, strength and hate, I have said it many times: They are the twin weapons that will drive forth the enemy; they are the hammer and anvil with which we will forge the coming victory. Soon the Passover feast will come. And then he'll be here, and———"

"Bar Abbas?"

"No, Jesus."

"But didn't you say that Bar Abbas was the man of hate?"

"Yes, but Jesus is the man of strength, of even supernatural power, and he can be led to be also a man of hate."

"I don't think so, Judas. I'm convinced that you'll never be able to mold him to your thinking. I trust he'll change yours."

Judas gripped her shoulder with his cupped left hand, pulled her playfully to him. "No, the man of hate will set the course for the man of love. And I am the man of hate. With his power, my dear, and my abiding hate, we'll do what Judas of Galilee and my Uncle Bezek failed to do."

They had reached the door. He rapped. As he waited for the servant to admit them he turned about to look southward above the city's ancient wall. His vision centered on an object high beyond the Vale of Hinnom, on the slope that pushed steeply up from the gorge where the fires forever smoldered. "The tree!" he said, almost shouting. "It's still there, strong and twisted and gnarled, fighting, and standing secure, confident and unrelenting in its strength, in its hate of the wind and the whirling sand that cannot prevail against it. I will borrow of its strength and its hate, Shelomith, and I will share with Jesus the hate I have borrowed. We will prevail, we will conquer and we will stand—he, and I, and the tree!"

Shelomith, hearing his wild laughter, wondered and was not a little fearful.

Chapter 15 ✠

WITH a flame in his heart Jesus of Nazareth journeyed toward Jerusalem and the great Feast of the Passover. Winter had gone with the suddenness of a door shut against the night, and spring had burst from winter's tomb to dress Galilee and Judaea in gorgeous colors unmatched in all the wardrobes of Herod's great white palace at Tiberias.

Sometimes Jesus, surmounting a slope that looked eastward to the greening gorge of the Jordan and the gaunt gray headlands of Decapolis, would pause and take a deep breath, as if to fill himself with the million mingled fragrances of apricot blossom, sweet herb, the flower of the pomegranate, the white and yellow narcissus, the crocus of the plain, gladiolus curving on one side of its spikelike stem, the rose of Sharon, the gay windflower, acre on acre spread along the smooth places in brilliant red and delicate pink and white, blue and cream and purple.

"Look you," he said one day to his friends, as he swept his arm in an arc that embraced the land from above the lake to below the Dead Sea far to the south: "What beauty, what divine truth and goodness! See—" he pointed toward a distant gentle slope—"see the silver sheen of the olive trees, and look at the gorgeous dress of the wild flowers. What is comparable to the flowers of Galilee? Can the looms and dyehouses of Tyre equal the blue of this one small hyacinth?" He reached down and plucked the flower, held it so that they might see it.

Jesus was silent a moment as he looked northward toward the silver-blue shimmering of the Sea of Galilee and along the twisting track of the Jordan framed in a welter of blossoming oleanders. "This, all this, is the Father's world. What a heaven, what a glorious heaven, if only man would will it so!"

But he could not often pause thus, for the flame burned in his heart and he must be about his Father's business. In the months that had followed his tremendous experience in the Wilderness of Judaea, a wonderful conviction had been taking deep root and growing within him: The time had come to do battle. With one bold stroke he would cut at the root of an unrighteous, cold and dead system of theology; he would plant in the hearts of those who would have them the seeds of a pure, warm, living love of the Father and all the Father's children.

So south from his new home at Capernaum, along the winding trails that bordered the Sea of Galilee's western shore, through the green meadows by the Jordan, across fords and over waterless wadis and up gentle slopes to the gates of Jericho, and past Jericho's walls along the steep and rugged climb to Bethany and Israel's pulsing heart beyond, Jesus journeyed with his friends in the stream of pilgrims moving toward the Passover.

Chapter 16 ✠

JUDAS came early to Jerusalem to sell his animals and doves for the Passover sacrificing. He rented stalls for his cattle and sheep outside the Dung Gate, where they were inspected by the overseers of Annas and his sons and, after much haggling, some were purchased and removed. Some others he had his servants lead up to the Temple. There he would deal further with the overseers and also sell directly to the pilgrims.

He had followed them to the Temple and was directing the placing of the animals in the stalls set up around the walls of the Court of the Gentiles. He was busily engaged in this when he felt someone touch him lightly on the shoulder. "Kind sir," a disheveled fellow said, "I'm a poor man seeking an honest penny. Would you hire me to help with the animals and the doves?"

"Gesmas!" Judas had seen through his disguise. "Why are you—?"

"Not so loud with the name, Judas. Someone hearing you might hold us both in suspicion. Let's move over there—" he flipped his head sideways—"and sit on that stone bench against the wall. The wall has no ears."

They sat down on the bench.

"Did you make the journey into Galilee, and did you see Dysmas and the others?"

"Yes." Again Judas recounted his journey, told of meeting the

tall Galilean carpenter, Jesus of Nazareth, of the water changed
into wine, of the strange withdrawal of Bar Abbas before the unas-
serted authority of the Nazarene.

"I know this Jesus, though slightly," Gesmas said. "You know
I'm a Galilean too and was brought up near Cana. I think his father
once helped my father build a barn, and I seem to remember that
the man fetched the son along to help. And I've heard more of him
in recent days. His fame is beginning to be noised through the land.
Another one of these evangelists, I'd say, softhearted and soft-
headed, a visionary like the Prophet John but lacking his fire and
thunder—and lacking the courage of Bar Abbas, as you'll agree
when you see him tonight."

"Tonight?"

"Yes, I came here seeking you to say we're meeting after dark at
the shop of Japheth the cobbler. Bar Abbas and Dysmas and the
other Zealot leaders will be there. Urgent plans are to be considered. We want you."

"But this Japheth's shop?"

"This side of Dung Gate, some hundred paces up one of the
narrow ways that run from the square in front of the gate. Someone'll show you." He sniffed. "When you come on a smell such as
this you'll be close to Japheth's. He buys hides from the sons of
Annas who have tanning shacks across the brook Kidron." Gesmas
lowered his voice. "Be careful of your tongue. Old Pilate has his
spies in Jerusalem as thick as the fleas on those dogs that paw the
filth of Hinnom's gulch. He always does during the Passover
season."

So after nightfall Judas started toward Dung Gate. He did not
take time to go to the inn and wash himself and change to fresh
clothing. A clean face and an unspotted robe would be conspicuous
in the stench and closeness of the Lower City.

In the square before the gate set in the eastern wall close to the
place where the Tyropoeon Valley and the brook Kidron came together at the Vale of Hinnom he accosted a man with a long hawk-
beaked nose. "Peace be with you, friend!"

"Peace be with you!" the fellow muttered.

"I'm seeking the shop of one Japheth, a cobbler. Could you direct me to it?"

"It would be closed now." The tone was gruff. "Nor do I see you carrying sandals to be mended."

"It was not to have sandals mended that I was wishing to see him."

The man eyed Judas sharply. "You're not of Jerusalem?"

"No, I'm from Kiriot, though of Galilean stock. I have business with Japheth. So if you'd——"

"Galilean, eh?" The thin face relaxed—grudgingly, Judas thought, though in the yellow light from the fogged window of a linen merchant's shop he could not see the features distinctly. "Japheth's a Galilean, and I too. You're a friend of his?"

"I'm a friend of several of his friends. I was to meet——" Judas hesitated.

Hawk-Nose laughed. "Don't be afraid to speak. I too am attending the meeting at Japheth's shop. I was on my way. You must be Judas son of Simon. We were told to expect you. Gesmas gave you the news today at the Temple?"

"Yes."

"Let us go. Bar Abbas likely has already arrived." Hawk-Nose pointed out a narrow alleyway. "It's just a few paces along there."

The cobbler's shop was closed, but through a slit they could see a feeble light. Hawk-Nose belabored the door with his fist. Sandaled feet came shuffling toward them and a rough voice challenged: "Who's there?"

"Unbar the door, Achbor. It's Ebal, and I've brought Judas of Kiriot."

They heard a heavy bar pushed across the door, and then it was opened.

"They're in the back," a short, swarthy fellow told them. "Bar Abbas is there." He slid the bar into place and followed them to the dimly lighted chamber beyond.

Bar Abbas sat slouched on a low stool facing the door. Light

from two sputtering candles seemed to emphasize the blackness of
his heavy beard and danced in his sharp eyes.

"These are Ebal—" Gesmas was pointing—"and Judas of Kiriot. I think you know——"

"Oho! So I do! Peace be with you, Ebal, and you, friend from
Kiriot!" Bar Abbas beamed. "Judas, I much regret I don't have
Shishak along to greet you properly by throwing himself on your
back, the stupid fat one! How have you been? I haven't seen you
since the night of the wedding feast at Cana when this brainless
one—" he ducked his head toward Dysmas, seated near him—
"came nigh getting his skull cracked by my sword, and that tall one
from Nazareth——"

"—drove you from the courtyard with one straight look of his
eyes," Dysmas completed the sentence in a merry tone.

"He did, I'll not deny," said Bar Abbas. "But to this day I can't
understand why I let him."

"Let's not go into that now," Dysmas said. "We've more important matters to consider. Judas, this one—" he indicated a man
at his left—"is Japheth the cobbler, and this is another Galilean,
he whom you failed to see when you visited us there, Simon the
Zealot."

Judas bowed to each. "Peace be with you, men!" he said. "I'm
glad to meet all brothers in the party." They acknowledged his
greeting.

"I heard after you had gone that you had come seeking me," said
Simon. "I'm sorry, my friend. They told me, though, that you'd
talked with the Master. In fact, he said he talked with you."

"The master? I don't understand."

"Jesus. He whom you saw change the water into wine."

"Yes, but——"

"I've joined his company." Simon smiled. "I'm one who holds
that he is the Messiah."

"Simon, let's not say anything to start dispute," said Dysmas.
"We haven't come to debate whether or not Jesus is the Messiah.
You haven't known him many months, and you say he is. I've

known him all my life, and I say that he's only the carpenter of Nazareth, though an estimable young man. Let it go now. The purpose of our meeting is to determine the most effective means of harassing the enemy during the season of the Passover. Isn't that it, Bar Abbas?"

"Yes." Bar Abbas flailed his knee with a hairy fist. "We want to do the pagan swine all the hurt we can, and this is a proper season. But not alone during the Passover. After it we must not slacken our efforts to plague them, to sally out upon them and rob and slay, and make them wish with all their hearts they had never smirched our land!"

Gesmas agreed. "That's as I see it. While the Roman soldiers are busy here in a city teeming with pilgrims, we can pick them off with an arrow or a javelin from a wall or out of an alley and quickly escape in the honeycombs of our ancient buildings."

Japheth spoke up. "Gesmas is right. We can make things miserable for them, even during the Passover. But we must look also to the days that follow, as Bar Abbas says. We're not strong enough now. We must recruit many more men. We must forge and buy weapons. We must have places prepared where we can hide, to emerge from when the occasion is ripe for striking. The day will come—may the God of Israel advance it!—when we'll drive the oppressor from our soil. But that day is not yet. The Romans are too powerful. We could stand against them only as the straw field against the racing flame. The Romans are——"

He cut short his impassioned words, for there was a sudden banging on the outer door.

"Open! Open in the name of the Emperor!"

"God in Israel! Roman soldiers!" Gesmas jumped to his feet. "The candles! Twist them out!"

"Hold, Ebal!" Japheth commanded, for Ebal was nearest the candles. "They've seen the light through the slit in the door. Bar Abbas, they seek you. And you, Dysmas, and perhaps Gesmas." He pointed toward a high chest against the wall two paces from where the Zealot chieftain had been seated on the stool. "You men know the way through the tunnel—under the wall to the sheep stalls outside the Dung Gate. Get you gone quickly. While I answer the door you others put the chest back in place. Hold your tongues. God in Israel—" the pummeling on the door was furious—"soon they'll be bursting in on us!"

He shuffled toward the front. "I'm coming!" he shouted in a grumbling tone. "Give a man time, won't you? Just hold your peace one moment. Let me get this bar slipped back." He fumbled with the bar, and finally opened the door.

"Peace be with you!" he said calmly. "Welcome to my humble shop! And though it be closed for the day, if I can serve you—— Is it sandals to be mended or—?"

"By Vulcan, we wish none of your cobbling!" declared the officer of the legionaries massed about the doorway. "But if there's one Bar Abbas in your smelly rathole, we're taking him, and you along with him!"

Though Judas was in the rear room, he could hear the Roman distinctly. That voice—it sounds familiar. Can it be that it's—? Oh, God, it's Longinus! He'll recognize me. With this red hair . . .

He clamped the cloth securely on his head, pushed down the black goat's-hair rings to hold it in place.

"Speak up, cobbler!" Judas heard the Roman's impatient words. "Are you sheltering that pig of a Jew? Speak quickly before we tear this sty into splinters!"

"Bar Abbas, did you say?" Japheth, standing in the light of the soldiers' torches, wrinkled his forehead as if in deep thought. "No, Centurion," he said, "there are just a few friends of many a year in the back room. They were helping me with the work, even though it's late. It's the Passover season, you know, and the work's heavy. But won't you come inside?" He stood politely to one side and held the door far back on its hinges.

"If it's not the truth you're telling, by Jupiter, you'll rue your lies, cobbler!" The officer turned to his men. "Publius, command

outside while I go in. See that no one slips past. The door at the
back is covered." He turned to another. "And now you, Quintus,
and you, Galba and Servius—that will be enough—inside, with
me!"

They rushed past Japheth, quickly examined the room, started
through the doorway between the chambers, with Japheth behind
them.

Judas was yelling, "It's an outrage! I'll not pay good coins for
this poor work! See how already the sole is pulling away." He
whirled around, with the sandal he had been shaking in Ebal's face
still gripped securely in his hand. "I'll not pay for such shabby
work. I . . . I . . ." He dropped the hand with the sandal to his side.

"Who's this fellow?" Longinus demanded, pointing to Judas.

"I've long been a customer of this cobbler," Judas spoke up, be-
fore Japheth could answer, "and I've paid out good coins. And
I deserve good work. But look at this sandal—ripping apart before
I've worn it a month." He started toward the centurion. "See?
Look, sir, how this cobbler would defraud me."

"Friend," said Japheth humbly, "I'm sorry the work was not
good. I have been so rushed with the great demands on me. So
many customers! But do not hold it against me. I—I—I won't
charge you, friend. Leave the sandal, and tomorrow you can have
it properly mended. It won't cost you a mite!"

"I wanted it to wear on the morrow," said Judas grudgingly.
"Well——" He shrugged. "See that this time you do a proper
job." He dropped the sandal onto the bench beside its mate and
started boldly toward the door.

One of the soldiers jumped quickly in front of him. Longinus
waved the legionary aside. "Let the Jew go," he said. "That'll be
one less quarrelsome knave to listen to."

Judas walked through the doorway. "Let him pass," the soldier
called out to those at the outer door. "Centurion's orders."

The Romans lost no time searching the room. One of them
walked over to the chest, raised the lid, let it fall. Japheth held his

breath while the soldier stood a moment staring at Ebal, who sat, his mouth crammed with cobbler's nails and hammer in his hand, before a last on which a sandal rested. The nails will help Ebal hold his tongue, Japheth thought. Then he spoke to the centurion. "This man—this Bar Abbas, didn't you say?—what has he done, Centurion?"

Longinus looked him straight in the face a long moment. "By the gods, I've a feeling, cobbler, that you know more than you pretend! We were told that the thieving, murdering scoundrel would meet with others of the Zealots in one of the shops along this foul gutter. There's something strange——" He hesitated. "I've a feeling I've seen that knave before—the one that quarreled about your work." He glared at Japheth, shook his fist under his nose. "We'll find Bar Abbas, and he'll talk when we get him. Jew, if you belong to his party, it'll go hard with you, too!" He kicked a stool out of his way. "Outside, men! The Jew is not here."

Chapter 17 ✠

THE next morning Judas went early to the Temple to complete his trafficking with the overseers of the sons of Annas. They pursued their usual course of hard and unfair bargaining, but Judas was crafty and a match for them. Though he kept back some of the animals for private selling to Passover pilgrims, his leather pouch already bulged with coins, many of them gold.

His business for the morning finished, he started to leave by the Gate Shalleketh that opened on the bridge over the Tyropoeon Valley. The gate stood at the southwest corner of the Court of the

Gentiles, centered between double lines of Corinthian columns. Far below, at the bottom of the fissure, flowed the brook Kidron.

"If any reason should arise for your needing me," he said to one of his servants, "you can find me at the inn, or else at the shop of Benjamin—or his house. See to it that you feed and water the stock in the stalls at the Dung Gate."

Turning around to leave, he collided with a man entering through the gate. The man started to mumble an apology, but suddenly his youthful face lighted. "Judas of Kiriot! Peace be with you, friend! We meet for the first time since the wedding feast at Cana."

"Unto you be peace!" Judas had recognized him as John the son of Zebedee. "How are Jesus, and the others? And the sun-baked prophet of the Wilderness?"

"The prophet is still thundering away, calling in dire words on the people to repent. The others have come with me to the Passover, even the Master. There—over beyond that group of black men from Cyrene, to the right of the gate."

Judas thought the tall Galilean's countenance seemed sad, troubled. Perhaps he was only fatigued; his white robe was filmed over with the soft brown pollution of the dust of travel, and his reddened face was streaked with it. Those about him also were stained from the Judaean roads, now trampled by the feet of pilgrim thousands. The black beard that framed the round face of heavy-jowled Simon, Judas saw, was browned almost to the color of the soil. The thin, ascetic face of Nathanael bar Tolmai was silted with grime.

"We've been traveling fast," John explained. "We're all greatly wearied, and soiled from long walking." He lowered his voice. "And we're a little fearful of the Master's zeal. He's been talking much of the new covenant to which he will bear witness, and of how the priests for long time have brought disrepute on the true worship. We hardly know what to expect of him. . . . But I must go back to the group or he'll think I'm lost. Judas, come see us. The Master will be glad, and so will the others."

Judas thanked him and watched him walk away. Hardly had John rejoined those about the Galilean when Jesus, his dust-streaked

face seeming suddenly to pale, strode quickly straight toward the
pens in which were confined the sheep and cattle that Judas had
sold to the overseers of the High Priest's family.

As he reached the first pen, in which were several small lambs,
one of them cried pitifully; two pens away the mother sheep answered its bleating. The Nazarene reached down over the rails,
grasped the lamb, lifted it up and carried it to its mother. "Get in
there, little fellow," he said, as he dropped it on the hay and struck
it playfully on its tiny round rump.

"What right has that man—?"

Judas, looking around quickly, saw that his servant had arisen
from the stone bench on which he had dropped to rest.

"Quiet!" he commanded. "Stay where you are!"

"But that lamb doesn't belong to——"

"Hold your peace, I told you!"

The servant stepped back, mumbling, and sat down.

Now Jesus, straightening to his full height, saw that already
many nearest him in the bustle and stench of the profaned majestic
Court of the Gentiles had turned to watch him. Saying not a word,
he reached for two small cords lying across the top rail of the pen.
He bent down and picked up another from the mosaic pavement
where it was not foul with animal dung and urine. Calmly he
plaited the cords into a rope the size of his thumb.

Then with his left hand, while he held the short rope securely in
his right, he jerked away the top rail, and then the next, and with
his foot he pushed free the two bottom ones.

A man came rushing toward him. Jesus, standing straight in his
path, seemed to Judas to flash a terrifying indignation. The man
hesitated, then turned away, muttering.

Now there was a stir among those who thronged the great ex-
panse of once proud and unstained marble. As the people surged
toward him, Jesus stepped up on the end of the bench on which
Judas' servant sat. The servant scurried aside. Jesus raised the rope
he had fashioned of the cords. His eyes blazed in fury.

"Call you this unholy trafficking, this filth and noisome odor, this blood and suffering of frightened animals—call you all this—" he swept his arm around so swiftly that the rope whistled—"the true worship of the Father? No, I tell you! This is an abomination in the sight of God, a foul smell in the nostrils of the Most High, a profanation of His holy Temple, a mockery of worship!"

One long instant he was silent. The people, watching the welling of his wrath, were speechless before him. He shook the brown fist that held the corded rope. "Know you that I have come in order that you may know and appreciate the true worship of the Father—and it is none of this!"

With a leap he was off the stone bench and racing toward the other pens. At the first one he whirled about to confront the startled watchers. "Is not this a house of worship?" His words were like lightning, and his face flamed. "And yet you have made it a veritable den of thieves!"

He turned again and with a mighty heave threw down one side of the pen. Then he tore away another. As he pulled down the rails and jerked open the stall doors he waved the animals out. They began to stampede into the large open space, and many fled through the gates.

The servant came running to Judas. "The cattle and sheep are running away. The High Priest's men will never be able to recover them!"

"Let them go," Judas said. "They'll go back to the stalls at the Dung Gate where the others are. Then we'll sell them again to these Temple thieves."

He had not taken his eyes from Jesus.

Jesus strode over to the place where the cages had been set up for doves and pigeons and began unfastening the latches that secured the doors. A white dove ventured out, rose with fluttering wings into the air, circled above the heads of the throng, flew aloft over the smoldering flames on the Great Altar. Then another, and another. In a moment the air was churning with the flutter of wings.

The cages lay broken and empty on the beautiful mosaic of the court.

But he was not finished, this dauntless Galilean with the straight legs, the browned, muscled arms and the flaming black eyes.

Twenty paces from him sat a cluster of tables at which huddled the cunning servants of the Temple in charge of money changing. Many pilgrims coming from distant places did not have the Jewish coins proper for use in Temple worship. Some brought Greek money, some that of Alexandria; some had come from Cyrene, some from Arabia, a few from as far away as Dacia. Many brought pieces bearing the image of Caesar. So they changed their money into Jewish coinage and in the changing they paid a heavy toll.

To the nearest of these tables Jesus walked. He held the rope doubled in his right hand, the loop circled about his wrist. A broker seated behind stacks of coins arranged neatly on the table leaned forward as if to protect his hoard. The edge of the table disappeared into the soft flabbiness of his paunch.

The Galilean looked sharply into the frightened eyes of the money-changer. "Come not into the Father's house to contrive your robbery of His people!" He darted a finger toward the little man. "Get you gone, lest your sacrilege bring down ruin on your head. No more from this table shall you carry on your evil trafficking!"

Jesus reached down, grasped the frame of the table, hurled it over. It fell on its side to the pavement, and the coins rolled in every direction beneath the feet of the crowd. Many snatched for them furtively and thrust them quickly into the folds of their robes.

In an instant he had pushed over the other tables, and the coins— copper, silver, gold—went rolling in a mad jingle and clash along the marble.

Judas stood immobile, as though he had taken root in the pavement, watching the tall man from Galilee country. Amazed, hardly believing what he saw, vastly excited, he gazed while Jesus walked calmly to one of the great Corinthian columns. There the Nazarene stayed quietly as the money-changers scrambled among the laughing, jeering people to seek their rolling coins. The twined whip, still looped about his wrist, trailed to the pavement. As though on looking down he had suddenly discovered it, Jesus with a deft fling of his hand hurled it into the muck of one of the stalls he had just thrown down. Then, without looking toward the angry men he had challenged so dramatically, he strode back to his friends.

Oblivious of the multitude, Judas was staring at Jesus when someone touched him on the shoulder. It was Simon the Zealot.

"Judas of Kiriot!" Simon cried and then lowered his voice. "You got away!"

"Yes," Judas said, "and I'm glad to see you did too."

"The soldiers left soon after you. I was afraid they might have followed you. Longinus said there was something familiar about you, and——"

"He did! It's a good thing I kept on my headcloth."

"You'd best be careful, Judas." Simon brightened. "You saw the Master just now? What do you think of him?"

"I've never seen anyone more courageous. He's utterly fearless. I remember what you said last night, Zealot. You may be—I suspect you are—right."

"Indeed, I am. Come, Judas, let's go over to him."

Jesus received him gladly. His tired features lighted up. "I am happy to see you again. Are you ready to go with us into Galilee?"

"But, Rabbi, my father expects me to take him the money from the sale of the cattle and sheep, and——"

"Were some of these yours?" Jesus signaled with his thumb, smiling.

"I had sold them, sir, to the sons of Annas. But I brought them into the Court of the Gentiles. It was my sinning. I'm truly repentant."

"When one truly repents, the Father is quick to forgive, my brother." Jesus laid a brown hand reassuringly on the Judaean's shoulder. "You are a man of business, Judas. We need such a man in our company. There's much to be done, and I must without de-

lay be about the task my Father has appointed me to do. When you
have gone to Kiriot and finished the immediate work there, return
to me in Galilee, and I shall make you a herdsman not of sheep and
cattle but of men." His smile proclaimed both tenderness and
strength. Without another word he grasped the arm of Simon the
burly fisherman and began walking with him along the row of
columns toward the Gate Shalleketh.

Exultant, Judas gazed after him until Jesus and his company disappeared among the throngs on the bridge. O God in Israel, what
valor, what utter lack of any fear, and what a flame of righteous
anger! A thought came sharp and thrilling to stir him: If the
Nazarene can thus hate, will not hate unleash at the proper time the
power held controlled within his usually calm soul?

If so, then indeed Jesus is the Messiah of God! He is the avenging sword which in due season will expel the pagans. With a small
whip of cords he drove the greedy money-changers before him.
What then can he not do with an army of Israel's youth supporting
him as the great new king of a restored and mighty land?

At Cana he made water into wine to please and befriend. He
demonstrated divine power in doing that. Yes, but today he demonstrated a divine hardihood, a divine anger in ousting the despoilers
of our majestic house of worship.

Bar Abbas? Did he escape the soldiers, or have they ferreted him
out of some crowded hole in Ophel? It doesn't matter now. Bar
Abbas beside this Galilean is an uncouth weakling, a slinking robber of women, children and oldsters, a cringing man of earth. Bar
Abbas is just a brigand of the rocks and hills, of the cellars and tortuous alleys of Ophel. But this Jesus is . . . is . . . yes, let me say it,
O God, let me shout it to these countless pilgrims of the Passover,
for now I know it, I know it indeed! He is that one for whom we
have looked long and with great hope; the Deliverer, the Saviour of
our nation, God's own Messiah!

He did not shout it. He held his peace, though his whole being
rushed to his lips. He looked over the heads of the multitude, be-

yond the fire and smoke from the Great Altar, to the Porch of the
House of God sheltering the Holy Place itself. It seemed to reach
to heaven.

A bright new hope leaped in his heart. Words came, and this
time he spoke aloud.

"And I am his man."

Part II

THE DISCIPLE

✣

THE flame had not subsided when he went to the house of Benjamin.

"He *is* the Messiah, Shelomith! I'm convinced of it. I guessed as much when I saw him transform the water into wine. But now I'm sure he is our awaited king!"

"But why, Judas? How do you know?" Her tone betrayed mild disapproval of his enthusiasm. "I've already heard of the Galilean's actions at the Temple—from the servants. I don't know whether the better people approve them. Uncle Joseph and those at the Temple are, of course, greatly angered. At most it showed only that the Galilean has nerve."

"The multitude gave warm approval, Shelomith."

"The multitude is quick to approve any new thing—and just as quick to reject it," Shelomith countered. "Do you think it will support him when the power of the priests and the best people of Israel is turned against him?"

Judas smiled wryly. "What difference does it make, if he is the Messiah? What does the mob count against the power of God? And you can't say all the best people are against him."

"I grant you that some are showing interest. Mother has heard that even Nicodemus wishes to have a talk with him. But if he does, I'll warrant it will be somewhere in private. Nicodemus is a worthy man and a bold one, but I don't believe he's bold enough to espouse the cause of your Galilean openly." Shelomith picked up a fat fig from the tray before them, pushed the tray toward him. Her face grew troubled. "Oh, Judas, it's not that I'm against him; it's just that I'm for you. I love you, Judas. I don't want you to take a false step, my beloved. I don't want you to get yourself too—too in-

135

volved with this Nazarene." She threw her arms about him in an impulsive gesture of protection, and then gently released them.

Judas was too absorbed in the great question to respond to her. "But if he is the Messiah——"

"The Messiah of God a simple carpenter from a despised Galilean village! It doesn't seem likely. Still, I don't say he isn't, Judas. I just want you to be cautious. Why must you so early identify yourself with him? Why not let him prove himself the Messiah before you——?"

"You'd have me a coward?"

"No, Judas. You couldn't be a coward. But you could be more prudent, not so quick to take a stand. You see, my beloved, this Jesus threatens the position of the Temple leaders. They're determined to end his influence, perhaps destroy him. They're angry and——"

"—and scared."

"Yes. He's a menace to their—their existence. It's not so much the animals they lost or the threat of other such losses. It's the loss of the people they fear, their support of the institution of religion."

"That's the word—institution. It's not religion, Shelomith. I'm a Zealot, and we believe in the religion of the fathers. But this Temple worship isn't religion. It's a system. Sacrificing. Blood for God. Blood to wash away sins. Animals to give their blood. Money to buy animals—money for old Annas and his family. Form and ceremony, but no true worship." Judas' eyes were fiery. "That's what he said. He flung it in their faces, too! It was stirring, Shelomith.

"You asked me how I know he's the Messiah." He leaned forward in his earnestness. "This is why: Jesus has not only power—as he showed at Cana—but a swift and terrible anger. He whirled that whip like a sword of vengeance. Today I saw he could hate."

Judas got to his feet. "Strength and hate, Shelomith! I have told you they are the sword and shield of the great king who will restore us, the conquering Messiah of God! Yes, I'll stand with him. I'll be one of his company."

His eyes glittered, his voice vibrated. "Now and through the ages, my beloved, my name will be linked with his."

Chapter 19 ✠

THE door of his sister's apartment was ajar as Longinus walked along the corridor. He peeped in.

"I was wondering when you'd return," Cynara said. "Come in, Longinus. I'll get you some wine and something to eat. You must be hungry." She smiled brightly. "Or have you been out celebrating with the Passover roisterers?"

"Would to Bacchus there were no such thing as this damnable Passover!" He sank wearily into a chair. "Keeping these Jews tractable is a hard assignment in normal times, but when you stuff Jerusalem with Jews from all over this side of the world and they all start mourning their old days of lost glory—well, Cynara, it's a task I don't relish one bit."

"It's a silly holiday, if you want my opinion. But then, most things in Israel are silly, I'd say. I don't suppose, though, that it matters to them what I think." She shrugged.

"That's the truth. Nobody can swerve them from their notions, especially when they get their religion mixed up in the argument. They're the most stubborn people Rome has rule over. If we didn't have many a soldier in Jerusalem tonight——" His eyes twinkled. "By the way, Cynara, I saw the centurion of Capernaum today. His legionaries are stationed down in Ophel—that's the poor and tough district—and he asked——"

"He's a good Jew," said Cynara, interrupting. "I wonder if he came here to keep order or to observe the Passover." She got up. "I'll get the wine."

"Good." Longinus affected a serious expression. "I was wondering, Cynara, if perhaps you wouldn't be returning to Capernaum and——"

"Marry the centurion? By the gods, Longinus, no! If I'm to marry a Jew, I'll take a real one—with a beaked nose and a great oiled and plaited beard; not a Jew with blue eyes and blond hair." She handed him the wine. "As a matter of fact, the centurion didn't ask me to marry him."

"Perhaps then, if you insist on his being a Jew, your next husband will be that—that—what's his name, the son of Herod's steward you were telling me about?"

"Paran?" Her laugh was shrill. "By Venus, you must be anxious to get me married. Hah! That mooning calf! I'd never be able to get out of his sight."

Longinus sipped his wine. "Maybe your husband, when you get another, would do well to keep you always in sight."

She pretended a pout. "You sound like Flaccus. Flaccus was old-fashioned in his ideas, particularly about matrimony. He thought that midnight should find a married woman in her own husband's bed. I just couldn't agree . . . and, well, he divorced me."

"It was Caecilius whose bed you——"

"No, silly. You forget, Longinus, you've been out here two years last summer. It was over Caecilius that Cassius divorced me. That was shortly after you were ordered to Palestine. Cassius and I were having our difficulties about the time you left. He was an interesting person. If he hadn't been so narrow-minded . . ."

"Who was the intruder then that roused Flaccus' ire?"

"You didn't know him, Longinus. He was a wastrel in Rome, the son of a wealthy senator. He became so profligate—after I refused to marry him—that his father sent him away, to manage some manufacturing establishment in Phoenicia, I heard."

Longinus sat up straight, put down the wineglass. "By Jupiter, Cynara! There's a Roman up at Tyre—I've heard the tribune at Caesarea speak of him—who manufactures textiles and glassware which he sells to Benjamin, a Jewish merchant here."

"The father of Shelomith, isn't he?" Cynara smiled mischievously. "I understand, Longinus, that you've suddenly taken a great interest in the wares sold at Benjamin's shop, and that sometimes you even have business at his house on Mount Zion."

"Inacha's eyes and ears are always open, eh?"

"And there's the daughter of your rabbi friend Nicodemus. Her name's Rebekah. I've seen her again, since returning from Capernaum. She too sees and hears—and remembers."

Longinus leaned back. "And tells," he added, while Cynara laughed. "I've seen Shelomith only a few times, and if I should get interested, I'd have no chance with her. She's betrothed already."

"Yes, I know."

"Inacha told you?"

"No, Rebekah, the first time she came to see me—just after I arrived in Jerusalem with Sergius. Tell me, Longinus, does Shelomith ever speak of her betrothed?"

"Not often. And then only indirectly. But I haven't seen much of her, remember."

"Brother, I wish you'd take her away from him."

Longinus looked at her, mouth open. "But I didn't know you'd ever seen her, Cynara."

"I haven't, though I hear she's beautiful." Cynara sipped from her glass, set it down, turned it slowly on its slender stem. "Longinus," she said, "do you remember the redheaded Jew in the tavern that day below Hebron—the day I first saw you after landing in Palestine—the one that sentry claimed had slipped into my tent the night before?"

"Yes-s-s." Something evidently puzzled him. "By all the gods, great and small—" he slapped his open palm against his knee—"I knew that face in the Ophel cobbler's shop was familiar! I knew I'd seen the knave somewhere. Surely I remember him, Cynara. A damnable revolutionary, one of the Zealots, every moment up to mischief against Rome! By all the gods!"

"That man is Shelomith's betrothed, Longinus." She smiled demurely. "Surprised, dear brother?"

"By the great Jupiter! You mean that beautiful, cultured girl is betrothed to that rebel, that—that nobody!"

"But he's not a nobody, Longinus. His father is a wealthy man whose lands and herds are tremendous. You saw that day he was a friend of the Rabbi Nicodemus."

"But he's a Zealot, a brigand, Cynara. If ever I get my hands on him again——"

"But you can't, Longinus. Don't you see? If you want to win the girl from him, you can't do him bodily injury." She sipped the wine again. "You understand that, I'm sure."

"Yes, but I'm a Roman centurion. I can't permit revolutionaries, enemies of my country, to escape me because of—well, any personal reason."

She met this with a shrug. "But you might fail to catch them, eh?" When he made no response she set down her glass and leaned toward him. "But I don't want you to take her away from him, Longinus, for her sake. I want you to do it for my sake—for me."

"What! You don't mean—?"

"Yes, I mean I want the big Jew myself."

"By Hercules, Cynara, you're inexplicable! Don't you know that's the skulker who slipped into your tent? You said he wasn't, but you——"

"—lied, yes. I knew at the tavern that he was the man. That's one reason why I want him, and, by Cypris, I'm going to get him, Longinus, whether you get his girl or not!"

"But, Cynara, why in the world——"

"—would I want him?" She twirled the slender, delicately molded stem between thumb and forefinger so that the red liquid rode high in the glass. "My dear brother, it's clear to me that you little understand women. I've wanted this Judas ever since I awakened and saw him beside my couch. When I get him, of course I may not wish to keep him long. Why do I mean to have him? I might say because he's big and auburn and bold and unafraid and he has money—well, the usual reasons. But they wouldn't be the main one." She was looking pertly at him from beneath long eyelashes.

"Well, by the gods, what is it?"

"Because he's the first man I ever saw whom I couldn't bend around my little finger, right from the start." She laughed. "Women are strange, eh, my dear brother?"

He shrugged. "You should know."

Chapter
20   ✠

COLOR flamed along the watercourses of the ancient land. The grapes ripened, and the sheep and cattle grew fat on the hillsides. Weeks passed and the sirocco blew hot out of Arabia, and the wet winds came eastward from the Great Sea.

Jesus was back in his beloved hills. Like Judas he had left Jerusalem without delay. With his Galilean friends he had gone homeward. This time he had journeyed along the higher western road through Samaria past Mount Gerizim, where the Samaritans had raised their own temple and on whose slope Jacob seventeen centuries ago had dug the well from which they still drew water.

He had chosen the way through Samaria because he felt that it would not be thronged with pilgrims returning from the Feast of the Passover. Already his name and the story of the frenzied day in the Court of the Gentiles were on too many lips. He knew that he had infuriated the leaders of the Temple, all the more because he had delighted so many of the people. Whispers had come to him that he would take the place of John the Prophet. John was bearing the fierce hatred of Herodias, determined to destroy him because he had dared to denounce her adulterous sharing of the Tetrarch Herod's bed. Whispers had even been brought to Jesus that shortly the Jews would make him their king.

He wished to avoid the crowds, for his hour, he knew, was not yet. He had only begun to proclaim his mission. Few persons if any, he reasoned to himself sadly, understood the great work he had been sent to do. In Galilee, at the Temple where he had talked to the multitude after he had driven out its profaners, many had heard him gladly, though often the scribes and Pharisees and Sadducees had been present to heckle and challenge. He knew, too, that many loved him—John, the gentle and yet at times fierce younger Zebedee, and James, the older and more deliberate brother; Simon, impetuous, frank, talkative, lovable, rough fellow; the quiet and intellectual Nathanael; and the other friends who were often with him. Yes, these Galilean youths loved him and were of all the world closest to him, but they too had only a vague comprehension of what he was seeking so earnestly to teach them.

He must have a longer time. In Jerusalem, and in other places where the people assembled, lay great dangers. The priests would destroy him. The Romans, should they get the notion that in him the Jews had a potential leader, would send him quickly to the cross.

There was so little time! Could the normal lifetime of a man— if he were spared for a normal lifetime—be long enough to teach the love of God to a dying world? Could people be made to understand the nature of the Father and their relationship to Him? Could he lead people—even Samaritans, even Romans, all God's children, people so unheeding, so perverse, and yet so lovable—could he lead all his brothers to see straight into the heart of God?

So little time for so great a mission!

Sometimes on a sultry summer's evening Jesus, seated on a level stone, his dusty homespun robe pulled high to let the breeze fan his legs, tired from tramping, would watch the moon climb above the gaunt headlands of Bashan across the little sea. Sometimes, lying stretched at night on his mat on the flat top of Simon's house near the seaside, he would ponder the great mysteries of the heavens and marvel at the far reach of his Father's dominions.

Great, utterly without limit, is the Father's world, and yet not so great as His love! thought Jesus when he was alone and in a mood of meditation. Great is the Father's physical universe, and yet not all this is so great as one of the least of God's children, Jew or Samaritan, Greek or Roman or man of Cyrene. For every man is a son of God.

"O Father," he would often pray, "cause Thy children to know that they *are* Thy children and, knowing it, to seek mightily to bring Thy kingdom to this world."

Sometimes doubt assailed him, and he would remember the travail of those days in the Wilderness when he had wrestled with temptation. But then he would recall also the glory that had come upon him in the knowledge that his Father was with him and His arms were strong about his shoulders; in the revelation, clear, sharp and wonderfully certain, that for him his Father had set out a mission and that he must be about the Father's business.

Looking out across Galilee's waters—now troubled with a squall come raging along the steaming trough of the Jordan, now mirroring in unruffled quietness the gray towering bluffs of the eastern shore—and thinking of his mission, Jesus would feel strength surging through the clean litheness of his erect frame, confidence, yes, and enthusiasm for the purpose ordained for him by his Father.

He would teach these his brothers, and unnumbered ones in future ages, that God is love and all the peoples of earth are His children, made in His image, wrought out of His very heart of love. He would turn men to God, show them the way and set their feet on the path home.

Yet, he said to himself, the time is so short, and so great is the task!

One Galilean youth, one lone and often lonesome youth, to transform a world perverted and perverse! Not with fire and sword and scourging legions of warriors. Not in vengeance and great hate and running rivers of blood. But in the outpouring of an infinite love and with the aid of my simple, earnest and loving Galilean young men and those who in my name shall follow after them through the long ages.

For love, and nothing else, is the key, the power and the strength of a world's redemption. There is nothing stronger than love. God is love.

This then is my mission—to show to my brothers of earth the way to the Father. And I—of all God's sons on earth—I am the way, and the light making plain the way, the way to the great and loving heart of God.

Chapter 21   ✠

MEANWHILE in the deep summer when the winds blew hot out of Arabia the flame continued to blaze in the heart of Judas in Kiriot.

"He is indeed the Messiah! He is that one of whom the prophets spoke. He will lead us to a great new day in Israel! I know it, Cush, Pethuel, Seba. I am convinced!"

Sometimes the Zealot companions came to visit him; sometimes he ventured from his father's lands to talk with them and make plans for the coming of the day. "We must be diligent, Nadab, Tola, Lamech. We must be alert. We must keep organizing. We must keep building up a strong secret army to support him openly when he's ready to take the throne. The time is not far off."

When he had finished his more pressing duties at home he strode northward with a spring in his stride and a burning eagerness in his soul. Northward in Galilee, serene in his divine strength and ready to be quickened into a consuming hatred of his nation's enemies, was the leader. . . . And I am his man! I will give purpose and direction to his strength!

Judas tarried in Jerusalem to see Shelomith. They walked out beyond the Vale of Hinnom to the place where he proposed to build his house. They ventured to the edge of the chasm to peer down into the evil depths. In gay spirit Judas even clambered up the twisted tree and pushed himself along a limb that overhung the gorge. He sat balanced on the limb, his legs swinging.

"Be careful, Judas," Shelomith warned. "One slip and you'd be killed on the rocks below!"

"I'm not afraid." He swung a leg higher. "I thrive on danger, my dear. All my life I've lived with danger."

"And I don't like it. Judas, why must you persist in this madness? Why can't you forget this . . . this dream, and live your own life?"

"It is a dream, Shelomith. But the dream must be made to come true. And it shall."

"You talk with such confidence, my beloved, and yet I'm fearful. I——"

"The way of a woman," he said, grinning. His red hair blew in the breeze. "Always practical, never seeing any reality in a dream. Yet the world is built on dreams, my dear girl. I'm going now into Galilee to help build a dream."

A glow came to her face. "Oh, Judas, perhaps I'll see you up there. I hadn't told you. Mother and Father and I are going to visit the family of Chuza, Herod's steward."

"I know who he is. A traitorous Jew! His son and daughter were at the wedding feast at Cana with the centurion of Capernaum."

"It was the centurion who fetched us the invitation. He had come to Jerusalem on business and Longinus brought him to our house."

"Longinus!" Judas frowned. "He comes often to the house of Benjamin, doesn't he? I don't like it, Shelomith."

"And I don't care for your dark looks, Judas. He's friendly, and——"

"He's a Roman."

"But are all Romans evil?"

"Yes. From suckling babies to toothless crones. The whole accursed tribe."

"We've been over all this before, Judas. I feel it more deeply
with every repetition. The fierce hatred you carry in your heart will
do you no good. In time it will destroy you. You must root it out."

"Hah!" His laugh was shrill, derisive. "Root out the very
thing that gives me strength? No, I will not! I'll water and nourish
it until it comes to full flower. Then we—Jesus and I and many
others—will attend to these Romans who have their feet on our
necks!" He slithered along the limb, jumped to the ground. "No,
Shelomith, I'll not root out hate. Hate gives strength to the sword
arm." He pointed to the trunk of the tree. "It's strong, isn't it? It
has thrived all these years on hating wind and sand, and fighting
them."

They walked back to her house on Mount Zion. Early the next
morning he arose and left his inn. Already Jerusalem was astir.
Across the bridge over the Tyropoeon, through narrow descending
streets, past burden-bearers bent under hampers of grapes, brick-
layers with trowels and leveling rods, carpenters carrying hammers
and squares, countrymen bringing into the city sheep and cattle
freshly killed, Judas made his way to the gate in the wall. High up
the Mount of Olives he turned to look back. The white walls of the
Temple, reflecting the light of the new day's sun, were resplendent.
But not more so than the singing heart of the man of Kiriot.

"The center and soul of the new Israel!" he said to himself,
though he spoke the words aloud. "There, in the midst of those
ancient walls, he will set up his throne! There will his last enemy be
slain, and he will rule unmolested over God's chosen race. And I
shall sit at his right hand to give counsel!"

He stood a long moment looking, in his imagination seeing
dreams rise into solid substance. Then he set his feet again to the
way and the task ahead.

At Capernaum Judas found the Nazarene. With him were several
Judas already knew. A newcomer was Philip of Bethsaida, whom

Judas took to be Nathanael's brother. He was introduced to two young men whom he remembered having seen across the chamber the night of the wedding feast. He was told that they were brothers of Esther, Dysmas' new sister-in-law. Their names were Jude and James, and because the second of the brothers was smaller than the older Zebedee and to distinguish one from the other, they were calling him "Little James."

"I'm sure you've heard of the notorious publican Levi at Capernaum," Simon the Zealot whispered to Judas when the two had drawn a little way apart from the group.

"Yes," Judas said. "Who hasn't heard of the traitor?"

"Make no reference to him. It will only bring sorrow to Jude and Little James. Levi is their brother."

Jesus welcomed him happily, inquired of Simon his father. "We've been hoping you'd join us, Judas," he said. "There's much to be done and a great harvest of souls to be garnered into the Father's storehouse."

A talk with Nathanael one day greatly heartened Judas. By diligent inquiry Nathanael had traced the lineage of Joseph the carpenter directly back to David, and beyond.

"A prince of the house of David!" Judas exclaimed. "This was the one thing needed. This answers the doubt that has plagued me."

Chapter
22   ✠

LONG after the lamps had been snuffed out in Chuza's house on the lake front near Tiberias, Shelomith and Berenice lay on their couches and talked. They had not seen each other since the last Passover, when Berenice had visited the daughter of Benjamin.

Inevitably their talk centered on men.

"Does the centurion of Capernaum come to see you often?"
Shelomith asked, her tone deliberately casual.

"No-o, not so often. When he comes it's usually on business with
my father, something about the government, you know." Quickly
Berenice changed roles, became inquisitor. "How often does the
Centurion Longinus come to see you? I've been hearing . . ."

Shelomith laughed. "Very rarely. He came with the centurion
of Capernaum to fetch your invitation. Sometimes I see him at my
father's shop, where he comes to inspect the new merchandise. And
a few times he has come to our house."

"What does Judas think of him?" Berenice's voice was merry.

"The mere mention of him—or any other Roman—makes Judas
furious."

"I noticed at the wedding feast at Cana that Judas scowled fiercely
every time he looked in our direction, except when he was staring
at Cynara, and then——"

"Was the Roman girl there? I didn't——"

Berenice was sweetly apologetic. "Oh, Shelomith, I didn't know
I was giving away a secret. I thought of course Judas had told you."

"No-o." In the darkness she attempted to sound little concerned.
"I've seen Judas hardly at all in recent months. I think he mentioned something about the wedding feast, but he seemed mostly
interested in the strange magic of the Galilean who changed water
into wine."

"Yes, that was remarkable. I heard of it afterward. I drank of
the wine; whether it was transformed from water that night I can't
really say. Well, Cynara—" Berenice was not to be diverted—
"was there with the centurion and Paran and me. She told me she
talked with Judas, though briefly—too briefly, she said." When
Shelomith did not respond after a moment Berenice raised her head
on her elbow. "Shelomith, have you ever seen Longinus' sister?"

"No, but Rebekah, Rabbi Nicodemus' daughter—you know
her—told me about her. Rebekah thinks she uses dyes from Germania to get her hair that color."

"No doubt she does. What else did Rebekah tell you?"

"That she'd already had two husbands and appeared to be in search of another."

"I think so, too. She's a dissolute woman. Not vicious, but she simply seems to have no morals, certainly no sense of what is conventional, among the Jews at any rate, when it comes to a woman's behavior with men. You understand what I mean?"

"Yes. I've never seen her. But I suspect she spends her nights going from one man's bed to another's."

Berenice was silent a moment. "Paran's wild about her."

"Does she care for him?"

"No, I'm sure she doesn't. He's too young—and inexperienced—for a woman like her. She's seeking a man who's older, more seasoned, a man like . . . like Judas, Shelomith. I don't wish to alarm you, my dear, but you'd best keep your eyes on——"

There was a sharp rap on the door.

"Berenice! Berenice!"

"Yes, Mother. Wait a moment until I can unfasten the door." She jumped from the bed, clutching her nightdress tightly about her waist.

Joanna stood outside. In the light of the lamp she held, fright was plain on her face. "Paran is very ill," she said. "His forehead is hot. He tosses in his sleep and moans dreadfully. Please put on your robe and come help us."

"I'll be but a moment, Mother."

"Your father has sent for a physician. We're keeping wet cloths on Paran's face, but I don't know whether they cool the fever."

Shelomith went to the doorway. "Can't I help, too? I've had experience with fevers."

"Yes, my dear," Joanna answered. "But try not to awaken your father and mother. They must be wearied by the journey from Jerusalem."

The women stayed with Paran until the sky grew light above the Sea of Galilee and the servant returned with the physician. All day the physician remained, and throughout that night. But by the morning of the second day the fever had not abated. Paran seemed to be weakening steadily. When the distracted parents cried out to the physician, he shook his head and confessed that he knew of no other treatment that might aid.

"Then my son will die?" Chuza asked pitifully.

"Unless, sir, the fever abates quickly," the physician said. "His strength is going. He can't continue to fight this devouring fever for many more hours."

"There must be something we can do." Chuza's eyes pleaded. "You must know something else."

"Nothing more, sir, except to continue applying wet cloths."

Suddenly Shelomith thought of the Galilean. But a certain apprehension kept her from speaking. Would Jesus intercede for the dying son of an officer of Herod, the apostate Jew, the servant of the Roman conquerors? Wouldn't Judas, probably now at the Nazarene's side, be infuriated if she sent for him?

Jesus could help Paran, would help him, if the stories she had been hearing about him were true. And if Judas should be angry, well, let him!

Without further hesitation she said to Chuza, "There's a man in these parts called Jesus who is reported to do wondrous works. He might come and heal Paran. I've heard Judas speak often of his remarkable powers."

"Indeed, I've heard of the man." For a moment a glimmer of hope came to Chuza's eyes. "But he's a strict rabbi, and I am steward to the household of Herod."

"But you might try him. Certainly he's worth trying."

"You're right, Shelomith. He can do no worse than refuse. I'll send servants for him at once. Here, Amram! Quick! Get your horses. No, wait. I'll go myself. Fetch my horse, and one for Jesus. And you on another. Make haste!"

Near Magdala they met a man who said that, three days before, Jesus and his small company had come south from Capernaum on a journey to Cana. "Go there and ask to be shown the house where the water was made wine," he said. "It's the home of Esther his cousin, and likely you'll find him there."

So they rode toward the southwest. Moment by moment Chuza's anxiety for his stricken son mounted. He felt he must turn back so he might be with Paran when death came. Sometimes a terrifying thought seized him: His son already lay dead in the great house! But they went on. It was almost sunset when they rode into Cana and drew up at the home of Cleopas' daughter.

Chapter | ✠
23

JUDAS sat on the left hand of Jesus at the table of Dysmas' brother. "Master," he said, as he set down his wine cup and leaned across to look into the countenance of the Nazarene, his eyes bright with dream, "tell us, when will the kingdom be established and the throne set up at Jerusalem?"

Jesus turned to reply, his own eyes aglow. "The kingdom must first be established in the hearts of men, my brother."

"But it has long been established in our hearts, Master. We have long prayed the God of Israel to overthrow our enemies and restore our power and prestige. When will He drive out the despoilers and give us back our glory?"

"The despoiler, Judas, is not he who robs us of our possessions or lashes our backs or even smites us with a sword. The despoiler is he who blackens our hearts and makes them unfit to be the abode of God our Father. Before the kingdom comes the heart must be cleansed."

"But, Master, the Scriptures tell us that when the Messiah comes he will lead God's chosen people to overcome their enemies and set up anew the kingdom of Israel."

"You have studied the Scriptures diligently, Judas, that is certain. The ancient prophets did so write, and they spoke the truth. But who are the enemies of God's chosen people, and who indeed are His chosen ones?" Jesus' smile was warm and compassionate.

"Are not the Romans enemies of God?" Judas' face was a mirror of his perplexity. "Master, they have enslaved our land. They worship not our God. They are worshipers of many gods, thieves and plunderers. Are they not our enemies, and are not we the chosen ones of God?"

"All men, Judas, who so will are the children of God. And every man is an enemy who would keep us from sharing in the love of the Father, who would turn us from Him."

"But, Master, the Romans are such——"

A servant came crying, "Rabbi, there's a man at the door who wishes greatly to speak a moment with you. He says he's the steward of the household of Herod."

Judas shouted, "Chuza, the henchman of that traitor! Master, bid him begone!"

Jesus looked at Judas. He said not a word, but the man of Kiriot ceased his protest. Then the Nazarene said to the servant, "I'll go with you." He arose from the table.

"Peace be with you, Chuza!" he said at the door. The rays of the dying sun lighted his face and danced along the reddish-brown hairs of his short, double-spiked beard.

"I seek the Rabbi Jesus. Sir, are you he?"

"I am Jesus. What can I do for you, my brother?"

"Sir, my son is dying. Will you come with me and restore him? All day I've ridden in search of you, and now he may be already dead. I've fetched a horse for you. Won't you leave with me at once? The time is short—so short! Oh, sir, I beg of you! At any moment . . . Oh, sir . . . "

"What trouble afflicts your son?" Jesus' voice was steady, soothingly gentle.

"A fearful ague has struck him down, Rabbi. The fever burns

him. He moans and tosses on his bed. And though the physician has labored diligently, he has been unable to break the fever. Sir, won't you go with me?"

"The Father is the Great Physician, my brother. He has all power. Calm your fears therefore and trust in the power and the love of the Father." Jesus laid a friendly hand on the shoulder of the troubled man. "Now come out to the gallery where there are waterpots and a basin, and wash from the long journey. Then sup with us—your servant, too."

"But, sir, time presses. Even now my son——"

Jesus cut short his pleading. "Leave your son in the Father's loving care." There was authority in his tone. "Call your servant. I'll show you where the waterpots are, and then you will sup." The level rays of the sun gave added warmth to Jesus' smile.

When they walked into the dining chamber he introduced the men about the table, the friends of his intimate group. He took the stranger's hand. "My brothers, this is Chuza of Tiberias."

Judas put down his wine cup and looked quickly at Dysmas, who in the absence of his brother was their host. Would he receive the servant of Herod hospitably?

Dysmas said, "Peace be with you! Anyone invited by Jesus is welcome to this house. Sit down and sup with us."

When they had finished the fish and the wheat cakes and had drained their cups, Jesus turned to Chuza with a questioning look.

"Oh, Rabbi, though it's late now, won't you return with me and restore my stricken son? I've heard that you have performed signs and wonders and that you have power to make whole those who are grievously ill."

Jesus sighed. Looking, his friends saw on his face a deepening sadness. "Always signs and wonders they seek," he said, as though to himself. "Only for the working of magic do they come to me, only for the accomplishment of wonders. But not for my love, not for the love of the Father."

Chuza seemed deeply affected. Suffering was in his eyes, pleading on his pained countenance. "Oh, sir, I hardly know what to say! I know only that my son is near death, that I love him dearly, and that if you were of a mind to do it you could restore him."

A look of infinite tenderness possessed the young preacher. He grasped with firm hand the sagging shoulder of Herod's servant. "Suffer no longer," he said. "In your heart I see great love and a growing faith. Strengthen your faith, my brother. The Father is able and willing to restore your boy." For a quiet moment Jesus' eyes were closed. When he opened them they shone with a new brightness. "Chuza my brother, the Father already, even now, has healed your son."

Chuza's face showed amazement, incredible joy. "You mean, sir, that he is not dying, is not dead? You mean that as we sit here now—far from him over there near Tiberias—you mean he is restored to full strength?"

The sun was dropping into the Great Sea beyond the rearing thrust of Mount Carmel. Its dying rays shone through the window full on the face of Jesus, and small reflected orbs danced in the shining film that glistened in his wide eyes. "Go you, my brother, and see. Learn the power and the love of God our Father."

"Oh, Rabbi . . . oh, my Master . . . " Chuza's eyes were lowered as he reached for the hands of compassion and held them gripped. When at last he looked up to Jesus, his tears were streaming. Suddenly he released his clasp and was gone.

For a long while after the door closed behind him the company about the table sat silent. Then Judas, leaning over, his elbows on the board, said, "But, Master, you knew this Chuza is Herod's steward."

Jesus looked deep into Judas' stormy eyes. At length, his expression stern but tinged with sadness, he answered. "Judas, can you have it in your heart to begrudge happiness to any of God's children?"

"But, Master—" Judas glanced toward Dysmas—"I didn't know that the servant of such a man as Herod could be a true Israelite."

"All men are created in the image of the Father; all are His children. This you would know, my brother, had you eyes to see, were your heart willing to discern. There is not room in the smallest corner of the heart, Judas, to harbor hatred of any man."

Chapter 24 ✠

As CHUZA and his servant Amram breasted the last rise that fell away into the plain where his house lay and he saw the lake behind it glimmering in the dawn, a great fear caught at him. Can my son be dead after all? Is it only a vain and foolish hope that has brought me cheered through the long night? Was the rabbi only a man, just a stalwart, noble, kindly, well-meaning young man?

He peered ahead along the road, anxious to see if any travelers were stirring, friends that might be going to the wake for his son. It's too early for that, he told himself, but the thought gave him no peace.

As he drew nearer and could see the house and the grounds about it, he could discern no unusual activity. It may be, he suddenly thought, that the boy has overcome the fever and is now still abed but slowly recovering his strength. He felt cheered again.

He came to a turn in the road where trees shut out the view. Then he heard a clatter of horses' hoofs, and, riding out from behind the trees, he saw some of his servants racing toward him.

A sudden fear sickened him.

They have seen us coming, he said to himself. My son is dead and they wish me to know it before I meet Joanna.

He rode forward as a man going to his death.

The servant on the leading horse could not wait to give his tidings. A hundred paces away he shouted, "Master! Your son is well again!"

Chuza reined in, sat waiting. A strange lightness seemed to possess him as he slumped wearily in the saddle. The long tension released, he felt he might float away.

"Master!" said the man when he came alongside Chuza. "You heard me? Paran your son is alive and well. He's having his breakfast at this moment, and a right bountiful one he's eating."

"Praise the Lord of Israel!" exclaimed Chuza. "God be thanked for His great mercy unto us! And how are Joanna and the others?"

"They're overjoyed, sir. It has been a wondrous time."

"Is Paran fully recovered?"

"Indeed, master. It appears that he has never been more in health than he is now."

"When did he recover, or was he restored gradually?"

The servant was thoughtful a moment, as if considering. "It's passing strange, sir. We servants have been unable to understand it. We've never heard before of any such thing among those afflicted with the fevers."

He stroked his horse's mane. He looked into his master's face. "Your son was very low, master. We were all agreed that shortly death would take him. The fever was consuming him, his brow was as though on fire. He lay flat on the mat and was too spent even to moan. And then, sir, then all of a sudden the fever broke, his brow was cool again, and he opened his eyes. He rose from his mat, as though he were arising in the usual way at the break of day, and he stood up, and in another minute he was calling loudly for his supper."

"What hour of the day was it the fever left him?"

"I well remember it, master," the servant answered. "I was standing where I could see out through the window in the bedchamber's western wall. The fever left him and he arose to his feet, sir, just as the sun was dropping behind yonder slope into the Great Sea."

Chapter | ✠
25

THE strange restoration of the son of Herod's steward so moved the people of Galilee that in the winter weeks that followed throngs pressed about him as he and his friends journeyed along the western shore of the little sea.

Many of these people were deeply interested in the Master and his teaching, Judas was confident, but others were only idly curious to see and hear the young man about whom everyone was talking. None was more interested than Judas. He stayed close to the Nazarene; he listened intently and with growing rapture to his powerful words; whenever he could he conversed with the Master.

Jesus sought to take advantage of every opportunity to proclaim his mission. So he preached and healed, he trudged up and down the hills and valleys and along the seaside and told the multitudes about the love of the Father for His children of earth, and he placed his hands on them and prayed to the Father and restored them.

In the midst of these busy weeks one day came foreboding news. Tetrarch Herod, goaded into action by Herodias, had ordered the Prophet John imprisoned in the dreary old fortress-castle of Machaerus, a headland of the Dead Sea's eastern shore.

No longer were the flaming calls to repentance being heard along the Valley of the Jordan.

Jesus was sad. Judas, too, was distressed, but the imprisonment of the prophet served to satisfy him utterly that John was not the Messiah, for of course the chosen one of God would not suffer himself to be thus dealt with. In the same way it strengthened his belief, grown now to a certainty, that Jesus was the Messiah.

In these weeks that had seen the oleanders coming to blossom again along the greening course of the Jordan, Judas had gained a

new appreciation of the Master, a strengthened affection, a developing faith in his divine appointment to restore Israel to her ancient
splendor. He looked forward with fretting impatience to the dawn-
ing of the Master's day. He could hardly wait.

One thing puzzled him greatly, however. Why does the Master
show no distinction between Jew and gentile, God's select people
and His enemies? Why does he heal those not of the ancient faith?
Why did he so gladly restore the son of Chuza? For days the Master's rebuke, given so pointedly when Judas mildly questioned the
healing of Paran, had rankled. But he had said nothing. He had
not even protested to Simon the Zealot.

The Master perhaps has his reason, Judas told himself, and one
day the reason will appear. But it does seem strange. This thing is
certain: He has power. He can do things that no other man has ever
done. Healing lepers, giving sight to the blind, straightening paralyzed arms and legs. And when the day comes, he will have whatever power is required to set up the throne of Israel in the ancient
city on the hills.

The power of the Nazarene, power not often used and never to
its full degree, had been dramatized one Sabbath when they went
with Jesus on a visit to his mother at Nazareth. Judas would never
forget that day.

The elders of Nazareth had invited the tall son of the village to
teach them in the synagogue, and the little stone house of worship
was filled long before Jesus seated himself in the chair on the raised
platform at the front, his head reverently covered with the corners
of his tallith. The tallith was new and the long fringes danced and
sparkled in the sunshine.

Jesus, when his time came, had read from the scroll on which
were written the burning words of the great Isaiah:

"The spirit of the Lord is upon me, because he hath anointed me
to preach the gospel to the poor; he hath sent me to heal the broken-
hearted, to preach deliverance to the captives, and recovering of
sight to the blind, to set at liberty them that are bruised, to preach
the acceptable year of the Lord."

As the Master was reading Judas recalled the day in Meshach's inn near Hebron—the day after he had seen Cynara in the tent—when he and Rabbi Nicodemus had discussed the nature of the Messiah and Nicodemus had quoted the strange, imageful words of Isaiah. . . .

Then Jesus had rolled up the scroll, handed it to the presiding official and, turning again to face his homefolks of Nazareth, had said, "This day is this Scripture fulfilled in your ears."

"He's telling them," Judas had whispered to Simon the Zealot beside him, "that he's the Messiah of whom Isaiah was speaking."

A murmur arose and grew into a loud muttering among the Nazarenes. A neighbor of Mary stood and, pointing his finger at the preacher, asked, "Aren't you Joseph the carpenter's son brought up here in Nazareth among us?"

"Yes, you know it," Jesus had answered, smiling, "and well I know you are thinking that if I did notable things in Capernaum, and healed lepers and the halt and the paralytic, why should I not do them here in Nazareth also? I tell you of a truth that no prophet is accepted in his home country. He must needs go to another before he is given the honor due him."

The tall preacher recalled the story of how Elijah in the days of great famine, when the rain had not fallen for three and a half years, had not been sent to a widow in Israel, though there were many widows and very poor, too, but instead to a widow away over near Sidon. And later Elisha the prophet had not healed a leper in Israel, though the land was teeming with lepers, but had cleansed one Naaman, a Syrian.

Judas remembered that he had wondered why the Master seemed always anxious to show that God's love was not reserved for the children of Israel. His words infuriated the Nazarenes. They had rushed upon him, and though his followers had struggled to rescue him from their rage, they had seized him and shoved him to the edge of a high cliff from which they were determined to hurl him to death.

But they had not done so! Though Herod had seized and imprisoned the courageous John, the angry Nazarenes had not been able to work vengeance on the stalwart son of their village.

At the edge of the precipice Jesus had turned about and faced his traducers so triumphantly that they had backed away from him in terror, and he had walked unafraid through the center of the wrathful throng.

Judas and Simon the Zealot talked late one night about the imprisonment of John. Judas recalled the Sabbath day at Nazareth. "There is proof indeed that Jesus and not John is the Messiah," the man of Kiriot declared. "John, though a mighty man, is subject to the rule of man, but Jesus is not, else he would have been killed that day at Nazareth. Will man kill God? Zealot, I think not. The Master is not subject to the power of man. He is beyond question the Messiah. Now I know it."

Chapter 26 ✠

ON A morning soon after he had established himself at Capernaum Jesus with Judas started early to the seashore, for the Zebedees and the sons of Jonas were returning from a fishing venture and he wished to see if they had caught much in reward for their heavy toil.

The little house of Simon sat behind a low stone wall at the end of a narrow way opening on the road to the seaside. Hardly had the two stepped from the door before Jesus was espied by a scattering of men coming past the customhouse where Levi the publican collected the duties. The men at once began whispering among themselves that this was the young rabbi from Nazareth who not many weeks ago had cured the dying son of Chuza. Soon a group was following him, so that when he and Judas reached the shore a throng had grown about him.

The people began to plead with Jesus to teach them. They were so insistent, and they pressed so closely upon him, that he was being pushed into the sea. They could not all see him because of the flatness of the beach. So Jesus, when he saw Simon, with Andrew, and the Zebedees pulling their boats into the shallows, called to Simon to move his boat out a short way from the shore. Jesus then waded out, his robe pulled to his knees, and clambered into the boat. From it he spoke to the multitude ranged along the water's edge.

When at last the crowd began to slip away Jesus suggested that they go fishing. "Float out the other boat, too," he said, "and we'll move toward the middle of the sea."

Judas, who had joined Jesus in the boat, noted with amusement that the usually agreeable Simon, busy with some of the gear, was solemnly shaking his head. "But, Master," the big fisherman protested, "we're fatigued already; we've fished all the night and caught nothing. It seems to me that now we should spread out our nets to dry and ourselves seek some rest." He looked out from beneath bushy eyebrows for the Nazarene's assenting nod, but when he saw that Jesus stood straight and unmoving he shrugged and smiled grimly. "Nevertheless, Master, if you wish to go fishing, then fishing we'll go." Cupping his hands to his mouth, he called to the Zebedees, who were sprawled in their boat, to push it out from shore.

Soon the boats were sailing eastward toward the distant frowning headlands of Bashan. Jesus sat relaxed in the stern of Simon's boat, watching the trough of water leveling in its wake as the vessel moved steadily into the rising sun. Judas, slumped on the deck, kept his eyes on the tall, calm Nazarene.

Suddenly Jesus stood up. "Furl the sail," he commanded, "and thrust out the anchor." When they had obeyed he pointed. "Now let down the nets there."

Simon directed the lowering, but Judas saw that the Bethsaida fisherman had no enthusiam for the task. Jesus pointed again. "A little way to that side." Small waves, stirred by the sudden anchoring and the dropping of the nets, slapped gently against the boat. The nets seemed to dance grotesquely beneath the thin greenness of the water. "Now! Begin pulling in the nets!"

The crew grabbed the nets. Judas sprang to help. They bent their backs, tugged hard.

"The nets have fouled on something," one of them ventured. "Maybe they've caught on driftwood or shoal rocks."

"No, the nets aren't caught," Andrew declared. "It's fish! Pull, men. Pull!"

They hauled up the nets until they could see the fish—perch, carp, bream, flashing their silver in the sunlight, slithering, slimy eels, crabs clutching with long fingers.

"The Lord of Israel be praised!" Big Simon's lethargy was gone. "What a haul! What a haul of beauties!"

They began pulling in the nets, and fish splashed and plumped about the deck under the feet of the straining men. "Hold! Wait, men, not so fast!" Andrew warned. "This net won't stand any more strain. It's beginning to break. Be careful or we'll lose all the fish that are in it."

"Pull over this way and give us a hand with this catch!" Simon yelled to those in the Zebedees' boat. "The nets are breaking; we'll be losing the fish."

The Zebedees pulled alongside Simon's boat, and with adroit handling of the burdened nets the men got so many fish aboard that the little vessel was heavily loaded. A few minutes later the Zebedees' boat was filling with fish, too, as the tortured nets were dragged one after another from the sea. When they had pulled up the last net and thrown it across the leaping, squirming fish, and had started for the western shore, the boats were so low in the water that some of the men feared they would sink.

But not the man of Kiriot. Brought up in the desert country of lower Judaea, he knew little of the sea and its perils. As he sat squeezed in among the slimy fish he kept his gaze on the quiet and unconcerned Nazarene in the stern looking down into the white wake cut through the green waters. Just now Judas was not thinking of the great haul of fish, destined for the markets at Capernaum or even for the Zebedees' market at Jerusalem.

Suddenly Jesus looked up, and his eyes fastened on the Judaean's thoughtful face. Judas said, "Master, I was there that night at Cana—at the wedding feast. I drank of the wine. I was there the night Chuza came seeking you. I heard of the restoration of his son. Now, Master—" he motioned toward the fish—"I look on this great haul. Oh, Master, the power you have! Truly you have been sent to deliver us of Israel out of our bondage!"

Jesus smiled as the sunlight shimmered and sparkled in the mist about them. "You have great discernment, Judas." In a graver tone he added: "Through good works and much prayer to the Father, my brother, see to it that you do not fail to understand."

Chapter 27 ✠

SIGNS and wonders, yes, that was still what the people wanted, Jesus perceived. Always signs and wonders. But not the precious seeds of his words sown in their hearts. Only here and there did he see the seeds fall on hearts warmed and stirred.

Jesus recalled sorrowfully how the people of Capernaum and the region roundabout had acted when he called Levi the publican to become a follower. They had shut their hearts to everything except the fact that Levi had been a collector of taxes, that he had been a hated small Mokhes, a douanier who stood in the customs booth and accepted the taxes from the fishing vessels and many other tolls.

Levi had given a great feast to honor his new Master and to signalize his casting off of the old life with its burden of sin and ugliness. The smug ones of Capernaum, Jesus remembered with revulsion, had scolded him because he had sat down and eaten with

Levi and his guests, many of them unacceptable to the piety-pro-
fessing hypocrites who knew every jot and tittle of the old covenant
but cared not a fig for the spirit giving life to words that without it
were dead indeed.

All they could see was that Jesus, the rebel against the ancient
teachings of the fathers, the flouter of old and empty tradition, of
narrow and killing cant, had broken bread with the despised agent
of a plundering oppressor. This recognition was all that mattered
to them.

They had refused to see the repentant Levi, hating forever his sin,
renounce his old life, break away from chains that for years had
shackled him, make amends to those with whom he had dealt un-
fairly, give his wealth in one generous gesture of gratitude to
those who needed it more than he, and pledge to his new Master life
and utter love.

Even Judas of Kiriot, his new follower of such capabilities and
promise, had spoken contemptuously of Levi as an outcast Jew, a
lover of Rome and a traitor to Israel. Judas too had refused to see
Levi as repentant and sorrowful, anxious to atone for a life traveled
along a wrong highroad.

The people had not tried to fathom the meaning of Jesus' words,
had not been striving to learn his straight and plain way and, having
learned, to walk in it.

They had wished only to see him perform his wonders.

Many sought only to criticize, and hedge him about, and put
obstacles in his way.

Judas also was disappointed at the outcome thus far of the mission
in Galilee. He had gone up to join the Nazarene hoping to see a
fast development of his plans. He had expected to see the fame of
Jesus spread quickly to the regions beyond Galilee, to the desert
country below Kiriot, to Phoenicia on the northwest and across the
eastern borders of Israel past Decapolis and down into Arabia. He
had hoped that by now the demonstration of Jesus' tremendous
powers would be hailed throughout the land. By now, he had been
confident, the people everywhere would be demanding that Jesus

be made king. He had even visioned the king about to be seated on a golden throne in Jerusalem, with not a Roman daring molest his reign.

But Jesus had put his great power to nothing except puny uses, Judas felt. Healing a young man near death of a fever—and he the son of a servant of old Rome-loving Herod—restoring a paralytic, soothing the raging mind of a village lout, cleansing lepers, opening the eyes of blind beggars—these things were all very well, but what large good did they accomplish? How would they help toward the great objective? How could such acts, limited to the personal aiding of some unimportant fellow, promote the struggle with Rome or increase the stature of Jesus as the restorer of the kingdom?

If only he would listen to me, thought Judas often as he watched the rabbi's healing works and heard his healing yet powerful words, if only he would heed my counsel, I could tell him how to hasten the day. Someday I'll dare suggest to him, yes, urge him, even demand of him that he utter words of fire and thunder, that he gird up his loins and unsheathe the avenging sword.

Then quickly, Judas asured himself, would come the full triumph.

And then he, the man of Kiriot, would be raised into a position of great honor and power. Judas had not forgotten the words of Jesus that day after he had cleansed the Temple. "You are a man of business, Judas. We need such a man in our company." Yes, Jesus will need me when he takes the reins of government.

But when, how, where will the Messiah come into the kingdom? Often Judas lay sleepless pondering the problem, reviewing in his troubled mind the ancient prophecies set off against the present sore condition of his loved land. In the center of all his thinking, tall, capable, commanding, stood the erect figure of the Nazarene.

If only I knew, if I could only reason clearly what course Jesus would follow, I would know how to act; we of the Zealot party could shape a definite course.

If the Galilean would but lift his hand and say the word, a legion of angels would descend and destroy Israel's oppressors. There'd be no need to keep on recruiting our youth into a revolutionary force.

No human army would be called for. Uncle Bezek and Elam and all the others who have died for Israel would be avenged and my oath fulfilled.

Without the intervention of Jesus the Messiah any struggle of swords would bring our quick defeat, though from reports I know of the steady growth of the secret army. Only the divine power of the Galilean, certainly in this day, can defeat Rome.

Jesus is divine, yet he is also a man. He is a man with unbounded love of his fellow men.

That may be the key! In the end, when the time ripens, Jesus may exercise his divine power to protect his friends, to prevent the Roman soldiers from destroying Israel's eager, excited, patriotic band. Perhaps an act of rebellion will be the signal for the Galilean to raise his eyes to heaven, call down the angelic hosts.

I'm not certain. I cannot fathom the mind of Jesus. But soon he will give us an inkling, will indicate his course. Then we'll know definitely how to proceed.

In the meantime we must continue—in Galilee, Judaea, Peraea and throughout Israel—the building of our clandestine force to plague the enemy day and night and to battle Rome openly when the opportunity comes.

Jesus in these busy, stirring days had no thought of an earthly kingdom. Though his heavy labors up and down the land often left him at a day's end worn and greatly fatigued, and the indifference of the multitudes would make him sorely troubled in spirit, he was young and strong and eager to be about his Father's business. As he sometimes expressed it, the fields were white unto the harvest.

The passing weeks had brought the full summer. Whenever he looked on Galilee's countryside he found himself lifted in spirit. Over the Plain of Esdraelon, soaked in the water and blood of centuries, waved now acre on acre of windflowers, the anemones— red, pink, purple, cream, white, blue—fashioned like small cups on slender stems. Great fields of them were a flaming scarlet, as thought they had drawn up into their fragile cups the blood of un-counted warriors fallen there over the long years.

Across the flatlands and up the slopes of rounded hills, down into wadis now dry with the ending of the rains, along the banks of trickling streams, across the changing hardened face of Galilee ran the flowers—daisies, tulips; cyclamen stupefying to the fish that nib-bled the gorgeous petals which fell into the stream from stems over-hanging the banks; gladioli swaying on spikes curved like the scimi-tars of Eastern warriors; the white and the yellow narcissus, hya-cinths, larkspur, the loosestrife with its brilliant purple cluster, marigolds, blue squill, jasmine, the mallows huddling in the marshes. Up and down the steaming cleft of the Jordan marched the tamarix with feathery thin branches and white-pink flowers and the reed grass and papyrus stems with their long knops of hairy streamers like an army gaily caparisoned and waving its banners.

Jesus had joy in the dark months at the year's ending and its beginning. They brought days of meditation and calm reflection, when thoughts like persons seeking shelter against the cold were turned within, when men and women worked at homecrafts, spend-ing most of their hours indoors.

But he gloried in the warming spring, with the greening hills and the flowers and the cattle grazing, and in the hot months of summer with the sun on his back, and arms and chest bare to the gentle cooling breezes. He loved the still summer nights with the overturned great bowl of the sky and its innumerable stars inviting him to contemplation of his Father's unmeasured dominions and unending stretch of boundless love.

All one summer night he spent alone in a mossy sheltered place on the side of Kurn Hattin. He stretched himself out in the fold of his heavy homespun robe. He had wished to be alone in order to think clearly of the task immediately ahead, to commune with his Father and learn His will, for the step he would take with the com-ing of the morning's sun would be of immeasurable importance.

The world was filled with men whom he must show the way home. The earth was alive with the harvest, just as the slopes of

Kurn Hattin in the darkness below were alive with flowers whose fragrance came up to him now in the cool air of the calm night. The harvest was plentiful and ready for the reapers.

He had determined to commission from his followers a small company who would give up their daily trades in order to remain closely beside him and be trained carefully. These men would then go out into the world and in his name teach as he had taught them: in his name heal the sick, give vision to the blind of eye and heart, and lead wayward men to the Father.

There had been twelve tribes in ancient Israel, and so he would name twelve whom he would call his apostles, or "those sent out." He had the soul of a poet and it would be a happy sentiment. Twelve would not make too cumbersome a company.

He had come high on the mountain to meditate on the twelve he should choose and to ask the counsel of his Father.

Now the sun was lifting out of Galilee's little sea and cleaving a shimmering, blinding path through the waters. Soon the throng would be here, and from them he would select his immortal band to take on their shoulders the burden of the glorious mission.

Jesus arose and threw aside his robe. He walked to the small stream near by, removed his loincloth, unlatched his sandals and bathed quickly in the cool water. When he had dressed again he opened his pouch and, having given thanks, took from it a loaf, cheese and some olives. After eating, he sat down to await the crowd which he saw a long way off already moving from Capernaum toward the mountain.

When they had come up the slope and grouped themselves about him, he told them of his determination. Having offered a prayer to the Father, he called out those whom he had selected: Simon, the fisherman of Bethsaida, whom he called in affection Peter the Rock; Simon's brother Andrew; the two Zebedees, James the elder and John, sons of his mother's sister Salome; Philip, also of Bethsaida; Nathanael bar Tolmai of Cana; Judas of Kiriot, the only Judaean in the group; Levi, the publican of Capernaum, who would be called Matthew, and his brothers Little James and Jude, the three of them, like the Zebedees, first cousins of Jesus; Thomas, called the Twin; and Simon the Zealot.

When he had laid his hands on them and ordained them to the great task, he dismissed the rest who had come, and he began to talk with the new companionship of his plans for carrying the good news of God's love to Galilee, Judaea and Samaria and ultimately to all the world. They would journey as brothers. God the Father would see to their wants, he assured them, and when they went forth to preach they should give small consideration to the needs of the body.

The Master named Judas to carry the pouch for the company, for he was a man of considerable experience in handling money. Judas, not at all surprised, was none the less delighted: the office promised opportunity. Money, even among members of a wandering band of evangelists, was power, and soon he would be in still greater favor. Soon he could begin to use his wits toward shaping a new course, one that would direct quietly but surely the marvelous endowments of the Master to the liberation of Israel.

He imagined the pouch within the fold of his robe beginning already to swell with silver and gold coins. He would be a leader in the land, keeper of the keys of the new kingdom's treasury. Treasurer of Israel! The rhythm of the words, the very thought of them, sent a fine tremor through his frame. Keeper of the treasury!

Chapter 28 ✠

ON ONE of the twin peaks of Kurn Hattin, the bright Galilean skies above him, the blue waters of the little sea glimmering in the distance, his twelve newly ordained brothers grouped about him, Jesus stood enraptured. He knew with a sure knowledge that his

Father ruled the universe, he felt his Father's arms about him to inspire, sustain, embrace. He could have shouted his joy.

So it was with light steps that he walked down to the place known as the saddle between the horns, where already the multitude awaited him. The returning crowd had spread the news of the rabbi's selecting an inner fellowship, and some whispered that he might work wonders among them. Now the throng had surged back to the mountain.

The Nazarene was tired and his reddened face was sweat-creased as he faced them from a small level place on the sharply descending hillside. But never had his friends seen him more radiant.

"How blessed are those without arrogance and false pride," he said, "for truly they dwell within God's kingdom. They stand not on their rights, nor do they carry their dignity before them as a shield, and yet of a truth they are triumphant.

"How happy likewise are those who are troubled because of the evil about them, for they shall be comforted.

"Blessed are those who are truly humble, for they shall be lifted up and attain all the treasures of the abundant life.

"Blessed are they who hunger and thirst for the good life, for they shall be abundantly satisfied.

"How happy are those who show mercy; mercy shall be shown them.

"Blessed are those who seek always to do the will of the Father, for verily they shall live in His presence and look into His face.

"And blessed, O blessed, my brothers, are those who strive for peace on earth, for they shall be known as the children of God Himself!

"Nor be you sad and disconsolate when men may malign you and persecute you because you love piety, for you shall dwell secure and happy within God's kingdom. And happy are you when for my sake you are reviled and lied about. Rejoice, and be happy, for your reward shall be great. Remember that the prophets of olden times were so dealt with in their day."

"What loveliness, what majesty in his words!" Judas whispered to Simon the Zealot standing at his side. "His sayings like doves seem to wing from his lips. And see how already the multitude listens enthralled."

So the tall Master stood in the sun on the small level spot and talked, his voice now smooth, cadenced and soothing, at other moments soaring and inspiring, and the people drank in hungrily the golden phrases. Jesus seemed to sense in this gathering an unusual number sympathetic to him.

But not all those listening were friendly. The idly curious were there, as always. Some were skeptical critics and some were avowedly hostile. Here and there was a Pharisee or Sadducee or scribe, and not far from him followers of the Temple leaders at Jerusalem stood with arms folded across their paunches and sneers on their lips. Now and then these men would challenge some statement of his, some interpretation of the ancient laws.

"I am not come to destroy the law or the sayings of the prophets, but rather to fulfill what has been written," he replied to one who had interrupted his discourse. "Of a truth, I say unto you that as long as the heaven and the earth remain, not a jot or a tittle of truth shall be destroyed. Nor would I teach men to go against the law of truth, and anyone who shall so teach will have small share in the kingdom of heaven. On the contrary any person who shall teach and live the truth and cause other men to do likewise, he shall have a great place in it."

He lifted his long arm, so that the robe fell away to reveal the swell of his muscles, and pointed directly toward the group of smug religionists smirking at him above their oiled and plaited beards. "But this I say unto you, and with emphasis let me declare it to all who are before me: Unless your righteousness—your right living—is of a kind far superior to that practiced by the scribes and Pharisees, you will have neither a great nor a small place in the kingdom of heaven."

Judas nudged the Zealot. "The Master is bold indeed," he said under his breath. "He fears no man. But I'm afraid he may so anger them that they'll do him violence before the time is ripe."

Not a man, however, offered to harm the Nazarene. The little knot of scoffers seemed content to appraise him in superior manner as if he were on trial before them. One especially attracted Judas' attention. He was arrayed in a priestly robe at the borders of which were knotted the fringes of his office. In a voice heavy with feigned deference this Pharisee said, "You have been speaking of the law and how you came not to destroy but to fulfill it. You said that one who broke even a small commandment would have a low place in this kingdom of heaven you talk so much about. What then do you say is the greatest of the commandments?"

Jesus, his face glistening, smiled, quite unperturbed. "Thou shalt love the Lord thy God with all thy heart, and with all thy soul, and with all thy mind. This is the first and great commandment. And the second is like unto it: Thou shalt love thy neighbor as thyself. On these two hang all the law and prophecies."

Then he turned away from the man to address the multitude. Through the warm afternoon he continued with beautiful clarity to expound the true meaning of the ancient writings. The people stood entranced, for never had they heard words fall in such mingled strength and sweetness from the lips of any man.

"You have heard that it was said of old, 'An eye for an eye and a tooth for a tooth.' But I say unto you that you should not retaliate if a man does evil unto you. If he strikes you on one cheek, then turn also the other to him. If he sues you and takes away your coat, then give him your cloak. And if anyone should force you to help him along his way for one mile, walk with him still another. To him that asks of you a favor, give; from him who seeks to borrow of you, do not turn away. You have heard it said that you should love your neighbor and hate your enemy. But I say unto you that you should also love your enemies, bless them that curse you, do good to them that hate you, pray for them that treat you with spite and injure you."

Judas, though he felt that the Master was eulogizing weakness, nevertheless was amazed at his genius in expressing himself with such pellucid clarity. And yet what strange words! What utterly strange words for a Galilean youth, even though he be the Messiah of God! The law of the fathers is the law of striking back. How can he drive out our enemies by turning one cheek and then the other to them?

A man whom he took to be a poor tradesman of near-by Capernaum gave voice to Judas' doubt. He asked Jesus how one could defeat his foe by such methods.

"I ask you," Jesus said with a quick smile, "how else can one defeat him?" He went on to explain in a simple, convincing way that a man can never depend on strength—the strength of his arm, the toughness of his weapon, the keenness of his eye—for victory. "For one day," he added, "the enemy may develop a stronger arm, a heavier shield, a clearer eye, and then he will overcome you. But there is one strength that can never be matched, one weapon that can never be beaten down, one sharpness of the eye that can never be dimmed even for an instant. That strength, that weapon, that vision is but one thing—love. And love encompasses all the strength of God Himself, for God is love.

"A man can never defeat God, nor can your enemy prevail against your love for him. You will defeat him, for you will make of him a friend. The strength of love, my brothers, is the superior strength. God is love, love is God."

Judas wished to cry out his protest, yet he could not. His mind was in a tumult as Jesus spoke to the multitude standing before him. What incredible counsel to give to men who must fight to make themselves what they were determined to be—the head of all mankind!

Now Jesus was taking a different course.

"You are the salt of the earth." Jesus emphasized the inclusiveness of his words with a sweep of his arm. "But if the salt should lose its sharpness, how then should one be able to restore it? It is thenceforth good for nothing but to be thrown out and trodden underfoot." He paused to permit them to consider the compliment, and the warning. "You are likewise the light of the world. Through you must the way be lighted to the Father's home so that your brothers seeing the way may travel along it. You must, because you are this light, so shine that the way is made clear. Look you!" He pointed afar off to the left toward Safed on the mount almost three thousand feet above the level of the Great Sea, and the people turned to see. "A city set on a hill cannot be hid. Neither do men light a candle and place it beneath a bushel measure, but on a candlestick so that it gives light to all within the house. Likewise you must let your light so shine that your fellow men, knowing you to be the children of the Father, may glorify Him because of you."

The force of his picturesque words held them, though the sun was warm and sweat seeped down faces turned earnestly toward him. He told them how they should pray to the Father. They were not to make a public spectacle of prayer like the hypocritical religionists who in the synagogues and at crowded street corners made long oratorical supplications that they might gain the attention and praise of men. They were to pray in secret, with their minds and hearts attuned to hear the soft answering voice of the Father. He even gave them a model prayer, a short communion in which they should seek forgiveness even as they willingly forgave their brothers who might have offended them, and seek deliverance in temptation and from evil.

Nor should they consume their days and their energies in nervous fear of a future that might bring them to hunger and nakedness.

"Is there not more to living, my brothers, than eating rich foods and wearing fine raiment, even raiment from the looms of Tyre and Sidon? Why not be as the birds, who neither worry nor fret? Nor do they sow grain and reap the harvest and store it away in barns. Yet the Father feeds them. And if He feeds even the birds, my brothers, will He not feed His children? I ask you: Will worry over these things add one cubit unto your stature?"

Jesus pointed to the plain stretching toward Capernaum. "And why worry about raiment? See the flowers. Consider these beautiful anemones, the gladioli, the hyacinths, roses of Sharon's plain, jas-

mine, narcissus—so many others, gorgeous in their beauty. Recall
the beautiful words of King Solomon's Song of Songs:

> For lo, the winter is past;
> The rain is over and gone;
> The flowers appear on the earth;
> The time of the singing of birds is come,
> And the voice of the turtle is heard in our land.
> The fig tree ripeneth her green figs,
> And the vines are in blossom;
> They give forth their fragrance.

"Look whither you will, my brothers, there are the flowers. Do
they toil for their raiment? Do they spin? Yet I say unto you that
neither King Solomon, nor Tiberius, nor Tetrarch Herod was ever
arrayed in a robe so splendrous." He pointed to a little flower at
his feet.

Jesus returned then to his argument. "If God the Father will so
clothe these small flowers that are here today and gone tomorrow,
will not He clothe you, O men of little faith? My brothers, let not
the small things of life—the food and the raiment—be of great concern. Trust in the Father to see to your needs, for He knows what
they are and He will supply them. Seek you rather the kingdom of
God and God's own right living, and all things needful will come
to you in due time. Be not today anxious about the things of tomorrow, for tomorrow will bring its own problems and perplexities.
Consider only today's anxieties, for each day has enough of them."

He talked on for a while, earnestly, his words by turn pleading,
warning, comforting, enspiriting. But Judas perceived that the
Master was beginning to tire.

Now Simon Peter was talking with him. Jesus nodded. When the
apostle stepped aside Jesus raised his arms, closed his eyes. Lifting
his bronzed face toward the sky, he prayed to the Father that He
hold all these His children in His loving care. Then he opened his
eyes and, smiling on them, he dismissed the multitude.

Chapter
29   ✠

FOR Judas the weeks that followed the Master's great sermon on
Kurn Hattin were filled with events strange and breath-taking. One
particularly disturbed him. It happened shortly after they returned
late that afternoon from the mountain.

Coming into Capernaum, they had been met by a group of Jewish
elders who had besought Jesus to go to the home of the centurion,
one of whose favorite servants lay desperately ill. They wanted
Jesus to heal the youth.

"The centurion is a good friend of the Jews here, Rabbi, as you
know," an elder declared. "He helped us build our new synagogue.
We think it would be entirely proper for you to oblige this upright
man by restoring his servant."

"Show me his house," Jesus said. "I shall go and heal him."

But before they reached the house the centurion met them. "Master," he said, "my servant has a palsy. He suffers greatly."

"I am going to your house to heal him," Jesus answered.

The Roman's face lighted, but grew serious again. "Master, I do
not deserve to have you enter my house, though you'd be welcome
indeed. But if you will only command the illness to leave him, it
shall do so and he will be restored. I know myself what it is to issue
commands and have them obeyed. I say to this soldier 'Go!' and he
goes, and to this other 'Come!' and he comes."

Instantly the Master's tired, lined face had rounded into a broad
smile. "I say to you, my brothers, that I haven't found faith like
this, no, not in Israel! I tell you that many shall come from the east
and the west and will sit down with Abraham and Isaac and Jacob
in the kingdom of heaven; but the children of Israel shall be

turned out into the darkness of the night, where there will be anguish and bitter weeping."

Judas had been standing beside Simon the Zealot while the centurion and Jesus were talking. "Can he mean that the gentiles, the pagan peoples, will have preference over us of Israel?" he whispered. "Can the Master mean that we Jews are to be despoiled further and even expelled from our own land?"

Simon made no answer, for his eyes were fastened on the Master. Jesus was speaking again, his face alight with happiness: "Go on about your business, my brother. As you have believed it would happen to your servant, so has it happened." He looked a moment into the Roman's eyes before he turned to Simon Peter. "Let us be going on our way."

The next day when Judas made inquiry he learned definitely that on the late afternoon before, at the precise hour of sunset when they had met the centurion, the servant's fever and paralysis suddenly had deserted him and he had been completely restored.

Once more Jesus had aided an enemy of Israel, he reminded himself. Judas had never been able to settle in his mind why the Master should extend his marvelous help to any person not of the chosen race. Perhaps I'll never fathom that mystery, he admitted. After all, the healing of the Roman's servant was significant for but one thing, one transcendingly important thing: The Master has power!

Judas was with Jesus one day across the Sea of Galilee in the country of the Gergesenes when they were abruptly accosted by a huge, demented fellow who came screaming and stark-naked, his body scratched and bleeding from falling and writhing among the rocks and brambles of that wild region.

The Master, seeing the man was mad, commanded the devils to come forth from him. "Who are you?" he asked the poor wretch.

"My name is legion," he answered. "We are a great many. But why have you come here to torment me, Jesus of Galilee, son of the Most High? I know you. Why come you here to torture us? Why command us devils to go forth?"

The Master saw that he was beside himself with madness and fear.

"He's completely crazy," Simon the Zealot said. "He not only believes that devils possess him, but he even believes he is all the devils, he believes he encompasses them. It is a frightful pity."

The demoniac had seen the calm, untroubled eyes of the man from across the lake. He fell at the Master's feet, his whole attitude imploring, beseeching. "Drive us not forth homeless and abandoned to the furies," he begged. "Send us not away homeless with no place to lodge." He looked about, his anguished eyes rolling.

Then he saw a great herd of swine feeding among the rocks at the edge of the precipice that fell away sharply into the sea. He pointed, his eyes ablaze. "Send us, Master, into the swine! There we shall abide, in the foul swine!"

Jesus, looking down on him with compassion, nodded.

In that instant the madman jumped to his feet and ran with a great shouting and screeching, toward the swine. When they saw him, they fled, grunting and squealing. At the edge of the precipice the first of them tried with stiffened legs to brace themselves and stop, but those behind, stampeding wildly from the grotesque, screaming lunatic, drove into them and the whole herd fell in a struggling mass into the sea below. In a few minutes the squeals of those who survived the plunge died away beneath the waters of the little sea.

The naked giant stood at the brink and looked down. Calmly he came back to where Jesus stood with his apostles. "Master, the devils that possessed me are gone, drowned with the swine." His eyes were clear now, and the torment had left him.

"Yes, my brother," Jesus said, "they are gone from you forever. Judas, he is cold. Find him a robe, and give him to eat."

Hardly had they crossed the lake again to Capernaum before there came to Jesus one of the elders of the synagogue, a man named Jairus. He was obviously in great distress. He bowed low to the Nazarene. "Master, my beloved daughter is dying. I beseech you to come with me to my house and restore her."

They started at once for the house. The report spread quickly that Jesus was about to perform another miracle of healing, and a throng formed to follow them. At Jairus' home they found the mourners already screeching and wailing, for the little girl, they told Jesus, was dead.

"She is not dead, but sleeping," the Nazarene replied calmly.

"Sleeping, indeed," one of them said, as others laughed derisively, "but it is the long sleep that will not be ended until the day of judgment."

But his smugness vanished in sudden astonishment when Jesus went into the child's bedchamber and, bending over her bed, spoke gently: "Little girl, wake up!" and she stood up, smiling and restored.

So through the late summer and into the autumn and the quick changing of the face of Galilee's countryside the faith of Judas in Jesus as the Messiah grew stronger as he looked on while the Nazarene did marvelous works of healing. Yet his anxiety also increased, for it seemed that Jesus was giving little thought to the restoration of Israel. The Master seemed content to speak oftener and with a deeper insistence on its all-encompassing importance of what he was wont to describe as his "mission."

Never would he dwell on matters of politics and government. When any of the apostles or others among his closest friends would report to him that people were saying he should be king of Israel, he would shake his head. "My kingdom," he would answer gravely, "is not of this world."

Chapter
30   ✛

TOWARD the end of winter Judas returned to Jerusalem. He was anxious to see Shelomith, for it had been months since he had been with her. He wanted to tell her of the Master, of his tremendous power exhibited in such a variety of ways, and of all that it foretokened for the nation and for them.

He was coming to Jerusalem for the ostensible purpose, however, of collecting money from a group of charitable women who contributed to the work of the Master and his apostles, though they wanted few people to know that they approved the actions of the strange young rabbi in Galilee.

Judas went first to Benjamin's shop, where he was told that the proprietor had gone on a visit into Galilee.

"To purchase homespun for the shop?" Judas asked.

"I don't know, sir. The master didn't say. I have the impression, however, that it was not a business trip."

Puzzled, Judas went to the house on Zion Hill.

"She's not here," the manservant told him. "She went with her father and mother and the maid Hagar to Galilee to visit in the household of Chuza."

"Again?" Judas frowned. "They must be unusually friendly with Herod's steward."

"They were urged by the centurion of Capernaum and Centurion Longinus, who fetched the message from Chuza."

"Longinus urged Shelomith, I suppose!" Judas' tone had a sharp edge.

"The Centurion Longinus came here with the centurion of Capernaum. He accompanied them northward. From there they're going—perhaps they've already started—in the entourage of the Tetrarch Herod for Machaerus beyond the Dead Sea."

"Machaerus?" Judas was incredulous.

"Yes, sir. I understand the Tetrarch is planning to give a great birthday party there."

"You mean that Shelomith is going with Herod to join in celebrating the birthday of that renegade! God in Israel!" He stood silent a moment, pained and angry. Then, his voice calmer, he asked, "How long will they be away from Jerusalem?"

"Not long, I think, sir. As soon as the feasting at Machaerus is over, they'll come home. They'll not go first to Galilee."

"Who will be coming back with Benjamin and his wife and daughter?"

"Only the servant Hagar, sir, and of course the Centurion Longinus."

"But Longinus will have soldiers with him, no doubt, as escort."

"No, sir. He took no soldiers. He wore the civilian toga. I don't think he wished it to be known generally that he was going. I trust, sir, that you'll be discreet."

"Indeed," Judas said from the door. "I shall return when Shelomith is home again. Thank you."

He went next to Japheth's shop. "Remember me?" he asked the cobbler.

"You're the man of Kiriot." Japheth smiled through his stubble of beard. "You've been away a long time. But I never forget the face of a friend—or an enemy. What can I do for you, Judas?"

"Let's go into the back room. I've business for no other ears." They walked into the rear. "Where is he now?"

"Bar Abbas?"

"Yes."

"Somewhere in the rocks between here and Jericho, I'd say, though I don't know of a certainty; he moves about fast."

"Could you get word to him?"

"Yes. Both Gesmas and Dysmas are in Jerusalem now. They can find Bar Abbas."

"Good, Japheth! Then tell them this for me——" He peered about cautiously. "Could other ears be hearing?"

"No. But keep your voice low, for someone might enter the front."

"Listen, Japheth. Tell Gesmas or Dysmas—or both—to bear to Bar Abbas the word that old Herod is going to Machaerus, his fortress-palace on the other side of the Dead Sea, for a season of drunken carousing. Tell him there'll be rich geese there, for easy picking, if he's careful. But this is what I want him told for a certainty: that one will be there whose——" Judas paused, and Japheth, grinning, drew his right hand quickly across his throat. "Yes, that's what I mean. The Centurion Longinus."

"But how can Bar Abbas get to Longinus with his century about him?"

"He won't have any soldiers with him. He's traveling as a civilian."

"Indeed! Perhaps Bar Abbas can slit his guzzle." He grinned again. "But why do you want it slit, Judas?"

"Isn't he a Roman centurion, an enemy of Israel?"

"Yes, but I suspect there's something more."

"He's trying to steal my betrothed away from me, Japheth. He's taking her and her parents to the Tetrarch's party."

"Well he deserves the knife then. I'll tell Gesmas and Dysmas what you've said. They'll get to Bar Abbas. They may stay and help him dispose of the Roman. But tell me this, Judas: how is it with the tall one in Galilee?"

"Things go well with the Master, Japheth. I'm a member of his company now and carry the pouch. I'm on my way to rejoin him. One of these days you'll be hearing great things of him. The day of our liberation is not far hence. Be patient and——" he held a warning finger to his lips—"guard well your tongue, friend."

"Have no worry, Judas. My lips are sealed. Nor will the others talk."

"That's good. I must be going." At the door between the two chambers he turned about quickly. "Tell them Longinus will be returning along the Jericho road. Ask them to be sure to warn Bar Abbas not to harm anyone else in the party—just Longinus— and to see that my betrothed and her parents are safely delivered in Jerusalem. Her name's Shelomith. She'll be the most beautiful woman in the party—" he laughed lightly—"and that's how he can identify her. She's tall, and her hair's black as a raven's wing. Warn him that not a hair of her head must be touched!" He had a sudden thought. "They should also tell Bar Abbas that there may be another young woman with Longinus—his sister, a golden-headed, blue-eyed woman. If so, she mustn't be molested either."

Japheth smiled. "Yes, even though she's Roman and an enemy. You wish her brother's throat cut and yet——" He laughed. "She's beautiful?"

"Yes. And it might be that . . . that . . ."

"That she might be useful, even in Israel."

Judas nodded, grinning. "Even in Israel."

"It would be vengeance on her brother. Very pleasant vengeance, eh?" Japheth picked up the sandal he'd been mending. "Most enjoyable, most diverting vengeance."

Judas went over it again. "Is everything clear, Japheth? Do you know exactly what they must say to Bar Abbas?"

Japheth set down his hammer. "It's as clear, friend, as the beard on the High Priest's chin. And I'll warn them to make it just as clear as that to Bar Abbas. Be content that no harm will befall either your betrothed or your woman of the corn-colored hair."

He was chuckling as Judas walked from the shop.

Chapter 31 ✠

EARLY the next morning, his business in Jerusalem finished, Judas went out through Dung Gate and climbed the Mount of Olives. At Bethany he tarried for an hour with the Master's friends Lazarus and his sisters Mary and Martha. Then he took the road that dropped down to Jericho through a wild region of rocks and stunted undergrowth.

He lodged that night at an inn north of Jericho. He planned to get an early start for Galilee to rejoin the Master. In the darkness of his unlighted chamber he considered what course he should take during the coming months. I'll work with hand and mind to gain

Jesus' complete confidence, he told himself; to establish myself in a position from which I may begin gently to direct him toward the liberation of Israel.

Judas was still thinking of the days immediately ahead when with the first light of morning he started north along the Jordan. The Master is being slow to move toward the throne, he reflected, but when his hour comes he'll ascend it and drive out the nation's despoilers. He has the power, he is the Messiah; all he lacks, no doubt, is the resolution to assert his authority. It shall be my task to speed him tactfully, and soon the great goal will have been accomplished. Then I'll be . . . Then Shelomith and I . . .

O God in Israel! He stopped in his track. Even now she's with the damnable Longinus, Israel's enemy, my enemy! With his staff he smote a loose stone at his feet. At this moment she's asleep in the great stone pile at Machaerus surrounded by old Herod and his concubines, perhaps even abed with Longinus—oh, no, not that! I do her injustice. God pardon me. But lust is contagious. And why would she, my betrothed, the betrothed of the man who's soon to be treasurer of the kingdom, be taking the hospitality of our pagan enemies? Let Herod have his orgies for his own kind. For all I care he may feast his mistresses, his notorious wife and her wanton daughter, his Roman guests, his Roman-imitating Jews. He can gorge himself on rich food and potent wines. He can loll abed with his women and satiate himself in long nights and days of lusting. It's nothing to me if his paramours wear their gowns of thinnest silk and parade before him until his thick lips drool and his eyes are blinded with the heat of passion. They can twist and writhe before him. They can stretch themselves on silken beds, clad in gossamer. Let them—— O God, Cynara! She'll be there. She's there now. It's all right for her to be at Machaerus, for she's heathen and wicked and wanton. But no one can know better than I that she is beautiful, that her eyes are the blue of the Great Sea on a calm day in summer, that her hair is the color of grain ripening in the sun.

There's another one at Machaerus, Judas said to himself as he started walking again, and it is not right for him to be there. John the Baptist, he of the flaming words and the flailing arms, languishes in the dungeon beneath that great pile of masonry. While Herod pursues his lust in the palace-fortress above him, the evangel of Israel's God lies fettered in a cold cell. . . .

At the first crossroads he turned right and with long strides walked eastward toward the Jordan and the gaunt granite ridge on the far side. Soon he came on a road that swung south to cross the river near the head of the sea. He took that road. Jesus and Galilee for the moment were forgotten. Judas had decided to go to Machaerus.

He crossed the pleasant valley, already greening with the promise of returning summer. He passed from behind clumps of oleanders and willows to view in its majestic aloofness the high, proud mass of Mount Nebo, from a shoulder of which Moses the lawgiver had viewed the Promised Land and died. By early afternoon he was trudging through a region of sand and gravel that skirted the shores of the salt sea into which the Jordan flowed to its death. But the sun was reaching low for the waters of the Great Sea far to the west when he began the steep climb up the face of the headland that brought him tired and breathing hard into the thin, high air of a wasteland of basalt and fused granite boulders.

For an hour Judas lay in the lee of a large rock and rested. It was late when he came to the wall of Machaerus. In the darkness he made his way stealthily to its foot and crouched there a long while listening. When he heard no sentry's steps he climbed the wall, dropped to the ground on the other side and hid behind a shrub.

Yellow light streamed through the windows of a large room and fell in warm squares on the broad terrace beneath. He could hear music and now and then a loud burst of laughter. It must be the great hall of the palace and Herod is entertaining his guests, Judas reasoned. If only I could slip unnoticed to the palace wall and see into the hall! But there must be many sentries. He lay still behind the bush, listened and watched. Fear and anger stirred him. Visions of Shelomith smiling on Longinus within there returned to torture him. He crept forward, keeping out of the patches of light, moving cautiously from shrub to shrub, until he gained the terrace. He scurried across it to crouch in the shadow of the wall. But he dared not stand upright in the light and attempt to peer into the great hall.

Why did I come here anyway? he asked himself. Why did I walk all those long miles through the sand and gravel and across Jordan's valley? Only to see Shelomith smiling on the hated Longinus? Or to see a Roman woman with a soft, white body and golden hair? I shouldn't be here—I, a Zealot of the Zealots, a follower of the tall Nazarene, that strong leader of utter purity of body and mind!

If I came to see Shelomith and carry her away from this den of evil, how can I remove her now I'm here? Would she go? Is she still my betrothed, or has she succumbed to the seductions—— O God in Israel, may it not be so! May it not be so!

If I came to see the Roman woman, hoping, though I'd not admit it even to myself, that I might bed with her, that I might finish out the night in the tent—God forgive me! Then, I, Judas of Kiriot, son of the worthy Simon, apostle of Jesus the Messiah, I am in danger of deep sin.

Voices. Defiant, protesting. Beyond the terrace, to the right and down somewhere below. Voices of Jews he could tell by the Aramaic, unlettered men of the countryside no doubt.

These angry voices may be related in some way, it flashed on him suddenly, to the imprisonment here of the bold preacher of the Wilderness.

In the darkness Judas moved stealthily toward the voices. At the end of a wing that jutted out from the great structure and ran down a declivity from the terrace off the dining chamber he discovered a group of irate men assembled before three small lighted windows. He was not challenged. After several minutes of discreet silence he pushed toward one of the squares of light and peered inside. As he did so a man nudged him with his elbow, pointed with a quick nod of his head. "He's pale, isn't he, and thinner?"

"Yes, he is," Judas agreed. The Prophet John stood in the cen-

ter of a large square cell whose floor was more than the distance of a
tall man's height below the bottom of the windows. He was gaunt,
and his head thrust up on the stem of his thin neck. The leathery
tan of the desert had paled to a sickly yellow.

John was conversing with a man at one of the small openings.
"I did not relent," he said. "I retreated not one pace. In fact—"
a wry smile lighted his haggard face—"I called on them again to
repent—Herod and the woman Herodias. I told them they were living in adultery. I declared to them that the great God of Israel
would hide His face from them. I besought them with earnestness
and vigor to repent——"

"The slimy son of perdition!" The man interrupted the Prophet.
"And his woman is a whore of hell! They shall be damned to the
bottommost pit!" He turned away from the window, reported in
excited tones what the Prophet had said, for only the few pressed
into the tiny openings could see and hear the prisoner.

A bedlam of rage swallowed the man's words as quickly as those
back from the windows caught their import. Other faces took their
turn at the small squares to catch a glimpse of the heroic man who
had dared stand before the wicked Herod and his brazen wife.

"Silence!" It was the same man. He was waving his hand to
quiet the passionate crowd. "Let's push into the banquet hall and
demand of Herod that he release the Prophet John. Let's speak
with courage, and the Lord of Israel will see that Herod dare not
touch us. Let's tell that son of hell——"

Suddenly he stopped speaking, and Judas, who had turned away
from the opening to listen, saw that he was staring, mouth open and
aghast, into the dungeon. Judas whirled about to peer through the
window again.

Four of Herod's soldiers had entered the cell. The doorway
through which they had come, in the wall opposite the windows, was
open. Judas ventured to lean inside, the better to see and hear.

The Prophet John stood facing the soldiers. He seemed utterly
calm. "The Tetrarch Herod cannot kill me; he has neither the

authority nor the power." A thin smile gashed his countenance. "If you like you may tell him that I, John, said it."

One of the soldiers laughed. "You'll soon see whether or not he can have you killed," he said sardonically. "In five minutes, old man, your head will be on a platter in front of the daughter of the Tetrarchess Herodias."

"But I'll not be dead, soldier of Herod," John replied, his voice even. "You may think so, but you do not understand. My God will deliver me from death, for the ending of this life is but the beginning of a greater one." Suddenly he held out his skinny arm, thrust a long forefinger toward the soldier's nose. "Repent of your sins, else you will never see that life! Repent! Repent!"

"Hold your peace!" Another soldier, with fierce eyes, faced John. "You've been condemned to death. It's the command of the Tetrarch that as a gift to the young woman we fetch your head on this platter!" Judas saw with horror a third soldier holding by one handle a huge silver tray that hung almost to the floor.

Still the Prophet was calm. "Have I not said unto you, soldiers of Herod, that man cannot kill man? It is meet that you should repent and seek forgiveness of the Lord God of Israel before He shall require of you even your——"

With one vicious sideways thrust of his right foot to John's shins the first soldier sent the gaunt preacher sprawling on his face. Instantly, as though by prearranged plan, another fastened his fingers in the long black locks of the Prophet's hair, held the head steady. In that same second a heavy sword descended—so quickly that Judas, watching appalled, hadn't seen it drawn from the scabbard—and the soldier, standing straight again, held up the severed head. Blood poured from it onto the jerking, twitching body on the dungeon floor. From the stump of the neck blood spurted in arching streams.

Judas turned from the window, his stomach churning with nausea.

Vile shouts and terrible imprecations descended on the four

bloody soldiers in the keep and rose high above the battlemented walls. Huddled in front of the narrow opening, Judas clutched his rebelling middle. O God in Israel! He said his God would deliver him. O God, why was he not delivered? Why?

The man of Kiriot knew that he must relieve the nausea that gripped him, but he could not hold his eyes away from the square of light. Once more he leaned over and peered into the dungeon.

The door that had admitted the soldiers of Herod was closed now. The walls were bloody, the floor was red with sticky gore that a moment ago had been the wine of life. The body of John the Baptist lay face downward, long and inert, in a mire of blood. Blood dripped, slowly now and more slowly, from the severed neck.

But what held Judas' eyes in horror and fearful wonderment was the bloody right hand of the Prophet. Six inches above the floor, unsupported save by the arm rigid and set in death, the hand, forefinger extended straight and stiff, pointed toward the door through which the soldiers had left. Repent! Repent!

Chapter 32 ✠

JUDAS stumbled away from the square of yellow light and the frightful sight of the headless body. He said his God would protect him. Yet there he lies, O Lord of our unhappy land, rigid in the wallow of his own blood. No more will his great voice thunder. No more will his long arms flail the air and call on sinners to repent.

The voice is silent, the arms are stilled and the blood of life is drained out on a dungeon floor in order that a drunken, fawning lover of evil Rome may make sport before his wanton women. In the feasting chamber above even now they jest as the head of the great John the Prophet, silent and bloody and eternally profaned, lies on a silver platter before them. . . . O God of ancient Israel, he said his God would save him.

Judas heard the soldiers coming. Herod was sending his palace guard to quiet the tumult of oaths and lamentations outside the cell of the Wilderness preacher. They were disturbing the merriment of the feast; they were showing poor respect to the Tetrarch of Galilee and Peraea on his birthday. Soon the soldiers would be clouting Jewish skulls. But not the red-thatched skull of the man of Kiriot!

He ran through the darkness around the wing of the palace, up the incline until he reached the terrace alongside the great dining hall and crouched in the shadows on the low stone balustrade. . . . He said his God would protect him. Of him Jesus had said that never a greater man had been born of woman. Yet there on the cold floor of the dungeon . . . Judas lifted his eyes to the stars and the moonless cavern of the sky. Why, O God in Israel, oh, why?

He sat a long while and his thought were as dark as the night. . . . Shelomith, my betrothed, lovely daughter of Israel . . . here at Machaerus, den of loathsome sinning . . . here with lovers of Rome, reclining at table beside a Roman soldier, enemy of Israel, my enemy! . . .

He stood up. He moved across the terrace, skirting the light from the windows. . . . How can I sit still when such thoughts oppress? Where is she? Oh, Shelomith! Can it be that my beloved has——

Two great doors were suddenly flung open almost in his face, and he stood half-blinded in the brightness of the lamps illuminating the dining chamber. Just then two men supporting a heavy, stumbling, retching, drunken fellow brushed past him to the edge of the terrace. Judas scurried out of the oblong of light and ran toward the balustrade where he had been sitting. . . . That big man, lavishly dressed—in a tunic of purple silk, grease-spotted from fallen food and wine-splotched—could that be old Herod? Yes, the Tetrarch himself, drunken and nauseated, his round paunch overstretched with gorging. . . . Judas sat on the balustrade in the darkness and listened, himself sickened, to Herod's loathsome vomiting. In another minute they were leading the Tetrarch away, around the other side of the terrace. In the palace, Judas could tell by the stir, the feast had ended and the guests were departing.

Let them go. Let them all go. Let Cynara go off somewhere to bed with one of the rich guests. Tonight she wouldn't want to share the silken couch of the Tetrarch. And let Shelomith go, too. Let her go from the iniquitous hall to sleep somewhere in this cursed pile. Let her—— O God, no! I'll kill Longinus! With one jab of my knife I'll be avenged for this night. I'll take her away, and then I'll go back to Galilee and the Master. . . . But the great Forerunner had said his God would protect him, and now he's only a stiffening corpse on a cold stone floor!

Judas would have cried aloud had not caution restrained him.

A long moment he considered the strange and troubled nature of this evil night. He thought of his father back home, and of his Uncle Bezek dying on a cross long ago in Galilee. Straight across the dead waters of the sunken sea he saw a hillside in Jerusalem and a twisted, gnarled tree. . . . The tree is I, Judas the man of Kiriot, beaten by winds of circumstance. Yes, but the tree fights; it has never yielded. And it stands. . . .

He thought of Shelomith. Her soft, white hands, her black hair, dark eyes looking out innocently from beneath long black lashes. A true daughter of Israel. A true——

In the light of the lamps Cynara's hair must have shone like gold. Now freed of the restraining golden net, spread over a silken pillow on a luxurious couch somewhere in the castle, it must be sending forth an aroma teasing, tempting. . . . Lord of Israel, I am of the company of the Nazarene. Protect me from evil conjurings, O God!

He thought of the dead John. What a strange, terrible gift for a young woman, even a pagan, wanton woman. The severed bloody head of a man on a silver platter, set on the board in front of her. Pain and blood before indulgence and fastidiousness. What sort of woman can this daughter of Herodias be? A heart cold as stone in a body beautiful, lips crimson as the platter's gory treasure, flesh warm and yielding, fragrant as the costliest nard which even now began to tantalize his nostrils. . .

He turned his head. A woman stood beside him, pressed against the balustrade, her bare arm lightly touching his.

"Cynara!"

"You know my name. At least I make some progress."

"But how did you know I——?"

"I was watching Herod when they led the drunken old glutton out on the terrace. I saw you when the doors opened. You were standing in the light of the lamps. When I got the chance I slipped out here. They don't know where I am. I . . . I . . . Oh, Judas, I'm glad you came here! I don't know why, and I care not."

He was lifting a leg over the balustrade to stand straight. She pushed him down, her hand soft on his shoulder. "Don't get up. Just let me sit a moment with you. It was so close in there, and the heavy drinking, the smell of meats . . . Oh, it's pleasant out here, Judas."

She sat down on the coping and settled her gown about her. She was close against him.

"But your brother—he'll be missing you."

"Longinus?" She laughed. "He has eyes only for that dark-haired Israelite. He could hardly wait for the banquet to be over so he could be alone with her . . . the rest of the night." She paused a brief moment. "I don't blame him. She's a beautiful creature. He'll not miss me."

"But——"

"Oh, Judas, why must you think of what might happen? Give yourself to the present. She leaned back so that her shoulders were against his chest and the odor of her body and her hair was around him. "I wish you'd——" She looked up into his face. "If you'd only——"

She could say no more, for his face was pressing hard against hers and his lips were tasting, savoring. With his right arm he held her, and in the timeless, unheeding darkness his free left hand was eager, searching. . . .

But not for long. Inside the great hall someone was calling her name.

"By all the little gods!" She pulled her lips away and twisted from his relaxing arm. "It's Berenice calling me—for her stupid brother Paran, no doubt. I do wish he weren't so persistent."

"Cynara! Cynara! Where are you, Cynara?"

She rose quickly. "I must be going, before they come out here and discover me. I'll get away from them, though, and quickly, on the pretense that I'm fatigued and want to go to bed. My room's there, Judas. See?" She pointed. "The one this side of the tall evergreen. It opens on that upper balcony reached by those stone steps there. I'll place a light—no, two small lamps—at the window. I shan't be long, and—oh, do not tarry, Judas!" Her laugh was gay, excited. "And now—oh, Judas, oh-h-h——" She held her lips quick against his and for an instant her warm hand strayed along his chest. Then she ran across the terrace and turned in at the open doorway.

Chapter 33 ✠

As JUDAS stepped through the window he saw the Roman girl lying stretched on the couch in the shadowy corner of the bedchamber. Cynara had removed the two lamps from the window soon after she had placed them there, and one of them she had extinguished. She had so screened the other that it provided little light.

He walked to the couch, stood looking down. She lay on her back, her right leg bent slightly, her head cradled on her arm, the silken yellow hair fanned outward to cover half the pillow. The sheer black nightgown concealed little.

"Do I look . . . the same?" She fluttered her eyelids. "Do you recognize the woman of the tent?"

Strange tinglings ran along Judas' spine. He knew that if he should try to speak his words would be hoarse, strained. He licked his lips, closed his fingers on cold, damp palms.

"Well—" Cynara sat up—"won't you take off your robe and . . . and visit with me awhile?" She patted the couch.

Hating this woman as he hated all Romans, hating his recreant self, he stripped off the robe, threw it across the back of a chair, unlatched his sandals, sat down beside her. She lay back on the pillow and straightened her legs so that the nightgown slipped above the knees. "Judas, why are you so . . . so timid? You of all men! Did anyone see you enter through the window?"

"No . . . no, I don't think so." His stammer betrayed the tumult of his thoughts. "There was a man down below—maybe a sentry— but he didn't see me."

"You're thinking of the sentry outside the tent, eh?" She laughed. "This is Machaerus; this isn't the camp of Sergius. Relax and——" She stopped. She was looking through half-closed eyes. "Oh, Judas, can it be that . . . that you've never before seen a woman . . . thus?" He was sitting against her, even with her waist. She reached up and with a warm finger stroked his forearm and the back of his hand spread palm-down on the couch.

"Certainly you're not disturbed about Longinus." She gave a merry laugh. "He's settled for the night . . . in one of the bed-chambers . . . with that dark girl. He's concerned with nothing else. He'd be a fool if he were."

Judas said nothing. He felt she lied. Her words seemed power-less to anger or to hurt. He sat absorbed, drugging the protests of his faith, his honor, his loyalty and the hate that was the nerve of his being, hardly seeing the film of her garment, hardly hearing what she said.

"Judas, you weren't afraid that day at the inn. It must be because I'm a Roman——" She lowered her eyes from his face. "But isn't a woman a woman?" She swept her hand across her body. "Aren't they all the same? Do you notice any difference?" She was laugh-ing, perhaps deriding him.

Judas sat against her right side and looked into her face. The soft light from the one faint lamp glinted on her hair tumbled about her head like a bronze halo; her mouth was half open, circled by hot, red lips; she lay flat, head pressed into the pillow, and her eyes searched him from beneath artfully lowered lids.

"You're so strong, Judas, so . . . so virile," she whispered. He saw the artfulness go from her eyes. Her breath came up into his face, panting and invitingly fragrant. "Oh, Judas, why are you so . . . so . . . Why must I entreat . . ."

Leaning over her, his right arm bracing him, her waist hot against it through the sheer gown, he felt her stir. Now her right leg was pulled up, so that he could feel it pressed hard against his back. Her hand that had been toying at his chest slipped around his body and her left arm came up to cup a hot palm about the back of his head. With the strength and ardor of abandon she pulled him down hard against her.

A sudden shout: "Cynara! Cynara!" A knocking on the door, loud and demanding. "Cynara! Are you all right? Cynara!"

She pushed him back with all her strength. "Judas! You must— Judas—— Oh, by the gods, why would he have to come now! Judas—" she shoved her palms against his chest—"Judas, you must——"

He pulled his mouth from her lips, loosened the grip of his arms about her, sat up. "By Beelzebub, who—?"

"It's Longinus. He's——" Another insistent pummeling on the door. "Yes! Yes!" she shouted, trying to feign sleepiness. "Who is it? What do you want?"

"Cynara, it's Longinus. Are you all right? The sentry——"

"Stupid, of course I'm all right, except that you've come banging on my door in the middle of the night to wake me when I was having such a nice sleep. Why on earth, Longinus—?"

"Sorry to disturb you, Cynara. But the sentry reported he saw a man entering your window. Get up, put on your robe and open the door. I must search the room."

"Longinus, have you lost your wits, waking me like this to

search my chamber for a man?" She whispered to Judas, "You'll have to leave. He'll never go till he gets in here and looks around. Oh, why did he have to come meddling in my affairs? Damn him! . . . Well, wait a minute till I can get my robe and light another lamp!" she yelled to her brother. "But of all the damnably silly foolishness——" She reached in the half-light for Judas to steady her as she got to her feet. "Kiss me, oh, kiss me!" She stood on tiptoe for his embrace. "Now, begone," she said, "but, oh, Judas, come again! Come back after he has left and everything has quieted. We'll not be interrupted. I swear it. Then we can——"

He pulled the latchets of his sandals, grabbed his robe as he ran past the chair. He heard the robe tear. A corner had caught in a crevice. He jerked it free. With one hand on the sill he vaulted through the window, landed upright on the terrace, raced through the cool darkness. . . .

When she knew he was safely gone Cynara opened the door.

Longinus looked about the chamber, studied the couch. "He has gone." He smiled grimly. "I'll say nothing to my men out there in the corridor. Who was he?"

"How do you know there was a man in here?"

"Do you think I'm stone-blind—and foolish?" He pointed. "The depression there—where he sat." Then his eyes lighted on a scrap of robe fastened in the chair between the arm and the frame. "And that bit of robe. He left in a hurry, I see." Longinus went over, pulled out the piece, examined it. "Huh! Galilean homespun. Could it have been—?"

"You came too soon. When will you learn to attend to your own affairs, Longinus?"

He frowned. "Haven't I warned you against that—?"

She whirled on him, her eyes blazing. "Who are you to come here from his woman's bed to prate your silly moralizing?"

"What woman's bed? Cynara, are you mad? What do you mean?"

"Now you affect injured innocence. You know perfectly well what woman—his woman, that girl Shelomith, the one you've been eying all night. Well, I . . . I don't blame you." She smiled weakly.

"I've not been in her room, nor she in mine, Cynara. She's a virtuous woman."

She gave a shrill laugh. "Perhaps you really believe it. Maybe she is. I care not one denarius. But I'd appreciate your staying out of my room—and my affairs. I'm old enough—and experienced enough—to know what I want. And I don't need any guardian over my virtue, either." She walked to the window, pointed out into the darkness. "Now your bird has flown—out the window through which he flew in. Once more he has escaped you." She held her head back and laughed in his face. "You think you're so clever!"

The centurion scowled. "Listen, Cynara, do you take me for a complete fool? I placed no sentry at the window on purpose to give him a chance to escape. I didn't want to embarrass you. I knew who the man was. The sentry saw his red hair." He paused. "I didn't want to embarrass his betrothed either." He walked to within an arm's length of his sister. "Now get back to bed, and say nothing of this night's business—to anyone. Do you understand? I warn you. Say not a word. I wouldn't have Shelomith know." He glared at her.

"Yes." She pointed to the door. "Yes, I understand. I very well understand. You, too, get back to your bed." Her face was dark with her suddenly flaming anger. "Get back to bed. Get back to the creature you're trying to take away from him." She shook her fist under his nose. "But don't you ever try again to keep me from him!"

He looked at her a moment, but said nothing. Then he went to the door, opened it, strode out, slammed it behind him.

Through the darkness Judas ran. Machaerus and the wall about it and the prowling sentry and the dimly lighted chamber were behind him in the night. . . . O Lord of Israel, I have sinned, I the servant, the friend, the apostle of the Good Master, the pure man of Nazareth, the Messiah of God, the coming king. I have failed him.

. . . I have let a sinful woman lead me from the path, O God. But the sin is mine. She is a woman of a gentile race, ignorant of the laws of God, ignorant even of Yahweh Himself. But I am a son of the chosen people, and a member of the Messiah's inner fellowship. . . .

He ran through the night until he could no longer make out in the eastern blackness the shape of accursed Machaerus. Then only he paused to rest. He fought to drive from his mind's eye the vision of yellow hair spread over a pillow to frame red lips and blue eyes and half-closed lids. . . . O God, forgive me, forgive my lustful heart! I blamed Shelomith for lust to justify my own concupiscence.

Chapter 34 ☩

IMPELLED by a sense of urgency, Jesus determined to send out his beloved twelve two by two to try themselves at the task of proclaiming his good news.

When Judas arrived from the south the Master completed the pairing. Having given them their instructions and his blessing, he dispatched them—talkative Simon the Rock with his quiet, deliberate brother Andrew, so that the one's boldness would offset the other's timidity, the one's calmness would slow the other's impetuosity; the Zebedee brothers—older, more mature, practical James with younger, more visionary, idealistic John; the scholarly Nathanael bar Tolmai with the slow and dull but earnest Philip; Thomas the distrustful, skeptical, slow to faith but soundly honest, paired with Matthew, the former publican who in one blinding moment of utter conviction and in faith never relinquished had turned about to walk steadfast and fearless along the way of an entirely different life; Little James and his brother Jude, sons of Cleopas and brothers of Matthew, the one the champion of duty, the other the exponent of the virtue of doctrine; and the two Zealots—Simon of the flaming fanaticism, seeking to serve God with the fire and sword of the word, the apostle of zeal, and Judas of Kiriot, Judaean among Galileans, fierce enemy of his nation's enemies, in whose heart the Master saw the seeds of avarice and a measureless ambition.

So they went journeying to preach and heal in the Master's name, each pair to the region seeming to offer the greatest opportunity. Judas and Simon the Zealot went southwest, for Judas secretly hoped that in the region of the Jordan he might come upon word of Bar Abbas. Perhaps the revolutionist had been able to recruit many for service in the army that would support the Master on his ascending the throne. And he might hear that already Bar Abbas on the road from Jericho to Jerusalem had slain Longinus, and that Shelomith, fearful and penitent, was back safe in her father's house.

He had said nothing of this—or of his visit to Machaerus—to anyone, not even to Simon the Zealot.

When groups gathered to hear them, Judas and Simon sought to give them the warm and heartening message of the Master. Simon emphasized the importance of the ancient law and how God required that they obey His commandments as laid down in the Scriptures; he told them of the purity of the Master and how he taught his followers to live by the law and keep themselves unspotted by the world.

Judas dwelt on the power of Jesus, the Messiah of God, and his ability to work wonders. He told them that one day the Nazarene would re-establish the ancient kingdom and all men would bow before him. He counseled them to be ready with good weapons at hand to fight for King Jesus with the coming of that day. He spoke of his own love of the Master, how Jesus would be a great ruler, even more powerful than King David, and how he would strengthen Israel against the proud empire of Rome.

But sometimes among them were certain ones who had heard

Jesus himself discourse on his favorite theme of God as the loving, kind, just Father of His people, even all men, and the duty and privilege of all to love and serve Him and their fellow men with joyous and thankful hearts.

"Your words are not his words," a tall, thin villager declared one day as he wagged a finger at Judas. "I've heard him, and he doesn't talk the way you do." There was much nodding of heads among them, and some even doubted that the two were of the Master's company.

Late on another day, as the sun was dropping toward the ridge of mountains, the apostles were about to end their labor in a huddle of vineyardists' huts on a hillside above the Jordan when several men fetched a young woman before them.

"She is possessed of devils," her father announced. "The devils, when they will it, throw her to the ground, and she jerks and struggles in their grasp. She foams at the mouth, and the devils speak through her lips in strange words and terrible mutterings and groanings. Some have told us that if the man of Nazareth were here he'd drive the devils out, and others have said that in his name you two could do this."

Judas prayed that the Father might use him to restore the young woman, who now stood watching him, obviously suspicious.

He raised his hand and placed the palm on her head. But when he closed his eyes and lifted his face in an attitude of prayer he felt no assurance that power was being given him. He was impressed instead with a sense of his own weakness and sinfulness; here before these people he should fall on his face and implore God's forgiveness.

But he kept to his feet, and, knowing he had failed to reach the Eternal Power, he opened his eyes and looked into hers. She jerked away from him. "He's no man of God!" she screamed. "He only pretends to be a servant of the Almighty. There's no healing in his hands. No! No! Away with him! Away! Away!"

Foam began to fleck her lips. Chewing her tongue, she sank to the ground and pounded it with her thin arms while she moaned in a strange tongue. When she was still and seemed dead, two of the men lifted her and stood her on her feet. After she had recovered sufficiently to walk with their help they led her away. Her father, following behind, turned to look in disappointment and despair toward Judas and Simon. In a short moment the company of villagers had left them.

So, weary and beaten, they retraced their steps to Capernaum and the Master. They had no good word to tell Jesus about their mission. And nowhere had Judas learned any word of Bar Abbas.

The day after their return the Zebedees came in, bursting with stories of the great success they had met with. In one place, they reported, they had come upon an unorthodox preacher healing and working wonders in the name of Jesus but not in the manner to which they were accustomed.

"We invited him to join us and follow our way, but the fellow refused, Master," John declared, his eyes warm with love for his tall cousin. "Then we warned him never henceforth to do any works of healing or teaching in your name."

"But in that you erred," Jesus said, not ungently, "for if he was doing such things in my name, though in his own way, he could not have been working against me."

In doing the will of God, he told them, one must not only act out of love and zeal, but one must also chart with reasoning the course of one's work.

The rabbi was happy in the measure of success reported by his returning apostles, but he saw that much yet remained to be taught them, and he felt that the time was not long in which the great lessons might be learned. For the day was coming when they would of necessity be his evangelists.

Then without warning, and before all the apostles had returned, frightful tidings arrived.

One of the servants of Chuza, coming back early to Tiberias to arrange Herod's palace before his return, reported the beheading of John the Baptist.

"I was helping in the dining chamber the night of the Tetrarch's birthday party," Chuza's man told Simon bar Jonas, who for years had supplied Chuza's kitchen with fish freshly caught in the Sea of Galilee. "There was much drinking and before long the Tetrarch had drunk himself well nigh into a stupor. When someone mentioned the Prophet John, who'd been there in the dungeon a year, the Tetrarch ordered him brought to the dining chamber to make sport of him before the guests.

"But John wasn't frightened. He shook his finger at Herod and the Tetrarchess and shouted at them that they were living in adultery because Herod had taken her away from his brother and she was not his lawfully wedded spouse. He spoke with great passion and it sorely angered Herodias, so much so that the Tetrarch ordered him returned to the dungeon."

"And there had him beheaded, the rotten heathen!" Simon's face flamed beneath the wild stubble of his beard.

"Not until later, after Salome danced. The Tetrarch had begged her to dance, had promised her anything if she would—even the half of his kingdom. So she danced—a wild and lewd performance that tickled old Herod. When he asked her what he should give her she asked for the head of the prophet on a platter. So he ordered his soldiers to go into the dungeon and get it."

Judas had been listening intently. "Had many of the guests left when you set out from Machaerus?" he asked.

"Most of them, sir. The Tetrarch and his party were to remain a few days longer. I came north with my master and his family in the company of the centurion of Capernaum and a half century of troops. The other half century were sent on a mission to Jerusalem with the Centurion Longinus and——"

"You mean Longinus had troops with him between Jericho and Jerusalem?" Judas interrupted, unable to conceal his anxiety.

"Yes, sir, he did. We learned this as we came around the head of the sea. Longinus and the soldiers had gone before us. And it's a good thing for him and the young women with him that there were troops along. That Bar Abbas and his men——"

"What! Did Bar Abbas attempt to waylay them?"

"Indeed he did, sir. But it turned out that the waylayer got waylaid."

"You mean Bar Abbas was captured?"

"He was, sir. He must have been surprised because of the soldiers. He and his men about nightfall came down out of the rocks to ambush Longinus, but the soldiers deployed behind the robber band and captured many of them. For a few minutes, though, there was fierce fighting, we heard, and Bar Abbas killed several Romans before they seized him."

"You say Longinus had some young women with him?"

"Two. One was his sister, a woman with blue eyes and yellow hair. The other was a dark-eyed, black-haired Jewish girl."

"What became of them?" Judas' eyes were anxious, though he tried to keep his tone casual.

"Oh, they escaped without a scratch, sir! They went on to Jerusalem with Centurion Longinus, I suppose, sir."

"And Bar Abbas? What became of him? Did you hear the names of any others who were captured?"

"Longinus' soldiers manacled them and took them on to Jerusalem—to the Tower of Antonia, we were told. I think they were Galileans for the most part. I remember the name of one, I think— Dysmas. And——"

Judas seethed with apprehension. "Do you remember hearing whether there was one Gesmas among those captured?"

"I believe I did hear that name called."

Still Judas could not bring himself to tell anyone about his journey to Machaerus. Too much shame was connected with it. He was deeply troubled. Bar Abbas captured! And Dysmas and likely Gesmas! "It was my fault. I have sinned. It was my sinning that led them to be captured by the Romans. I conspired murder, the slaying of Longinus when he was on a peaceful detail. Now our Zealot leaders will be slain instead. They'll die on the cross. Perhaps already they have gone to their deaths." Through the night, sleepless, he punished himself.

Before the sun had risen out of the little sea he started for Jerusalem.

Chapter
35 | ✠

WHEN he found Shelomith at her father's house, he said abruptly, "I had to see you. I've been upset because of the way you've acted lately. I've wondered if you still consider yourself my betrothed, or if the Roman has stolen you away from me."

She tossed her black head. "You've had no cause to be troubled, Judas. Have I said I was no longer your betrothed? What have I done to indicate—?"

"What have you done?" His tone was sharp. "What haven't you done? Didn't you go with the Roman to Herod's drunken party at Machaerus? Weren't you there when that turncoat had John beheaded? I don't even know—" he turned his head away, but she saw the frown creasing his forehead—"that you disapproved the horrible murder."

She whirled on him. "Judas, how can you say such a thing! You know I didn't approve it, that I was deeply hurt by it, greatly angered. Didn't I leave Machaerus as soon as the sun rose the next day?"

"But, Shelomith, why did you go to such a place, and with a Roman centurion of all people? Why in the first place—?"

"You talk as though I went with Longinus alone. Yet you know I didn't. Of course my parents went to Tiberias with me, and we accompanied Chuza and his family——"

"—and Longinus."

Her eyes blazed, but when she spoke her voice was restrained. "Yes, and Longinus. But I was not with him alone."

"But you sat with him at the birthday feast, and——"

"How do you know that?" Her black eyes snapped. "Did
Cynara tell you? She was there." She looked him full in the face.
"Have you seen her since she got back to Jerusalem? Did you go
first to her house to—to find out about me, or just what did you go
there for?" She was furious.

"No! I haven't been to her house," he answered truthfully. "I
don't even know where she stays. I didn't know she was in Jerusalem. I haven't——"

"Oh, you protest much, don't you? But you've seen her."

"That night in the tent when——"

"No, I'm not talking about that night in the tent. Since then.
You didn't suppose I knew, Judas. You think I'm just a simple
Jewish woman without eyes or ears. Hah!" She threw her head
back. Her cheeks were flaming. "No, not that night. Another
night. The wedding feast at Cana. After the feast. In the darkness
along the gallery. Her arm was warm and soft, wasn't it? And
her voice was pleading, seducing, so charming, eh, my beloved?
'Oh, Judas, do come! Oh, please come to see me at Capernaum,
Judas! Oh, Judas-s-s!' " Suddenly she laughed, but there was no
mirth in it. "You didn't guess I knew, did you? You never told
me, though you talked much of the wine made from the water.
You spoke at length of the power of your Master, but you——"

"I never went to Capernaum to see her, Shelomith. I didn't know
she'd be at Cana." He laughed with a trace of bitterness. "You
seem to have the full story. The Roman woman told Berenice, no
doubt, and that dear girl couldn't wait to tell you all about it."

"Yes, Berenice told me. She said the Roman woman wants you,
Judas, is determined to get you." Her voice was calmer. "Oh, how
I despise her!"

"But you don't despise her brother. You go with him on jour-
neys. He comes to your father's shop. He comes to your father's
house. He seems to have much business here."

"I don't love Longinus, Judas, and you know it. He has acted
with courtesy and propriety toward my family and me. If he
weren't a Roman you'd not feel this way about him."

Judas laughed again. "And if Cynara weren't a woman, a woman with golden hair, you'd not despise her, eh? No, Shelomith, it isn't because Longinus is a Roman that I hate him—not that alone. You know why. How often I've told you! It's because he's an enemy of my land, a soldier in an invading army that has Israel prostrate. That's why I'm his sworn foe, why I'd kill him——"

Shelomith was looking at him with a strangely puzzled expression, her mouth half open. "Judas, if I thought you——"

"What do you mean? I don't understand."

"You and your Zealots! Judas of Kiriot, you knew I was going to Machaerus. The servant told me you were angry. You knew that Longinus would be there. If I thought you'd plotted with that terrible Bar Abbas——"

"Shelomith, what are you talking about? Explain yourself."

"Bar Abbas lay in wait for our party on the road from Jericho. But he hadn't guessed we were being escorted by half a century of soldiers. He killed several legionaries, but he didn't kill Longinus—" she looked straight at Judas—"and he got captured himself, and some of his men with him."

"God in Israel, you might have been hurt, Shelomith!"

"Yes, it wasn't the protection of your Zealots that saved me. Now tell me the truth, Judas. You knew about this, didn't you?"

"Yes. A servant of Chuza returning to Galilee from Machaerus told me. I suppose Bar Abbas will go to the cross."

"No, but he'll die—and he deserves to. You'd never agree about that, I know."

"But why not on the cross?"

"Because tonight they're taking him and a few of the others to the dungeons of the Amphitheater. They'll fight wild animals at the next games."

"O God in Israel! How do you know this, Shelomith? The centurion told you?"

"Yes."

She had never seen such furrows in his brow. "And you'll go with him to the games, I suppose?"

"No. You know I won't, Judas. Jews have nothing to do with that pagan sport." For a moment she said nothing. "Oh, Judas," she began again, "why can't it be as it was before you became so— so fierce in your hatred? Why must you spend your waking hours in plots against the Romans? You say you love me, and you say you love the Nazarene. Why not be content with my love? Or why not be happy following him? Or return to your father's home and look after his business? Or settle here in Jerusalem? I'd be glad to be with you wherever you are. Why must you endanger yourself— and me—by getting involved in this Zealot movement? Oh, my beloved, be willing——"

"—to be a herder of cattle at Kiriot, or run a shop in Jerusalem and sell meat and hides?" He laughed mirthlessly. "Not me, Shelomith. I'm aiming for higher things." He pleaded with her. "Have patience. Have faith in me, beloved. Only a little while longer, only a few more months. Then we can settle down. Yes, then we can build our house above Hinnom, with a wall to keep the children from falling into the gulch!" He stood up. "Then we'll be great ones, Shelomith, next to the king himself!"

He did not mention Bar Abbas again. Shortly he told her good-by; he had business to see to in Jerusalem, he said.

From her house he went straight to the shop of Japheth the cobbler. His secret information, the plot he had promoted had resulted in the capture of Bar Abbas, Dysmas and Gesmas. The Zealots would have small use for him now. He must square himself, devise what he could.

Chapter 36 ✠

"Take the four of them, Flavius—Bar Abbas and his two lieutenants and that fat man." Centurion Sergius grinned. "Though how the roly-poly will be able to fight a lion or a bear I don't see. At that, he may make finer sport for the spectators than Bar Abbas."

"And a finer meal for the lion, too," Flavius agreed. "How many men shall I take in the detachment, Centurion?"

"A dozen should serve. Manacle the prisoners' wrists well and put them in the center. Don't worry about the fat one; he couldn't escape if unfettered. Go by way of the bridge, then skirt the foot of Mount Zion until you come opposite the Amphitheater, turn there and go along a street that leads straight to the square in front of it. Let the men carry their shields, and also their broadswords, though they'll not need them. You'll meet with no trouble."

"I trust not, Centurion. But these Jews—" Flavius shook his closely cropped head—"you never know what they may try to do. They're an obstinate, rebellious race."

Night had fallen on Jerusalem when they brought Bar Abbas and his three comrades, Gesmas, Dysmas and the waddling Shishak, from Antonia's dungeon and began the march across the city toward the Amphitheater, hated by the Jews more intensely than even the frowning citadel of Rome on the summit of Mount Moriah. Having crossed the bridge over the Tyropoeon Valley, the detachment turned left and moved south through the darkening, narrow streets. When it came opposite the arena it turned right through a defile of houses and shops.

"This is the street, Varro," Flavius called out from the rear of the double file surrounding the four Zealots. "Keep on it. A half mile up will bring us out on the square in front of the Amphitheater, and then we'll——" He stopped abruptly. Varro, the shaft of an arrow sticking out from his toga above his chest, was slowly crumpling to the cobblestones. "By Jupiter and all the——" From high windows a shower of javelins descended on the soldiers. Two others swayed and went down. "Run, Publius!" Flavius shouted. "Fly to Antonia and bring aid! We're ambushed!" He sprang beneath the overhang of a careening, ancient house. "Back against the wall, men! Hold onto your prisoners. If one tries to escape, thrust him through with your sword!" He bent down to grab a fallen soldier, dragged him over to the wall. "Get the others back, too!" he commanded.

In the tumult Flavius had not seen a door on the street level open noiselessly and a long, hairy arm thrust out to seize Bar Abbas and pull him inside. "Quick!" a voice whispered to the Zealot chieftain. "Out through the door at the rear! Down along the passage to the valley! Stay in the shadows. Cross the valley and get through Ophel to Japheth's shop. They're waiting to rid you of the manacles."

Against the wall and under the projection of the old house, with their shields protectingly in front of them, the Romans awaited reinforcements. Varro was dead. Several others were wounded; it appeared that one of them would die. And two of the Zealots, Bar Abbas and a Galilean called Dysmas, had escaped in the darkness.

"Damn Sergius!" Flavius was furious. "I wanted to bring half a century as an escort. Then we'd never have been ambushed. If these beasts had tried it, we'd have rounded up every damned Zealot on Mount Zion and slit his throat!" Roundly he kept on cursing the centurion. "He doesn't realize how devilishly set the Jews are to do us injury. By the time he or Longinus gets here with troops the villains will have melted away in this jungle of streets and dives."

Chapter 37 ✠

ALWAYS now for Jesus the hours were filled with ministering. The throngs pressed upon him, bringing pathetic ones that he might lay his hands on them and heal them of their infirmities.

The Master could not shut the doors of Simon's house against them or retreat into the hills to avoid them. With a great joy he

brought them the healing and comfort of his strong brown hands
and warm, loving heart. And he brought them the words of life.

Judas of Kiriot stayed near Jesus and watched the working of his
wonders with mixed emotions. . . . He is so good, his heart is as
large as the earth, so willing and happy to help even the least of
men. O God, how I love him! But why does he dally so? He has
all power, and his is the task to restore his suffering nation to its
ancient glory. How can he do that by giving a blind man his sight
or a foolish fellow his sanity? With one sweep of his long arm he
can heal all infirmities, straighten all twisted limbs, give sight to all
sightless eyes. Why bother with one poor fellow at a time, when
the hours are flying and Israel remains in subjection? Restore his
nation and then heal with a mighty proclamation all those who suffer and sorrow—that would be the right way. O God, help me, his
friend and his apostle, his devoted servant, to make him see that his
way is not effective, taking decades to bring in his kingdom, if it
ever can! Give me words to incite him to glorious action, weapons
with which to speed the fight for our deliverance. . . .

But the only weapon Jesus had was love.

To wield that weapon he had himself—and the twelve, all of
them now back from their missions.

There was still much, however, that they must learn. The task
ahead was one to test the souls of men. He must teach them,
strengthen them. For soon the task would be theirs alone. The day
was imminent when they no longer would have him to guide them.
He would lead them apart where they might spend a short season
together away from the multitude.

So on a day set—it was spring again and he was eager to be much
on the waters and in the fields among the flowers—Jesus and his
company sailed in a Zebedee boat across the northern curve of the
Sea of Galilee to a level green spot beyond the mouth of the upper
Jordan. It was near the city of Bethsaida Julias in the Tetrarchy
of Herod Philip, named for Julia the daughter of the Emperor
Tiberius. The Master planned for them to enjoy a quiet day or two
with one another. He would teach them the things of the spirit.

In relaxation and calmness he would instruct them in the task of carrying the good news.

Jesus had failed to reckon with the determination of the people to seek him out. Hardly had he and the twelve landed when they spied many Galileans coming around the bend from the direction of the other Bethsaida just across the Jordan in Galilee. These had heard early that morning where the Master was going, and they had followed by land. Others had joined them along the way.

The Master had not the heart to disappoint them, though their coming brought to naught his hope of an intimate communion with the twelve alone, and though he was tired with laboring through the winter and saddened that so few had taken his message to heart. So he bade them sit down on the grass and he expounded in words of grace and magic strength his interpretation of the writings of the olden prophets. As he taught and healed, the shadows lengthened and began to climb the steep ridge of Gaulanitis on the eastern shore.

"Master, the day grows short," one of the apostles said. "Many have come long distances and have far to return. They're hungry. Shouldn't you dismiss them now and let them start for their lodgings?"

Instead Jesus proposed to feed them, though the apostles had no food and the multitude had grown to thousands. A small boy standing near offered him five barley loaves and two fishes. Jesus took the food and, offering a prayer to his Father, began to divide it into portions and hand them to the twelve, who in turn passed them among the seated throng.

So were five thousand fed.

Afterward they collected the uneaten fish and bread, and it was reported that there were twelve full baskets left.

"When the Master is king there'll be no problem of feeding our army," Judas observed to Simon the Zealot. "He could open the very storehouses of heaven to give them food and drink."

The Zealot shook his head. "He'd never do that. It wouldn't accord with his teaching."

Many in the throng, rubbing full stomachs and sucking particles from between their teeth, shared the opinion of Judas. The tall Galilean, they were saying, should be king. He could expel old Herod and the Procurator Pontius Pilate. And he could feed them. They would not have to work for their bread.

Chapter **✠**
38

IN GALILEE the spring flowers were gone and the white blossoms of the juniper had fallen, leaving the dark green leaves to provide a haven for the birds or some weary traveler resting beneath them. Fallen too were the crimson flowers of the pomegranates, and soon now the round yellow-pink fruit, red and sweetly acidulous beneath the tough rind, would be ripe. In the deep gorges some oleanders still retained their flowers, though most of the blossoms floated slowly along the lazy summer streams. On the hillsides grapes in countless vineyards were fat and deep red and purple, ready for the winemakers, and olives were ripening in all the Galilean orchards.

Weeks ago Jesus and the twelve had gone northwest from Capernaum into the borders of Phoenicia, toward Tyre and Sidon. From this region, where the Master had healed and taught many who had heard tidings of his powers, they had journeyed east to come again into the Jordan Valley above tiny Lake Merom. After crossing the Jordan and turning again to the south Jesus with the twelve had gone through Gaulanitis into Decapolis. He was still seeking a season of rest and seclusion.

Little privacy with his apostles had Jesus been able to procure, for news of their coming went ahead of them, and everywhere great crowds pressed him, bringing the sick and the paralytic, the blind, the maimed, the demented. Weary and spent, he determined to return to Galilee. So he took ship and landed at the hamlet of

Dalmanutha a few miles from Tiberias and the palace of Herod Antipas.

From there he would walk or sail north along the coast until he came to Capernaum. Then he and his close friends would be home again in their own part of Galilee, and surely this time they would be permitted seclusion.

But hardly had they landed before the news of his presence, flying along the coast and out into the hills like a bird before the storm, brought hundreds rushing again to see him. With them came the usual Pharisees and scribes, Sadducees and rulers of the synagogue and some in that region who held places in the Temple of Jerusalem, for they never relaxed their efforts to confuse and discredit him before the people.

On this day they urged him to perform some wonder, like the great prophets of old, to prove that his works were of God and his words were true. The Master refused. "Always you must have signs and wonders! When it is evening you say, 'It will be fair weather, for the sky is red'; and in the morning, 'It will be foul weather today, for the sky is red and lowering.' O you hypocrites, you can discern the face of the sky; why can't you discern the signs of the times? You have lived in a generation privileged to know the Father, to read His word and have His love proclaimed to you. Yet you must have a sign to prove what is good." There was fire in his eyes. "No sign shall be given you."

Sad at heart, he called the twelve and they took ship again. In his beloved Galilee he could have no seclusion. And seclusion with the twelve he must have, if these brothers were to turn to God the Father the hearts of a lost and bewildered world.

He knew where they would go. They would stop for a short time at Capernaum and then move on to Bethsaida. Leaving their ship there, they would journey far beyond little Lake Merom to Caesarea Philippi at the foot of snow-capped Mount Hermon. On the slope of the cold, majestic mountain he would find the timely solitude in which to weigh and warm their hearts.

So they took ship again and crossed the head of the little sea and,

after much journeying along the upper Jordan, came to Caesarea
Philippi and passed through that city. From a high place on Hermon's side they looked back along the way they had come. Immediately below lay the new city, built by the Tetrarch Herod
Philip in honor of Caesar Augustus. Beyond it wide pasture lands,
hemmed about by forests of great oaks and noble cedars, ran rolling
toward Lake Merom. South from the lake twisted the Jordan
through a maze of oleanders and paper reeds and here and there
orchards that came down to the valley; then it fell into the wide and
glimmering sheen that was the Sea of Galilee.

In this bracing air he could begin revealing to them the instrument through which man's salvation would be achieved.

What could change the heart of man? What could erase hatred
and error and make of man the image of God he was destined to be?

Only God could. And what is God? God is love, and love is the
touchstone that will change a corrupt world and make all men
brothers of one another and sons of God.

If he was the Messiah of God—and Jesus knew he was—how
could he best proclaim his Messiahship? How show himself of a
certainty to be God on earth? How demonstrate what God is like?

It was in his heart that if he would do this he must show forth
the love of God utterly; he must meet hate at its worst with love at
its best; he must prove that love inevitably triumphs over hate.
Nothing halfway would do. He must suffer the uttermost. He must
be the Lamb of sacrifice, and his brothers must know that he was the
Lamb.

Here on the heights of snow-crowned Hermon, up in God's
heavens, he would endeavor to teach them the Great Plan, to prepare
them for hard days, to strengthen them for their own great trials
when the burden would be theirs alone to bear, to thrill them in the
knowledge that victory would be the final fruit of their labor.

They climbed higher still, and after a time they paused to rest and
eat. When they had eaten they stretched out on the grass or sat on
rocks and talked of their travels together, and their hearts responded
to one another and to the Master.

At length, his eyes bright and hopeful, he spoke to them: "You have been journeying about the country, mingling with the multitudes, and you must know what the people hold in their hearts concerning me. Who do they say that I am?"

Simon bar Jonas did not hesitate. "Some say you're John the Baptist returned to life. That, I hear, is the belief of Tetrarch Herod, who has been shaken and fearful since he ordered John beheaded."

Others of the twelve said they'd heard people explain the Master as a reincarnation of one of the great prophets of old times, perhaps Elijah, or Jeremiah, or even Moses the lawgiver.

"But who do *you* say—" this was the great question and the earth's future would be determined by the sort of answer they gave—"that I am?"

Once more the burly fisherman of Bethsaida was the first to answer. There was no reservation in his tone. "Master, you are the Christ, the Messiah of God long promised to His people to lead them forth; you are the Son of God!"

"Happy are you, Simon bar Jonas!" Jesus' voice was vibrant, his face glowed as with an unearthly light. "Flesh and blood have not revealed this truth unto you. It has come to you from my Father in heaven; He has put it into your heart." For an instant he meditated. "Simon, you are like a rock. Do you remember that day I called you 'the Rock'?" His smile was joyous. "From this day you shall be called Peter—a stone. Do you see yonder rock bastion on the edge of the cliff?"

Jesus pointed toward a stone fortress which served as garrison post for Roman legions. According to tradition it had been erected by the ancient Phoenicians. It sat above a deep gorge through which roared a mountain torrent that disappeared into an underground channel. Because of its dismal and frightening look the place was called locally Gates of Hell.

"That pile of masonry has endured through the years and still stands safe and secure above the Gates of Hell. And so are you, Peter; you're a rock. I will erect upon you—and those whose minds and hearts reflect the faith and the love you reveal—my brotherhood of love. Nor will all the gates of hell be able to prevail against it!"

They remained for a spell on Hermon's side, and Jesus talked with them, taught them and dealt gently with them, for he knew that before long they would be sad of heart and for a time like sheep lost from the shepherd. The pattern of the Great Plan was outlining itself more clearly as the summer days waned and the air began to grow chill, and in its center Jesus already saw the familiar and terrible shape of the cross.

"Soon I must leave you," he told them one day. "The powers of evil are determined to slay me, and I will be delivered into the hands of wicked men. At Jerusalem I shall be rejected by the rulers and bear insults and shame and torture, yes, and death itself. Have no fear, though, my brothers, for within three days I will triumph even over the power of death!"

Instantly bold Simon's face was aflame. "But, Master," he said, excitement and alarm sharpening his words, "nothing like that must come to pass! Tortured and slain! Of course not! We'll lay down our lives before such a despicable thing can happen!"

The Nazarene showed no pleasure in Simon's declaration. Sad and shocked, he turned away from the impetuous apostle. "Get you behind me, Satan!" he said sternly. "Would you circumvent the will of the Father?" Quickly he was gentle again. "You don't comprehend, Peter. Your words grieve me; they are stumbling blocks in my path. I must walk the road I was sent to tread; I must walk it wherever it may lead."

To all the twelve he said: "If any man will come after me, let him deny himself, and take up his cross, and follow me. For whosoever will save his life shall lose it; and whosoever will lose his life for my sake will save it." They saw on his face a new radiance. "For what is a man profited if he shall gain the whole world but to lose his own soul? Or what shall a man give in exchange for his soul?"

Judas, seated with Simon the Zealot on the fringe of the circle facing Jesus, whispered to his comrade, "What does he mean? That he's soon to die, and we also?" He shook his head gravely. "He is so—so inexplicable. But what a leader he is! How can one help loving him?"

On another day while they rested in the region of Caesarea Philippi Jesus called to his side Simon Peter and the Zebedees. With them he went far up the mountainside until they had gained the altitude of eternal snows. All about was light and the air was thin, and it seemed that from here one might almost reach up and touch the stars.

Jesus drew the three close to him and talked to them of the purpose for which he had been sent and of the burden which would be settled on their sturdy shoulders. As he talked of the nature of his Father, of His great goodness to men, and how He would have them dwell always in righteousness, the Master seemed to grow in stature and a great light from within seemed to transform him. The beauty of his soul was revealed to them in a melody of words. Beside him and conversing with him they fancied they saw returned to earthly life great Moses and the stern and mighty Prophet Elijah. It seemed to the three that on this mountain and issuing out of it they could even hear the voice of God Himself in warm praise of His beloved Son.

Knowing themselves to be in the presence of God they fell on their faces in the snow.

They would never forget that solemn, sweet hour on the mountaintop. Nor would the carpenter of Galilee.

They walked down to join the others of the twelve as men who had seen a vision. They knew. The three knew of a certainty that their beloved Master was God's anointed. And Jesus knew that he was ordained of the Father to point the way. For him that way led unalterably to ancient Jerusalem and a hill outside its walls.

He would walk that way even to the end.

Judas of Kiriot, waiting with the other eight apostles who had not gone to the higher eminence with the Master, was not thinking of that way. Out of his own scheming he was evolving another plan.

At its core was no cross, but a crown.

Chapter
39   ✠

FAST developing events at Jerusalem hastened the unfolding of the
plan that was taking shape in the busy mind of Judas of Kiriot. He
had come with Jesus and the eleven to attend the Feast of Tabernacles.

The streets were swarming with pilgrims. Some had come from
as far away as Macedonia, Asia and Galatia; others from the region
above Antioch. Dark-visaged Jews had trudged west through the
deserts of Arabia. From many nations the dispersed people of God
had converged on the ancient citadel of Israel. Some called the occasion the Festival of Booths because of the booths set up as shelters
along the hillsides and around the walls. They were packed with
people of all ages, from infants to old men and old women bent and
hardly able to get about. They were crammed, too, with offerings—
baskets of finest grapes and olives and measures of full-headed
grain. Dogs and goats were everywhere.

Like other great festivals of the Jews the Feast of Tabernacles
was related to the agricultural life of the people. It served, like the
others also, as an occasion that recalled past years of glory when
Israel was an independent nation. At such festal times a nationalistic fervor often swept through the land. The Romans would rein-
force the military units stationed in the larger centers, especially
Jerusalem, to prevent any disturbance that might cause critical reports to get back to the Emperor.

Judas was confident that Bar Abbas and Dysmas would come to
the Feast of Tabernacles. They would probably be as safe in Jerusalem as anywhere else. He was anxious to see them, to be sure they
held no grudge against him and to concert measures with them. We
must do something to spur the Master's interest in the early liber-

ation of Israel, he told himself as he went toward Japheth's shop. We can't let him pursue the method of individual restoration. It's too slow. We must evolve some plan that will lead him to effect this grand purpose overnight—in the twinkling of an eye. And we must have our forces mobilized, ready to seize arms and take their posts once the Master acts.

Neither Bar Abbas nor Dysmas was at Japheth's.

"They've been here," the cobbler reported. "I can get a message to them. But they must be very careful. If they're captured again, Judas, there'll be no escape. It will certainly be the cross then."

The sound of heavy boots in the front room of the shop and a coarse voice demanding the cobbler put a stop to their talk.

"Romans again!" Japheth grabbed a broken sandal from the bench beside him, thrust it into Judas' hands. "Be mending it." He opened the door and walked into the front chamber.

Four Roman soldiers glared at him.

"What sort of a shop is this where the cobbler's not at hand to serve his customers?" one of them demanded.

"Sir, I'm sorry. I was back in my workroom. I've been rushed, with but one helper. How can I serve you?"

The soldier dropped a pair of heavy short boots and two sandals on the counter. "Centurion Longinus bade me take these to you for mending. He demands excellent work, and he wants them before sunset. We'll be here for them then."

He opened his pouch and dropped some coins beside the boots. "Here's your pay. If it's not enough, we'll give you the rest when we come for them. Are you content?"

"Indeed, sir." Japheth fingered the coins. "These are enough. The boots and sandals will be ready when you return."

"Good!" The Roman's gruff manner smoothed. "Remember to do what you say."

When they were gone Japheth went back to the workroom. "Soldiers of Longinus," he told Judas. "Boots and sandals to be mended."

"Yes, I heard. Friendly fellows, eh?" Judas tossed the sandal

on the workbench. "I must be going, Japheth. Get word to Bar
Abbas and Dysmas to meet me here two days hence. Tell them it's
urgent. Warn them to take care."

From the cobbler's he went to visit Shelomith. He had seen her
that morning briefly, and neither Longinus nor Cynara had been
mentioned. Perhaps, he concluded, I was hasty in thinking she
might have become interested in the Roman. .

He had been in Benjamin's house only a few minutes when the
Rabbi Nicodemus entered. As always he was exquisitely dressed.
He greeted Judas cordially and inquired after the health of Simon
his father.

"I haven't seen him in months, Rabbi," Judas answered. "I trust
he's well. Since my last visit to Jerusalem I've been all the time with
the Master, most of it in Galilee."

"It was to talk with you about your master, Judas, that I came.
I hoped I'd find you here and am not surprised." He smiled. Then
he went on gravely: "Judas, the Galilean is in great peril. I'm here
to tell you so you may warn him. He'd best leave off his teaching at
the Temple and depart from Jerusalem. His enemies—and there
are many, Judas, among the Temple leaders—would not stop until
they had him slain." The rabbi cleared his throat. "This I know.
I was at the meeting of the Sanhedrin called by the High Priest. I
was there while the plot was hatched. I would not have gone if I'd
known that the purpose of the session was to sit in judgment on the
wonder-working Nazarene.

"The captain of the Temple Guard came before us. It developed
that he'd been given orders to arrest Jesus if he should appear again
at the Temple. Now that he was proclaiming his mission to throngs
in the Court of the Gentiles it was presumed that the captain
would carry out his orders and fetch Jesus before the Sanhedrin.

"But he didn't have the prisoner with him and this enraged
Caiaphas. When Caiaphas demanded why he hadn't arrested the
Nazarene, the captain confessed he hadn't dared to challenge either
the power of the teacher or the anger of the multitude by laying
hands on him. 'No man ever spake as this man,' he declared."

Nicodemus leaned back in his chair, unclasped his hands, held each palm downward on a sharp knee. "But Caiaphas was not so easily to be thwarted. He told the members of the Sanhedrin that Jesus had blasphemed the Holy Name in his discourse at the Temple by speaking of himself as the water of life and the bread that came down from heaven."

"Didn't they understand that the Master uses figures of speech in his teaching, that he colors his discourse with forceful pictures which help reveal the deeper meaning?"

"I told them that," the rabbi hurried to say. "They admitted it, but they hate him, especially the High Priest, and they do not care to understand him. Caiaphas insisted that Jesus was falsely teaching the multitude; if Jesus were permitted to continue it would lead to sedition and so cause the Roman authorities to deal harshly with the whole Jewish nation. For that reason, he insisted, it had become necessary to put at naught the influence of Jesus over the people."

"And to do that they'd have to concoct some evil trickery?"

"Yes, exactly. Openly arresting him would stir a tumult that would bring the Roman troops on the run, Caiaphas said, and broadswords would be cleaving Jewish skulls. To this they agreed."

"How, then, sir, did they propose to entrap him?"

"They were at a loss how to proceed until Annas spoke up."

"A man of great cunning."

"Yes, Annas suggested that a woman be employed. He proposed that a sinful woman, perhaps a woman of the streets, be taken— maybe from a booth convenient to the Temple while in the act of sinning with some pilgrim—and brought before Jesus while he was teaching the people."

"But, Rabbi, how would that be a snare for the Master?"

Nicodemus smiled. "I understand your bewilderment. Judas, you know we have an ancient law demanding that a woman taken in adultery be stoned. If one of his enemies asked the Nazarene what should be done with the woman, Jesus would have to say, under the law, that she be stoned to death. But old Annas knew Jesus would never give a judgment like that. On the one hand, how

could he say the law of the fathers should not be followed? On
the other, how could he permit her stoning and uphold his own law
of love and forgiveness? Do you see now the cleverness of the
scheme?"

"Yes, I see. They'd put the Master in a quandary where any
answer would condemn him."

"Exactly. A diabolical design. I opposed it, with vehemence.
But I was overruled, of course. I'm deeply disturbed. You must
warn Jesus."

"Rabbi, I'm happy that you, a member of the Sanhedrin, feel
friendly toward the Master. I thank you. But I'm not worried. I've
no fear for his safety. He has the strength of the God of Israel in
his arms. He's——"

"He's the Messiah of God, you believe, Judas?"

"I do, Rabbi. He's the chosen one sent to deliver us. He awaits
only the coming of his hour, and then his enemies will be prostrate
before him. He'll be our king."

Nicodemus leaned forward, his forehead crinkled in little lines.
"I've heard that he speaks of his hour, Judas. What does he mean
by that term? I've been puzzled by it. When will his hour come,
and what will it mean when it comes? I—I cannot fathom it."

"Nor I, Rabbi. In recent weeks, when we were on Mount
Hermon and since, he has often spoken of it. 'My hour is not yet
come,' he said time after time. Recently, too, he has declared to us
that here in Jerusalem he will be scorned, persecuted, and even
killed, but after three days he will raise himself up again. We do
not know what he means by that—whether he's speaking in figures
or words of literal meaning."

"Some of his words indeed seem puzzlingly profound and ob-
scure. Yet at other times he speaks with marvelous simplicity, and
the common people hear him gladly. Isn't that so, Judas?"

"Yes, Rabbi. The captain of the guard was right: Never has a
man spoken like the Master."

"But, Judas, reverting to the phrase he uses—'my hour'—what

do you think he means? That question stirs my deepest interest. Surely you have an opinion."

Judas was silent a moment. "I've often wondered, Rabbi, as have all of the other eleven. Simon bar Jonas even remonstrated with him one day at Caesarea Philippi when the Master told us that he would be killed."

"What did Jesus say to Simon?"

"He said he was Satan tempting him."

"But his prediction that he'll be killed and then raised up?"

"Maybe, sir, he means—speaking in figures again—that he'll be raised to a throne after being 'killed' as simply a teacher and worker of wonders. This effort to entrap him may lead to that. His life as a teacher may be put to an end. Then he'll have vengeance on his persecutors by proclaiming himself king. But I don't know. What do you think, sir?"

"I don't think your answer explains the mystery of the Nazarene. His words must have deeper meaning. I only wish I could get to the bottom of them. But this I know: He is a greater man than many in Israel suspect. It may be, Judas——" He stopped.

"You too think he may be the Messiah?"

Nicodemus nodded. "Yes, my son, it may well be that he is. I wish I knew."

Judas spent the night in Jerusalem. He would see the Master early on the morrow, when Jesus had come to the Temple from his friends' home at Bethany, and tell him what Nicodemus had reported.

But when Judas, with Shelomith who wished to see and hear the strange rabbi from Galilee about whom all Jerusalem was talking, entered by the Gate Shalleketh and walked through the Court of the Gentiles they found that Jesus had already begun his discourse. Judas would have no opportunity to warn him.

Hardly had they pushed forward into the throng ringed about him as he stood on the steps before the Beautiful Gate when the assemblage split apart into two pushing, excited masses. Shelomith and Judas, on the edge of the resulting corridor, were amazed to discover several burly men dragging down it a young woman, shamefaced and scared and clutching at her sadly disarranged clothing.

"It's—it's the woman Nicodemus was telling about last night," Shelomith whispered. "Oh, the poor creature!"

Before Jesus they loosed her and stood away. She ventured with eyes of fear and not of insolence to look at the rabbi, while she sought to smooth her torn robe.

"Rabbi," said one of her captors, "this woman only a few moments ago was taken in adultery in one of the pilgrims' booths. Just down the slope toward the brook Kidron." He paused. Jesus made no comment. "A woman so apprehended, the Lawgiver Moses decreed, should be stoned. But you're a great teacher. We'd like to know what you'd decree."

Shelomith clutched Judas' arm. "Surely he won't order her stoned to death."

Judas saw ornately robed Pharisees and others of the Temple leadership watching intently. Their scornful eyes and leering lips betrayed their contempt for Jesus.

But the Nazarene seemed not to be hearing the questioner or giving heed to the Temple circle. Instead, as the eyes of the immense concourse never left him, he bent down to the marble of the Chel.

"What does he mean, making no answer?" Shelomith asked Judas in a low tone. "He seems to be writing with his finger in the dust of the pavement. If he doesn't answer, won't he lose face before all this gathering?"

Judas seemed unworried. "I don't know when or what he'll answer, but the fellow who asked the question is the one more likely to be confused."

That fellow would not be turned aside. "Maybe, Rabbi," he said, advancing a step nearer, "you didn't understand what I asked you. Do you agree with our father Moses that this adulterous woman should be stoned? Tell us, Rabbi."

Jesus, straightening to full stature before the breathless congre-

gation, studied the man. "I heard and understood both the words
of your lips and the dark thoughts of your heart," he said. Shelomith fancied she detected a faint smile on his face. "And I say
unto you—" his eyes lifted to the hypocritical group at the corner
of the Chel—"let him that is without sin among you cast the first
stone." Once again he stooped down and wrote.

"Oh-h-h." Shelomith's hand was at her mouth. Then she whispered, "Oh, Judas, look! Her accusers are slipping away. He has
indeed confused them! Oh, how good, how noble, he is!"

The priestly party had slunk away, without a word, around the
corner of the Chel. Only the woman stood there.

"Where are your accusers?" Jesus asked her as he straightened
himself again. "Has no one condemned you?"

She lifted tearful eyes to him. "No one, sir. They have gone."

"I don't condemn you either, my sister. Go now, and avoid the
paths of sin."

Chapter 40 ✠

"I've never seen a nobler act, nor one so clever," Shelomith said
as they started across the bridge from the Temple. "Your Master
is a brave man, Judas, and wise and good."

"And powerful, too," Judas added.

"Isn't there power in goodness and wisdom?"

"Yes, but also in wickedness. Aren't the Romans powerful?"

Shelomith touched his arm impulsively. "Though you've been
months with Jesus I don't think you fully understand him."

"Who could fully understand the Messiah of God, Shelomith?"
He turned it over in his mind. "Of course I don't entirely understand him. But there's one thing about him I believe I understand

better than any of the other eleven. That is the power held leashed
within him."

"Leashed? Haven't you told me how he works wonders of healing, opens the eyes of the blind, restores the use of paralyzed limbs,
cleanses lepers crying their———"

"Yes, of course. But that isn't the power I'm thinking about.
Those things are, to my mind, only minor proofs of this tremendous
potency. His great strength has not yet been shown."

"I suppose you mean he'll show his greatest strength against
Rome."

"Exactly. These works for the ill and the maimed are good. I
don't disapprove of them. But they accomplish good only for a
particular person here and there. What I am thinking of is salvation for the whole nation—in an instant, by one mighty act."

"But will that be his way, Judas?"

"I think so. It's my task to speed the day." He looked at her with
a strange light in his eyes. "Shelomith, I've talked often and in hazy
fashion of a plan. I haven't been able to see it clearly—yet. But
we're recruiting men right along, and a pattern is beginning to take
shape. The core of it is the mighty power of the Master. I'm going
down to Kiriot to help my father finish the harvesting. While I'm
there I'll be doing some hard thinking. Out of it I'll evolve the full
shape of the plan and how it may be implemented. Before the coming of the next Passover, my beloved, we'll begin our life together."

So while Jesus and the eleven were returning to Galilee Judas
went down to his father's country. As he trudged south he pon-
dered the course to pursue. He had not seen Bar Abbas since the
night when by his contriving they had stolen him away from the
Romans on the way to the Amphitheater's dungeons. Perhaps
Japheth had been unable to get the message to him. Maybe Bar
Abbas had been afraid to risk a visit to the cobbler's shop during the
Feast of Tabernacles.

He would manage some way to communicate with Bar Abbas. In
the meantime he must weigh the situation carefully. I must be log-

ical and take the facts into account, he told himself. That's how the
eleven err. The Master so stirs their emotions that they're content
with the surface meaning of his words. I go deeper, trace the hidden
truth beneath the symbols. It's a boon to Israel that I can keep a
calm mind and use cool reasoning.

Soon would be the Feast of the Dedication, when throughout
Israel but especially in Jerusalem patriotic Jews in a surge of devotion would celebrate the ancient deliverance from the Syrians. Two
hundred years ago Judas Maccabaeus had been the great hero of the
Jews. Now—the man of Kiriot let the thought run through his
brain—through the design of another Judas the nation might once
more be delivered. The Feast of the Dedication might signalize the
beginning of release and victory.

He revealed this surmise to Cush, Pethuel, Lamech and other
Zealots when they came to see him. "It's when they'd most likely
demand that the Master be made king. You must redouble your
preparations. See that the recruits have adequate weapons. Every
company must have capable leaders, and they must be trained so
that their fighting, when the time comes, will be co-ordinated."

"But, Judas—" Cush's brown, bearded face revealed doubt—
"are you certain Jesus is the man to be king? We've heard of his
marvelous deeds and the might of his sayings. But is he a warrior?
Isn't Bar Abbas the better man to lead us?"

"Have no fears, Cush. I once had the same doubts, but I'm no
longer puzzled. The Master's a man of peace, but he has power.
He's the Messiah. Of this I've no doubt—none. He's the man to
be king. Perhaps Bar Abbas will be the chief military leader. He's
quick with the sword, and unafraid. The Galilean Zealots may
favor him for that position. But Jesus will be king."

"Then the uprising will come during the Feast of the Dedication?" Seba asked.

"It might well come then. I don't know when he'll take the
crown. But if we're ready, perhaps we can hasten the hour."

"We'll be ready, Judas." Nadab was unsmiling. "We haven't
been asleep; we've done much already. We'll sharpen our spears

and put new edges on our swords and go to Jerusalem. And we'll slice many a Roman gizzard."

"Perhaps even the gizzard of that damnable Longinus," agreed Pethuel. "He should be long dead."

Seba smiled. "Speaking of Longinus, Judas, reminds me: What became of his sister, the one with hair the color of rich goat's milk? Have you ever visited her—again?"

Before Judas could answer Cush nudged him. "I'd have bet the hairs on the High Priest's chin that you'd go to see her and finish out that night in the tent."

"No, I never was able to finish my visit," he said truthfully. "I don't know where the Roman woman is—nor do I care." He wondered about this, but said no more.

During the remaining days of his visit he went about with Zealot friends and talked often with Judaean youths whose hands itched to cleave Roman skulls. He urged Cush and the others to organize additional companies. Before Judas left Kiriot it was agreed that the leaders would bring the spirited young men at different times and by devious ways to Jerusalem in advance of the feast. There they'd be ready to take advantage of whatever opportunity might arise.

After that Judas went north again to Galilee. One day he ventured to tell Simon the Zealot what had transpired during his stay in Kiriot, to hint that the Master's hour might come during the Feast of the Dedication. Simon seemed uninterested. "That's not his idea, Judas; I'm convinced. I can't grasp it, true. But I'm certain we should not seek to shape his course. Our part is only to follow him."

Judas was not deterred. In the dark days of early winter he worked to advance his ambitious scheme. Often he talked with Jesus in the hope that the Master would let fall some word of his own intention, if indeed he had one. But Jesus, if he knew his hour, spoke of it only in general terms that to Judas seemed more confusing than revealing. The Master's vagueness, his apparent inability, as Judas reckoned it, to step forth boldly, only increased the determination of the man from Kiriot to perfect his program.

Its general design he applied to the occasion. Bar Abbas would slip into Jerusalem from his hiding place in the hills a few days before the Feast of the Dedication. He would lead the fighting Zealots. Dysmas would be one of his lieutenants. With the storming of Antonia and the release of the prisoners in its dungeon, Gesmas would be another. From the Kiriot region would come Cush, Seba, Pethuel, Nadab, Tola and numerous other leaders of the aroused youth. They would assemble in Jerusalem and lose themselves in the teeming ways of Ophel. So too the bands from the other districts. In the city, crowded for the festival with a million Jews fired with frenzy to drive the hated invaders forever from their beloved homeland, Bar Abbas and his men would be safe until the Master's hour struck. Thereafter no Roman in all Israel could call his life his own.

Judas smiled as he contemplated the great day. King Jesus, seated on a golden throne, perhaps on the Pavement at the Praetorium, would assume the character as well as the accouterments of his ancient forebear David. And Judas would be keeper of the royal treasury, seated by the king to whisper counsel.

Chapter 41 ✠

IN THE mind and heart of Jesus, too, a plan—the Great Plan—was evolving. The sands in his glass of life were running fast. Shortly he must go forth from Galilee to meet his supreme test. He must proclaim himself before the people the long awaited and earnestly looked-for Messiah of God. And having done this, he must be prepared to become the Sacrifice.

Where better to accomplish this supreme mission than at Jeru-

salem during the Feast of the Dedication, with all the world gathered before the great white Temple?

So with sad heart he determined to leave beloved Galilee and
go south on the great adventure, this time through Samaria, proclaiming the good news to that land despised of the Jews. Perhaps
in Samaria the bread of life refused by the elect sons of Galilee
would be accepted with thankful hearts by the outcast.

As he topped a hill that afforded a view of the shining little sea
he turned for a lingering glance.

"Woe unto you, Chorazin! Woe unto you, Bethsaida!" He looked
straight north along the shore where he had spent so many happy
hours. "If the mighty works had been done even in Tyre and Sidon
which have been done within your borders, those cities a great while
ago would have repented, sitting in sackcloth and ashes. And it
shall be more tolerable for Tyre and Sidon in the day of judgment
than for you!"

He lowered his eyes to gaze down on Capernaum, its rooftops
shining in the winter sun. Over beside the sea he could pick out
the square bastion of the Roman garrison. Not far away was the
flat roof of Peter's house, where on nights when the stars were his
only companions he had lain wide-awake thinking how eager his
beloved Galilee would be to receive the message of the Father's
love. He groaned within himself and strove to keep a despairing
cry from his lips.

"And you, O Capernaum, you that are exalted even unto
heaven——" A shudder ran along his tall frame. He thought of
the terrible words of the great Prophet Ezekiel when he had fore-
told the doom of a thriving metropolis:

"For thus saith the Lord God: 'When I shall make thee a desolate city, like the cities that are not inhabited; when I shall bring
up the deep upon thee, and great waters shall cover thee; when I
shall bring thee down with them that descend into the pit, with the
people of old time, and shall set thee in the low parts of the earth,
in places desolate of old, with them that go down to the pit, that
thou be not inhabited; and I shall set glory in the land of the living;

I will make thee a terror, and thou shalt be no more; though thou be sought for, yet shalt thou never be found again, saith the Lord God.'

"And you, O Capernaum," Jesus said, with face set, "shall be thrust down to hell."

With a vision that held clear and frightening through long centuries he saw a flattened, desolate place in a great marsh, thrust through with unsightly wild grass and paper reeds, and in the matted tangle at their roots here and there cut stones fallen as if from some antique structures. He saw the hand of a man pointing to this desolation and heard his voice saying, "This may be the site of ancient Capernaum where for a season dwelt Jesus of Nazareth."

Solemnly he turned to the twelve and the others who were accompanying him. "He that hears you hears me and he that despises you despises me; moreover, he that despises me despises Him that sent me."

Without another backward look he started toward Samaria.

But in Samaria too he would be rejected. When he sought food and shelter for the first night in one of its villages, hospitality was bluntly refused him. It was evident that his party was on its way to Jerusalem to worship in the hated Temple of Herod, and he and all his group were therefore an abomination in the sight of the Samaritans. In abrupt manner they warned the Master and his friends not to tarry.

The Zebedees were infuriated.

"Master," said one of the Sons of Thunder, his eyes blazing, "it was here that Elijah called down fire from heaven to consume the enemy. Won't you command fire from heaven to destroy these wretched villagers who refuse you even a crumb of bread and a mat for the night?"

Judas nudged the Zealot. "Did you hear the apostle of love? He doesn't sound like a turn-the-other-cheek advocate now, eh? But I think he's right. A little singeing would teach these people better manners. Word of it, getting to Jerusalem ahead of us, would add to the Master's popularity with the Israelites. . . . But he'll not do it."

Jesus, who had been looking in silence at the Zebedees, said, "You have spirit, but it is the wrong sort. Don't you understand that the Son of Man has come, not to destroy men's lives, but to save them? You will not call down fire to destroy them. We shall go into another village."

So they spent the night at a small place nearer the Jordan, and the next morning they continued their journey.

Sometimes Jesus would stride along, his head up and his arms swinging, as though he would push ahead of the other pilgrims. Again he would tarry in some warm place in the lee of a boulder to talk with his followers, to bless small children, to heal the sick and maimed, and soothe and comfort the distressed and weary in heart. Often he found himself heckled by the usual emissaries from High Priest Caiaphas, for the Temple group were determined to destroy his influence with the people before they murdered him.

The crowds grew larger as he moved south. At Jericho pilgrims who had traveled on the other side of the Jordan and those from the eastern lands increased the press around him. On the day they went through that city an incident occurred which made Judas fear it might lessen the popularity of the Master and delay his crowning.

Judas had seen the short, ponderous fellow earlier that day as they went past the customhouse. He had recognized him as the publican to whom he had paid a tax—an exorbitant tax, he was convinced—on a previous visit to Jericho. He even remembered the name was Zacchaeus. The man was held in contempt not only as a traitorous Jew because of his office but also as a dishonest one.

That night Judas discussed with Simon the Master's extraordinary attitude toward this notorious person. "I can't understand why the Master insults the feelings of devout Jews to gain the doubtful support of a reprobate," he said.

"Judas, the Master wasn't insulting the devout Jews. Haven't you heard him tell the story of the shepherd who lost one of his hundred sheep, and how he searched and searched until he had found that one? The shepherd wasn't insulting the other ninety-nine. They were safe in the fold. Well, Zacchaeus was the lost sheep. The Master wanted to restore him to the fold. And he did, judging by the publican's giving back the money to those he'd defrauded."

Judas shook his head. "I don't know. I'd have let the wretch stay up that tree until he shriveled like a last summer's fig. Telling him to come down, that he was going home to dine with him— this was not calculated to make good men think more of the Master."

"It should have made many of them happy," Simon answered with his genial grin. "They got back many a coin because of it."

Judas shrugged. "I wish nevertheless that the Master would be more careful not to offend the people who count most—especially with the Feast of the Dedication just ahead. The news will reach Jerusalem before we do. It can't do him any good."

"You'd still lead the Master, Judas."

"Isn't it obvious someone must direct him? If he had been directed today, Zealot, do you suppose he'd have dined with a scorned publican, a tool of Rome, almost on the eve of a great national feast?"

"You're right." Simon's eyes shone. "Only the Master would have thought to do such a thing. That's why I want him to lead, Judas, and I'll be content to follow. And you, my friend, will never be happy until you've surrendered your—your obstinacy and let him lead you."

Judas laughed stridently. "You preach to me! Wait till you see what happens in Jerusalem!"

Chapter 42 ✠

WHEN they reached Bethany several days before the beginning of the feast Jesus found Lazarus ill. An ague which had persisted through the early winter was proving serious. Jesus' friend was a frail, gentle fellow, quiet and contemplative, more like his introspective sister Mary than busy Martha. Jesus agreed to stay at the house during the festal season.

Judas was glad they'd arrived early. He had much to do and many persons to see in Jerusalem. Bar Abbas he must see; Dysmas, too, if possible; and the chiefs from the Kiriot region. He should get an estimate of the number of recruits who had slipped into the city in the streams of pilgrims. The wily Japheth could bear messages from one leader to another. It would be dangerous for many to meet at any one time in his back room.

He went to the cobbler's.

"Bar Abbas is in Jerusalem," Japheth told him. "And so is Dysmas. They're anxious to see you. But they must be careful. Longinus and Sergius would like nothing better than to get hands on them again. Many are here from southern Judaea. The city swarms with fanatical youths eager to rise against the Romans. They await only a signal from somebody."

"That could be bad, Japheth. An overexcited fellow might start the revolt before we're ready."

The second day he went to the Temple. Inside the Gate Shalleketh he almost stumbled over a slovenly beggar, soiled and forbidding, crumpled against one of the great columns. This heavily bearded man, a black patch over one eye, extended a grimy hand. "Alms, kind sir! Alms for a poor, blind wretch! Pity, sir! Alms!"

"But you have one good eye. And you look strong enough. Why can't you—?" Judas fancied he saw a quick smile light the darkly matted face. The impudent fellow mocks. He bent nearer. "Bar Abbas! How in the world—?"

"Not so loud with the name, Judas." The chieftain's finger was on his lips. "I thought you'd come to the Temple. I got the message you sent through Japheth, but I was afraid to come to the shop. I didn't have much use for you when I was captured trying to ambush Longinus on your information. But I'm told I owe my escape to you. So all's forgiven. Sit here on the base of the column, where we can talk in low tones. We've got to get our plans arranged. I'm perplexed, and not a little fearful."

Judas told him of his visit to lower Judaea. He would see the Judaean leaders, learn the strength of the force in Jerusalem. "Then we, you and I, will meet again here at the Temple. You can change your disguise, if you think best. We'll arrange the placing of the men about the courts."

"Tell me, Judas, do you think your rabbi will take the crown at this feasting season?"

"Maybe he plans it, Bar Abbas. He has been speaking of his hour. In any event, we must be ready. We'll have our men carefully disposed, yours of Galilee in one area and the Judaeans in other places about the Court of the Gentiles and outside the walls. Unprompted, the Master may declare his Messiahship. In that case there'll be no need of soldiers. He has sufficient might, I'm convinced, to sweep away our enemies with the waving of his hand. This he may do."

"But if he doesn't, Judas? Where'll we be then? I'm not clear about this design of yours. We might be getting ourselves in a very bad situation. I'm not so certain of your rabbi's powers. I——"

"He's the Messiah, Bar Abbas. Believe me. This is how it will be: He will be here at the Temple. He will take his place—perhaps before the Beautiful Gate—and there proclaim the restoration of our nation with himself as king. Then our armies will surround him as the army of the new Israel. We'll not be called on to fight. His power will be sufficient."

"But, Judas, he may not do it. He may be content to talk, to——"

"If he doesn't, then will be our turn to act." Judas' eyes were bright, his voice was eager. "You and I, stationed where our men can see us, will give the signal and the Zealot youth will fall upon the Romans. We'll give them a good fight, and——"

"You're mad! We can't defeat Antonia's soldiers, Judas, pouring down upon us."

"You don't understand, Bar Abbas. You have little faith. When we begin shedding our blood for Israel the Master will be forced

to intercede to save us from the enemy. Don't you see, my friend?
He'll never let us be overthrown. He'll call down the armies of
heaven to fight beside us." Judas' eyes were burning now, as in his
mind he saw the coming of the new glory. "So, if Jesus doesn't act
of his own accord, we will force him to become our king!"

From the Temple Judas went toward the shop of Benjamin. As
he neared it he suddenly slowed his pace. Longinus and Shelomith
were coming out. They turned down the street that led to her house.

"Damn the thieving pagan!" Judas' hands clenched into hard
fists. Then for a moment his lips stretched in a cold smile. "Only
give me time, O Lord! Only give me time. When the Master is
king and I sit beside him———"

He walked into the shop and greeted Benjamin. "I've been to
the Temple," he said. "I wanted to see Shelomith and I thought she
might be here rather than at home. But I don't see her, and———"

"She's been gone but a moment. She can't have got far."

"Then I'll run and overtake her." Judas started for the door.

"No, stay!" Benjamin betrayed confusion. "Tell me where you've
been since last I saw you, what you've done, how fares the
Galilean."

Judas was nearing the doorway. "I'll see you tonight, sir."

"No! No! Wait. Judas, it wouldn't be best———"

Judas wheeled about. "What do you mean, sir? Isn't Shelomith
my betrothed? How say you?"

"Calm yourself, my son." The merchant recovered his poise. "It
will save you embarrassment if you go later to my home to see her.
She's walking with the Centurion Longinus. He was here———"

"Longinus! I'll slit his throat! I'll kill the———"

The stout, bewhiskered Benjamin stepped in front of the
Judaean. "Wait, Judas! Don't be rash. Longinus came here in your
behalf. He's———"

"In my behalf! What do you mean, sir?"

"He came here to ask me to tell Shelomith so she might warn
you. It happened that she was here when he came."

"That happens often, doesn't it?"

"No." Benjamin caught Judas' arm. "She loves you, Judas. She's true to you. She doesn't love the Roman, though he's shown himself a friend to my house. You may refuse to believe it, but he's just shown a friendly spirit toward you too."

"But what had he to tell? Why do you think he bears me no ill will?"

"Longinus has just got word that the Zealots were plotting a revolution against Rome during the season of the feast. A traitorous Jewish servant at Antonia broke the news to the centurion; he'd heard it from the careless lips of some Galilean boaster."

Judas gave a start of surprise and indignation. Benjamin continued without interruption. "Longinus came to warn Shelomith not to let you get involved; the revolutionaries, he said, will be severely dealt with."

"So he'd protect me? I don't believe it, sir. He wants to appear concerned for my safety only to advance himself with Shelomith. That's what I'll tell her. And if the Roman comes here again you may tell him that my leader can brush his old Tiberius off the earth. Let him look to himself and his own safety."

Jesus was glad to have a few days at Bethany with the twelve. There was much he wished to tell them, much of faith and enthusiasm for the great assignment to be implanted, watered and warmed. Within another few days the stir and excitement of the feast would be upon them.

At this gathering of all Israel into her capital city, if he saw that the time was ripe he would assert the true nature of his Messiahship. He would challenge the authority of the leaders, and in their consuming fear and anger he would become the Great Sacrifice through which His errant children would be reunited with the Father. In Jerusalem he would be lifted up before the people, and thus lifted he would become God's Symbol of His love for His children. He would be unto all generations the eternal Signpost to the Father's love.

So Jesus talked to them earnestly but tenderly of the days ahead: How he would be given over into the realm of death and yet would rise again to testify to the omnipotence of God and his own oneness with the Father, and of how shortly he would leave them. But he would not leave them comfortless, for the Spirit of the Father would abide with them always to comfort them, strengthen them and make them sufficient for whatever trials might come.

They listened, striving to grasp his singular words, to be reconciled to a course that seemed shrouded in a mystery at once dreadful and glorious.

One afternoon when Judas had returned from Jerusalem Jesus walked with him and Simon the Zealot down to the stables behind the house of Lazarus and his sisters. They slumped onto the straw. Jesus, his long brown legs stretched from beneath his robe to catch the winter sunlight, talked to them of his life's purpose. He sensed that the Judaean's thoughts were wandering. "Judas, something seems to be weighing on your mind. Are you troubled, my brother? I've noticed that you've been going often into Jerusalem. Does something there give you concern?"

"Master, as you know, I bear the pouch for our company and—" Judas smiled faintly—"sometimes it must be replenished. . . . I've been thinking much of the coming days of the feast. You've told us that your hour approaches." He stopped, his eyes on the straw.

"But don't be sorely troubled in heart, my brother." Jesus' voice was comforting. He looked deep into the black eyes of the man of Kiriot. "Judas, do you remember that once before, when we were high on Hermon, I asked who men were saying that I am?"

"I do, Master. And I remember well the answer of Bar Jonas."

"I ask you now that same question, Judas. What is your answer?"

"The same he gave, Master: you are the Messiah of God, sent to deliver us from bondage, to redeem the chosen people." He said it in all earnestness. "That's why I'm concerned these days, Master. I look anxiously for the coming of your hour. I would see you lifted up before the people, the king come to his glory. So would all Israel. We can hardly wait for the day, Master, when you're en-

throned above all the hosts, above all the nations of earth!"
Smoothed of its frequent scowling, Judas' dark face was lighted in
rapture. "When that day comes, Master, I crave to sit near the
throne. And, Lord, speed the day!"

"Do you love me, Judas?"

"You know I love you, Master. You can see in my heart that I
love you dearly."

"Yes, I know you love me." The whisper of a sigh escaped
Jesus. "But I greatly fear, my brother, that you do not understand
the nature of love or the purpose for which my Father sent me into
the world. Strive in these remaining days to comprehend. Pray to
the Father that you may grasp the truth."

Chapter 43 ✠

JUDAS came whistling over the Mount of Olives and down the
fall of the hill toward the brook Kidron. Today was the great day,
the climactic day, of the feast. Today could well be the greatest day
in history.

He paused to look across the walls and roofs of Jerusalem. Once
again the city overflowed with pilgrims. Its roofs glowed as though
they knew that soon the proud invader would be no longer beneath them. Under those flat roofs devout pilgrims were stirring to
ready themselves to go up to the Temple. And under many robes
were daggers freshly edged.

The course of action had been set. The Zealot commanders had
laid their plans with care. Each had been assigned to a location in or
near the Temple courts. The artfully disguised partisans had been
carefully instructed. The Master would come to the Temple to
teach, as he had been doing since the beginning of the feast. At the
propitious moment he would proclaim his Messiahship, announce

the liberation of Israel, and to the accompaniment of the joyous shouts of the assembled Jews accept the restored ancient throne. Then on all sides Zealots would draw out their hidden swords and surround their king.

Each day the leaders and their companies had taken their stations in case the Galilean should choose that day. But Judas had been confident Jesus would wait until today to make his world-shaking declaration. Today he would certainly act.

But suppose he didn't act. What then? They had made provision for this eventuality. If for any reason the Master should fail to move, the Zealots at a concerted signal from Judas and Bar Abbas would lead the throng in a frenzied and tumultuous exhortation to the Galilean to take the crown. Then with drawn swords they would fall upon the Roman soldiers in the Temple precincts. The Master, to restore peace and prevent the effusion of blood, would be constrained to supernal succor.

Last night Shelomith had protested. "Oh, Judas, do not stain your hands with blood!"

He had laughed at her alarm. "Isn't it blood well spilled? By the blood of a few pilgrims and the blood of many Romans Israel will be lifted from slavery and set free. Are you afraid the centurion who's so anxious for my safety may lose some precious blood?"

"You might lose blood yourself, Judas." She was not reconciled to the venture.

Judas crossed the brook Kidron, went along the road toward the city's upreared eastern wall and entered through the Dung Gate. As he was crossing the square before it he heard horses' hoofs clattering on the cobblestones, and along the narrow way to the Temple he saw Roman cavalry spurring their mounts. At that instant a man came running into the square, breathless and wildly excited. Out of the clutter of Ophel's dens a mob of gesticulating Jews swarmed about him.

"It has started! The hour has come! I've seen it! I've seen with my own eyes the coming of the day! O God in Israel, it has come to pass!" The fellow thrust out his arms. Sweat poured down his face, though the morning air was crisp. "Yes, men, the day is at hand! The day—the great day!"

"What possesses him? Do evil spirits control his tongue?" A woman, her front teeth missing, tugged at Judas' robe. "What can he mean? Is he mad?"

The man heard her. He swung around, glaring. "What can I mean? I mean the day of Israel's deliverance! Didn't you just now see the Romans charging up the Mount of the House? Damn the beasts! They too shall perish. The swords of Israel flash in the sun! The Court of the Gentiles already runs with blood—the blood of Romans mixed in the blood of the sacrifice! Go, you men, to the Temple and fight with your brothers! Go fight—fight——" He panted for breath.

Judas had heard enough. He sped along the narrow street. . . . O God! It has begun too soon. The Master's not here. O my God! . . .

On the bridge he was almost trampled by a century of Romans galloping over the Valley of the Tyropoeon. As he jumped out of the way he glimpsed grim faces, uniforms torn and battered. The brown smear of drying blood on tunics showed that they had been in the center of fighting. Judas thought he recognized Centurion Sergius in the lead as the horsemen dashed toward Mount Zion.

"It's all over," a man told Judas at the Gate Shalleketh. "You'd better not go inside. The Romans are on the rampage. They lost many soldiers. But we fared worse—far worse."

"What happened? What started the melee?"

"I'm not sure. It began in a flash. I heard that a pilgrim stabbed a Roman soldier who ordered him to stand aside. A patrol of Longinus' century was taking its station. The soldiers thrust their spears into the Jew, killing him. Other pilgrims, waxing furious, assailed the soldiers and killed several. That set it off, they say. Now many of our men are dead. Others they've bound and doubtless will send to the crosses. Two of my Judaean friends were among those slain. They were leaders of a company of Zealots from down near Beersheba. They——"

"From lower Judaea, you say?" Judas fixed startled eyes on the forlorn face. "Who were they? What were their names?"

"Pethuel," the man said, "and Cush. There may have been other Judaeans slain."

Judas felt as though he might sink down on the pavement. "They were friends of my youth. I knew them well. O God in Israel!" He sat down on the pedestal of a Corinthian column. "If the Master had only been here—in time! If only he'd been here!"

Through eyes that hardly saw he looked across the defiled marble of the great Court of the Gentiles.

Chapter
44 ✦

JESUS and several of the apostles had crossed the brook Kidron when they saw Simon bar Jonas, who had gone early into the city, running to meet them.

"Master, oh, Master——" He was breathless and red of face. His mouth was wide open, gasping. "Master, the soldiers of Pilate—" he sucked in a great mouthful of air—"have slain many of the pilgrims . . . in the courts of the Temple. It was fearful. The soldiers swarmed down from the Tower of Antonia. They fell among the pilgrims, killing right and left." He caught his breath again. "There are stir and commotion throughout the city. The anger of the Jews is hot against the Romans and the tyrant Pilate."

For a long moment Jesus said nothing. His look reflected the gravity of this news.

Finally he said, "I am grieved for those slain and their loved ones.

Many will say they were justly punished for rebelling against the Roman authority; others that their sinning brought this evil fate upon them. But I say to you that this is not the way of the Father. This is not how He accomplishes His divine will."

His friends stood silent about him. When he spoke again it was as though he were reasoning with himself. "My hour has not come. This is the message the tragic incident brings me. I must await another day. That is the Father's will, and it is my will that always His will be served."

He knew that if he should go into the Temple now and proclaim himself the Messiah, with all Jerusalem in an uproar and the people in a ferment of nationalistic devotion intensified by the massacre, his act would be misinterpreted, its purpose defeated. In this hour of grief and anger the Jews would hail him as an earthly deliverer, clamor to make him their temporal ruler, their leader in a war of arms.

From the Messiah of God, the brother of all men, the Son of the Father, they would seek to reduce him to a small ruler of a poor, benighted kingdom of Israelites.

But now in his eyes they saw the fire of the Galilean days and the same strength and warmth. He stood erect and square on his sandaled feet. "Nevertheless, we shall go to the feast, and I shall teach again in the Temple."

Judas was leaning against a column near the Gate of Shushan when Jesus strode through the Court of the Gentiles and took his usual place on the steps in front of the Beautiful Gate. He's too late, Judas said under his breath. If only he'd been here an hour ago! He couldn't have let the pilgrims be killed.

They had removed the bodies of the slain soldiers and pilgrims, but the gorgeous mosaic marble was stained in many places to mark where they had fallen. Disappointment and chagrin were as crimson in the heart of Judas as those awful bloodstains on the marble.

Nor did the Master's homilies serve to dispel his gloom. The crowd was hearing him gladly, but present also were the inevitable scoffers—the Pharisees, Sadducees, scribes, the priests and the hangers-on of the Temple—to dispute and cross-question. He said nothing to indicate that shortly he would be enthroned, that he would call down on the enemies of Israel a thundering vengeance. In fact, he seemed rather to avoid making a direct claim that he was the Messiah. He spoke in a sort of beautiful mysticism, Judas felt.

"How long will you keep us wondering?" a man asked Jesus. "If you are the Christ, say so plainly."

"I have told you and you wouldn't believe me," the Master answered. "The works that I do in my Father's name bear witness. But you don't believe me because you are not my sheep, as I have already told you. My sheep listen to my voice. I know them and they follow me, and I give to them eternal life. They shall never perish, neither shall any man wrest them out of my hand. My Father, who has given them to me, is the Lord of all, and no man can snatch them out of my Father's hand." Jesus let this sink in before he concluded: "And my Father and I are one."

Beautiful words, Judas said to himself, but the same message he has so often brought. No hint in it of action today. O God, if he had but come in time!

Judas saw a man push toward the inner rim of the crowd with a large chipped stone in his hand, a jagged fragment thrown aside in the building of the still unfinished Temple. Jesus too had seen him. Judas noted that the Master's eyes betrayed not the slightest evidence of fear.

Now others, burly hirelings of the priests, snatched up broken pieces of marble left by the stonemasons. Several men came through the Gate of Shushan with stones hastily collected on the edge of the Kidron gorge. They ringed themselves about Jesus.

Undisturbed he watched them. "Many good works have I done among you through my Father's power. For which of them do you take up stones against me?"

"We aren't going to stone you for any good deed you've done," a ruffian answered, "but because you utter blasphemy. You, a man, claim to be one with God!"

Jesus tried to reason with them, but they would not listen; and they began all the more to menace him. But his eyes stayed their arms. Not a stone was hurled.

"Let us be going," he said to Simon bar Jonas and the other apostles there with him. "I must wait until another season."

Throwing the corner of his long robe over his shoulder, he walked toward the Gate of Shushan. His friends fell in behind. Not once did he look back.

When they had disappeared Judas sat down on the pedestal of the great column. His gloom weighed heavily on him. The Master is unafraid, he said to himself. He has power. His goodness and his wisdom have no limits. Alas, he will not on his own declare himself, and ill luck and some fool's rashness robbed me of the chance to make him act!

Judas sat a long time looking across the Court of the Gentiles, which was emptying of the pilgrims. His eye fell on a hulking beggar hunched forlornly against the wall near the gate through which the Master had passed. Judas went over to him. "We've failed," he said, his voice low. "We must look to another day. The Master came too late. If our man had not struck too soon——"

"Your master came too late indeed!" Bar Abbas growled. "And what would he have done if he'd come before our man drew his sword! Do you think he'd have led us to victory? No! All he wants to do is talk! Words! Words! Words! I'm sick of the sound of them. I'm through. From now on I'll carry on the fight my own way. You've led me off the track once too often with your plannings and promisings. Every time you start anything, somebody else gets hurt—or killed—or captured."

"Remember that I rescued you. Where would you be now but for me? Still fighting beasts in the Amphitheater? You're stupid, Bar Abbas. The worst of it is you don't understand the Master. Didn't you hear him say he must wait till another season?"

Bar Abbas held up a quick hand in caution. "Haven't I told you this wall may have ears? Yes, I heard him! I heard all his clever words." He got to his feet, stood as though crippled. "They're pleasant on the ears, but what do they mean? I can't make out in them a promise of death to the pagan whelps! I can't hear in them the crack of a sword on barbarous heads! No, ask me no longer to wait for his day to come. I'll see to my own——"

He stopped short, conscious that he had not taken his own warning. A man had drawn near them. "You needn't be cautious, Bar Abbas," he said. "I'd know that voice anywhere, though your disguise is clever. If you hadn't spoken I'd never——"

"Abihu! God, man! Have you just come from Galilee, or were you here for all the feast?"

"I arrived in Jerusalem this morning. I've been looking for you, my friend. I first went to the cobbler's, and then I came here." He took Bar Abbas' hand and said gravely, "I bear grievous tidings from Nain."

"Demas?"

"Yes. Your sister Eunice bade me say that if you'd see him alive you'd best hasten to her house. He lies desperately ill, and he hardly leaves off calling for you."

"Demas?" Judas' face revealed his concern.

"My son." Bar Abbas stared at the pavement. "The one the soldiers' horses trampled." He raised his head quickly, and his expression was frightful. "May the God of Israel damn the heathen race of them to hell! Now they've killed my boy. Oh, Demas! Oh, my son!" After a moment he mastered himself. "I'll go to him, Abihu. I'll leave before sunset."

Judas grasped the big, coarse hand. "I grieve with you, Bar Abbas, my friend. May God restore your boy! May you find him recovering!"

"I'm grateful, Judas," Bar Abbas said calmly. "Go back to your Nazarene, if you want to." A shadow darkened his stubbled face. "But I'm finished with him. I'll have no more of your wonder-worker."

Chapter
45   ✠

JESUS and the twelve went north to Jericho from Bethany. Eastward from the old walled city they crossed the Jordan into Peraea.

The rabbi knew he was a hunted man. He knew Caiaphas had sought to have him killed during the Feast of the Dedication. But his Father had kept him safe.

At Jerusalem he was a visible and audible threat to Caiaphas and Annas. But here, surrounded by his apostles and friends, he could await in comparative security the coming of the Passover. The greatest feast would bring the hour that would see him lifted up.

Here on the eastern side of the river he could commune with the twelve. The Pharisees and Sadducees, the critics and the scoffers even in this remote region continued to plague him, but they would never be bold enough to attempt to do him physical harm. In Peraea he could teach and heal and hold fellowship with his apostles as he awaited his destiny on a hill in the ancient capital.

James bar Zebedee had gone to Jerusalem with a catch of fish which had been brought from Galilee by one of his father's men. He returned troubled. "Coming back, Master, I paused at Bethany. Lazarus is seriously ill. Mary and Martha importune you to go to them. They're in deep distress."

Judas immediately protested. "But, Master, you remember how they tried to take your life when we were in Jerusalem. If you went to Bethany——"

Jesus looked deep into the black eyes of his keeper of the pouch. "How well, my brother, you know these things." To James he said, "I am grieved at the news you bear. Lazarus has been in poor health, but his illness is not fatal. It shall be used as an occasion to glorify God, and the Son of God also will be glorified through it."

He did not explain his meaning. Instead, he called the twelve to him and told them a story. He had told them many parables, especially during these days in Peraea. This one was about a prodigal son who had demanded his inheritance of his father. After getting his money the boy had gone into a foreign country and spent it all in boisterous and intemperate living. But he had repented, and when he returned home penniless the father had forgiven him and with great joy restored him to his place in the family.

On a later occasion, when others were with the apostles, he used a story to picture the smallness and meanness of a spirit constricted by avarice and covetousness.

"There was once a certain rich man whose ground brought forth plentifully. So he began to consider how he should store the abundance his lands were producing. He reasoned to himself that he should tear down his barns and storehouses and build greater ones, so that he might have room in which to provide for the produce.

"Then this rich man said to himself, 'I will say to my soul, "Soul, thou hast much goods laid up for many years; take thine ease; eat, drink, and be merry." '

"But God said to the rich man, 'Thou fool, this night thy soul shall be required of thee. Then whose shall those things be which thou hast provided?' "

His eyes rested for a moment on Judas. Then he said:

"So is he that is content to lay up treasures for himself, but is not rich toward God. See to it that you are not satisfied with hoarding treasures here on earth that have no permanence, that may rust away or be eaten by moths or stolen in the night by thieves. But be determined rather to lay up permanent treasures that will forever be safe in heaven. Instead of seeking to accumulate great possessions on this earth, strive to store your treasures in heaven by giving away that which you have here. Only by giving, my brothers, can one truly have. Only by recklessly sharing of your treasures and of yourselves can you be certain of possessing forever the untold treasures of heaven. That is the supreme law. Lay up your treasures in the Father's storehouses, for where your treasures are, there also will your heart be."

For another long moment he scanned the man of Kiriot, and there was pleading in his look.

"Good Master, what can I do to obtain this treaure in heaven of which you speak?"

Jesus turned to face a youth standing near the Zebedees. He was struck by his look of utter sincerity. He recognized him as a person of standing in the neighborhood. His dress and general demeanor bespoke wealth. Jesus' heart went out to the young man.

"Why do you call me 'good'? Do you not know there is but one who is 'good' and that is God the Father? Do you see the Father in me? Or do you mean by 'good' what the world means by goodness, the keeping of the commandments?"

The youth was puzzled, but he was intently interested and eager to pursue his questioning.

"But, Master, from my earliest days I've kept the commandments. Isn't there something else I must do if I'm to lay up in heaven the great treasures of which you've spoken?"

Jesus felt his soul lifted as he looked on the handsome lad so deeply touched, so noble in his possibilities.

"Yes, if you would gain these immeasurable treasures of heaven, if you would secure for yourself throughout eternity the very riches of the Father Himself, there is one thing yet you must do." A film of tears glistened in his eyes. "My beloved young brother, you are close to the Father's kingdom. How I would that this day you would enter into it! What one thing is needful for you still to do?" There was earnest entreaty in his smile. "If you would gain the unmeasured riches of the kingdom, you must first give yourself— utterly." He gazed pleadingly into those sober eyes. "If you would gain this treasure, go sell all you have and give it away, divide it among those whom it will best serve, and then, free and unencumbered, come and follow me!"

Again he studied that perplexed face before him, and he lifted silently a prayer to his Father.

The youth stood before Jesus. His eyes lowered. Jesus saw him quickly brush away a tear. Slowly he turned and without making reply walked from the circle, shoulders drooped, away from the tall Galilean.

For he had great earthly possessions.

The next day Jesus told them he was going to Bethany. "Lazarus is asleep," he said. "I must go and awake him."

Puzzled but fearful, they began to protest.

"But, Master," said Andrew, like Judas the day before, "Bethany is nigh Jerusalem. Do but remember how bitterly hostile the Temple leaders were during the Feast of the Dedication, how they sent men to take up stones against you. Now they'd be more bent than ever to harm you."

"Yes, Master, and if Lazarus is sleeping, isn't it a sign he's mending fast? Don't the physicians say so?" Bar Tolmai's ascetic face was anxious.

Judas said nothing, for he recalled the rebuke in the Master's eyes when he had remonstrated yesterday and the strange words that had hinted more than they had said. But Judas did not want Jesus to go to Bethany. His presence so near Jerusalem might precipitate events before the Judaean was ready. For now Judas was revising his first plan. The new one, beginning to take shape, must be absolutely workable. It simply must not fail. When the Passover came, his ambition for Israel, for the Master—and for himself— must be realized. There must be no slip this time.

But he held his peace.

Jesus, letting his eyes circle the protesting apostles, smiled. "You don't understand. I must go to my friends. They are in great distress. They need me. Lazarus sleeps the sleep of death. Even now he lies in the tomb."

Chapter
46 ✠

THE amazing report swept through Ophel on the tongues of excited tradesmen, water carriers, tailors, workers in many crafts. Housewives shouted it across the cobblestoned alleyways. . . . "Have you heard? . . . Isn't it past all believing, Rachel, and yet . . . My man knew Lazarus well, and he knew last week he was nigh to death. And now they say . . . The Pharisees, Jacob heard this morning at the Dung Gate, claim it was trickery, yet how . . . Yes, how indeed can such a thing have happened? . . . Leah, going for a pitcher of water, heard a man at the well say that he had just come from Bethany, and he said . . ."

The stories overflowed Ophel and spread through Mount Zion. They ran up Mount Moriah to the Temple on the summit. They were carried into the homes of the defenders of orthodoxy; quickly they gained the ears of the Temple leaders.

Shelomith first heard the tidings from Rabbi Nicodemus. She had met Rebekah at Benjamin's shop and had walked the short distance home with the Sanhedrinist's daughter. Nicodemus had come in a few minutes later from the Temple, where he had heard the story. He was excited, hardly paused in his recital. "His sisters had sent word to the Nazarene, who was then somewhere in Peraea, to come save their brother's life. But he delayed. When he got to Bethany this morning Lazarus had already been in the tomb four days. The sisters warned Jesus, when he ordered the men to roll back the stone sealing the tomb, that already the body had begun to decay and the odor would be offensive. They were deeply distressed that the Nazarene hadn't come sooner, but——"

"But, Father, what did he do? What did he say? Oh, Father, do hurry."

Nicodemus smiled. "If you wouldn't interrupt, Rebekah, I'd get along faster. Well, he told them to roll back the stone, and when the opening stood revealed the people backed away. But the rabbi walked right up to the cave's mouth. He stood there a moment, his eyes closed, his face to the sky, and prayed. Then he opened his eyes and called out in a loud voice: 'Lazarus, come forth!' "

"Oh, Father! What—?"

"Everybody was tense, looking into the tomb. Then they saw Lazarus, bound head to foot in his grave wrappings, come shuffling out. The Nazarene ordered them to unbind Lazarus and let him go." Nicodemus relaxed. "That's the story they're telling. And it must be true. It's given the High Priest and his supporters a shock. They're furious."

"Shelomith, Judas must have been there. When he comes to see you, bring him here so he can tell me more about it. I've never heard anything so thrilling!"

"No, my daughter, you haven't. Nor anything so important. It proves, doesn't it, that the Nazarene is——" He said no more, and in another moment he left the room.

"Your father meant that Jesus is the Messiah?"

"Yes, I think so, Shelomith. He's long been interested in the Nazarene. But he takes issue with those who think that the Messiah will become our king and restore our liberties."

"Judas thinks he will."

"How long since you've seen Judas, Shelomith?"

"Not since the Feast of the Dedication. I hardly ever see him now that he's become a member of the Nazarene's band."

Nor did Judas come to her house that evening.

But the High Priest did.

"I was hoping to find your betrothed here," he told her.

"He's out at Bethany, I think. I'm told he was with the Nazarene when Lazarus was raised from the dead." She watched her uncle's face betray a mounting anger.

"Surely, my dear niece, you don't believe such nonsense. Don't you know it was only a clever bit of trickery?"

"I wasn't there, sir," she answered. "I only heard the report from Rabbi Nicodemus, who'd got it at the Temple. The rabbi seemed to believe the man was actually raised from the dead."

Caiaphas' scowl was black as night. "Nicodemus is a follower of the Nazarene wonder-worker. But he hasn't the courage to confess it."

Within an hour after he left his sister's house Caiaphas sent an emissary to Bethany to visit the house of Lazarus and at a favorable time gain an audience with the rabbi from Galilee. Beneath his cloak the man carried a dagger.

But he was not to execute his mission.

The rabbi was no longer at Bethany, Lazarus told him. Jesus and his friends had left long before sunset. They had gone into the mountains north of Jerusalem, Lazarus thought.

Chapter 47 ✠

SPRING was fast coming again. From his retreat beyond Ephraim in the hills Jesus and the twelve could look down on the newly greening valley of the Jordan. The roads beside the stream of pleasant memories would soon be alive again with Passover pilgrims.

The stalwart Galilean looked forward to the feast with conflicting feelings. Sometimes, as in the high, clean hills he contemplated his coming immolation, a choking horror seemed to seize him. He fancied himself being sealed away, inert and helpless, within the damp walls of a secluded tomb. Sometimes, even in the midst of the friends with whom he had lived and worked, taught and journeyed up and down the land, he felt desperately lonely. Doubt threatened to overwhelm him.

But never did his Father desert him as he awaited his tre-

mendous hour. More often he looked forward to the Passover
with a lifting of spirit, a soaring of his innermost emotions. Love
possessed his heart, and soon before thousands gathered in Jerusalem love through him would find for time and eternity its supreme expression. He knew that through it all his Father would
be near him, around him, within him—his Father would be loving him.

So he gave his heart and his days to the twelve. Soon they would
be sheep with no shepherd to lead them, to fold them from the
alarms and storms of wandering. He revealed to them the goodness of God. He told them that in Jerusalem he would be lifted
high that men might see in him the propitiation for their sinning,
the door newly opened to the Father's house. He bade them be of
good courage, for the Father would send His own Spirit, when he
their earthly shepherd had left them, to warm them, support them
and give them peace.

But even yet they were frightened and could not understand.
Sometimes one or another would speak out, voicing his fears.
Simon bar Jonas said to him one day, "Master, must you go again
into great danger?"

Jesus knew that the impetuous fisherman said it out of love for
him, and he was not offended. "Would you tempt me again?" he
asked gently.

"As you will, Master." The stout fellow's eyes began to well
with fresh tears. "It's just that we love you so much."

The rabbi laid his hand gratefully on the apostle's shoulder.
Peter the rock. Yes, this Simon would be an unyielding founda-
tion stone on which the church would be built. This Simon and
this beloved little band, now so troubled, so filled with apprehension of what early days might bring, would be the bottom rocks.
These utterly human young men, now gay, now anxious, now
bickering among themselves, now securely bound to one another
in warm and intimate fellowship—they would be the pillars on
which through the long years men of good will would build the

new order. These obstreperous, trying, rough, gentle, sad, joyous young men would be the bedrock—sturdy Simon, and gentle John of the smoldering fire and his brother James of a flashing but quickly spent anger—his beloved Sons of Thunder and the Rock, the three of them his most constant companions—and the others.

Eleven Galileans, so different and yet so alike, so truly of Galilee, and Judas the Judaean. Eleven and Judas.

Often now in the desolate highlands he prayed for Judas. He besought the Father to cleanse his heart of hate and open it wide to the sunlight of love. Jesus, preparing himself and striving to prepare his brothers, carried a great heaviness because of the strange waywardness of Judas. Of all the twelve he seemed to have by far the least comprehension of what Jesus had so earnestly been trying to reveal, appeared more determined to set his own course.

The days passed, and on a thousand hillsides poppies, anemones and lilies flamed into color, and blossoms of the oleanders marked the turnings of the streams in the ravines.

Though he gave himself in devotion to his twelve, he did not withdraw from serving the others around him. He journeyed about the countryside and sometimes ventured far north of the region of Ephraim. It was on one of these trips that his compassionate soul was most plainly and beautifully revealed.

They were returning to a lower Galilean village to spend the night after a day filled with acts of charity and mercy. The sun was reaching low for the hills toward the Great Sea. As they walked along the narrow way suddenly they heard a great wailing and lamenting that steadily grew louder, and presently around the curve came a funeral procession. At the head stalked a tall man, sparse and angular, whose nasal recital of the deceased person's virtues provided a rising and lowering cadence for the long file of mourners.

As the cortege advanced toward them Jesus and his friends withdrew into the shrubs at the side of the way and stood respectfully silent. It was then that they saw the bier.

On it lay the body of a young man, wrapped in preparation for entombment.

Behind the bier, bent with the burden of her sorrow, her drawn, thin body convulsed with low sobbing, walked a woman in the garments of heavy mourning. Following her came others, of varying stations in life but all of them sorrowful.

As the woman came opposite him Judas saw a tear course down the Master's cheek. Then—it seemed as though by sudden impulse—Jesus stepped forward a pace and patted the woman gently on the shoulder.

"Weep not, my sister. The Father will sustain and comfort you."

She lifted her tragic face to him. "But, sir, he was all I had. All I had!" And she fell into a passion of weeping.

The Master caught her arm. "He is not dead; he is but sleeping."

"Oh, sir—" her voice was anguished—"oh, sir, do not mock. You see, we bear him to the tomb. O God, have mercy! Have mercy, Lord!" She dropped her head and the tears flowed unchecked.

Jesus loosed his grip on her arm, strode straight to the bier. "Set it down!" he commanded. The startled bearers obeyed. The mourners, their cadenced wailing suddenly quieted, drew around him in wonder and awe. A moment he stood beside the bier, unmoving, his eyes closed. Then he opened them and looked down into the face of the dead youth.

"Young man, I say unto you, arise!"

Some on the fringe fell back in abject terror. Others, their eyes fastened on the dead boy's bandaged face, saw him stir feebly. His eyes came open, and his arms moved as his hands felt for the side of the bier.

He sat upright.

Some sprang away from him as though he were a spirit from another world. Some screamed. Some fell prostrate in the dirt.

Judas, looking again at his Master, saw the glory of heaven lighting Jesus' face. With a vibrancy the Judaean himself could almost feel the Nazarene bent down, took the bound hand of the young man, lifted him to his feet, began to loose him from the windings.

"Now," he said when this was done, "go to her."

The young man stepped quickly around the bier and caught the woman in a crushing embrace. The two stood knotted together, weeping and laughing in uncontrolled emotion.

A man near them shouted, "His crutches! He has no crutches. He walked! He stands! God in Israel, he has not walked in ten years until this moment!"

It was then that Judas first saw the hulking, dark-bearded man pushing through the rim of those who had been mourners. He rushed to the boy and the woman in the center of the loudly rejoicing circle.

"Demas! Oh, my boy! Oh, Demas, my son, my son! See the boy, Eunice! Look: he's not only alive again, my sister, but his legs are straight and strong. He can walk! He can run and leap!"

"Bar Abbas! It was his son!" Judas clapped a heavy hand on the shoulder of Simon the Zealot. "See you, Zealot? The boy is Bar Abbas' son!"

In all the happy noise Bar Abbas did not hear the Judaean. His back to Judas, he stood crushing the stripling and the woman in his long arms.

Suddenly he faced about. Out of the black mat of his beard his shining eyes fell on the tall, smiling Nazarene. He dropped to his knees. "Oh, sir . . . Oh, sir, I . . . I . . ." he stammered, his gaze fastened on the rabbi's coarse sandals. "I have been wicked, evil in the sight of the Lord. I scorned you, sir, and scoffed." He raised his face to look in humility and with unmeasured thankfulness into the eyes of Jesus. "I was evil, and my stubborn heart knew you not. But now . . . now . . . Oh, sir, I thank you! I thank you, my Master, my Lord, the Son of the living God!"

The chief of the Zealot fighters leaned low to kiss the feet of Jesus of Nazareth.

Chapter
48   ✠

AGAIN Jerusalem was in a fret of excitement. All the roads into the city were choked. To a devout Jew, or to one craving merely the thrill of adventure, nothing was quite so important as to be in Jerusalem for the Passover.

Not all the arrivals were Jews. Pilate had taken quarters in the sumptuous palace of the Herods, while Herod Antipas, Herodias and Salome grudgingly had moved into the damp and drafty old Maccabaean palace. Both Pilate and Herod had brought soldiers to supplement the usual garrisons, for it was necessary that the political authority remain adequate to any sudden needs. Herod was anxious that no disorder develop to displease Pilate, and Pilate was fearful that should any outbreak occur grave reports of it would get to the Prefect Sejanus at Rome or the Emperor himself. So the Tower of Antonia bulged with soldiers, and Herod's guardsmen stalked through the desolate corridors of the old palace or camped on its grounds.

To add to the excitement of the pilgrims and the apprehension of the authorities a rumor was going about the city that during the feast the revolutionaries might attempt another rebellion. On thousands of lips were the whispered words, or boldly spoken joyous words, that the young rabbi, Jesus of Nazareth, would attend the feast. Some declared that he would permit himself to be acclaimed king. Already, they were telling, he and his company had reached Bethany, where they tarried at the house of Lazarus and his sisters.

Centurion Longinus had little fear that the Nazarene teacher would lead a revolt. He had heard much of Jesus and had formed the opinion, largely as the result of what Shelomith had said, that he was a mystic, an Oriental wonder-worker interested only in spiritual matters, in the relationship of man with the incomprehensible Yahweh, the god of the Jews.

But he was afraid that Bar Abbas might cause trouble. He was determined to catch the wily brigand and see him shackled to a wall of Antonia's lowest dungeon before the festival had got well under way. He would set a trap.

Early in the week before he had summoned Flavius. "Reports have come to me that the Jews may attempt an uprising during the Passover, in stronger force than during the Feast of the Dedication. I believe there may be some truth in them. At any rate, we must be unusually alert. If anything of the sort is contemplated, Bar Abbas will be at the center of it. So we've got to catch him." He smiled. "I have a scheme. I want you to execute it. Listen, Flavius——"

"I'm listening, Centurion. I'd give my left eye to catch that knave. I'd——"

"Here's the plan: I want you to have the fat fellow who was seized with Bar Abbas, the big dullard——"

"I know whom you mean. His name's Shishak. He'll make many a laugh at the games."

"Have him brought to you. Tell him that during the Passover season—he'll know it anyway—it's our custom to release one Jewish prisoner as an evidence of good will toward the people. Then let him go. But have several men designated to follow him. Don't let him know it. Tell them to keep out of his sight, but don't let him get out of theirs. Stay with him day and night. It's my guess he'll try to find Bar Abbas. He'll come on some of his Zealot friends and they'll lead him to Bar Abbas, I'll wager."

"A good trap, Centurion. I think we'll track down that murdering scoundrel."

"When he's located have one of the men report to me as

quickly as possible. We'll go nab him. Do you understand, Flavius?"

"I do, Centurion. I'll carry out your orders to the dot."

Beyond the Mount of Olives at Bethany Judas of Kiriot, too, was interested in finding Bar Abbas. He hadn't seen him since the afternoon on the road below Nain when Jesus had restored his crippled son Demas to vigorous life. He had talked with Bar Abbas then after he had fallen at the feet of the Master and professed his faith in Jesus as the Christ.

"I'd give my life for him," Bar Abbas had declared. "I'll spend whatever time I have left fighting in his cause. It's different now, Judas. Before I had little heart in your plan, but now I'd give the last drop of my blood to have him enthroned."

They had agreed to meet at Japheth's shop early in the festal season. There in company with Dysmas and others they would complete their program.

This time, Judas was sure, the Master would accept the crown and scepter. In the mountains north of Jerusalem he had been talking often with the twelve about the imminence of the great moment, its importance and significance. He would be lifted up before all the world.

Simon bar Jonas, the Zebedees and many others had been sad and at times almost disconsolate, for they had come to believe that the Master was speaking literally when he said that he would be treated shamefully and give his life as a sacrifice for man's sinning, an atonement to the God of Israel. But Judas held firm in his belief that Jesus was still employing his figurative method of teaching and that he did not contemplate actual physical death. How can the Messiah of God die? he asked himself to strengthen his own belief. How could a man laid away in a tomb be the saviour of his nation, the shepherd of the flock of Israel reassembled in the ancient fold?

This time he will assert himself. This time we'll see to it that he does not evade his great opportunity, his responsibility to God and Israel. He'll not walk out through the midst of a people demanding that he lead them to the enjoyment of freedom and the good life as the chosen of God.

He has always had the power, Judas told himself over and over. And this time he will use it. The Zealots and countless others will then rally to him. Bar Abbas will spring forth to lead them.

Jesus, lying sleepless in the house of his friends, called on his Father for strength to endure the terrible time now almost upon him. . . . When I proclaim myself the Messiah the Temple leaders will rise against me, seek to destroy me. If they have not done so already it's because they are afraid, for they know that my Father and I are one. Their minds tell them, but their hopes deny it. They fear me, and they hate me. But the little people, and a few who are great, like the Rabbi Nicodemus and Joseph of Arimathea, know in their souls that I am the Son of God. They cannot understand, but they can love. On the bridge of love they venture toward faith. . . .

The Master was greatly concerned for Judas. . . . He cannot, he will not, understand. His mind and his heart are set. He would put a limit on love. He would exclude all outside Jewry from the food of the Father's table, the shelter of His house. He thinks he loves me. But he cannot love me when he hates my brothers. All men are sons of God and brothers one of another. . . .

In the darkness of the small chamber he prayed for light to shine in the heart of the Judaean, light from the face of God. "Take out hate and fill him with love, O my Father; remove avarice and ambition and give him a generous and contrite heart. Turn him from his stubborn way."

Only tonight at the ending of the Sabbath his friends had given the Nazarene a dinner at the house of Simon the Leper. It had been a time of joy though the Pharisees and scribes and Sadducees, ever determined to deride Jesus, had shown up there. But they hadn't hurt him. Only Judas had caused him pain.

It was when Mary, overjoyed at the Master's presence and lifted

out of herself in the radiance of the moment, had come up to
Jesus and broken open a vial of costly nard to anoint him with it.
Judas, his dark face darker still, had protested the waste. "Why
pour out this valuable spikenard?" he had grumbled. "The woman could have sold it for three hundred pennies and given the
money to the poor."

"Why speak scornfully of Mary, Judas?" Jesus had asked, his
tone rebuking. "Let her alone. She has done a good deed. You
have the poor with you always and you can help them when you
will. But you won't always have me. With this ointment she's
anointed me for my burial. And wherever the good news is
preached this good deed of hers will be reported. She will not be
forgotten."

Judas had not been greatly perturbed. He remembered how the
Master had reproached him that night at Cana when he had said
something about the healing of Chuza's son Paran. Jesus would
still love him. And soon Jesus would be king and in the rejoicing
over great things matters of small moment would be obliterated.

Chapter
49   ✠

THE Roman—Judas could tell he was a Roman by his blue eyes,
cropped head, leering face—had succeeded in enmeshing the man
in the net. He was groveling in the dust and blood of the Amphitheater arena. Thousands of cold eyes looked down on him.

The pygmies, misshapen gnomes brought in from every region
of the empire to provide sport for Pontius Pilate and his friends,
had hurried out to surround him and hurl their tiny javelins into
his naked body threshing helplessly about.

Judas, looking closely, saw that the man in the net was Bar
Abbas.

Pilate was pointing, leaning out from the Procurator's box. As he pointed Bar Abbas seemed to fade away, and now Judas saw that the black mat of hair had turned to red and . . . God in Israel, the netted gladiator was himself, Judas of Kiriot! Pilate was pointing to him. "The keeper of the treasury of the great kingdom of Israel!" the Procurator shouted, his thick lips leering, and from the circle of faces rose a mighty laughter, ribald and heartless. "He would overturn the throne of the Emperor Tiberius! He would defeat Rome! He would tumble our empire in ruins; he—that conspiring redheaded fool of a Jew!"

The Procurator was seized in a paroxysm of laughter. He recovered slowly and considered the victim. As the spectators watched breathlessly he extended his right hand beyond the railing and slowly turned it until the thumb pointed downward. A savage roar burst from the throats of the blood-hungry horde.

Twisting in the net, pricked and stinging with the barbs of the dancing dwarfs, Judas with dim eyes saw a shape loom above him. The gladiator, his spear poised, waited for the right moment to thrust it down . . . down . . .

"Judas, wake up! Wake up, man! Must you sleep away the morning?"

He opened his eyes. The Roman . . . No . . . Someone was shaking him, fingers clutching his shoulders, the nails pinching.

"Get up, Judas! The others have almost finished their breakfasts. Soon we'll be leaving for Jerusalem. The Master has been inquiring for you."

He shook his head and struggled out of the straw. "I—I—was having a horrible dream, Zealot. The Romans had me in a net and were sticking barbed lances in me."

"The nettles in this straw," said Simon. "You were so buried I hardly found you. I was asleep when you crawled into the loft."

"After the dinner I went into Jerusalem. I was late getting back. I wanted to see some friends." He didn't say that he saw Bar Abbas, Dysmas and other partisans.

"Well, hurry. Water's been freshly drawn, and your breakfast's

cooked. We'll be ready to leave as soon as the man returns with
the white ass for the Master to ride into the city."

"What!" Judas clambered to his feet. "A white ass?"

"Yes, he told the man to go over to Bethphage and there he'd
find it tied. If the owner should raise any question he was to tell
him that the Lord had need of it. He said it would be a colt never
before ridden."

Judas' eyes were ablaze. "Listen, Zealot: don't you know what
that means? Riding a white ass in a procession, with men following?" He doubled his fists and raised them aloft. "May God be
praised! The Master is going to do it! He's going to do it!" His
red hair seemed ready to flame. "Don't you know, Simon, how the
Scriptures foretell that the king shall come riding on an unbroken
ass? Remember how the Prophet Zechariah wrote that Zion should
shout and the daughters of Jerusalem rejoice because, he said,
'Behold, thy King cometh unto thee, lowly and riding upon an ass,
even upon a colt, the foal of an ass.' "

"It's what the Scriptures say. Judas, could it really be that today
the Master will—?"

"The prophet declares also," Judas kept right on excitedly, "that
the chariot will be cut off from Ephraim and the horse from Jerusalem, the bows and arrows of battle will be done away with, and
'he shall speak peace unto the heathen, and his dominion shall be
from sea even to sea, and from the river even to the ends of the
earth!' "

"Those are Zechariah's very words. The Master is a man of
peace. Hasn't he said so often? But how can his dominion be from
sea to sea unless with the sword he expels the conquerors?" Simon
shook his head. "This is a mystery to me."

"Let's go to him. Let's go to the king!"

In a few minutes the colt had been fetched. When they had
placed on it a folded robe they helped the solemn rabbi to mount.
The little procession of disciples moved toward the Mount of Olives.

Once Jesus spoke to Judas, who walked beside him. "Troublous
hours lie ahead, my brother. Seek the guidance of our Father and

trust not to your own wisdom. Pray the Father to keep your feet from stumbling."

He might have said more, but a throng had begun to gather behind him and people along the way were leaving their work to follow. As the strange parade breasted the summit and began to descend toward the brook Kidron others came to meet the rabbi. The volume of their cheering and chanting grew into a roar.

Not on this glad day were the Pharisees to leave the rabbi unmolested. One of them pushed close. "Master," he yelled to be heard above the noise, "you hear your followers calling you king of Israel and shouting hosannas to the son of David. You know this will come to the ears of the Romans and inflame them against us. Rabbi, rebuke your mad supporters."

Jesus held up his hand, signaling silence. "I tell you that if these friends should hold their peace the very stones themselves would cry out."

When he ceased speaking the people began to shout with even livelier spirit. "Blessed, blessed, thrice blessed is he who comes in the name of our God!"

Several ran forward to a clump of palms beside the way and began to break the green branches. Others tore limbs from shrubs. They began to wave the branches and with screams of joy cast them in the path of the burdened white ass. Some in ecstasy jerked off their gaily colored cloaks and sashes and spread them in the dust as a carpet over which the little beast might walk. "Hosanna! Hosanna! Know you that the rabbi of Galilee will be our king! Hosanna! Blessed is he!"

Judas, still walking beside the slowly trudging colt, across from Simon bar Jonas who held the halter, could hardly restrain himself from leaping into the midst of the hysterical shouters and shrieking his own great joy.

The plan would succeed! It was on the way to fulfillment. Soon they would enter into the precincts of the great white Temple, into the kingship itself! Soon now, very soon.

They came around a bend. Suddenly Jerusalem, its ramparts

circling a sea of housetops as far as the smoking Vale of Hinnom
to the left and on the right the Temple, resplendent in the morning
sunlight—Jerusalem lay gloriously before them.

The king's capital city, Judas thought. This day we shall raise up
a great golden throne, seat the Master on it, give glad obeisance to
King Jesus, son of David.

The little ass had halted. Judas turned to look at the Master,
expecting to see his face wreathed in a smile.

But Jesus had not paused in order to contemplate his coming
glory. He was not smiling. He showed no sign of joy or elation.
Instead, his face was set. The shadow of a passionate sorrow spread
over it as he looked westward on the bedecked streets. He held
out his arms as though he would draw the proud city into his embrace. Tears began to run down his cheeks.

"O Jerusalem, Jerusalem," he cried in tones of utter woe, "if you
had but known—if you could but know now—those things that are
required if you would have peace! But they are hidden from your
eyes. The days shall come upon you when your enemies shall ring
you about and be entrenched on all sides. And they shall throw
down your walls and your great houses on your children, until not
one stone remains upon another, and you are leveled utterly to the
ground."

He was oblivious of the suddenly silent crowd about him. His
tears rolled freely and without shame down his cheeks. "All this
shall come upon you, O Jerusalem, because in your stubbornness
of heart you knew not the day your God Himself came to visit you!"

For a moment more he solemnly regarded the city before him.
Then he nodded to Simon bar Jonas and the procession started
again. As they trudged down the Mount of Olives they were silent
for a time. Judas could make no sense out of Jesus' lamentation.
Whatever it meant it increased the need of action. He said nothing.
Only the angry murmuring of some Pharisees disturbed the quiet.
The agonized words of the rabbi seemed to them terrible
blasphemy.

Now Jesus' expression brightened, and the people, noting it, began again to hail the king. More and more fell in with the procession, increasing the tumult. They passed by the gate into the Garden of Gethsemane, at length crossed the brook Kidron, and entered the city through the Dung Gate. While they moved slowly through the Ophel squalor the hosannas merged into a mighty chorus of acclaim. All the lowly men ran out from their hovels and ill-smelling shops to greet the rabbi of Galilee.

From one of the high places in the Temple the chief priests watched the procession thread its sinuous way up Mount Moriah. Now and then they could see the white ass and its rider. The glad shouts made a terrible dissonance in their ears.

"They've gone mad," Caiaphas observed. "The sight of him deprives them of their senses. What a hold the fellow has on the poor and despised! See him? His long legs almost touch the ground. A comical sight. A strange way for a king to enter into his kingdom!"

Annas regarded his son-in-law sternly. "Don't you remember the words of the prophet, how he said that the king would come riding on an ass, and a colt the foal of an ass? My eyes are old and they no longer discern things at a distance. But isn't that white ass a colt?"

"You mean—?"

"I mean the Nazarene must be destroyed, and speedily."

"If he makes one overt move the soldiers will be upon him. Our spies and Pilate's are everywhere." Caiaphas pointed. "The mob's already on the bridge. Let's move so we can see better into the Court of the Gentiles. They'll be coming through the Gate Shalleketh."

As he stepped onto the bridge Judas brushed against a servant from the household of Lazarus. The man was shouting and clapping his hands frenziedly. Judas tapped him on the shoulder.

The man turned around. "Judas! What a great day! A great day for Israel! The rabbi goes to the Temple to——"

"Hold, Amnon!" Judas fumbled in his pouch for a coin, pulled it out. "Will you take a message for me—in a hurry? You can be back almost by the time the Master is inside the Court of the Gentiles?"

Amnon nodded.

"You know where Benjamin's house is, don't you?"

"Yes, Judas."

"Run and tell Shelomith my betrothed that tonight I'll come there—that it's important I see her. Come back quickly with her answer. I'll be waiting near the Beautiful Gate."

As the man ran toward the Mount Zion end of the bridge Judas pushed ahead to come abreast of the Master, now nearing the gate. There Jesus stepped down from the white ass, and Simon bar Jonas handed the rein to a man who came forward to take it. He hooked his arm in the crook of the rabbi's. Together they led the procession through the gate into the court.

Judas, trembling with expectation, pushed through the crowd, keeping at the Master's elbow. . . . In what stupendous manner will it be accomplished? Is the Master walking toward the Beautiful Gate to take his royal place on the steps before it? Will it be that simple, O Lord, or will it come in rivers of blood?

He looked toward the frowning Tower of Antonia. Along the gallery sentries walked with measured tread, apparently oblivious of the mass of Jewry hailing a new favorite. He knew that beneath their stolidity was a cunning wariness. Let rioting break out and a detachment would sally forth, or else a shower of javelins would descend from the gallery, or a flight of arrows from bows held always ready.

His eyes went back to the tall Galilean. Calmly the rabbi walked about the Court of the Gentiles as thousands watched him. He paused to look into the stalls of sheep and cattle, which had been set up again in desecration of the dignity and beauty of this glorious edifice raised to God. Once he stopped before the table of a money-changer, but he raised not a finger against him. He turned toward the steps to the Beautiful Gate. Here he had admonished those

without sin to cast stones at the poor sinful woman. Straightway
he mounted the steps and stood above the people.

Again their voices welcomed him to this heart and center of
Israel. Pilgrims who had just learned of his presence there came
running. From the pinnacles of the Temple, from the topmost
ramparts of Antonia, startled pigeons lifted swift wings into the
air.

"Hosanna to the king! The Messiah is here! Glory is come to us!
May the God of Israel be praised, for he has brought deliverance
to our troubled land! The Messiah! The Messiah!"

Judas riveted his eyes on the serene and majestic figure on the
steps. Now . . . Now . . .

Jesus said nothing. Indeed, as Judas watched, he seemed to
ignore the clamorous mob. With a solemn and almost sorrowful
smile he gazed on the people, but as though without seeing them.
His mind appeared somewhere else. It was as if he looked far out
across the gash of Kidron, past the summit of the Mount of Olives,
past the Dead Sea and Arabia's burning wastes, beyond the reaches
of this world.

Still saying nothing, he walked down the steps, nodded to Simon
bar Jonas, who stood on the first rise, and, turning to his right,
began to retrace his way through the assemblage.

The Master is leaving! *It cannot be!*

He is leaving as he came.

He is leaving though under the very noses of Jewish priesthood
and Roman soldiery the people demand that he become their king.

Judas felt a sudden faintness. He leaned against one of the
columns.

The Master is leaving! Caiaphas makes no attempt to arrest him.
With his spies everywhere, his Temple guardsmen strolling disguised among the pilgrims, the strong arm of Rome supporting
him, the High Priest is doing nothing.

My plan is falling to pieces. Again Jesus walks boldly from the
presence of friends and enemies.

But why? Why did he come into Jerusalem riding on the white

ass, the symbol of authority, the fulfillment of ancient prophecy?
Why did he go this far, and no farther? Why? Why? Weakness
ran down into Judas' legs. He felt he would collapse on the marble
pavement.

It was then the servant of Lazarus spied him and shouldered his
way to the great column. "I delivered your message. She said she
can't see you tonight. She won't be free."

"Another guest, did she say?"

"No, sir. Her message was brief."

"I . . . I . . . thank you, Amnon."

As the servant was swallowed in the throng Judas stepped up on
the base of the column so that he might see above the bobbing
heads. The sun was toward the Great Sea. Now it fell on a knot of
young men moving out through the Gate Shalleketh—Simon bar
Jonas, the Zebedees, Nathanael bar Tolmai, Andrew, Thomas, the
others. In their midst walked a tall Galilean. He wore no crown.

Judas turned his eyes away. High above the Temple's north wall,
poised and masterful, the Roman sentries kept post along Antonia's
gallery. Closing his eyes, he envisioned a hillside in Galilee, and
rocks, a tall cross, a tormented man on it. . . . "He could have!"
he groaned to himself. "He could have, and he did not!"

He stumbled toward the gate like one in a trance. . . . I must go
somewhere and think. I must try to see clearly. I must recast and
build anew. Yes, by the God of Israel, I must start all over again.
I must find a means that will work, that cannot be thwarted. He
could have, and he did not. Or if he could not, he led us to believe
he could. Either way he has betrayed us. Either way . . .

Part III

THE TREE

✠

Chapter 50 ✠

THE afternoon spring sun was warm on their faces as the two young Roman women, wrapped comfortably in their cloaks, gazed out over Jerusalem's roofs from couches on one of the Antonia galleries.

Cynara pointed. "Just look at the people! They're scurrying about like ants. I remember, Inacha, you said it would be that way the day Nicodemus' daughter was here. Blood sprinkled on a doorpost! By Apollo, what a strange myth to bring so many people together! Inacha, I didn't imagine there were so many Jews in the whole world!"

Sergius' wife smiled. "The Jews, you can depend on it, will attend their feasts, and the Passover is the greatest. It brings them all! I'm always happy when it's over. They get so excited. There's always a chance the Zealots will murder somebody. And Sergius is so reckless. It keeps me worried."

"The wife of a soldier, I can see, leads an anxious life, particularly when he's stationed in Palestine." Cynara shrugged, grinned. "But having no husband at the moment, I haven't that worry."

"It's your own fault—having no husband. Cynara, why don't you marry the manufacturer at Tyre? He's Roman, and rich. What more would you want?"

Cynara gave a laugh. It sounded loud in the crisp air. "I might not even want that much. Both my former husbands were Roman and rich, and I didn't want them—long—any more than they wanted me."

"Well, if you aren't interested in him, there are several clever and handsome young men in the army out here. But—" Inacha giggled—"just don't let your eyes fasten on Sergius."

"Little chance I'd have to fasten my eyes on Sergius," Cynara said. "He's too busy keeping these Jews quiet—or trying to. Sometimes I wonder if you ever see him yourself."

"Well, it isn't often. Right now he's at Herod's palace—" she motioned toward the great stone pile—"getting orders from Pilate to keep an alert against the Zealots during the feast days. Isn't Longinus with him, by the way?"

"I think so—if he isn't at the dark-haired Jewish girl's, or her father's shop."

Inacha sat up. "Cynara, does your brother want to marry that girl, or just—?"

"Just to sleep with her?" The centurion's sister laughed merrily. "How could you blame him—either way? By Venus, Inacha, she's beautiful. What a figure! What hair and eyes!"

"Cynara! I didn't mean that! You——"

"I shock you? Inacha, you've been out here with these Jews so long you've become . . . prudish." Cynara chuckled. "But I insist I wouldn't blame Longinus."

"But, my dear, didn't you tell me she——"

"—is betrothed to a redheaded Jew named Judas? Yes. And he's the one——"

"Oh, I remember." Inacha's face lighted quickly. "The one in the tent and——"

"—at the wedding feast up in Galilee and at Herod's Machaerus party. May the little gods damn Longinus! Inacha, I'll never forgive him for breaking into my bedroom! At such a wonderfully promising time!"

"Yes, you told me about it. Cynara, you amaze me."

"By Cypris, why? Wouldn't you have been angry? Why not say so? Is there any virtue in not speaking frankly?"

Inacha laughed. "I suppose not. But you speak so very frankly!"

"A Roman custom, my dear. Have you forgotten it?"

"But that Jew, Cynara . . . your thwarted lover—" Inacha laughed again—"isn't he a revolutionary? I seem to recall hearing Sergius and Longinus speak of him as a dangerous Zealot."

"Yes, one of the most rabid. But Longinus can't do anything about it for fear it will hurt his prospects with Shelomith. Isn't it a strange situation? Still, he doesn't want me to get involved with the Jew. Complicated, isn't it?"

"But do you want to . . . to get . . . involved?"

"I've been trying to get involved with him for one long night." Cynara laughed so loud that the sentry walking the gallery around the corner paused to listen.

"Can you actually love the man, Cynara?"

For a moment she was thoughtful. "I don't think it's love. No, it isn't that. I think it's—it's his virility, Inacha. He's big and tough—and redheaded." She crinkled her nose. "But that's not all of it, either. Maybe it's the Roman in me—desire for conquest." She laughed. "He . . . he challenges me. I'd like to shake his Jewish superiority, if that's the word. He feels he's better than any Roman, I'm sure. By the gods, I'd like to make him beg a little!" She broke off, chuckling. "I've done all the begging so far, I'll confess. I'd like to make him lose his . . . his . . . "

"Virginity, maybe?"

Cynara burst into laughter. "Inacha, you shock me! How could you say such a thing?"

"It's being around you, my dear. But I believe I know what you mean. You'd like to break down his assurance that he's always right, the member of a superior race?"

"Maybe. Anyway, if I ever see him again—and I intend to— I'll tell you what happens."

Chapter 51 ✠

WEARY in mind and limb, dejected at heart, Judas stumbled down Mount Moriah from the Temple. I'll go out to Bethany, he told himself, and tonight I'll climb into the hayloft and try to think out a new course. If he's really the Messiah . . .

He stopped for a moment at Japheth's. None of the Zealots was there. Bar Abbas had not been in since last night when they had planned today's hapless venture. Japheth did not know when he'd return.

When Judas reached Bethany Jesus was unusually quiet. He talked little. His mind seemed in some other region, on another plane. He repeated briefly that soon he'd be leaving them, urged them to pray to the Father, assured them he would not leave them disconsolate.

They went to bed early. But Judas was a long time falling off to sleep. When he did, his dreams were troubled.

The next day the Master and the twelve went again to the Temple. Once more he drove out the cattle dealers and the money-changers. Once more the people approved and the authorities snarled their fear and wrath. And once more Jesus returned to Bethany uncrowned.

At the Temple the second day after the triumphal entry and the—to Judas—humiliating departure Jesus mounted the steps before the Beautiful Gate and taught the assembled pilgrims. He spoke with great earnestness, as though he would never have a chance to teach them again, and indeed his words seemed to prophesy it.

"The time has come," he said at one place in his long discourse, "for the Son of Man to be glorified. I declare unto you that unless a grain of wheat is buried in the ground and dies, it remains sterile; but if it dies it brings forth a great increase. Whoever therefore clings to his physical life loses it, but whoever is willing to sacrifice his life in this world will save it in the eternal world. If anyone would serve me, let him follow me; then what I attain he also will attain, and my Father will honor him."

At another point he said: "My soul is now troubled, but shall I ask my Father to save me from this trial? It was to endure this trial that I am come!"

Judas wondered what he meant then, and when a little later he referred to his being "lifted up."

"This world is to be judged and the prince of this world will be deposed," he said. "And I, if I am lifted up, will draw everyone to myself. Moses lifted up the serpent before the people in the desert, and in the same way the Son of Man must be lifted up, so that everyone who trusts in him may have eternal life."

So he talked on, and many listened with a deep yearning to comprehend, and many seemed enthralled, while others scoffed, and some refused even to pause in their moving to and fro through the Court of the Gentiles. When the shadows grew long and the sun dipped low he and the twelve left the Temple and walked out to Bethany.

That night Judas again lay sleepless. The days were passing and soon another Passover would be ended. . . . We will have no king in Israel, we will be doomed to another season of wandering over the face of Galilee and Judaea, and I . . . I will remain a nobody in Israel, and even my beloved may be lost to the Roman. . . .

And then in the darkness of the night and his heart, suddenly he saw it—sharp and clear and wonderfully simple—the infallible new idea.

Chapter 52 ✠

"I VOTE 'No.' I won't have on my hands the blood of this innocent, good man!" Nicodemus sternly addressed High Priest Joseph Caiaphas. "I'm against your proposal. I wish so to be recorded."

Caiaphas gave a cynical smile. "I'm not surprised. Many reports have come to our ears of the rabbi's interest in the Nazarene carpenter."

"I don't deny it," Nicodemus replied resolutely. "Interest in
both his message and his works. I've talked with him——"

"By night," the High Priest interjected. "And well so. It
would have been humiliating for all of us if it had got abroad that
a member of the Sanhedrin kept company with this blaspheming
impostor."

"Why do you say Rabbi Jesus is a blasphemer? Is it blasphemy
to teach the love of God for His children, to heal the sick, to restore
lepers, yes, and—I'll say it—bring forth from the tomb one who
has lain dead four days?"

His words provoked an angry hubbub. About the conference
room in Caiaphas' house beards wagged and bobbed—oiled and
braided beards, long beards and short ones, beards twin-pointed
and stubby or straight-cropped and combed out to transparent thin-
ness. The shadows on the wall from the lamps behind the high
court's members danced in a spectral weaving.

Caiaphas' voice rose above the others, drowned them. "Don't
you know, Rabbi Nicodemus, that the man Lazarus was in a trance,
that it was all a piece of sleight of hand devised by the Galilean
upstart to beguile the people?"

A paunchy Pharisee in gorgeous habiliments, his fingers heavily
ringed, stood up, licked his thick lips. "Or else, if he were dead,
he was raised to life by this Jesus through the power of Satan, to
whom evidently he has long since sold himself." He settled heavily
in his seat.

"No," Nicodemus answered, "I know none of this. I know only
that many eyewitnesses have testified the man was dead, laid away
in the tomb, and that the Rabbi Jesus, coming to his tomb after four
days, called him forth, and he came forth, bound in the wrappings
of the grave."

"No, no!" A bony Pharisee waved his bloodless hand protest-
ingly. "Say not so, Nicodemus! It's nigh blasphemy, if indeed it is
not!"

Caiaphas raised his palm to bring the assembly to more orderly procedure. "Rabbi Nicodemus protests, as we supposed he would. But with the exception of him, and perhaps Joseph of Arimathea—" the High Priest glanced at the man next to Nicodemus—"it is the will of the Council that——"

"I stand with Nicodemus," declared Joseph of Arimathea. "He has voiced my views."

Nicodemus said, "We two are not murderers, nor will we connive at murder."

"He's right. Our hands shall be clean. With Nicodemus I vote against the proposal."

Caiaphas smote the arm of his chair, sprang to his feet. His fierce eyes ran along the half circle of the Sanhedrin's membership. He shouted, "Who's afraid of this man's blood? He is an enemy of Israel. He jeopardizes the lives of our people. He will have the Roman armies down on us with fire and sword. I ask you: Is it not expedient that one man should die rather than a whole nation suffer?"

He paused. Solemn heads nodded assent. Nicodemus and Joseph the Arimathean sat silent and unmoving. Caiaphas, looking toward the two dissenters, doubled his hand into a fist. "The brothers fear to have this rebel's blood on their hands. Then let it be upon our heads!"

Fists went up around Jewry's highest court. "Yes, yes, upon our heads!"

Caiaphas reached backward for the arms of his chair and sat down. Only for a moment was he silent. "You have decreed that the blaspheming Jesus of Nazareth shall die. How shall his death be accomplished?"

A member at his left arose, straightened his attire, cleared his throat. "It must be recognized, most worthy High Priest, that this man has great influence with the people, superstitious and easily led as they are. Many have for him even a fanatical attachment; perhaps there are some who would die in his defense. Knowing this unfortunately to be true, we must take great pains to be wary in apprehending him. The mere fact that he's from Galilee warns us, for Galileans are quick to resist and eager to dispute any assertion of authority over them."

"The brother is wise in counsel," another said. "It would be prudent not to try to arrest him at the Temple, in the midst of his followers. That would provoke disorder and bring the soldiers from Antonia."

"Indeed, he's right," still another chimed in. "We must seize the Nazarene when he's alone, if that's possible, or with only the few coarse fellows of his inner group, who can have little cunning. Otherwise we raise an outcry against us."

"Brothers—" at the farther side of the chamber, a stout Sadducee had arisen—"we must proceed with great circumspection in this dangerous matter, as our fellow members have just cautioned. Galileans are a bold and violent people. They're in Jerusalem in strength, and their numbers will increase their reckless zeal. I think the best plan would be to wait until they've left before we lay hands on this Nazarene." Again heads wagged agreement as the Sanhedrinists solemnly looked from one to another.

A sleek Pharisee got to his feet. "But will not the carpenter himself have left? He has escaped us before on feast days. I'm for ending now the blasphemous preachments and magic workings of this enemy of our established religion. I'd rather see some risk taken of arousing the Galileans than let him get away again."

Now Nicodemus stood again. All faces turned to regard him. His face was grave, his bearing calm. "I cannot let the name of the rabbi of Nazareth be traduced and not lift my voice against it. He is a young man of perfect deportment. He has done no man ill. He'll rouse no Roman soldiers against us. This you know full well: He seeks to rule no temporal realm. His is a spiritual kingdom. He seeks to show forth the kingdom of the great God, Whom in perfect humility and understanding he calls his Father. He seeks only to be enthroned in the hearts of his brother men. This is plainly what he teaches. You cannot deny it."

A new murmuring began, but he refused to heed it. "I charge

that you, O High Priest, and you fellow members of the Great Sanhedrin understand this, but close your hearts and minds to it. I charge that you are interested rather in the maintenance of a cold, heartless, formal system of religion."

"Enough! We'll not hear him!" shouted the stout Sadducee, his heavy lips sagging, his eyes aflame with fury. "He must not so impugn our leaders! Nicodemus must be expelled."

This let loose a general storm of invective against Nicodemus. The High Priest, springing to his feet, began waving his hands in an attempt to restore decorum.

Before he could quiet them the door to the passageway opened, and a servant stepped unobtrusively inside. Seeing that he wished to speak with him Caiaphas signaled him to come forward.

He whispered in the High Priest's ear.

"Go fetch him." Caiaphas turned back to the members of the court, whose curiosity had now silenced them. "One has come who may have news for us of much interest and value." The door opened, and a man entered. Caiaphas bowed to him. "Welcome, Judas of Kiriot."

"Judas of Kiriot?" Incredulous, the stout Sadducee stared. "High Priest, isn't this redhead a follower of the Nazarene, a member of his company? What mischief is he planning here?"

"He *was* a follower of the Nazarene, carried the pouch for the company. That's true. But no longer, he says." Caiaphas looked questioningly at Judas as if for confirmation.

Judas nodded. "You have said it, O High Priest. I was deluded. But not any more."

Caiaphas explained. "This afternoon he came to me. He told me he had been disappointed in the Nazarene. For a long time he thought—God forgive him!—that this carpenter was the promised Messiah. But after months with him he came to the conclusion that Jesus was just another itinerant rabble-rouser, a menace to Israel. So he came to me to discuss means——"

"—whereby he might betray his master?" Nicodemus' eyes flashed scorn. "Judas, Judas, how could you? How could you?"

Caiaphas whirled on him. "Rather, Rabbi Nicodemus, whereby he might save his nation from the peril of following after this blaspheming magic worker. Wasn't that your motive, Judas?"

"You have said it, O High Priest."

Caiaphas' ascetic face relaxed into a smile. "That having been established, Judas, tell us now what word you fetch from Bethany, where the Nazarene and his company are stopping for the days of the feast."

"I've come, O High Priest, hoping that I might prevent further bloodshed and hurt of our land by the Roman despoilers. This would certainly be our lot should the rabbi of Nazareth attempt——"

"And you think——" Caiaphas' black eyes were bright with sudden intensity—"in the remaining days of the Passover he may seek to make himself Israel's king?"

"You've said it," Judas answered. "He rode into Jerusalem on a white ass the day after the Sabbath, you remember. He did not go on to the final attempt. But, if reports that have come to my ears be true, he'll soon make the real effort. Then it will have been carefully timed, and it will have great strength. As long as the pilgrims are in Jerusalem and Ophel's excitable thousands hang on his every word he'll have at his side a host of fanatical adherents willing to die for him." He paused. "Isn't that so, O High Priest?"

"Indeed," responded Caiaphas. "The man has a mob of followers of the type that dwell in Ophel—the coarse men of earth, the vulgar, the scorned, the wretched."

"This once you've spoken aright, High Priest," declared Rabbi Nicodemus, rising. "The Nazarene has a following among the poor and despised; they appreciate him and they love him. Now having heard you for once speak truth, I'll depart. I can't stay and listen to the words of a traitor, a man who'll sell his master and his own soul! How much are you paying him for this, Caiaphas? Thank God, his good father Simon in Kiriot can't hear him! I've had enough. In all the scrolls of Israel's history I've never read of such a meeting of our Sanhedrin. Never before has this body stooped so low."

A rising storm of outraged protest drowned his voice. For just a moment he surveyed them, a figure of nobility and elegance. Then, shrugging his shoulders in sorrow and futility, he started toward the door. Without saying a word Joseph of Arimathea arose and walked behind him.

At the door Nicodemus swung round. "Peace be with you," he said as the uproar quieted, "but not upon your undertaking. We leave the Great Sanhedrin and its honored guest, the betrayer who'd sell his master for a pittance!" He turned his back on them and strode through the doorway, Joseph of Arimathea at his heels.

As soon as the door had slammed behind them Caiaphas said, "Now we can get down to business. What do you suggest, Judas?"

"He must be taken in secret or his followers will start a riot. Then it must be made certain that he doesn't escape. Several times he has walked boldly through the midst of his enemies."

"That's true. What do you propose? Have you thought of a proper way?"

"I have a plan, High Priest. I don't think it will fail."

"What is it? Let's hear."

"I've learned that at sunset tomorrow Jesus will come into the city to eat the Passover with the twelve of his inner company. I'll be one of them. Of course I needn't tell you, High Priest, that there's some dispute this year about the proper day for the Passover's observance, since the customary day of the month falls on the Sabbath."

"Yes, there's argument whether the Passover or the Sabbath shall take precedence."

"The Nazarene wishes to offend no man, so he'll certainly eat the Passover at sunset tomorrow. He'll go to a certain house on Mount Zion." Judas hesitated.

"Go on," Caiaphas commanded.

"Afterward he'll return to Bethany, likely pausing awhile, as his custom is, to rest in the Garden of Gethsemane in solitude and darkness."

"Admirable! Proceed."

"If a company of Temple guardsmen and a detachment from a Roman century——"

One of the Pharisees jumped to his feet. "What would this Nazarene do then? Would he submit meekly? Would he offer to fight? Would he attempt some trick of magic?"

"The rabbi is unduly fearful," another said. "Surely he can't imagine that this rebel has supernatural powers."

"Let's not be critical one of another," Caiaphas cautioned. "Judas, do you think Jesus would yield to arrest, or would he offer resistance?"

"If he were taken in some solitary place, in the nighttime, with none except the others of the twelve to aid him, he'd do nothing. He's a man of peace. He abhors bloodshed. That's his great weakness. That's where he's vulnerable."

"What do you mean by 'the others of the twelve?' " a member asked. "Wouldn't you be there?"

Judas smiled. "I was thinking I'd lead the soldiers to the place where he and the eleven would be resting."

"Yes, that would be the wise course." Caiaphas nodded. "Then there could be no slip. This time he couldn't escape us."

The heavy Sadducee cleared his thick throat. "O worthy High Priest, I suggest that this body adjourn. We've agreed that the Nazarene deserves death, and this man seems to have been sent of God to effect it. I suggest that we leave to the High Priest the arrangement with Judas for the consummation of our purpose. That's wise, I think. The hour grows late, and we should be seeking our beds."

It was agreed. The Sanhedrin adjourned. For half an hour Judas remained with Caiaphas. When the business was settled he took his leave. Along the cobblestoned way from the palace he jingled the coins in the fold of his robe.

Thirty pieces of silver! he said to himself. The price of a slave accidentally killed. The price of blood. A token, Caiaphas said, to seal the bargain. Hah! Little he knows that with this paltry sum he has sealed his own fate. When the Master is king and I am his chancellor I'll fling these coins in Caiaphas' face and laugh.

Whistling and chuckling, he moved briskly along. Almost before he realized it he was near Shelomith's house. A light from one of the upper windows cast a checkered pattern on the pavement. A faint glow came from the corridor on which the street door opened.

Shelomith! My beloved! She has not gone to bed yet. I wonder ... Yes, yes! Of course. Why not? A great day is almost upon us, the day she and I have long waited for. Why not stop a few minutes and tell her, though it must be close to midnight?

Chapter 53 ✠

JUDAS had hardly gone when Caiaphas set out for the palace of the Herods.

"Tell the Procurator that the High Priest Joseph Caiaphas apologizes for coming at this late hour," he told the soldier at the door, "but say, even if he has gone to bed, that the High Priest must see him. Tell him I bear news of a plot against his life."

A moment later the soldier returned and showed him into the Procurator's small private sitting room. Outside in the corridor two other soldiers kept watch. His wife Claudia Procula, a wistful, slender woman whose dark-brown hair was tinged with gray, was with Pilate. She sat near a small charcoal brazier, a large square of needlework on her lap.

Pilate came forward, while Claudia bowed. "You bear news of a plot against the Empire, High Priest?"

"I do, Governor. I learned it only within the hour. That's why I came, even at such an unseemly time."

"Go right on. Don't hesitate to speak before my wife."

"Would you rather I withdraw and let you two talk alone?" Claudia dropped the needlework onto the small table beside her.

"No. No, indeed. Stay, Claudia. I want you to stay."

She settled back in her chair and picked up her sewing.

"Now," Pilate said, facing Caiaphas, "let me hear your story."

"The Great Sanhedrin was in session tonight, Governor, when a man was admitted. He was excited. He reported that a conspiracy had been formed, with a host of Galilean pilgrims at its core."

"The Galileans are always making trouble. Proceed, High Priest."

"Tomorrow or the next day they plan to revolt under the leadership of one Jesus of Nazareth, a despised village of their province."

"I'm acquainted with Nazareth."

"This Jesus schemes to be king of Israel. He's a spellbinder. It's astonishing how he can rouse the mob. And he does tricks of magic. A crazy tale went around only last week that he'd revived a man at Bethany from death."

"I heard that story. The servants were in a frenzy. But tell me, what force does this man hope to get together? How could they expect to stand against our centuries?"

"Of course they couldn't, Governor. But the Galileans are violently opposed to the Roman rule. They'd willingly risk their lives though they felt their revolt would fail. You remember how they fell on the ground at Caesarea and bared their necks to your soldiers' swords."

"Yes, yes. Say on."

"As I said, the Nazarene knows how to sway the people with his speaking, particularly the common men of the countryside and the poorer sections of the city. Of all Jews they're the ones who hate Rome most."

"But just how does he threaten my authority?"

"In this way, Governor. He's going to start an insurrection to make himself king. He won't succeed, of course. But his attempt will cause much blood to be shed—mostly blood of Jews, it's true, but also blood of Roman soldiers. There'll be disorder throughout the land. When noise of it comes to Prefect Sejanus and to the great stepfather of the Governor's noble wife——"

Pilate broke in: "The Procurator will attend to his duties. When and where can this man be seized?"

"I've made plans for his arrest. If you'll assign soldiers from one of your centuries to assist the Temple guard——"

"I'll order Centurion Longinus to attend to it. If the rebel seeks the injury of Rome I'll try him. But if it's some religious rivalry that's at the bottom of this——"

"Governor, there is a religious issue involved," the High Priest admitted. "The man's a rebel too against the God of Israel. He ascribes to himself the authority of the Most High. He makes himself even with God."

"I'm not interested in that. If that's what you have against him, try him yourself. I'll have nothing to do with it."

"But of course that's only one side of the matter, Governor. The other side I've already explained." The High Priest smiled, his teeth bared. "He would drive out the Romans, have you slain, take this palace for himself, be Israel's king. If the Emperor and his minister got wind of that, well . . . "

"I warn you I'll not be involved in religious quarreling among you Jews. I've enough to do without interfering in your religion, even if it weren't against our policy. High Priest, you'd better try him before your Sanhedrin, if his case deserves such a high tribunal—" his tone bore a trace of derision—"and I'll likely approve the judgment reached."

Caiaphas saw that the Procurator had become restive. He thanked him for the audience, bowed to Claudia and departed.

"A fawning Jew," Pilate's wife said. "I don't like his looks."

"Nor I. But I wonder about this Nazarene."

"The High Priest is envious. The Nazarene is a good man. I've heard much of him, and only good. The servants have brought tales of his miracles, and their stories disturb me strangely. He's devout, interested only in spreading the worship of his god. He has no notion of starting an insurrection."

"I don't know. But if he doesn't try it, some other damnable Jew will. I pray the gods to prevail on Sejanus to assign me to some other province. None can be so trying as this Palestine hole. No people can equal these Jews in utter contemptibility."

Claudia put aside her needlework, looked up at her husband. She seemed not to have been listening to him. "Have nothing to do with that just man," she said earnestly.

Chapter
54   ✠

"I KNOW it's late, my dear, but I just couldn't wait to tell you! It's all fixed now! Tomorrow . . . What's wrong, Shelomith? You look as though you'd——"

"Oh, Judas, why have you come here from—from there? I—I can't understand." He could not read her face. Worry, fear, pain? He had never seen her look that way before.

"Shelomith, what do you mean? What's troubling you?"

"It's just as though you'd come straight to me from a woman of the street. Though you were willing to betray him, how could you so dishonor me? Can I ever understand you, Judas? Can I ever fathom your mind . . . and your heart?"

"What do you mean—betray him, dishonor you?"

"Why appear so innocent, Judas? I've heard all about it. Rabbi Nicodemus came to see my father, right after he and Rabbi Joseph from Arimathea left the meeting of the Sanhedrin. He said he couldn't stay and hear the dastardly plotting against Jesus—your revealing how he could be set upon and dragged before the San-

hedrin to be condemned to death." Both sorrow and contempt were
in her eyes. "There's no need denying it."

"I don't deny going before the members of the Sanhedrin. But
I didn't betray the Master. Anything but that, Shelomith! I came
here to tell you about it." He shrugged, thrust out his hands. "But
you don't care to hear it. You choose to condemn me. But you don't
condemn Longinus. You betray your people when you see him." He
looked morosely at her.

Anger struggled in her voice. "Judas, why must you forever
bring up Longinus? Why are you jealous of him?"

"Didn't you refuse to see me, in order to see him?"

Her eyes were incredulous. She choked. But in a moment she was
icily calm. "Judas, do you have faith in anybody? You have none
in me. You scowl at me and scold me and charge me with foolish
things. You have no faith in your leader. You betray him for——"
Suddenly, her face pale, she held her hand before her eyes. "Oh,
Judas, it could not be that you took money!" She sank into a chair.

"No, your words are not true! I betrayed no one. I came here
happy, excited, eager to share my joy, my early triumph, with you,
and how am I welcomed? Didn't *you* begin to denounce *me* the minute you came into the room?" His lips curled. "And you haven't
denied that you refused to see me in order to be with the Roman."

Anger flowed over her. "I'm sick of this. I shouldn't honor
such a charge by denying it, but I do. I had no arrangement to see
Longinus. I didn't see him. But hereafter I shall, whenever I want
to." She threw her head back. "The night you spoke of I was with
Berenice, her father and mother, and her brother Paran, whom the
Rabbi Jesus healed. They had come to the Passover from Tiberias,
and they asked us—my parents and me—to dine at their inn. Now
I've told you, though you deserve no explanation."

"I beg your forgiveness, Shelomith," he said. "I was wrong.
But I bore the grudge because I love you."

"How can you love me and yet hate others so? How can love
and hate be compounded? Can you be faithful to me and betray
your master?"

"I tell you, Shelomith, I haven't betrayed the Master. Can't you understand? What I did tonight was just a step in the plan to make the Master king. This time we won't fail. He won't be able to get around it. He'll be put in a position where he'll have to make himself our ruler. He'll be simply forced to."

She shook her head sadly. "I don't like it, Judas. I've told you many a time you're in a desperate enterprise that will come to no good. You profess to believe in Jesus, but you have no faith. You should trust him to lead. You have no right to set his course."

"You're upset, Shelomith." He sought to soothe her. "Rabbi Nicodemus didn't understand. But he will—when we make him High Priest. He gave you a fright. Before you know it everything will be settled. We'll have our home and——"

"Yes, I am upset, and a great deal more than that. It was not just the rabbi's report that did it. It's your way, Judas, your utterly wrong way. Unless you go back to Uncle Joseph, throw his evil money at his feet and abandon this wretched scheming——" Her voice failed her. She seemed on the edge of an outburst of weeping. "Oh, Judas," she said after a moment, with a pleading urgency, "abandon this course before it's too late, forever too late."

"Shelomith, why can't you—?"

"Why can't *I* understand? It's *you* who can't—or won't." She had stood all she could. "It's your ears that are deaf to all reason, all pleading. You won't listen. You're bent on your way. All right, then follow it, Judas. When you've ruined your life and caused great misery, don't come sniveling back to me!" Her tongue became a whiplash. "Go then to your Roman wench! Can you understand *that!*"

The fire ran up his face into the flaming redness of his hair. "Yes, I understand it." He fought to keep his voice steady. "And I'll remember your words—when the king rules and I keep his treasury." He lifted his chin as he turned toward the doorway. "Now I'm going. And I won't come 'sniveling' back."

For a long breath she stood defiant. Then she ran into the corridor after him. "O Judas! O my poor Judas!"

But already the door to the street had closed behind him, and he was walking the rough way in the darkness.

Chapter 55 ✠

AT FIRST, as he stumbled down the cobblestones toward Ophel and the Dung Gate that would let him out on the Bethany road, his feelings were only of resentment and outrage. . . . She told me to get out. She dared me to go to the Roman woman.

. . . Maybe I shall. Cynara's in Jerusalem surely. At her brother's, not a mile away. Along Mount Zion to the bridge and across it to the Temple, and there's the Tower of Antonia. . . . He looked that way, but the darkness shut the tower out. . . . Why should Shelomith always be abusing Cynara? She's the sister of Longinus and for him Shelomith always has a good word. Maybe more than that. Shelomith wouldn't send the centurion off into the darkness. And Cynara will welcome me, will have endearing words for me and warm embraces. . . .

The vision of the night at Machaerus came haunting, enticing. As he walked his mood began to change. . . . Her words cut like a knife. But all the same she loves me. She was upset by what Nicodemus told her. She had a right to be. She didn't see through it, any more than Nicodemus. It *is* a bold scheme. Who but me would have conceived it? To dare propel the Master into the king-ship! No one else has a love for him that would venture so far.

As he pushed through the blackness the light of other days brought a warming glow into his perplexed soul. In the center of every vision was the Master. . . . The morning when he saw Jesus walking the highroad above the Jordan ford where the Prophet John was baptizing . . . The supper at Cana . . . Lepers stumbling and moaning their misery, and then suddenly healed and shouting

their joy . . . The darkness was aglow with Jesus' smile as he blessed
the people, healed them and gently set their feet on new and happy
paths. Above all the memories of the Master's works and deeds
he heard his voice, clear, beautiful, comforting, inspiring.

Judas could hear Jesus talking—to big-shouldered, shaggy Simon
Peter; to the excitable, intense Zebedees; to philosophical Nathanael bar Tolmai; to the others of the twelve. And to Judas of Kiriot.
Plainly now he saw the Master look at him and heard the Master
speak to him.

Suddenly the thought smote him: Am I trying to direct the hand
of God? Can Shelomith be right? Am I attempting to set my wisdom against the divine wisdom? No, O God, no! Deliver me from
that supreme effrontery!

He shuddered. What if the Master has another purpose, one I
can not envision? What if he actually meant a cross when he spoke
of being lifted up? O Lord, let not Thy Son become as poor Uncle
Bezek, a suffering sacrifice! Let me be the instrument to fulfill Thy
holy will.

The Master is so good, O God, he loves every soul—not just of
Thy chosen people, but every outcast gentile, every vile Roman—
that of his own he would never wield Thy sword of justice. Someone must guide him, direct him, push him into the full might of
Messiahship.

I am not afraid to be the one. I shall point him out, say the word.
He will have to act. We shall have a glorious king. He will thank
me and make me great. . . .

Judas had come near enough to Japheth's shop to see a light glowing inside. He hurried, knocked on the door. Shuffling steps
answered. "Who is it?" Japheth's gruff voice asked.

"Judas. Open, Japheth!"

The cobbler pulled back the bar, let him in. "I thought maybe
you were another customer with sandals to be mended. That's
why I'm up so late, Judas. The Passover season works me to death."

"Did you get word to Bar Abbas and the others?"

"Yes. They'll be in before the middle of the morning." In the thin light of the smoking lamp Judas saw his frown. "But I don't like it. They're going to get themselves snared by the Romans, and me with them."

"After tomorrow we won't be troubled with the Romans."

Japheth shook his head. "I don't know. I don't put much faith in you and Bar Abbas. It's my notion we'll have the Romans with us a long time."

"You'll see, cobbler." Judas reached for the door handle. "I've got to be getting on to Bethany. A long walk." He smiled. "Have faith, friend."

"Sometimes it's well to use caution, man of Kiriot." Japheth shuffled behind Judas to bar the door. "Oh, I was about to forget! There was a man here today with a message for you—from the Tower of Antonia."

"The Tower of Antonia! What man! Who from there could—?"

"He said he'd been out to Bethany. They told him you were spending most of your time in the city, and suggested he leave the message for you here."

"What did he want, Japheth?"

Japheth grinned. "He came from the woman of the corn-colored hair. She wishes you to visit her at the Tower. Said she'd arranged with the guards there to let you into her quarters. I asked the fellow, a Jew who's a servant of Centurion Longinus, if it was a trap. He swore it wasn't. Said the woman was bent on seeing you."

"Longinus' sister. You mean, the one—?"

"The Roman woman, yes, of course." Japheth's hand was on the bar. "Well, that's what he said, Judas. Do as you like about it. I'm not telling you what to do. But I believe—" his leer showed yellow teeth and sunken gums—"if I were a strapping young man like you I might just slip over there some night and pay her a visit."

He chuckled as Judas went out again into the night.

Judas started toward the Dung Gate. But halfway across the square he turned left, entered a narrow street up Mount Moriah.

He crossed the Temple region on the western side, a huge, looming shadow on his right hand, past the Gate of Asuppim.

In the thick gloom he approached the grim fortress of Antonia. By the flickering wall torches he could discern a guard at the entrance. Here and there a light streamed out through an upper window.

The guard had received instructions. He took Judas to Cynara's apartment.

When she came out from her room she was wearing a thin light-blue silken stola. It was bound beneath her breasts by a wide yellow girdle the color of her hair.

For a moment she stood in the doorway smiling but silent, her feet apart. The light from the bedroom lamp revealed every line of her lovely figure. Then, her head back slightly and her eyes half closed, she said, "I knew you'd come, Judas, though it takes courage to enter the quarters of Longinus. Have no fear; my brother will be gone all night. He's out keeping your Jews quiet and tractable. No one . . . nothing . . . to interfere . . . "

"I'm not afraid of your brother," he said evenly.

She straightened. "Oh, Judas, I didn't mean to offend you. I meant only that it was a brave thing to do." She smiled sweetly. "It flatters me all the more that you should be so eager to . . . to . . . "

"I got the message that you wished to see me. Why?"

"Why?" She leaned her head back and laughed. "Why be so naïf, Judas? You know perfectly well why. Did you think I wanted to eat the Passover supper with you?"

He paled. "You jest about our sacred customs. But that doesn't surprise me in a pagan."

Quick anger flushed her cheeks. "You may be joking, but I don't like it. You Jews believe you're better than we Romans. How absurd! We conquered your nation. We hold you under the authority of our legions. In all the world Rome is supreme."

He laughed in her face. "Today, yes. But tomorrow Rome will cry to Israel for mercy."

She stepped forward a pace. "You make me laugh, Judas. You'll never live to see the day when Israel triumphs over Rome! You—*you*—pretend to look down on me! Yes, I sent for you. And you know why. Don't try to tell me you didn't know what you came for."

"At Machaerus I was tempted. But I've sought forgiveness for that night's sin. . . ."

"Sin! Sin! Oh, you Jews! Always you ask for forgiveness for having sinned. If you break down and have a moment's pleasure it's sinning, and you must beg pardon of your Jewish god! Oh, you cold-blooded, hypocritical Jews!" She stamped her foot. "You'd lecture me on my paganism and your goodness, would you? I'll have none of it! And nothing of you! Get out!"

He stood his ground. "I didn't come here to go to bed with you. I thought you might possibly have some news for me. And I wanted to prove to myself that you have no power over me. I'm a follower of the Nazarene. Yes, and I'm betrothed to a daughter of Israel."

She slapped him. "Get back to your swarthy Jewess! See if you can take her from Longinus, drag her from his bed! Go! Get out before I call the guards!" She stepped back into the bedroom and slammed the door.

Chapter
56   ✠

DYSMAS was in the back room when Judas returned to Japheth's the next morning. The Judaean greeted the Galilean warmly. It was the first time they'd met in this room since Dysmas and Bar Abbas had, with Judas' aid, escaped from their Roman captors.

Soon others began coming in, each bearing a broken sandal or boots or some other article to be mended as though he were a customer. They kept the door between the two rooms ajar. After

a while Judas noticed through the slit that a man with a heavy
waterskin suspended from his shoulders by a huge strap was
giving Japheth instructions.

"It needs to be mended here," Judas heard the man say. He had
a big black patch over one eye. "I'm afraid it'll break and the skin
will fall to the cobblestones and burst. A small reinforcement, a
bit of good sewing . . ."

"When filled this skin must be quite a burden to carry, a cross
on the carrier's back." Japheth's eyes seemed merry.

"Yes, it's a burden to carry—a cross indeed. But one must be
content to carry whatever cross he's been given, eh, cobbler?"

"That's true," Judas heard Japheth reply. "Even if it's the cross
of slavery to the conquerors." He grinned. "They're waiting in the
back room, Bar Abbas, as you've guessed."

"It's a good disguise," Judas told him when Bar Abbas joined
them. "If we hadn't been expecting you we'd have thought you a
water carrier. Do you suppose anybody else knows? The square
in front of the Dung Gate was filled with Roman soldiers
patroling."

"I think not, Judas."

"If you can keep out of their net another day or two—until the
Master becomes king——"

"I'd gladly give my life to see him king," Bar Abbas said with
simple sincerity. "It's different since he restored Demas. I used
to scorn him, look on him as a man of womanish heart; now I
want to serve him, Judas. Like you, I want to bow down to him.
I want to be——"

He stopped. Through the street door a man was entering the
shop. He was a great, hulking fellow. His shadow carpeted the
floor as he waddled in.

"Shishak! Hail! I thought you'd perished in the dungeon."
Bar Abbas clapped a big hand on his beefy shoulder. "How'd
you get out, man? How'd you fly the Romans' coop?"

"The Romans freed me," Shishak said. "Couldn't afford to feed
me. I ate too much."

"Leave off the joking, Shishak. Why did they release you?"

"The Roman Flavius said it was ordered by Centurion Longinus. Custom of releasing one prisoner each Passover season."

"Then you just got free?"

"Yes, since the feast started."

Judas scowled. "It may be a trap, Bar Abbas. To catch you and Dysmas they may have baited a trap with this great tub of flesh."

"This time I didn't fall on your back, did I, Judas?"

"Be silent, Shishak! Judas may be right. Likely they're counting on you to lead them to me and Dysmas. Where have you been since you got out? Have you seen any friends? Did anyone say you'd find me at Japheth's?"

"I've seen only Chisleu. He said you were to meet with the man of Kiriot and others here at the cobbler's."

"O God in Israel! And you came here! The soldiers will have followed."

A sharp rap on the street door left no doubts.

"Open, cobbler! Quick, in the name of the Emperor!"

"Lord of heaven! Shishak, damn you to——"

"There's no time for that, Bar Abbas!" Judas said, closing the connecting door. "Pull out the chest! Into the tunnel, Bar Abbas! Dysmas! Fast!" The two disappeared into the subterranean passage. "Shishak, they saw you enter. Stay with me. Put the chest where it was."

They could hear Japheth slide back the bar. The sound of men shoving inside. The door between the two rooms was flung open. Two Roman soldiers entered. They glanced about the room. Then one of them stepped back to the doorway. "Centurion, he's not here."

"Where is he, cobbler?" Through the doorway Judas saw Longinus confront Japheth. "I warn you, no lies, no evading! Where's Bar Abbas?"

"I know no one here called Bar Abbas. Is he the one you asked about the last time, that Zealot bandit who robs—?"

With his open hand one of the Romans struck Japheth in the

face. "Didn't the centurion warn you not to lie to him? Now answer him, or you'll get more, and worse."

Japheth rubbed his reddening cheek.

"Cobbler, you'd do well to speak quickly and freely." Longinus glared. "We followed Bar Abbas' man, that fattened hog, to your door and saw him enter but a moment ago. Now he's gone. Where? The man he talked to at the bridge told him Bar Abbas would be here at a meeting of conspirators. We know all, cobbler. Now, where'd he go?"

The soldier who had struck Japheth moved menacingly in front of him.

"Centurion, he was here—and the big one. But they left—out through the back."

"We have men posted at the back door, you fool. They went out some other way. You aren't going to tell, eh?" The soldier drew back to strike. "No, Pluvius." Longinus folded his arms across his chest. "Cobbler, by Mercury, you're going to be surprised." He signaled. "Move the chest, men." Smiling, he turned to the stunned Japheth. "Clever, cobbler; simple but effective cover of the tunnel opening. We didn't find the hole the last time we looked. But we have ways of learning things."

Suddenly they heard voices in the tunnel. The next moment two Roman soldiers emerged. Behind them, dejected and sullen, his arms pinioned to his sides with leather thongs, walked Bar Abbas. After Bar Abbas came Dysmas. Other soldiers followed.

Longinus stood a moment regarding Bar Abbas. "Oho! So we meet again, you brave chief of Zealots who swoop down on unarmed caravans and grab coins from babies, women and old men? You killed Varro and other good Romans and would have slain me on the Jericho road that day if I hadn't been ready for you." Longinus walked up to Bar Abbas, looked him over coldly and then lashed the palm of his hand squarely across his mouth.

Surprised at the suddenness of the attack, Bar Abbas staggered, but quickly caught his balance. He stood steadfast before the Roman. Fire smoldered in his eyes.

"This time you'll not escape, Jew!" Longinus scowled. "Tomorrow you'll stand trial before the Procurator, and by the gods, I'll wager my head you go to the cross—you and these with you!" His eyes circled the room. "Manacle them! The cobbler, too. He's one of the chief conspirators. We'll wipe out this den." The soldiers sprang to carry out his orders.

Then he seemed for the first time to notice Judas.

"Hold! Don't touch this redhead. I—— Let him be. I know him. He's a friend of a friend of mine. But, by Jupiter, it was a poor time to fetch sandals to be mended, wasn't it?"

"It was indeed, Centurion." Immediately Judas hated himself for having said it.

Chapter 57 ✠

AS DARKNESS began to envelop the city they went through the Dung Gate and entered Ophel. With Jesus, the Zebedees and Simon bar Jonas leading the way they threaded the narrow streets, climbed Zion and came after a while to a house not far from Shelomith's.

Here the owner led them to an upper room, where they found the lamps lighted and a table spread for the feast. Couches were about the table.

On a low stand against the wall near the entrance stood a large earthen jar filled with water, and beside it lay a towel neatly folded. There was a basin close to the waterpot. Stools and a long wooden bench were alongside two walls.

The owner retired. Once more—for the last time, Jesus knew, and the realization tore his heart—he was alone with the twelve. Never again with them assembled together would he be privileged to teach them, to quiet their sudden fears, to console them and guide them to the Father's house. They were about to be leaderless and lost, fishermen in a rudderless ship beaten by storm-driven waves. Eleven Galileans and Judas of Kiriot—lonely, determined Judas, going his own way.

O Father—his thoughts were a prayer—it is not Thy will that my brother should accomplish great tragedy. Thou hast known, O Father, even from the beginning all things that have been and are to be, and I have known. Yet, O Father, it is not Thy will that any of Thy children should sin.

Sadly, for the awe of this solemn hour was heavy upon him, Jesus crossed to the couch at the head of the board and sat down. The others held back. They stood against the wall, or sat still on a stool or the wooden bench.

Even in this sublime moment, Jesus realized, they think of precedence; they bicker over high seats at this last table. O Father, forgive them, for they are but children! They sin and come short of their great promise. Have patience, O Father, and grant them time! In time they will be instruments in Thy hand. They will accomplish great things. Through distant years a mighty host will rise up and call them blessed, these eleven my brothers, Thy sons. . . . And Judas, who follows his own way, for whom there is now no turning back, on whom countless generations will pronounce anathema and whose very name will be a hissing, do Thou, O Father, forgive him, for he also is my brother and Thy son. Forgive him, O Father, forgive!

Jesus rose from the couch and walked over to the water jar. He laid aside his robe, took up the towel, unfolded it and wrapped it about his waist, tucked the corners into his loincloth. Then he poured water into the basin and carried it to the nearest of the twelve. He dropped to his knees and began to wash the tired and dusty feet of the astonished disciple.

Jesus moved from one to another. When at length he came to Simon bar Jonas the fisherman drew his feet back. "Master, I don't want you so to abase yourself as to wash my feet."

Looking up, Jesus smiled. "If you do not allow me to wash your feet, you have no part in the work that I do."

Quickly Simon lifted one foot into the basin. "Then, Master, wash not only my feet, but my hands, too, and my whole body."

It came Judas' turn. He was slumped down, his restless hand combing through his thick red hair. As Jesus went on his knees before him Judas said not a word. Tears fell on his wet feet before Jesus began to wipe them with the towel, but Judas gave no sign he knew it.

When he had finished washing and drying the feet of the twelve, the Master summoned them to the table. The younger of the Zebedees he placed on his right, and then, nodding to Judas of Kiriot, he stationed him at his left hand. So they reclined at the board.

"Do you understand what I have just done?" he asked them.

When none answered he said, "You call me Master and Lord, and you are right, for I am. And if I, your Master and Lord, wash your feet, if I enter on the task of the most lowly servant, then should you not be willing to wash one another's feet?

"I have done this as an example to you," he went on. "Faithfully I tell you that the servant is not greater than his master, nor should he refuse to do what his master does. And you, my brothers, should not hesitate to serve your brothers, for in so doing you serve the Father truly and in humility."

He closed his eyes, bowed his head above the board and said the blessing. As they ate, Jesus talked. Now, he told them, he would be going forth as a lamb to the slaughter ring beside the Great Altar in the Temple. Before another day's sun had set he would have become the paschal lamb for all mankind.

Familiar words, but never before so imminent. Familiar words and still unfathomed. They ate in silence, sorely disturbed. Then once more the Master, perceiving the heaviness of their hearts, assured them that when he was gone the Father would send them a Comforter, even His own Spirit, Who would remain always with them to strengthen them and give them peace.

Judas, sitting beside the Nazarene, listened closely. He sensed the Master's own depth of sorrow. He thought Jesus had the look

of a man going to his doom. For the first time Judas wondered if
this plan, too, might fail, if Jesus was destined never to become
Israel's king. Instantly Judas dismissed the thought from his
mind—but in this moment he could not keep from the reflection that,
whatever happened, he would not fail to profit. If the Master's
enemies should prevail, Caiaphas would not forget the man who had
delivered the trouble-making rabbi into his hands.

Out there in the darkness, he knew, across the Vale of Hinnom,
near the twisted tree, Temple guardsmen and hangers-on, with a
detachment of Roman soldiers, were assembling for their night's
duty. This afternoon he had gone from Japheth's shop to the
Temple to complete the arrangements. The arrest of Bar Abbas
and the other Zealot leaders had shown him there could be no
turning aside from his desperate gamble.

It is well I thought of that place, he told himself as he leaned
against the board. None will know. It's outside the city, beyond
Ophel's hordes, and the Master's circle will never suspect. They'll
have no chance to interfere. The course from the tree to Gethsemane
lies all the way outside Jerusalem's walls.

. . . An admirable arrangement I made with old Caiaphas. If I
can only find a plausible excuse to get away from here, I can guide
the guard to Gethsemane. It's well I went to Japheth's and saw my
friends led off in shackles and headed for the cross. I know now
that nothing can be expected from the Zealots. They're done for.
Only the Master can vanquish our enemies.

His thoughts were recalled to the upper room, for Jesus was
speaking.

"How I have looked forward with great desire to this hour when
I should eat this last supper with you." He handed the wine cup
to John. "Drink of it and pass it among you, for I declare to you
that I shall not drink again of the fruit of the vine until the kingdom of God shall come."

Exultation buoyed Judas. Jesus forecasts the kingdom will be
here before tomorrow's sun! The kingdom of God—no ethereal,
idealistic state of mind, no vain visioning of some future ecstatic

state, but the real land of God, Israel, revived under the leadership
of His Son to ancient power and glory!

Lifted out of melancholy, Jesus spoke again: "Be not sad and
heavy of heart, for, though I am leaving you, the Father will sustain you. Let not your hearts be troubled, for as you believe in God,
believe also in me. I tell you the truth. In my Father's house are
many chambers and room enough for all; I am going there to prepare for your coming. Believe me, for if this were not true I would
indeed have told you."

Thomas' brow was corded in puzzlement. "But, Master, if we
do not know where you're going, how can we know the way to
follow after you?"

Jesus looked along the board. "I am the way, Thomas, and the
truth, and the life. Nor is there any other way by which to approach the Father."

Glancing about him, now to the left and now to the right, Jesus
swept his long arm above the table. "How good it is to be here!
How I love you all, my brothers! How my heart is poured out to
you! And I know with what love you love me. And yet—" a tragedy
of spirit seemed to possess him; his bronzed face was tortured—
"there is one among you here who is about to betray me."

Unbelievable, terrible words. Appalled, mystified, horribly
frightened, eleven men stared at Jesus. Each thought, Can the
Master be speaking about *me?* Can *I* betray him whom I love better than life itself?

But the heart of Judas cried, He knows! He must be Messiah!
A mere man couldn't divine what I've so closely guarded. But why
should he say I'll *betray* him? That's not the word for it. Not at all.

His eyes were on the flat matzoth cakes before him, but he did
not see them. The fitful lamplight mottled his beard, glinted in his
perplexed eyes, cast black shadows on his fiery hair.

"Lord, is it I?" Simon bar Jonas leaned forward to look past the
younger Zebedees. Jesus did not reply. Along the table others
took up the query: "Lord, is it I? Lord, is it I?"

Their sunburned hands before them on the long board, they

stared at the Master, seeking yet dreading to hear his answer. Those hands . . . eager, frightened, trembling, brave, tired, strong hands . . . hands to remake a world. My own hands extended, Jesus fancied them, my two hands multiplied, extending and multiplying through the long ages.

"The hand of him who will betray me dipped with mine into the dish but a moment ago. His hand is even now on the board."

"O Master," asked Nathanael, "not I?"

"Nor I, Master?" Andrew's grizzled face was anguished.

Jesus answered nothing.

Simon bar Jonas nudged John. "Ask the Master who."

John whispered into Jesus' ear. When he answered it was in a voice so low that only John and Judas heard. "He it is to whom I first give a sop." Leaning forward, Jesus picked up a morsel of bread and dipped it into the charoseth, fruits, nuts and spices chopped and mixed together, sweet and richly fragrant.

He handed the sop to Judas. "O Master," said the man of Kiriot, as though he were utterly taken aback, "it can't be I?"

"You have said it," Jesus answered. He watched Judas swallow the sweet morsel. "And what you are to do, do quickly."

Without a word Judas got up, pushed back his chair and left the table.

When the door closed behind him one of the apostles whispered to another, "It must be that the Master has sent Judas on an errand."

"Yes. Maybe the wine runs low."

Chapter 58 ✠

WHEN Judas emerged from the house he found himself engulfed in darkness. A sinister cloud had swallowed the moon. All the city was lost under the warm pall of thickening night.

He felt his way along the terrace to the stone steps and with his hand sliding on the wall walked cautiously down to the cobblestones. He waited. Some wealthy man would come by, borne on a litter and with servants walking ahead and behind carrying lamps. He would join the procession and cross the darkened city.

But no one came along. So with his hand in front of him he started through a twisting alley that came out on the broader street of Benjamin's house. This would bear more traffic; on it he'd not be so likely to stumble in finding his way to the gate onto the Hebron road.

"What you are about to do, do quickly," the Master had said. What had he meant? Was he eager to take the throne? Anyhow, there's no turning back now, Judas told himself. Over there near the tree they'll be waiting. They've had time to assemble.

When he came even with Benjamin's house he saw torches and soldiers—Roman soldiers—and horses in front of it. The horses pawed impatiently, their iron shoes striking fire on the cobblestones.

Without pausing to consider, he went up to one of the legionaries. "Any trouble in that house, soldier?"

"What concern is it of yours, Jew?" the Roman replied insolently.

Another trooper intervened. "Why be so curt with the fellow, Quintus? There's nothing amiss in there, friend. The centurion said he was stopping to get information, but considering who's inside and the time he's taken, he must be after more than information." He winked. "They say the centurion's a great one for wenching."

"The centurion?"

"Yes, Jew, Centurion Longinus."

"I . . . I thank you. I was just wondering——"

Without looking back he hastened along the street. Beyond the range of the torches he was lost again in the gloom.

His passion loosed itself in the comfort of grandiloquence. Let her dally tonight with the damnable Roman! Let her look to the

Roman eagles! It's a false strength. Tomorrow the Roman centuries will be ropes of sand vainly trying to hold resurgent Israel
in check. Tomorrow she'll come back to *me*.

He went through the Eye of the Needle at the gate and took the
Hebron road. Beyond the Vale of Hinnom he turned left. As he
rounded an outthrust rocky cliff he saw in the dimness the tree
vaguely outlined, and back from the edge of the gorge torches
flickering, and men, their shapes revealed in the wavering torchlight.

Judas walked toward the group, picking his way, taking care to
keep away from the rim of the chasm. When he neared them he
was challenged by a man who seemed to materialize out of the
night.

"He's all right, Aaron," said another, whom Judas had not seen.
"You're the fellow from Kiriot, aren't you?"

"Yes. Will you take me to the captain of the guard?"

They led him past the tree. He saw Temple guardsmen and a
rabble of cattle drovers from the Temple, stonemasons' helpers,
petty thieves, procurers and other frequenters of Ophel dives.

"The Roman soldiers haven't come yet," the captain explained.
"We can't move till they do."

"That'll give the Nazarene and his followers time to get to
Gethsemane and be settled," Judas said. "Just now they're likely
no farther than the Dung Gate."

Before long the Romans arrived. Longinus seemed to take no
notice of Judas. The motley company, with the Judaean leading
them along the precarious way round the Vale of Hinnom, began
its circuit of Jerusalem's southern wall. When they came to the
road along the brook Kidron they took it northward.

Shortly they reached the gate into Gethsemane. There they
halted.

"I've heard a good deal about this rabbi from Galilee," the
guards' captain said to Judas. "Will he try some of his magic
on us?"

"He's a man of peace. He'll come meekly. There's no cause to

fear him." Judas added, "If you arrest him quickly there'll be no
trouble. His company will be about him. I'd better point him out
to you." He considered a moment. "This will be my signal: The
one I greet with a kiss will be the Nazarene."

As they walked toward the center of the garden, Judas wondered in an ecstasy of self-delusion how the Master would bring
about the discomfiture of his enemies when he saw he could not
evade them. By fire and earthquake? By legions of angels bearing swords of lightning?

A hundred feet ahead a group, evidently but a moment ago
aroused from sleep, were stumbling in retreat along the path.

"Followers of the Nazarene," Judas said. "They must have
been on guard near the gate. See how fearful they are?"

Their torches held high to show the way, the soldiers and the
Temple hirelings pushed forward. Presently they came to a clearing in which were an olive press and just beyond it gnarled olive
trees.

In the heart of the clearing, beside the olive press, stood the
Master in his white robe.

At his right was Simon bar Jonas, rubbing his eyes with thick
fingers.

Soon *I* shall stand on his right hand, Judas told himself.

A little way off, toward his left, were the Zebedees. Back
farther, as if they tried to evade the torchlight, were the others.
Judas caught a glimpse of Simon the Zealot, with eyes wild, peeping out from behind an olive tree.

Jesus stood silently regarding them as the torchbearers encircled
him and the eleven.

Judas walked up boldly and kissed the rabbi on the cheek. "O
Master," he whispered, "your hour has come. Take now the crown
of Israel!"

No one save Jesus heard him. Eyes of infinite sadness pierced
his soul. "Judas, my brother, would you betray me with a kiss?"

Judas slipped back into the ring of soldiers and Temple ruffians. He ventured a glance at Jesus. At that moment the Master

in firm voice seemed to address the whole throng circled about him: "Whom do you seek?"

The captain stepped forward a pace. "We're looking for one called Jesus of Nazareth."

"I am he."

The moon sailed suddenly free of the great cloud. The small open place, the olive press, the men crowded into the clearing, stood sharply revealed in the new light, but, clearest of all, the tall rabbi in the white robe of the Passover.

The throng, suddenly fearful, began to push away from him. When some in the rear stumbled and fell, others tripped over them. A panic came upon them. But the soldiers held their places.

Jesus, standing calm, his arms folded across his chest, spoke again: "Whom do you seek?"

Again the captain of the guard answered: "Jesus of Nazareth."

"I am he," the rabbi told him. "If you seek me, let my friends depart."

For another moment no one said a word or made a move. Then from the edge of the circle a man near Simon bar Jonas—one of the Temple guardsmen—stepped forward as if to lay hands on Jesus.

Simon whirled about. His sword flashed. The blade was aimed for the man's skull, but he dodged, and the weapon struck him on the right ear. Blood spurted, and the ear hung by a sliver.

Jesus said sharply, "Put your sword back into the sheath, Simon. Don't you know that he who takes up the sword will perish by it? The sword only begets the sword."

He turned to the wounded man, who had stepped back, blood streaming over his robe. The rabbi lifted the ear into place and held it there a moment, while all watched in amazement.

"Do you think that at this moment I could not pray the Father and He would send more than twelve legions of angels to stand at my side?" he asked them. "But then, how could the Scriptures be fulfilled? The cup that my Father has given me to drink, must I not drink it?"

Judas, in a curious fascination, kept his eye on the man whom Simon bar Jonas had wounded. The blood had ceased to flow. He saw the guardsman when he felt the ear gingerly and then pulled it. It stretched, but it held.

Now the rabbi spoke again, standing intrepidly in the glory of the moon before this mob that had come against him. "Why have you come forth in the nighttime, carrying swords and clubs, to seize me as though I were a thief? Didn't I sit daily in the Temple, where you were stationed, and teach? There you laid not a hand on me. Now you come stealthily during the hours of darkness." He seemed to grow taller and his eyes to take fire.

. . . Now, Now, O Lord! The healed ear, healed in an instant by a touch of his hand. The firm, courageous, commanding voice. The Messiah of God indeed. Now is the appointed time. O God, send down those twelve legions to smite right and left! Open the earth to swallow Thine enemies! Now! . . .

Nothing happened. Jesus had stopped speaking. The circle drew in a little nearer. Longinus took a small rope from a guardsman and knotted it quickly about the rabbi's wrists.

"The orders of the High Priest were that this man be brought before him," the centurion said. "Let's be off."

The eleven took to their heels. As Longinus started toward the gate with his prisoner, the moon was lost again in cloud.

But the cloud was not so black as the heart of Judas, stumbling along in the rear.

Chapter 59 ✠

As THEY came out of the gate on the way down the hill Judas tripped on the heel of a Roman soldier.

"Why such haste, Jew?" the sneering legionary asked. "In a great hurry to betray someone else?"

Judas answered nothing, slunk farther behind.

. . . But I have not betrayed Jesus. If I delivered him to his enemies, it was only because I thought he'd have to assert himself then and take the throne.

Take the throne? Where? How? There was no throne back there in the garden. Only an olive press. O God, in my distress I can't reason. The garden was no place, before a straggling mob and a few Roman soldiers. Ahead, in Jerusalem . . .

Judas' spirits rose. Tomorrow at the Temple in Israel's capital, before the host assembled for our great feast, the Master will become king of our land. Or he may choose to seat himself in the Procurator's chair on the Praetorium Pavement and there proclaim the end forever of Rome's tyranny.

Judas walked with renewed assurance behind the procession. . . . He is ahead, fettered and led by a Roman, and I stumble after, despised even by a pagan. But tomorrow will see the world a different place. All will be changed, in the twinkling of an eye. . . .

He kept well behind while the procession wove its way through sleeping Ophel, climbed Moriah, crossed the Tyropoeon bridge and pushed up Zion. At the palace of Caiaphas it stopped, but when a servant came out and spoke to the centurion it began to move again.

Judas shouldered nearer and ventured to ask a bystander why the Nazarene had not been taken into the High Priest's house.

"Caiaphas gave orders to take him to Annas, who'll examine him. After that he'll be returned here to stand trial before the Sanhedrin, which has been summoned. You know it wouldn't be lawful for the Sanhedrin to convene at this unseemly hour."

When they reached Annas' house the officers, several soldiers and their shackled prisoner were admitted. The others slipped through a gate into a courtyard. Judas pushed in with them.

Under ominous clouds the air grew chill. A servant fetched out a brazier of glowing charcoals and set it at the edge of the gallery. Everyone crowded around it. The torches made strange silhouettes dance grotesquely along the wall. Judas stayed back from the circle of light.

Several servant maids, awakened by the commotion, came out to exchange banter with the soldiers. They were astonished when they heard the rabbi of Galilee was being examined by Annas. One, a buxom, large-boned young woman bringing more charcoal, glared at the soldier who had told them.

"But what's he done?" Judas heard her say. "Who's he injured? Hasn't he healed sick people? Didn't he raise a Bethany man from the dead? We heard he did."

"Am I a Jew, wench? What do I know or care about the Galilean? All we have to do is take the Tower's orders. You'd better keep those big lips buttoned and those fat legs moving."

"That for you!" She snapped her fingers. "I wouldn't eat from your trough or sleep in your sty for a million sesterces!"

"By Jupiter, the wench has spirit!" The Roman laughed while his comrades guffawed. "I might come here again some night."

She turned her back on him. "Where are those men who were always with him?" she asked one of the guardsmen.

"They fled—away through the olives in Gethsemane like young harts."

"Strange they'd desert him at such a time." She stooped to drop charcoal on the brazier. "You'd think some would have followed——" She stopped. Judas saw her staring. "You over there—you're one of them, aren't you?"

The man she spoke to was Simon bar Jonas. The light from the torches fell full on his round face.

Simon shook his head. "No, you're wrong."

. . . Simon's afraid. Even bold Simon bar Jonas, impulsive, reckless Simon is afraid to admit he's one of us. . . . Judas slipped farther into the darkness.

The girl was not to be put off. She walked over to Simon, studied him. "This *is* the man I saw with the rabbi not long ago in the Court of the Gentiles. He's a Galilean. His speech—it's of Galilee. Can't you tell?"

A man near Simon bore down on him. "Does the maid speak the truth? Do you belong to the Galilean's party?"

"Man, I don't. The wench is mistaken."

She looked at him again. "I'm not." She walked into the house.

They waited wearily. Some lay on the flagstones, their robes pulled closely about them. Others stood with backs to the brazier, shifting their weight, turning now and again to rub their hands together above the glowing charcoal. But Judas kept undercover. He didn't want Simon bar Jonas to discover him.

When a soldier came outside from Annas' chamber one of his comrades asked, "How goes the hearing?"

"The old fox has been trying to question the Galilean about his teaching, but the man answered little. He said that after all the talk that's been made about him, everyone should understand what he's trying to teach."

"An insolent way to talk to a former High Priest," a guard commented.

"Yes, you Jews would think so," answered the Roman. "A Jew slapped the Galilean's face when he answered the old bag of bones that way."

"Isn't there anybody in there to take the prisoner's side?" the other soldier asked.

"None. Every single follower of his ran off."

"One's here. A servant maid a moment ago said she recognized him." The soldier pointed to Simon bar Jonas, who lay on his back in the shadows. "That man. But he denies it."

The soldier spoken to walked over and looked. "This fellow *is* of the Galilean's band. By the gods, he's the very one who cut off Malchus' ear. When Malchus comes out and spies him——"

Simon scrambled to his feet. "Soldier, I don't know what you're talking about. I never saw——"

"By all the gods on Olympus, you are the shaggy fellow who stood beside the Galilean in the olive grove. Yes, Jew, I know you."

"You're mistaken! I tell you I don't know that Galilean in there. I had nothing to do with him. I swear I don't know him! I swear——"

Just then, over the sleeping city from the Tower of Antonia,

shrill and harsh on the crisp air, came the blare of Roman bugles
blowing the second cockcrow.

In that same instant a door on the gallery opened and soldiers
and Temple guards came out. In their midst walked the Master,
his hands still fettered and a red smear across one cheek. As he
stepped from the gallery to the courtyard pavement Jesus saw
Simon bar Jonas. But he said not a word.

Judas slunk farther into the shadows.

"Where are they taking him?" he heard a serving maid ask.

"To the palace of High Priest Joseph Caiaphas," a guardsman
told her. "The Sanhedrin gathers there to sit in judgment on him."

Already the procession had started through the gate. The man
of Kiriot followed.

Chapter 60 ✠

JESUS stood silent, dignified, aloof before Caiaphas and the others
of the Sanhedrin hastily assembled in this dark hour before dawn.

. . . I must show to all men, now and through ages to come, that
I am the chosen of the Father; that love is light and strength and
eternal survival; that I am love personified, and that God, the
Great One, the Eternal, the Good, is love. . . .

Caiaphas had failed. Bitter, ranting, mad with hate and fear, he
had sought by hastily procured witnesses to condemn the rabbi of
Nazareth. But the witnesses had told conflicting stories. On the
evidence brought, the Sanhedrin's majority, though determined to
see Jesus condemned, could not justify a verdict of guilty.

Nicodemus and Joseph of Arimathea had nettled the High Priest
throughout the proceeding. When two new witnesses had testified
that one day they had heard the rabbi stand up in the Temple and
declare he would destroy that great edifice and in three days raise

up another not made with hands, Nicodemus had charged that the
High Priest was trying to give the words quite unintended meaning. Jesus, he had pointed out, had been speaking in spiritual
terms and, as was his custom, had used a dramatic metaphor to
emphasize a spiritual truth.

So the High Priest had failed utterly. Nicodemus was pressing
for Jesus' release. Under the law, Caiaphas realized, he must free
the accused unless he could promptly incriminate him.

So Jesus stood unperturbed, his manner that of judge rather
than judged.

Caiaphas sprang from his chair. "You have heard what these
witnesses have said. Can't you speak in your defense? Have you
nothing to say?" . . . If only I can make the fellow talk, say something! . . .

But Jesus remained silent. His fettered wrists crossed, he gazed
at the High Priest. He knew there was no need to speak; Caiaphas
was not interested in the truth. How could reason find hearing
in the cruel and narrow souls before him, hypocritical supporters
of a crafty hypocrite? Whatever he might say would be distorted.

The wily High Priest paced the chamber, back and forth.
Abruptly he whirled about, thrust his fist close to Jesus' face and
said hoarsely, "I adjure you, by the living God, are you the Messiah, the Son of God?"

All in the chamber held their breath.

The prisoner's eyes swept over the whole tribunal and finally
rested on Joseph Caiaphas. Now is the time, he thought. The
High Priest has at last given me the opportunity. He has centered
attention on the one issue. . . .

"You have said it," Jesus answered. "And one day you shall
see the Son of Man sitting on the right hand of power, and coming
in the clouds of heaven."

Caiaphas wheeled to face the Sanhedrinists. "What further
proof do you want?" he shouted. "You've heard his words. Can
you have any doubt now?"

He caught the edge of his resplendent robe in his two hands
and with a jerk tore a long rent. Along the semicircle of seats
others tore their robes. But not Nicodemus or Joseph of Arimathea.

The High Priest's little black eyes glistened like a serpent's.
"You have heard his blasphemy. What is your judgment upon
him?"

"Death!" one member shouted. A chorus took up the cry. "He's
worthy of death! He has blasphemed the Holy Name! He would
make himself equal with God! Death to the blasphemer! Death!
Death!"

They began to rise from their seats, their rent robes hanging
askew. Many walked from the chamber, though a number of the
more venomous remained. Of these some pushed forward the
better to see the prisoner, still majestically detached.

One of those who had brought him before the High Priest, a
Temple loiterer, walked up to Jesus and spat in his face.

"By the God of Israel," he said, "you won't act so almighty
when they start nailing you to the cross!" Laughingly brazenly, he
saw his spittle crease past the corner of Jesus' nose to cross the
closed lips and drop into the stubble of the beard. In Jesus' eyes
was a look he had never seen in any man's. Horrified at himself,
he ran from the room.

Chapter 61 ✝

PILATE's round face, red and glowering, betrayed his irritation.
"By great Jupiter, why must I spend my life among these miserable
Jews! Husband of the Emperor's stepdaughter and yet consigned
to live my days in this hellhole! A little more of this and I'll order
the army to wipe out half Jerusalem if it costs my head!"

"What's the trouble now?" Claudia, sitting up from her pillow, dropped her long legs from beneath the covers and searched with her feet for her sandals.

"I thought I was the Procurator." Pilate glared at his wife. "I must be wrong. I'm always at the fetch and call of the Jews and their damned High Priest. He must be the Governor, not I."

"Why all the temper? What new difficulty plagues you?"

He sat down heavily beside her. "Oh, nothing, I suppose—in itself. I'm just exasperated. It's not so much the trial of this Galilean magician, but Caiaphas always telling me in his damnably clever way what I should do, and when. I'm tired of his hectoring. You'd think I was only——"

"What's this about trying the rabbi of Nazareth?"

"Their high court met this morning before dawn—they've just finished the session, I understand—and found him guilty."

"Guilty of what?"

"Oh, he broke some of their silly religious laws, I suppose. At any rate, they gave him the death penalty, and they want me to confirm their finding by sentencing him to the cross. Claudia, they not only tell me what judgment I must render, but they make me get up at this unearthly hour to hold the trial. They want the fellow condemned and nailed to the cross and dead before sunset, because it's against their foolish laws to have a man hanging on the cross on their holy day! By Jupiter, Claudia, these Jews test a man's patience past endurance. I wouldn't offend them, for it might make Sejanus froth at the mouth. Word might get to your dear stepfather that another tumult——"

Claudia's suddenly stricken look stopped him.

"What's . . . what's disturbing you, my dear? I meant no disrespect to the Emperor."

"The cross!" She held her hand in front of her pale face, palm outward. "Oh, no! Not that! Not the cross!" She dropped her hand and showed her anguished eyes. "I say again: Have nothing to do with this just, this holy man. I dreamed last night a terrible

dream about him—and you. Your hands were red with his blood.
It must not come true! Oh, I beg you not to stain your hands with
the blood of Jesus!"

Chapter
62 | ✠

AFTER the trial before Caiaphas they brought Jesus out and placed
him at the center of a company of guards. They started north.

They're taking the Master to the Praetorium, Judas said to himself as the procession moved off; I must follow so I may stand at
his right hand when he smites his enemies. Judas took care not to
get too near the marchers.

Crouched in the shadows across from the entrance to Caiaphas'
palace, he had waited impatiently for Jesus to act. Would the
great palace be suddenly thrown to the ground, its stones crashing
and rolling?

But when not a stone, not a tile had been disturbed, he had
chided himself for being unrealistic. No triumph for Jesus in
overwhelming Caiaphas. The High Priest is his foe, but the victory must be won over the chief power, the greatest enemy. That's
Rome. Brought at last face to face with Rome, he'll assert himself.

When Judas reached the square in front of the Palace of the
Herods the Master had disappeared within. A throng was gathering. In it he recognized several of those who had tried most per-
sistently to entrap Jesus. Servants were bringing a litter. When
they stopped on the Pavement before the Praetorium the curtains
parted and the High Priest emerged. Caiaphas smoothed his robe,
tightened his sash.

A man near Judas asked, "Is the High Priest so bent on killing
the Galilean he'll defile himself by going inside?"

Judas shrugged. "Strange if he'd enter a pagan's house."

"Yes, with all these eyes watching. It's whispered he goes there at night when no Jewish eyes see."

A sudden hush fell over the growing crowd. Pontius Pilate stood on the Pavement. "What charge do you bring against this man? High Priest, what's the accusation?"

Caiaphas stepped forward. "O Governor, if he were not a malefactor we would not have brought him to you."

"Very well then. Take him yourselves, try him and pronounce judgment."

Judas' neighbor nudged him. "A smart answer to insolence."

"But, Governor, you know under the rule of Rome we haven't the right to send any culprit to his death, however outrageous his crime. The Great Sanhedrin has found he merits the death penalty. We bring him to you to ratify our verdict and sentence him."

"Well, what is his crime?"

"We've found him perverting the people. He charges them not to give their taxes to the Procurator's collectors, saying that he himself and not Rome should be the authority in Israel."

"So you charge?" Pilate turned and went inside.

Judas held his breath. . . . Now, O Lord of Hosts, let the Master step out to the Pavement, and his reign begin!

But no thunder reverberated, no fires flashed. The morning sun rose higher and the air stilled to a thickening closeness.

After a little while the Procurator came again from the judgment hall. "I find no fault with this man. Rome is not concerned with your religious feuds and squabbles. I shall release him."

"No, Governor, no!" Caiaphas shouted. "The man is dangerous. He's a threat to Rome. You can't ignore him!" He appealed to the rabble he had hired, saying "Isn't that true, men of Jerusalem?"

"Indeed! Indeed! He'd overthrow the government! He'd drive out the Romans!"

"You hear, Governor. They speak the truth. This man incites to violence. He's a rebel against all authority, religious and civil.

Beginning in his native Galilee, he's gone all up and down the land inciting the people."

Pilate pounced on this. "You say he's from Galilee?"

The High Priest replied, "One of the most turbulent of Galileans."

"Very well. Then he's Herod's subject." Pilate spoke to the guards inside the judgment hall: "Take the prisoner across the square to King Herod at the Palace of the Hasmoneans. The Procurator recognizes Herod's right to try him. Tell him this man's the king of the Jews. Go."

Turning his back on the fierce scowling of the High Priest and the mounting clamor, Pilate strode inside.

Now Judas' one idea was escape from there. He fought to keep his feet from breaking into a run. That would draw attention to him, but panic was about to overwhelm him.

. . . I must get away. Somewhere. Where, God? O Master, it would have been so easy for you! Who could stand against you? Could Pilate raise Lazarus, Demas, Jairus' daughter? Could Tiberius or Sejanus still the tempest, feed the multitude?

He got beyond the bend in the narrow street that led to Ophel. Some of the Zealots who were still free might have gathered in the square near the Dung Gate. . . . My hope is almost gone. All seems over. But maybe when the Master faces Herod he'll raise his omnipotent hand.

He ran blindly over the rough cobbles. Terror drove him down Mount Zion, down Moriah, down, down.

Chapter
63   ✛

JUDAS knocked on Japheth's door. The cobbler's wife might be inside. She might have news of the imprisoned Zealots.

"No use belaboring the door," a scurvy loiterer called out from across the alley. "Roman soldiers came yesterday and carried Japheth and Bar Abbas and some others to Antonia."

"Ophel seems deserted. Where's everybody?"

"Gone to the trial of the rabbi of Galilee. Should have gone myself, I reckon, seeing the High Priest was offering good coin to witness against the Galilean." He looked intently at Judas. "God protect us, aren't you one of the rabbi's men?"

"Me? I came here to get my sandals mended."

"What sandals? Those on your feet look good."

"I was to fetch others if he could mend them today." Judas started to leave.

The Ophel resident reached under his headcloth to scratch his pate. "Strange. I could've sworn I'd seen you with the rabbi."

Judas hurried across the quiet square. He saw few people—none he knew. Where to now? Bethany? O my God, no!

He climbed the hill to the Garden of Gethsemane. It was cool there. Birds sang in the shade of gnarled olives. As he reached the opening where the olive press stood a snake slithered across the path, sunlight dancing along its mottled skin.

At the farther edge of the cleared space lay a crumpled robe. Someone flying from the soldiers last night must have dropped it. . . . Last night—O God, have mercy! . . . Judas sank wearily onto a tree trunk. . . . If I could but recall the fled hours! If only I had remained with them in the upper room! The night before I had almost abandoned my plan. Through the weeks and months, though I hardly knew it, there were moments when I wavered. . . .

Again visions crowded upon him. That day long ago—not long as time is reckoned, but long in the changes it had worked—when he first saw the Master on the road above the ford. The days since, pushing one on the other, when he stood near the Master as he prayed and taught and healed. . . . Yet I saw not and heard not, he reproached himself. I would not heed. I was bent on my own way. But I meant no evil, O God, Thou knowest. I meant only to hasten his day of salvation.

His day! Judas still could not think of the day of freedom without hope reviving. All was not yet lost. He clung to his hope. He must keep trying to do what he was contrite for having attempted. He might praise the Sun of Righteousness and Peace, but he must do his utmost to make him the avenging Lord of Hosts.

He sprang to his feet and walked fast to the garden gate. In the old Palace of the Hasmoneans Jesus might now be sitting on the throne the Tetrarch had usurped, with Herod cowering before him! . . . That would be sweet vengeance.

He hurried back into the city, stopped when he saw a crowd had assembled in the Ophel square. Men came from their shops. A water carrier, his half-filled skin slapping against his hips, scurried over the cobblestones. Grimy children, their eyes aged and insolent, and mangy dogs with ribs thrusting through their hides poked about the edges of the circle.

Ophel's come to life again. Many must have returned from the Praetorium, Judas told himself. He slipped unobtrusively through the mass of people milling about a man who seemed greatly agitated. Judas was unable to hear what he was saying because everyone else seemed to be jabbering too and gesticulating excitedly. ". . . to the cross instead of him. But the High Priest was bent on having me released and him crucified . . ." He caught that much. Then he saw the big man as he turned round, his hairy arm upraised.

"Bar Abbas! God in Israel, man! How'd you—?"

"Judas!"

The man of Kiriot broke through the dense rim of people to reach the Zealot. "Tell me, Bar Abbas, has he proclaimed the new day? Did his word bring you out of the dungeon? Speak, man! Has the hour come?" His eyes blazed, his whole frame trembled. He seized the burly shoulder, held it fast.

Bar Abbas' eyes were on the cobblestones. He lifted them sadly. "Your plan has failed, Judas. I'm amazed you didn't know. When I was released I rushed here hoping I might raise a mob, charge the soldiers, steal him away." He shook his head. "Vain wish. No chance. I'd gladly change places with him, but they wouldn't have that. They want only *his* blood."

Judas' face paled. "Then Herod——"

"Herod sent him back to Pilate. It was Pilate who did it—pushed by that Caiaphas, son of hell! Caiaphas demanded that Pilate release me, and he did. Dysmas and Gesmas he ordered scourged along with the Nazarene. The last I saw of them they were dragging their crosses toward the Place of the Skull a little way ahead of him."

"Him? The Master?" Judas felt an intolerable weight.

Bar Abbas stared at him. "They say you delivered him to the authorities. Part of your scheme, I suppose. Strange you don't know what all Jerusalem knows—that Pilate ordered him to the cross."

"The Master—to the cross?"

Grief veiled Bar Abbas' eyes. "Yes, by now they've likely nailed him on it."

"O no! God above, no!"

Judas backed through the surging circle of the curious and the uncaring. He broke free, dashed across the square, panted up Mount Moriah. . . . My poor Master! I did not know. I did not mean . . . O Lord, have mercy on me!

Chapter
64   ✠

In Ophel rumor flew like chaff from the thresher's floor in a strong wind.

"He's already stretched on the cross," a shopkeeper on Mount Moriah was telling his neighbor, a tentmaker. He wagged a dirty finger with a broken nail before his neighbor's nose. "But, I tell you, he's only biding his time. I've heard a man named Judas say so. When he gives the sign the sky will split open. Angels will come pouring out. He'll command them. They'll smite the Romans hip and thigh. The heathen will rage in vain. It's in the holy scrolls."

On Mount Zion too the rumòr spread, though in rich and powerful homes it did not provoke the wrathful consternation it aroused among the poor and scorned.

Shelomith heard it from Hagar, who had it from a servant of the High Priest. She was terrified. Judas had betrayed his leader! Nicodemus was right. He had sold Jesus out. She went into her chamber and flung herself sobbing on her bed. . . . He didn't mean to do it. No! Never! He never thought Jesus would let himself be killed. He thought Jesus would—— He had planned—O God, that damnable plan! I warned him, but he would not listen. He wouldn't hear me.

Where can Judas be now? She'd had no word since the night he'd stopped in on the way from the Sanhedrin's session. He'd come excited, confident; she'd sent him away angry and perhaps shaken. Now he must be mad with dismay and anguish. His master had been raised aloft indeed, but pinioned to a cross. . . . Can Judas be over there on that frightful hill?

Sometimes from her rooftop she had caught glimpses of crosses on the evil Mount of the Skull, and always she had run from the roof in horror. . . . Are the twelve with the Nazarene, watching him, fearful and helpless, as death comes in slow torture?

With fresh alarm she thought of Judas' hatred of the Romans. He might strike one of them; in a burst of fury he might lose all control. There at the foot of the cross and surrounded by legionaries he might incite to rebellion. . . . Where can Judas be? Why was Longinus so secretive last night when he asked me how to find the twisted tree beyond Hinnom? Why did he have soldiers with him? . . . Then she saw why. They had told Hagar the Nazarene was arrested by soldiers in the Garden of Gethsemane. Last night Longinus had been on his way to seize Jesus. Judas was involved. Only from him could Longinus have heard of the tree. The tree was the rendezvous.

. . . But where is Judas now? On this bitter day, when he must

be drinking his rueful cup to the dregs, where would he go? Has
he fled? Has he left Jesus to endure his fate friendless and
alone? . . .

She arose from her bed, washed her tearful face in a bowl of
cool water. . . . I must go search for him. . . . She called a manservant. "Abiathar, I must go to the Place of the Skull. I must try
to find Judas. He needs me." When she saw he was about to protest, she was not surprised, "Yes, I know our customs forbid.
Nevertheless I'm going. He's in sore trouble. I'll get ready at
once, and you'll go with me."

Chapter
65 | ✚

RUNNING, walking, running again, his mouth open, his tortured
lungs heaving, Judas came to the foot of the Place of the Skull.

The multitude was at the summit. He could see Roman soldiers
in their bright uniforms now dulled by treading through the city's
filth out to this loathsome hill. About them swirled the rabble—
jeering youth and heartless age—pushing and shoving to see the
soldiers at their work. Judas could hear the dull blows of hammers.

The noise of hammering ceased. He struggled up the steepening
rise. In vain he tried to close his ears to the raucous laughter, the
coarse banter, all the pitiless mob sounds. In vain he held his head
from looking.

Above the surge of the throng two crosses raised groaning bur-
dens. He lowered his eyes. But a compelling power forced him to
look again toward the top of the hellish hill. He stopped, flattened
the palm of his hand against his pumping heart, strove to focus his
weary eyes on the crosses.

Dysmas. Gesmas. . . . Have pity, Lord! . . .

He bent his face toward the loose pebbles of the steep way and stumbled forward. Dysmas and Gesmas were to have been leaders under Bar Abbas in the war for freedom. Alas, now——

Bar Abbas is loosed to fight the Romans. But where is the Master? They said he was being led to the Place of the Skull.

Once more the heavy blows of hammers. No sound except that thudding, rhythmic, sickening beat.

Judas pushed up the frightful ascent. . . . I can't look. I can't go on. I must turn and rush down. . . .

But he climbed on. For a second time the hammers ceased their pounding. A chorus, savage, beastly, the snarling rage of the jungle, the mob cry of heartless humanity, rose above the mount of horror.

Judas looked. He ran. . . . I must see. I dare not, but I must. . . .

He saw a heavy beam, with a crosspiece fastened near the top, sweep upward. Stretched on it was a man, naked save for a loincloth. The man lay still, unprotesting, silent with the now hushed mob about him. The beam came upright, wavered and twisted an instant, and then dropped, with a sickening thump, into the hole.

As the cross fell into place the man's body swung forward, the arms jerked straight and tense, the fingers of each hand stiffened outward from the iron spike through the palm. The short block protruding from between the loins kept the full weight from the tortured palms; the spikes held their burden.

At the top of the beam was nailed a small board to which the accusation was affixed. Judas could read the legend, for the lettering was large:

THE KING OF THE JEWS

On the head of the crucified was a crude crown fashioned of a common shrub, deeply green and having small thornlike spines. Blood, dried and brown, had run down across his forehead to his drawn and haggard cheeks. His whole body, strangely pallid, was a crisscross of cuts and welts and purpling bruises.

. . . I can't look longer. Master, my Master, I have sinned the unpardonable sin. . . .

But he looked yet once again. Jesus opened his eyes, and Judas fancied the Master saw him.

Jesus smiled.

Down the steep way Judas fled. The small pebbles rolled under his sandals. He stumbled. Once he fell to his knees. He got to his feet and ran on, crying out his anguish. He clamped his eyelids tight to shut out the vision, but ever as he fled from the Place of the Skull he saw looking full upon him the Master's tortured, smiling eyes.

Chapter 66 ✠

CRYING to himself as one possessed of devils, Judas fled along the beaten road and came at last into the city.

Aimlessly he walked and ran, knowing not where he went, having no place to go, his thoughts endlessly turning on themselves. . . . No, he was not the Messiah. I must believe it. He was only a man. Only a man with a cunning to work wonders. I've been following a false leader, another false leader of Israel. How many we've had through the long years! A handsome, strong, winning young man. I loved him, but he was not that one for whom we've waited. And yet——

He wandered through the tortuous streets. . . . Where can I go? To Ophel? Who'd be there? Who'd listen? To Shelomith? I must pull myself together first. She might not be home anyway.

As he walked among the Passover throngs, alone and lost, tor-

mented with thinking and visions he could not put away, he began to
notice that the sun's light was failing. . . . The heat is oppressive,
though it's early spring. The air is a damp weight. A cloud is
over the sun. Or have my eyes lost their keenness? Am I going
blind? Through all my frightful days shall I see only the hated
hill? . . .

Exhausted, he sat down in a deserted doorway. But only for a
moment. He was up again, to blunder through the thickening air,
which had settled with a pale greenish eeriness over houses, streets
and pilgrims. The world had suddenly grown unfamiliar.

. . . Is a plague sent upon me? What I did I did for my people.
Yes, and for *him*. Not just for the good feel of money between my
fingers. Not just for thirty pieces of silver . . .

Out on the bridge above the Tyropoeon he heard the coins jangle
as he walked—the coins within the pouch hidden in the fold of his
disheveled robe.

. . . I'll fling them over the railing into the valley. I'll never
hear the sound of them again, or feel the touch of them in my
palm. . . .

He pulled out the pouch, fumbled at the leather thong that closed
its mouth, reached in with trembling fingers. . . . I'll rid myself
forever of these symbols. Caiaphas said they'd be symbols. Symbols
of what? Of guilt? My guilt? . . .

Judas put the pouch back in its place. . . . I'll take the coins to
Caiaphas, throw them in his face, tell him they're symbols of his
guilt, not mine; I unwittingly betrayed an innocent, helpless man,
didn't know what I was doing. . . .

He dodged as best he could through the pilgrims who streamed
over the bridge toward the Temple or away from it. They were
pushing, shoving, jostling, laughing. Here and there one of them
looked uneasily at the sky now fast darkening though it was hardly
midafternoon.

He gained the end of the bridge, darted through the Gate Shalleketh, crossed between the rows of tall Corinthian columns and
squirmed through the crowd in the Court of the Gentiles.

Chapter 67 | ✠

. . . For this I was born of Mary. O Father, protect her now, comfort her! This is why I was sent into the world, to be lifted up before the world. Soon now, O Father, the Sacrifice for all men of all ages will have been offered. Accept it, O Father, of Thy Son! . . .

Jesus felt the muscles in his right leg quiver. He had felt the same tremors many times: as a child after a long summer's afternoon swimming, as a man walking the hills and hollows of Galilee. Often they followed strenuous exercise. Today he had struggled under the heavy cross until he had fallen and black Simon of Cyrene had been pressed to bear it the rest of the way.

Cramp gripped the muscles, and they bulged into a knot hard as stone. Sweat burst from his forehead. In other days he had known what to do when his leg cramped. Many a night after a hard day's journeying he had wakened suddenly with the pain and pummeled his calf until he had beaten the rigidity away. But now spikes held his hands fast to the beam; another spike transfixed his crossed feet. He held under the torture of the cramp, and the muscles relaxed. His head fell forward, and he was quiet.

He heard the jeers of the throng. He strained his filmed eyes, tried to make out what they were crying. . . . The same tools of the High Priest, the same Pharisees and Sadducees and scribes who were always trying to snare me! But forgive them, Father. They think they're men of wisdom, but they're only foolish children; they know the teachings of the scrolls but not the lessons of the heart. . . .

"He saved others, but himself he cannot save!" He heard a Pharisee's thin, high voice and the laughter that ensued. "Yes, if he be the Messiah let him come down from the cross and we'll follow him! Let him work a wonder to loose his hands and feet from the nails!"

He heard all the scoffing, all the cruel jesting. "Come on down, Nazarene! You're a carpenter, aren't you? Pull out the nails and come down."

. . . O God, hold it not against them! They are Thy children.

Another man began to speak, a man uplifted. His voice came from the cross to the left. Jesus twisted his heavy head to see him. The man was adjuring him. "Yes, you of Nazareth!" The voice had the shrill born of torture. "You, Jesus, if you're the Messiah, save yourself, and us! Do you hear me, you there? Get down, if you be the Son of God, and then release us!" He burst into ghastly laughter.

"Silence, Gesmas! Hold your peace!" Jesus painfully turned his head to the right, for this command came from the other cross. It was Dysmas. "Don't you know you're speaking to the Son of the living God? Keep silent, if you have no other words to utter!" He panted, gathered breath. Then he said in a lower tone, "Jesus, I beg your forgiveness. Not until now have I known. O Jesus, Son of God, have mercy on me!"

A great elation lifted Jesus. His spirit soared high and free. The nails, the cramp, the searing torture vanished. . . . Father, I thank Thee. Thou art good. Dysmas, my childhood playmate, now my faithful friend on the cross . . .

Tears streamed from his eyes, clear and bright with triumph, tears of joy. His voice was vibrant. "This day, my brother, even before the sun has set, you will be with me in Paradise!"

Exhausted by the surge of emotion, he began to fall into unconsciousness. His head dropped forward to rest on his heaving chest.

Chapter 68 ✠

HALFWAY up the Skull Shelomith stopped. "I dare not go farther," she said to the manservant. "Go, see if you can find Judas. If you can't, try to discover from the soldiers where the Centurion Longinus is."

She sank down on a smooth stone beside the path.

After a while the servant returned. Longinus was with him.

"Centurion, I didn't think you'd be here. I was looking for Judas." She paled. "I—— Oh, surely you haven't been in charge." She put her palm to her mouth. Amazement, pain were in her eyes, her voice.

"Yes, I was in charge . . . up there," he answered. "Not because I relish it. Pilate ordered me. I hate it."

She looked away, out toward the city, and for a moment said nothing more. Then she turned again to face him. "I'm afraid, Longinus, neither you nor Judas will ever outlive the shame of this monstrous murder. You've heard that Judas was responsible for the Galilean's arrest? You heard he sold him to the High Priest?"

Longinus did not answer.

"You needn't be afraid to speak, Centurion. I've known it— since it happened."

"Yes, I heard that he betrayed his master for thirty pieces of silver. Last night, in the Garden of Gethsemane, he pointed him out."

"Then you were to meet him last night? That's why you stopped at my house—to locate the meeting place already appointed?"

"Yes."

She burst into weeping. "Don't think too hard of him, Centurion. Judas is not despicable. He thought he was doing his duty—as you thought you were when you . . . you obeyed orders. Judas is ambitious, but not just for money. He was trying to carry out a plan which has been his very life these last months. He had complete faith in Jesus' supernatural power. He thought he could impel Jesus to exert that power to drive you Romans from the land."

"I've known for many months that he hated us, Shelomith."

"I warned Judas, but he wouldn't listen. His plan failed because it was counter to Jesus' will. If Jesus had willed to be king, I firmly believe——" She stopped.

"Shelomith, you may be right. I have seen many men die, men famed for bravery and endurance, Stoics, gladiators, soldiers in battle. But never have I seen a man go to his death like this man. He may well be a god. He comports himself like one."

"Is he . . . dead?"

"If not, almost. All three must die by sunset, if their legs have to be broken. The Jewish Sabbath, you know."

"Yes." She fell to weeping again. "Oh, Judas, where are you?"

The centurion put his arm about her shoulder to support her. "We'll find him, Shelomith. You must go home. This is no place for you. I'll send one of my men with you."

"I don't need him," she said, quieting. "Abiathar here is sufficient."

"Go then, Shelomith." He smiled. "We'll find him and send him to your house. Now I must go back up there. Soon I hope in mercy to end the dreadful business." Abruptly he turned and went up the path.

On the way down the hill Shelomith and Abiathar paused for breath. The air was utterly still. Darkness descended on them. The earth beneath their feet trembled. They felt the Place of the Skull quiver.

Abiathar pointed up to the faint shadow of the central cross. "God shows His anger at the murder of His Son."

Chapter | ✠
69

JESUS struggled to raise his aching head. . . . The watchers have begun to depart. Many who came to scoff have gone back into the city. The soldiers lie huddled, impatiently waiting for me to die— even the one who lifted the vinegar sponge on the reed when I cried out my thirst. Father, forgive them, for they know not what they do this day!

John my beloved cousin is gone and she whom I gave into his charge and keeping, my own mother. No one remains with me. All have fled. O Father, where are the eleven? Where is poor Judas? Forgive him, too! Damn him not forever, O God. Save him in Thine own time and way. Men for a thousand years and longer will call down curses on his name, but do not Thou, O Father, condemn him utterly. . . .

The sky was growing black. The timetable of nature was upset. The people fled in terror before the frightful darkness and the earthquake.

Hear my prayer, Father. . . . No answer came. Only the lowering skies, the gloom, the shaking, the doubt and panic . . . Can it be that the Father no longer hears, no longer cares? That I am not His son? . . .

"O God, my God, why hast Thou forsaken me!"

The stragglers at the foot of the cross, startled at the despairing cry, pushed back, some fearful that it might provoke another tremor, some expecting a visitation of angels or demons.

. . . Darkness. Darkness and death. The stillness of the tomb. Forever and forever unending. Men, my brothers, going down to death and eternal night. O God, I sought to do Thy will. I sought to lead my brothers to Thee. And now I die, and all to no avail. My Father, why hast Thou left me to die alone on this hated hill in agony and sore distress, abandoned by all, abandoned even by Thee? O Father, my Father . . .

His head slumped on his chest. But not for long. He raised it again, though it was a fearsome burden.

. . . O my blessed Father, my kind and loving Father, the sky opens and heaven shines upon me. The hosts of heaven, the songs, the praises. Thou art good. Thou art love. Thou lovest me. Thou approvest my course. The gates of heaven swing wide. Thou comest! . . .

His blood-crusted face lighted with an eternally triumphant smile, Jesus of Nazareth fell into the great sleep.

*

Chapter 70 ✠

JUDAS raced through the Court of the Gentiles. Up the steps and through the Beautiful Gate he ran, fear-driven, intent on finding Joseph Caiaphas the High Priest of Israel.

He dashed across the Court of the Women, up the rounded marble steps and through the Gate of Nicanor into the Place of the Great Altar. Nor did he stop until he was on the porch of the Sanctuary, past which none but the priests dared ever tread.

There he spied Caiaphas. He was talking with several priests. They were telling him that ignorant people attributed the strange look of the sky and the trembling of the earth to the crucifixion of the Galilean magician.

"Superstitious pagans, shaking in silly fright at storm clouds and rumblings familiar to our region!" Caiaphas exclaimed. "Afraid of the Galilean rebel who'd bring ruin upon——"

Judas of Kiriot, his eyes glaring, his clothes awry, his chest heaving, stood before them, his money pouch clasped in his hand.

"What does this intrusion mean, man of Kiriot?" The small black eyes glinted. "Why do you come bursting into the Sanctuary?"

"I've come to bring back your thirty pieces of silver. I don't want them! I didn't know what I was doing when we made the compact. Now I want to be freed from the symbol of guilt. I don't want it said that I sold my Master the Messiah to death."

"Aren't you a bit late?" The little eyes danced. "Isn't your master dying on the cross right now?"

"Yes, I'm late! But I knew nowhere else to go. I don't want

this money! It's unclean! Do you hear me, High Priest? I've betrayed innocent blood! I've sent the Christ to the cross!"

"Hah! What's that to us, man of Kiriot? You've well earned the
money. Keep it. And now get you gone!"

"You'll not have it? Yes, but you will! It won't burn my soul in
hell!" Judas caught the pouch by the bottom, whirled it about. The
coins rang out on the marble pavement, rolled under the feet of
Caiaphas and the priests.

Judas rushed out toward the Great Altar. The skies were almost
black now. They seemed to smother the Temple.

A flash of lightning brought to startling brightness all the precincts of the Temple area. Judas heard a great tearing and ripping.
Looking over his shoulder into the Sanctuary, he saw the Veil rent
from top to floor, so that the Holy of Holies stood fully revealed.

He fled through the enveloping blackness, screaming his contrition and terror.

Around the corner of the Temple he ran, along the double
cloister of columns, out through the Gate Shalleketh.

He raced across the bridge. Now he was back on the cobblestones again, sobbing, crying. Down the maze of streets edging the
Valley of the Tyropoeon he hurried. Then, turning westward, he
panted up Mount Zion. When he could no longer run he staggered
in the greenish haze.

He rapped on Shelomith's door. "Your young mistress," he
gasped to the servant. "I must see her!"

"She's not here. She went to look for the Centurion Longinus."

Judas stumbled back toward the gate onto Hebron road.

On he went by blind instinct until at last in the now thinning
darkness he came to the place where the tree stood.

He sat down to get his breath and try to think. . . . I have sold to
his death the Messiah of God. Evil, I rejected good. In hate I rejected love. I am forever damned. I wavered and might have
turned away from my insensate plan. I heard the voice of the Master and my conscience, pleading, warning. But I would not heed.

I wished to save Israel from the Romans, yes. But I also craved honor and riches for myself. . . .

He sat near the tree at the edge of the chasm. . . . Here was my house to rise. Here were my children to run and play and shout delight. The window of my bedroom was to look out on the tree, to remind me, seeing it the first thing when I awakened, that, like it, I was to be unyielding, tough and twisted but strong. Twisted . . .

He saw the limb on which he had once sat while he talked with Shelomith. Flashes of lightning now and again revealed it starkly.

Judas felt the long rope girdle tight about his middle. He walked to the tree. He stood beneath it. One glance he gave in the direction of Shelomith's house. . . . I cannot live under the weight of my guilt. A man cannot sell God and live. God, have mercy! . . .

He unwound the rope girdle. He swung up on the limb, clambered out until he was well above the chasm. He tied the rope to the limb. He knotted the other end about his neck. . . . Master, do not forget me!

Judas of Kiriot fell.

Chapter 71 ✠

THROUGHOUT the Sabbath day Shelomith kept close to her chamber. Grieving, apprehensive, she wished to see no one. Her mother and Hagar said Judas would return and all would be as it was before yesterday's terrible events. But she knew this could not be.

The household learned that Rabbi Nicodemus and Joseph of Arimathea had obtained Pilate's permission to bury the body of Jesus of Nazareth in the new tomb lately procured by Joseph. The body had been anointed and wrapped and properly entombed, and a great stone had been rolled in front of the opening. Jesus was dead and buried. The story of the strange, magnetic young man of Nazareth—the man of the winning smile and the beautiful, flowing words, the man whose touch was said to have healed hundreds— was ended. Another great teacher in Israel had lived and died.

Shelomith knew in her heart that the story of Judas of Kiriot had ended too.

So when Longinus came early on the morning after the Sabbath she was reluctant to leave her room to see him. He insisted that he must speak with her. She bathed and dressed in fresh garments and went down.

He was smiling, excited. "Have you heard the news, Shelomith?"

"No. Is it about Judas you've heard?"

"I'm sorry, no. But it's bound to concern him, too."

"What have you heard?"

"The story is abroad in Jerusalem that Jesus has risen from the grave."

"Impossible! It can't be true—even of Jesus."

"It must be true. Incredible as it sounds, the report seems carefully verified. Several of his devoted disciples, as well as some of the women who worshiped him as a god, saw him this morning at the tomb. When she first saw him, one of the women thought he was the gardener, but when he spoke to her she recognized him."

"Longinus, of course I can't believe——" But could she? A thought had struck her. "Before the Sanhedrin they accused him of saying that if the Temple were destroyed he would raise it on the third day. Rabbi Nicodemus told me. He must have meant the temple of his body. *This is the third day.*" Her face was all alight. "Oh, wonderful above all wonders! Think, Longinus: the Conqueror of Death, the Messiah who frees us from the fear and dominion of Death! How pale beside this grows poor Judas' dream of the conqueror of Rome, the liberator from Roman domination!"

"Yes, Shelomith, you make it clear to me that I must find this risen Lord. He must be more than a god. He must be God. And I must beg his forgiveness. Who would not give him allegiance?"

"I feel as you do. Perhaps together—— Oh, if Judas only knew of this! If we could tell him! Too late. He'll never know. We'll never see him again."

"Surely you can't mean that. He'll return, and his master will forgive him, and he'll start hating all over again."

"No. He could not live with himself when he knew what he had done. Our ways had parted—his and mine. There was no help for it. He knew it, and I fear this was one more reason why he——"

"You don't mean you think he has—?"

"Yes. The realization of how he had deluded himself, his thwarted ambition and, above all, his grief and contrition would be more than he could bear."

"Where—how—would he—?"

"One place keeps coming to me. I have dreamed about it. I don't ordinarily put reliance in dreams, yet that place—it meant so much to him. Perhaps, Longinus——" She questioned her courage, his regard. "I wonder if I could. Yet I must. Longinus, would you go with me?"

They walked together the long way to the level place where the twisted tree stood by the Vale of Hinnom.

Fifty paces away, where the house would have stood, Shelomith screamed, "O God! . . . Look! Knotted around the limb over the gulch. Go, look, Longinus. I cannot!" She sank to the ground.

Longinus peered into the chasm, where sharp boulders thrust out from the precipitous wall.

Judas of Kiriot lay on a rock, a short length of his girdle knotted about his stiffened neck. His widespread robe revealed his body torn and bloody.

Longinus came slowly back to her. She had got to her feet. "Yes?" she asked.

He nodded.

"I was sure of it." She looked steadily into his eyes. "I'll be all right in a little while. It's all over and ended. I've already had my fight." Once she glanced at the tree. Tears welled in her eyes. "Think not too ill of him, Longinus. He loved his Master, and he loved Israel. He loved almost as passionately as he hated. But he chose the wrong road. He . . . he was lost. Ah, Judas, Judas!"

Longinus held his arm about her shoulder. She leaned her head against his chest. The tears fell.

"Let us go," she said at length, calm again. She gestured toward the tree. "You'll see to—?"

"Yes, Shelomith, I'll see to everything."

"You're so kind to me, so considerate. I can never thank you enough." Impulsively she put her hand in his.

Once, from the Hebron road, she glanced over her shoulder. The tree stood out in the crisp sunlight. One limb, lean and shriveled, seemed to point down.

All the way back Longinus held her arm, steadied her. "Shelomith, you said that together we might——" His voice was warm and low and tender. "This is not the place, my dear, nor the time, but someday, someday soon, I want to . . . to . . . "

"Yes," she whispered, "someday soon I want you to."